FROM THIS DAY ONWARD

Elizabeth Kary

VIKING

VIKING

Published by the Penguin Group
27 Wrights Lane, London W8 5TZ, England
Viking Penguin Inc., 40 West 23rd Street, New York, New York 10010, USA
Penguin Books Australia Ltd, Ringwood, Victoria, Australia
Penguin Books Canada Ltd, 2801 John Street, Markham, Ontario, Canada L3R 1B4
Penguin Books (NZ) Ltd, 182–190 Wairau Road, Auckland 10, New Zealand

Penguin Books Ltd, Registered Offices: Harmondsworth, Middlesex, England

First published in the USA by Jove Books, New York 1989
First published in Great Britain by Viking 1989
1 3 5 7 9 10 8 6 4 2

Printed and bound in Great Britain by
Richard Clay Ltd, Bungay, Suffolk

A CIP catalogue record for this book is available from the British Library

ISBN 0-670-82094-6

To the members of the
Missouri Chapter
of the Romance Writers of America,
in appreciation of
their friendship and support

Acknowledgments

MANY PEOPLE SELFLESSLY offered their services and expertise to me as I was researching this book. I would like to thank Dr. Russell S. Gilmore of the Harbor Defense Museum of New York at Fort Hamilton, who gave me pertinent information on Forts Hamilton and Lafayette and who was kind enough to read the Prologue of this book and pronounce my hero's escape feasible. I also owe a great deal to Kathy Bills at the Western New York Landmark Society for her assistance in making the Rochester section of the book true to the time in which it is set.

The help I received from Donald Loker, director of the local history section at the Niagara Falls Public Library, was invaluable in helping me to see the city where I grew up in a totally new light. The information he made available to me added a wonderful veracity to the narrative.

In addition, I would like to offer my sincerest gratitude to the staff of the St. Louis Mercantile Library Association and, in particular, to Mark Cedeck of the Barriger Railroad Library branch of this wonderful institution. His patience in providing me with everything from timetables to descriptions of the railroad cars and pictures of the U.S.S. *Michigan* and the *Philo Parsons* is very much appreciated. Another enormous, heartfelt thank-you goes to Charles Brown of the same institution. He is a librarian's librarian, and no request for information was too obscure for the multitude of talents he brings to his vocation. His help in researching this small but fascinating footnote to the Civil War is one thing that made the history live for me and, I hope, for my readers.

Another thank-you goes to the staffs of the Olin Library at Washington University, the Webster Groves Library in Webster Groves, Missouri, the Missouri Historical Society, and the Toronto Public Libraries.

I would also like to offer my gratitude to my aunts and uncles, Tom and Thelma, Ray and Muriel, and Bud and Barbara Sparling, who remembered how Niagara Falls looked in the 1930s and 1940s when many buildings of the Civil War period were still standing along Main and Falls streets. Their reminiscences helped me to reconstruct the Niagara Falls of days gone by. Another thank-you goes to my sister-in-law, Renée Witmer, for her company and her patience while I explored and took notes and pictures of the Cave of the Winds area and other parts of Niagara Falls.

Without the help of these generous people, *From This Day Onward* could not have been written. Any inaccuracies in the narrative are the fault not of their scholarship but of my own.

August 11, 1864
Fort Lafayette Prison
in New York Harbor

Prologue

IT WAS MADNESS to even consider escape on such a night. In the last ten months only a handful of men had been courageous enough or desperate enough to risk the treacherous tides and unpredictable currents of the Narrows between New York Harbor and the vast Atlantic in an attempt to win their freedom. And only God knew how many had succeeded. But tonight Ryder Bingham was such a man.

Bracing against the wind, he rose from where he had lain on the mossy, shingled roof of the prison and, as he did, felt the gale force of the rain for the first time. The sheeting fury of it took his breath as the storm wrapped itself around him, but Ryder stood his ground, defying the elements like a lighthouse on some lonely spit of land. Far to his right he could make out the faint glimmer of lights along the shore from Fort Hamilton and the town of New Utrecht, but nothing penetrated the darkness from across the Narrows to the west where Staten Island lay.

With a flare of lightning to show the way, he began to move along the lip of the slippery, slanted roof that capped the two tall stories of casemates. Below him he could see the lintels of the gunports protruding slightly from the fort's heavy brownstone wall, and he knew that the force of the wind must be blowing rain into the cramped quarters the guns and prisoners shared. Farther below him the water of the channel churned and foamed, crashing over the shores of the narrow island to lick at the very foundation of the prison.

As he moved toward the corner of the building, he tightened his grip on the rope he had fashioned from strips of his single woolen blanket. He had done it secretly and deliberately three days ago, just before he had begun to tunnel upward through the vaulted ceiling of his cell. It had taken him every minute of those three days, scraping and gouging with a common folding knife, to loosen and remove the heavy red-brown stones that lay between him and the prison roof. They had been days of grief and guilt, of grim, determined work. Ryder had been silent, fierce, driven, and the other men within his casemate had not offered to help with what they considered a completely hopeless effort. But neither had they betrayed Bingham to the prison authorities.

When Ryder had finally cleared a passage through the deteriorated masonry and wormed his way up to the shingled roof, he had known grim satisfaction, and not even the violence of the summer storm could dim his will to escape. He would get away, or he would die in the attempt. For him there had never been another choice.

Having reached the corner of the prison closest to the center of the channel, Bingham knelt to fasten the end of the makeshift rope to one of the roof brackets. The wool was rough and resistant beneath his raw fingers, and Ryder struggled with the knot for a full minute before he was convinced it was secure.

This route of escape, from the corner of the prison farthest from the land might have seemed unlikely to most, but in the long days while he had waited for his brother Mitchell to die, Ryder had spent hours staring out the casemate window, studying the Narrows with his seasoned sailor's eyes. He had made note of the currents, of the water's daily ebb and flow. This was where he would catch the incoming tide to freedom; he was staking his life on his calculations. In the past months, he had borne all he could take of confinement, had accepted all he could stand of responsibility. There was only death or freedom now, and to him they weighed the same.

With a single tug to test the rope, he eased over the edge of the roof. As he lowered himself toward the fringe of island below, he felt the slight give of the line between his hands, smelled the musty scent of the wet wool, heard the fabric creak with the strain. But the knots held fast, and he hung suspended for what seemed like an eternity in the desolate half-world between earth and sky. Spume dashed high to welcome him to the turbulent sphere below, and finally he touched the gravelly ground at the base of the thick fort wall. The moment he gained his feet, he made for the water's edge a dozen yards away, praying no one would see him and sound the alarm. But the fury of the storm must have driven the guards inside, and as he lowered himself into the water, there was no sign of discovery. Slipping deeper, he felt the storm-swelled waves swirl cold against his hips and thighs, sucking him toward the bay, drawing him into the darkness. There was a moment when he tried to fight the pull, but there was no hope of resisting. For good or ill, Ryder resigned himself to the water.

Once he was free of the island prison, Bingham lost all sense of time and place. He might as well have been in the middle of the ocean as six hundred yards from the Long Island shore. The swells were broad and deep enough to hide everything from view, and the rain closed in around him until all the world was dark and wet. At first he struggled toward where he knew the land should be, but his strength was as nothing against the currents in the open channel. He could only hope that he was being carried toward land, not dragged out into the endless sea.

How long he drifted Ryder did not know: skimming the swell of the waves, being buried in the trough when the crests broke over him. Salt water was constantly in his nose and mouth, and it took all the strength he could muster to fight for air to breathe. He could not see for the rain in his eyes or hear for the roar of the water around him. Above him the sky quivered bright, then dark, and the sound of thunder reverberated around him. In time, the insistent cold of the channel began to penetrate his limbs, and as the chill crept deeper, he fell victim to a seeping lethargy, an insidious resignation. Yet even as his perceptions began to dim, there was the conviction that he would not die at sea. That belief, couched in the vagaries of his subconscious mind, had been part of what made him such a sure and courageous captain, such a daring and successful blockade-runner. But just as the skein of rational thought ran out and his will to struggle ebbed, something hard and rough grazed his cheek. Blinking to clear his vision, he found an empty wooden crate an arm's length away, lying in the hollow between two waves. Even through the fog that enveloped him, Ryder recognized the crate's providential arrival, and he wrapped his arms around it, clinging to it determinedly as something to keep him afloat.

But again the cold and exposure clouded his reason until he was roused by the sound of breakers against a shore and the feel of gravel and sand beneath his knees. He was too weak to struggle as the tide tossed him up on a beach, then tried to reclaim him, thrust him a little higher and abandoned him to the land. Ryder dimly recognized that he was safe but lay immobile, unable to think or stir.

Finally a modicum of sanity returned, and he forced himself to stand and look around. Beyond the hummock at the edge of the beach he could see the roofs of what he thought must be New Utrecht. There was a Mrs. Gelston from the town who visited and sent supplies to the fort, and Ryder had made careful inquiries as to the location of the Gelston home. As he lay gathering his strength on the beach, the storm abated with a last flicker of lightning and a final dousing of rain, and he set out through a drifting mist in the direction of Marine and Fourth streets.

New Utrecht was a rural community nestled in the shadow of Fort Hamilton, and Ryder was able to move through it unseen by following the hedgerows that hemmed most of the properties. He approached the Gelstons' tall stone house through an old-fashioned garden behind, and though it was very late, a single light burned from a window on the second floor. Gathering a handful of pebbles, he began to throw them at the window. The night was dank and still, and the sound of the tiny stones hitting the glass seemed loud as cannon fire. He had thrown no more than three or four when the window opened and an older man, apparently Mr. Gelston, leaned out.

"Who are you?" he demanded in a whisper.

"I'm from Fort Lafayette," Ryder replied in the same hushed tone.

The man muttered an imprecation and closed the window, but he appeared at a rear door a few moments later. "Damn fool!" he growled. "Don't you know this house is watched?"

Ryder shook his head. "I didn't know where else to go."

"How did you get here from Fort Lafayette?" the man demanded.

"I swam."

"Swam?" Gelston muttered, half to himself. "Swam the Narrows on such a night? It's a wonder you made it." The man sighed. "Well, after all you've been through, I'm sorry I can't take you in. The Yankees know my wife has done charity work at the fort, and they're suspicious. As soon as they find you're missing, troops will show up to search the place."

Ryder stared at the man in the doorway, and in the silence a faint breeze brought the sound of voices from the front yard.

"You see? They're out there even at this hour," Gelston breathed.

"But where am I to go?" It was more a demand than a question. "I won't be taken alive."

Gelston hesitated, unwilling to help the man before him but aware of the desperation in his reply. He could offer him a chance, at least. Glancing to the right and left as if afraid they might be overheard, he whispered, "There's a house just down the road, a small frame place with a porch on the side. Their name is Smithers. Tell them I sent you. They'll take you in."

Before Ryder could mutter so much as a word of thanks, the door closed silently, and he was left alone in the misty night. Aware now of the troops standing guard at the front gate, he crept toward the rear of the property. Gelston had not said in which direction the Smithers house lay, and Ryder headed north, praying that he would find the place before the Federal troops discovered him. He moved with exaggerated stealth, staying in the shadows of the woodlot that edged the Gelston property, trying to slip away from the sentries he could see dimly outlined by the glow of a single lantern. But instead of avoiding them, Ryder stumbled on one of the troopers who had stepped into the trees to relieve himself.

For an instant both Ryder and the sentry stood staring in stunned surprise; then Bingham turned to flee while the soldier pulled his pants together. "Halt!" the sentry shouted finally as he leveled his gun at Ryder's back. "Identify yourself."

But instead, the Confederate continued to run, moving diagonally across the woodlot. Behind him he heard the soldier's two companions join him, and Ryder dodged right and left in a valiant attempt to elude them. His movements were swift and sure, and he was faster alone than the three armed men together. Behind him he could hear the crushing sound of pursuit, the curses his hunters gave as they stumbled through the underbrush. A gunshot rang out and then a second. A powder of wood and bark sprayed over Ryder as the second ball came dangerously near its mark. He did not hear the retort of the third musket, but the impact of the bullet knocked him flat. Hardly realizing what had happened, he staggered to his feet and moved ahead, unaware of the blood streaming from his shoulder or of any hint of pain. The soldiers paused to reload, and in the seconds that took, Ryder managed to dodge to the right, then double back and hide in the lea of a fallen tree. As he waited, the sentries stumbled past him, so close that he could hear their heavy breathing and smell the faint scent of the whiskey they had drunk to ward off the dampness and cold.

He lay hidden for a few minutes to be certain that the troops were really gone before venturing from his hiding place. It seemed wise to move in the opposite direction from the one the sentries had taken, and by chance he found the frame house with the side porch three lots beyond the Gelstons'. The place was cloaked in darkness as he approached, but he pounded on the door, desperate for help. His wound was beginning to throb, and he could feel his own blood warming the clammy clothes he wore. His knees were growing weak, and there was a catch in his side from the strain of running hard after nearly ten months of inactivity.

The sound of his fist against the stout wooden panel seemed to echo through the darkened house, and he had nearly given up hope of help from this quarter when the door opened. A grizzled, white-haired man stood watching him, a flickering sperm candle in one hand and a cocked pistol in the other.

"I'm from Fort Lafayette," Ryder managed to tell him. "Gelston sent me here."

There was an instant of silence, and Ryder felt the old man taking the measure of his words, studying his wet clothes now stained with blood, his unkempt hair and beard, the exhaustion on his face. As if satisfied that he was all he claimed to be, the fellow opened the door a little wider and gestured Ryder inside.

The room was spare and inhospitable, but the man was suddenly solicitous, offering Bingham a chair at the wide pine table, then closing and locking the door behind him.

As the bolt snapped in place, a woman in a nightdress and shawl appeared from a curtained alcove at the opposite side of the room. "What is it, Jed?" she asked.

Jed frowned before he answered. "It's one of them fool Confederates escaped from the prison."

The woman nodded as if in agreement with Jeb's view of the South and its defenders. "Well," she answered slowly, pushing back a lock of gray-flecked hair, "Confederate or not, we better help him anyway."

"That better, son?"

Ryder nodded as the woman in the nightdress wrapped a bandage around his left shoulder. He watched as she worked over him, the gruffness of her voice and features belying the tenderness of her touch.

"You were damn lucky," she went on, tying the ends of the bandage together. "That ball passed clean through you without hitting anything that won't mend. You've lost a bit of blood, and with any wound there's danger of fever. I'll warrant you feel a little shaky now, but with a few hours' sleep you'll be able to travel. And the sooner we get you on a train headed north, the less chance there is you'll be recaptured."

Ryder moved his shoulder gingerly to test for pain, then turned to his benefactors, his face grim. "I'm not going north. I want to get back into battle as soon as I can. I've got a score to settle with the Yankees, and I can't very well do that from up in Canada."

"You'll be back in battle soon enough," Jed assured him. "Once you get across the border, you'll go to see a man named Holcombe; Jeff Davis sent him to Canada 'specially to see that loyal Confederate boys like you have a way to get back home. They'll ship you out of Halifax to Bermuda, and then the runners will take you into Wilmington or Charleston by the dark of the moon."

Ryder Bingham well knew about running into Wilmington by the dark of the moon; he had done it more times than he could count. He knew all the tricks of sneaking past the blockade squadron, could remember the fierce excitement of passing unseen within a hundred yards of the enemy cruisers.

"I can't wait that long to get back into action," he insisted, thinking of the havoc he would wreak in the name of revenge. "I'm going south now, tonight."

The woman sat back and looked at him, her mouth drawn narrow and tight at the corners. "That's crazy," she insisted. "If you do that, you'll be retaken by noon tomorrow."

"Listen, son. What Willa says is true. When a prisoner escapes, the police chief has his men watch the trains. They concentrate on the ones headed south; it's where an escaped Confederate is expected to go. That's why it's wiser to head for Canada."

Ryder saw the logic in their words, but felt a surge of fresh frustration. "I have a score to settle with the Yanks," he repeated.

Jed nodded. "I guess we all do this late in the war."

Bingham could see agreement in Willa Smithers's eyes, and he wondered, for the first time, why these two people were willing to help a Confederate escape from a Federal prison. What were their ties to the South? What score did they have to settle that made them flout the Yankee laws?

When she had finished bandaging Ryder's shoulder, Willa applied a soothing salve to the graze on his cheek and then began to work the same medication into his torn and blistered hands.

"Did you tunnel out?" she asked.

"The walls are ten feet thick at Fort Lafayette, so I worked my way up to the roof."

"To the roof, you say?" Jeb's voice was touched with awe. "I wouldn't have thought of that myself, not tunneling up." He chuckled suddenly with appreciation. "Bet old Lieutenant Wood has never seen the like!"

Ryder flexed his ravaged hands and smiled grimly. It had been a wild scheme born of grief and despair, but it had worked. The blocks he had systematically removed from the ceiling of his cell and hidden beneath his cot had opened a way to the roof and freedom. Nor did he intend to be retaken. If remaining free meant returning to the Confederacy by way of Canada, then he would head north as the Smitherses suggested. It might take longer to get back into the fight, but he would make up for the time he lost. He would see that the Yankees paid dearly for Mitchell's death if it took him the rest of his days.

Willa Smithers saw the determination in Bingham's face and drew a long breath. "I reckon what you need now is some sleep. There's a bed up in the loft. Once you wake up, we'll wash and barber you and send you on your way."

"Think Jonah's clothes will fit him, woman?" Jeb asked. "He's built tall and rawboned like him."

Willa Smithers looked at her husband, her expression suddenly bleak. "I suppose they might at that, old man. He puts me in mind of Jonah, too."

"Won't Jonah be needing the clothes himself?" Ryder asked, unwilling to take any more from these people than they had already given.

"No, Jonah won't be needing them," Jeb began with a shake of his head, but Willa finished for him.

"Our son Jonah won't be coming home. He died with Lee at Gettysburg."

Chapter One

RYDER BINGHAM ENTERED the passenger car just as the train began to roll, and he braced himself against the motion, taking time to observe his surroundings. He was struck first by the relative opulence of the northern train: by the double rows of wrought-iron seats padded in durable leather, the brass oil lights suspended between the windows, and the multicolored carpet on the floor. The wooden car did show signs of heavy use, but the last time he had gone home to Wilmington, in March of 1863, the southern rolling stock had been like the people he had seen, showing the wear of war. His attention quickly passed from the physical surroundings to the people in the car.

Jed Smithers had insisted that he catch the northbound train at Fort Washington, the second station on the Albany line. It was a precaution in case there were detectives watching the busy New York City station at Thirtieth Street. But because of Jed's caution, many of the seats in the sixty-passenger coach were already taken. Carefully, Bingham assessed his fellow travelers.

There were a large number of Union soldiers in the car, probably men on furlough from camps in Virginia. At the sight of their blue uniforms, Ryder felt the familiar hatred for his enemy swell through him. It was coupled with a sense of impotence, the frustration of not being in control of his own life. If he wanted to escape, he knew he would have to wait to avenge Mitchell's death, bide his time until he was free. But only the conviction that he would have his revenge one day made restraint possible. The time would come when he would force the murdering Yankees to their knees, and when he did, he would show them not one ounce of mercy. But for now he must rein in his strong emotions, ignore the enemies who surrounded him, and decide his course.

The soldiers on the train were in all attitudes of repose. Some slept with their heads thrown back against the headrests they had bought from vendors in the station to make the low-backed seats more comfortable. Others played cards or read. Many talked and joked among themselves, embroidering greater daring and valor into the tales of battle they would tell once they arrived at home. None of them could have known there was a Confederate among them, and while he longed to shout the truth, Bingham was very glad.

His gaze moved beyond the soldiers to several pairs of older men sitting together. They were probably salesmen, he surmised from the sample cases at their feet and thrown into the overhead racks. A salesman's samples, the miniature furniture and appliances or bottles of patent medicines and swatches of cloth, were too valuable to be trusted to the vagaries of checked luggage. A man could lose his livelihood as easily as a bag.

There were pairs of older women, too, traveling together for companionship and propriety. This war had drawn many women from the safety of their homes and made it necessary for them to travel, sometimes without the protection of a man. Were these women returning home from visits with sons or husbands, from nursing in hospitals at the front?

There was a flurry of activity from the front end of the coach as a child escaped the clutches of his mother, a young matron with a brood of five to tend. The child, a bright-eyed boy of about four, tore down the aisle toward the back of the car until a sergeant snatched him up and settled him on his lap.

"I have one at home about your size." The sergeant grinned. "And about as full of the devil, too. What's your name, son?"

"Teddy," the child answered, regarding the man's uniform carefully. "Are you in the war?"

"I surely am," came the reply.

"My pa's in the Union Army, too, only he has two more stripes here." The child pointed to the sergeant's arm.

The man laughed. "He does, does he?"

The child's mother came up the aisle in a swish of skirts. "I'm sorry, Sergeant," she began breathlessly. "Here we've hardly begun our trip, and already Teddy is misbehaving!"

The sergeant laughed again. "Oh, he's not misbehaving, ma'am; he's just high-spirited. I was rather enjoying getting acquainted. If you don't mind, I'll look after him for a bit."

"He's a handful," she warned.

"It'll get me in practice for the two at home."

With a grateful smile, the woman agreed. "If he gets to be a pest, just bring him back to me."

"We'll get on famously," the sergeant assured her before she turned to go.

Ryder watched the young matron's retreating figure. For a moment he had considered attaching himself to her party for the safety it could provide. A healthy military-age man out of uniform and traveling alone might well arouse either animosity or suspicion: animosity because with the advent of the draft he would have to have bought himself out of military service; suspicion because he might be just what Ryder was, an escaped prisoner. If he seemed to be traveling as part of a group, his presence on the train would not be suspect. Well, Bingham reflected, joining the young matron's party was out of the question now that she had attracted the attention of a Union soldier. Still, he watched her retreating figure appreciatively. He had always liked redheads, and it had been a damned long time since he had seen an attractive woman.

As she slipped back into her seat, his gaze drifted to the figure sitting across the aisle. It was another lone woman, this one dressed in widow's weeds.

Having weighed the advantages of attaching himself to just such a person, Ryder watched her more closely. Sitting with her head turned toward the window, she was staring at the world outside with singular concentration. A heavy mourning veil obscured her features, and nothing about her gave a clue to her age. Her shoulders were slender and straight, but he could tell nothing more from her demeanor. He sighed and glanced down at his deep blue frock coat and trousers and noted the black mourning band fastened around the sleeve. The last time Jonah Smithers had worn this suit of clothes, it must have been to a funeral. The black armband seemed somehow providential, and Ryder tightened his grip on the valise the Smitherses had given him, then started down the aisle toward one of the few empty seats in the car—the one beside the widow.

The woman did not even glance up as he tossed his bag into the overhead rack and took the seat beside her. Settling himself more comfortably, Bingham stretched his long legs before him and tried to wiggle his toes in Jonah Smithers's too-tight boots. Though the tailoring was not all he might have demanded in other circumstances, Jonah's clothes fit him tolerably well, except for the boots. He had always had the biggest feet in his family, even bigger than his older brother Wade's, and Jonah's boots pinched.

Well, at least he wouldn't have to walk all the way to the Canadian border, he told himself, resigned to the discomfort.

Bathed, barbered, and dressed in his borrowed clothes, Ryder had been shocked when he realized the stranger in the speckled mirror at the Smitherses' house was he. During the months in prison, he had lost considerable weight, and he did indeed look as Jed had described him, "tall and rawboned." At Fort Lafayette, he had been painfully aware that Mitchell was wasting away, and he had given his brother most of the food the guards brought. But until Ryder stood staring at the tall, gaunt man in the looking glass, he had never realized that the scant rations had affected him, too. Still, he was not sorry he had gone without. Perhaps the extra food had bought Mitch a little time, had given him at least a little better chance to survive the consumption brought on by the unaccustomed cold of the northern winter and the dampness in their cell. If only he had been able to convince the commandant and the guards of the seriousness of his brother's condition, Mitchell might have received the care he had so desperately needed.

Ryder cursed under his breath, though he knew there was no point in useless recriminations. Try as he might, he had not been able to gain concessions for Mitchell's failing health, and his brother had died a useless death.

Swallowing his bitterness with an effort, Bingham turned his attention to the woman who occupied the seat beside him. She still seemed engrossed in the view beyond the glass, and he let his leisurely gaze wander over her. She was covered from head to toe in black: a heavy mourning veil cloaking her features, a severe long-sleeved gown giving her a dowdy air, thin black mesh gloves conforming to the shape of her slender hands. The dress was of a common fabric, but as he studied it, he began to notice the delicate details of braid on the skirt and sleeves. With the sunlight streaming through the window, he could also detect a faint pattern in the cloth and suspected that the dress had been dyed when her household had gone into mourning. Even the buttons along the front of her gown and on the cuffs had been dipped in lye to remove any hint of luster, as the first stage of mourning demanded. Absently he wondered whom she had lost—a father or a husband?

She did have a fine figure, he went on to note, slender but with a fullness to her breasts that could not be achieved by the ruffles some women sewed into their bodices. And she must be tall, he calculated, judging from where her shoulder brushed his arm. He could feel her warmth along his left side and smell the faint, tart scent of lily of the valley that wafted up to him. It stirred more than his curiosity. Was she young? he found himself wondering. Beneath the heavy gauze of her wrist-length mourning veil, was she pretty?

It was probably just as well that she seemed disinclined to conversation. He had more important things to think about than a strange woman on a train. He looked past her out the window to where the Hudson River lay sparkling in the summer sun and found himself wondering for what must have been the hundredth time how he would get across the Canadian border once he reached Niagara Falls.

The train stopped to take on passengers at Spuyten Duyvil and Riverdale, then continued along a narrow shelf of rock that traced the eastern bank of the river. The train had just begun to resume its speed, its regular swaying motion, when three rough-looking men entered from the door at the rear of the car. Ryder watched their progress down the aisle, the way they slowed to look at each male passenger and paused to question a few. Totally alert, he strained his ears to catch some snatch of conversation. Could they be detectives? he wondered. Were they looking for him? His heart beat wildly with anticipation. Would it be wiser to stay and brazen it out or rush to the front door of the coach and jump from the train?

As if in confirmation of his worst fears, the phrase "escaped prisoner" drifted to him from where the men had stopped several seats behind his own. There was a leap in his pulse as he judged the distance to the door, then to where the detectives stood. The spaces seemed almost equal and his chance for escape frustratingly small. His decision was made by the lack of options. He would stay.

Surreptitiously Ryder dipped into his pocket, closed his fingers around the derringer Jed Smithers had given him, and withdrew it. Under the cover of his free arm, he pressed the snub barrel of the gun into his companion's side.

The woman turned to him with a start and seemed to grasp the seriousness of the situation instantly.

"I'm the man those detectives are looking for," Ryder said in an undertone. "Do as I say and live to tell your grandchildren how you helped a Confederate prisoner escape. Betray me and you will die!"

"What?" the black-clad woman gasped, going hot and cold as she stared at the man sitting beside her. She could feel his pistol jabbing her ribs and see the dangerous glitter in his eyes. In a split second she recognized that he was indeed ruthless enough to do exactly what he'd threatened, and the realization turned her numb.

The men her companion had identified as Union detectives were at the seat behind them now.

"Tell me your name," he demanded in a whisper.

"Jillian," she replied, forming the word with difficulty. "Jillian Chandler—er—Walsh."

"Which is it?"

"Walsh. Jillian Walsh."

Before either of them could say more, the three men had come to stand beside them. The tallest one, who seemed to be their leader, nodded and raised the corners of his mouth in the semblance of a smile. He had bad teeth, discolored and uneven, and one or both of his companions smelled of sweat and whiskey.

"Where're you folks bound?" he asked conversationally, rocking back on his heels as he eyed them.

"We're—we're going to Niagara Falls," Jill heard herself stammer in response to a prod in the ribs. "We're going to visit my father-in-law."

"He's been unwell," Ryder improvised by way of explanation.

"And your name, sir?" It was a demand, not a question.

"I'm Roger Walsh, and this is my wife Jillian," Ryder complied.

"You're not visiting Congressman Walsh, are you? Congressman Gerald Walsh?"

Her captor's head snapped around as Jillian answered. "Why, yes, we are. Do you know him?"

"I've met him once or twice. He's a fine man. It's a shame about him losing the last election." The detective's manner changed, knowing now who they were. "And I'm sorry to hear he's feeling poorly."

"Oh, he tells us it's nothing serious," Jillian went on, wondering where the words were coming from. She had never been able to fib to anyone without giving herself away. She only prayed that the derringer in her side and the fact that her life hung in the balance would make her unusually convincing. "But we'll feel better once we've seen him."

The three men nodded in unison, taken in by her story and suitably understanding.

"I'm Detective Brenner, with the New York City Police," the leader told them and tipped his hat. "We're looking for a Confederate blockade-runner named Ryder Bingham. He escaped last night from Fort Lafayette Prison, out in New York Harbor. That's not an easy thing to do; he must be a wily one. And you know, it's odd, Mr. Walsh," he went on, "but the description we were given suits you to a tee: a tall, black-haired man with blue eyes."

"There must be thousands of men who fit that description, Detective Brenner," Ryder observed with apparent calm. "But why are you searching the northbound trains? If I were an escaped Confederate, I'd head south as fast as I could."

"Oh, we've got men searching the trains going that direction, too. But this Bingham fellow was wounded when he stumbled across some Federal troopers on the Long Island shore. Police Chief Kennedy of New York City thought he might be headed north to Canada to throw us bird dogs off his scent."

With the Confederate pressed close beside her, Jillian felt the tremor that passed along his limbs in response to the detective's words. Was this the man they were seeking? she wondered, stealing a look at her "husband." Could this be Ryder Bingham with his gun pressed hard against her ribs? A dizzying swell of fear washed through her at the possibility.

"Well, I certainly hope you find your escaped blockade-runner, Detective Brenner." The words sprang to Jill's lips of their own volition, and the quiver in her voice was totally genuine. "He sounds like a very dangerous man."

"Oh, we'll find him, all right, Mrs. Walsh. Don't you worry none," he assured her. "And you tell your father-in-law that Zeke Brenner hopes he's feeling better."

"We'll do that," Ryder agreed as the detectives moved away.

Jillian sagged the moment the men turned their backs to go, the tension of her impromptu performance giving way like a broken spring. But beside her, the stranger remained alert even after the three detectives had left the car.

"That was very convincing," Bingham complimented her in an undertone, never taking his eyes from the front door of the coach.

"Are you Ryder Bingham?" she breathed after a moment, wishing he would put away his pistol now that the immediate danger was past. "Are you the blockade-runner they are looking for?"

As if sensing her fear of the gun, Bingham palmed the derringer and slid it back into his pocket. "Does it matter?" he asked and then shrugged. "For the duration, why don't you think of me as your husband, Roger Walsh? It seems to me that we make an unusually compatible couple. Don't you agree?"

For a long moment Jillian stared at him through the grayish film of her mourning veil. Consider him her husband, indeed! It was men like him who had killed Jeff Walsh. And then this Confederate had the gall to suggest that they made a compatible couple. She was appalled both by the observation and by the hint of humor in his tone. Humor at a time like this!

"We're not the least bit compatible," she snapped as she turned back to the window, surprised and oddly pleased by her own temerity.

Before her the Hudson River was widening, sparkling deep marine blue in the morning sun. Its shimmering surface was alive with ships: vessels with sails unfurled and flapping like sheets on a washerwoman's clothesline; small paddle-wheel boats, their streamers of smoke and steam mingling as they curled upward. Larger vessels nestled against docks along the bank, waiting to be relieved of their cargoes. But Jill was hardly aware of the scene before her. All she could think about was the man at her side and the past minutes when her life had been in imminent danger. Was it in danger still? She dared to sneak a look at the fugitive who shared her seat. She had lied to the detectives for his sake; she had done exactly as he'd asked. What was it he wanted from her now?

Using the cover of her mourning veil to hide her scrutiny, Jillian studied her companion. He was a big man, tall and broad through the shoulders and chest. But he was thin, too thin for his height. The bones beneath his skin were too sharp, too prominent, giving his features an almost menacing mien. His face was hard and impassive and might well have been fashioned from wood, the kind of carving New Englanders did of the weathered fishermen who plied the North Atlantic. It was a high-browed, broad-cheekboned countenance, and there was an inflexible look to the set of his chin and jaw. His lips were chiseled, too, narrow and harsh, and fine lines webbed from the corners of his eyes as if he was used to squinting into the sun. There was nothing soft about him, from the rigid line of his shoulders to the expression in his eyes, which were a dark and fathomless blue, like a midnight sky. Was he Ryder Bingham, the escaped Confederate prisoner the New York detectives had talked about?

She looked at him more carefully, noting that his skin was pale and colorless against the silky black of his hair, that there was a dark red graze across one sallow cheek. She glanced down to where his hands rested in his lap. They were rough-skinned, and there were scrapes and cuts around the knuckles. If he touched her, she was certain his palms would be horny and abrasive. Had he tunneled out of the prison, she wondered, dug his way to freedom? In spite of her fear, she knew a touch of awe. He must have wanted very badly to be free, to work so hard and risk his life for a fleeting chance to escape.

Jillian turned her attention once more to the scene outside the window, unwilling to find anything brave or admirable about the man beside her. He had forced her to lie for his sake; he had threatened her life. How could she feel the slightest bit of empathy or even grudging respect for a ruthless man like this one?

She drew a long breath and released it slowly. Dear God! How had she come to this? Less than a month ago she had been content and protected in her father's house. It was true that Benjamin Chandler had been desperately ill, dying in fact, but in spite of it she had felt sheltered and secure in the cozy brick cottage at the edge of the grounds of the private school where he had been headmaster. When word came of her new husband's death, it had been her father and not Jill who had been overwhelmed by grief. With the news, Benjamin Chandler had turned his face to the wall as if he could not bear the destruction of the future he had so carefully engineered for his only daughter. He had given up the fight and succumbed to his illness, leaving Jillian just as he had always feared he would, alone and in debt.

Jill had been forced to sell everything except a few of her father's books, her mother's heirloom necklace, and the red silk shawl Benjamin had bought his wife on their honeymoon. With nothing more than a trunk full of her own hastily dyed mourning clothes and the money from the sale of her parents' things, Jillian had left Harrisburg, Pennsylvania, for New York City. There she had visited her father's broker to settle what he owed, then boarded the train to Niagara Falls to take up a new life with her father-in-law.

Gerald Walsh's invitation had been a grudging one, couched in unwelcome responsibility and grief. It had been issued only for the sake of propriety and duty to a woman he'd never seen, to the wife he had never approved of for his only son. Still, Jillian knew she had no alternative but to accept what Walsh was offering. She was not prepared to make her own way in the world; she had no skills with which to earn her keep. Nor did she want to be on her own. She had been sheltered all her life and needed a man's protection. Surely this incident on the train proved she was incapable of living by herself if she had ever doubted it. She had been on her own less than seventy-two hours, and already some madman had made her his hostage.

In spite of the sunshine streaming through the window, Jillian shivered, terrified by what the day and night ahead might bring. Was this man indeed going as far north as Canada? Would he let her go when he reached his destination, or would he silence her forever once he had no further use for her? Jillian shivered again and forced her thoughts from the round of questions she did not want to answer. Instead she stared all the more intently at the scene before her, willing herself to deny her mind-numbing fear, to think of nothing more than the view beyond the glass.

Though he sat menacingly beside her, Ryder's head was filled with some of the same questions that were plaguing Jill. To save himself from discovery, he had allowed the woman beside him to learn his name and destination. Because of it, would he be forced to keep her with him until he found a way to cross the border into Canada? And, Christ! How had he managed to pick a hostage who was married to a Yankee congressman's son? He had gone cold all over when she had calmly told the detective who it was she was going to see. Being with her had given him an advantage with the New York City detectives, but what would happen when they reached Niagara? Would Congressman Walsh be on hand to meet this woman's train? Would he order Ryder arrested within sight of the border and freedom?

The engineer whistled to signal that the train was coming into a station, and with a wheeze of steam and a cacophony of bells the train drew up to the wooden platform. The sign on the station office read "Poughkeepsie," and Ryder felt a rush of relief when he saw the three New York detectives leave the train. Was he safe for the moment? Could it be that now the only danger of discovery lay with the woman beside him?

Through his haze of concern, Ryder became aware that a number of soldiers were shuffling along the aisle toward the front of the coach. He heard their last ribald comments to one another and their parting laughter. Then outside the window he began to see reunions, families come together to welcome their men back from the war. He saw women turning glowing, tear-streaked faces up to be kissed by their returning men, saw children clinging tight to their fathers' knees, saw parents clapping their sons on the back in joyous welcome. And as he watched them, Ryder's bitterness was renewed.

These men had come home to snug houses, prosperous farms,

well-fed children. The people who had gathered to meet them were fit and strong, untouched by the war. These Yankee soldiers had homes to come to, unlike so many of the Southern men. Unlike Ryder himself.

For the first time in months he let himself think about home: about the stately pillared plantation house that overlooked the Cape Fear River, about the people he loved who were waiting there for his return, and about the ones he would never see again.

Unwillingly his thoughts strayed to his mother, Alysse, the soft, serene presence from his childhood. And for the first time he was glad that she was dead. If his father's demise had robbed her of her will to live, what effect would Mitchell's passing have had upon her? Nor would Ryder have known how to face her with the news that he had failed to care for her precious youngest son. A knot of grief rose in his throat, a despair that swelled to define the horrendous scope of his own loss. Alysse would not have blamed him for Mitch's death; she had loved him more than that. But Ryder blamed himself, would blame himself for Mitchell's death as long as he lived.

Taking a ragged breath, Ryder swallowed the useless emotion and welcomed the rage that took its place. This was not the time to mourn, he chided himself. It was a time to fight to escape, to fight with everything in him. He would make his way to the Canadian border and somehow win his freedom. He would use whatever means were necessary to reach Canada.

Abruptly he realized that the train was leaving the Poughkeepsie station, having deposited some passengers and taken on new ones. As they rolled beyond the outskirts of the town, food vendors began to come through the cars selling fruit, bottles of cider, and maple sugar candies wrapped in paper. One of the boyish vendors stopped to sell his wares to the woman and her brood who occupied the seats across from where Bingham sat with the widow. As the boy stood waiting for the young matron to take money from her reticule, the sweet scent of the peaches in his basket tickled Ryder's nose and made his stomach roll with hunger. For all their generosity, the Smitherses had barely been able to scrape together money for the train ticket, and the few dollars Ryder had had with him when he was captured had long since gone for food and medicine for Mitchell. Hunger was not a new companion, and Bingham forced the thought of the soft, tantalizing peaches from his mind, realizing that the bread and cheese he had eaten early that morning would be the only food he'd have until he crossed the border and made contact with Holcombe in Canada.

It was a small enough sacrifice, he reasoned, but once the vendor was gone, the child, Teddy, toddled across the aisle, a ripe peach clutched in one grubby hand.

"Didn't you want a peach?" he demanded of Ryder, eyeing him speculatively.

Without thinking, Ryder reached out to steady the child as the train nudged around a curve in the track, then shook his head. "No, I wasn't hungry," he lied.

"Didn't you want one?" Teddy asked the black-clad woman at Bingham's side, obviously unable to understand how these two grown-ups could pass up such a treat.

Jillian hesitated one second too long before she answered. "No, I wasn't hungry, either."

As the child made his way back to his mother, Ryder turned to Jillian. It had not occurred to him that she might have wanted a peach or perhaps something from one of the other vendors. In spite of his need to control her and her actions, he had not intended that she go hungry for his sake.

"If you wanted a peach, you should have asked for it," he admonished her softly.

"Oh?" Jill replied, turning to him with marked disbelief. "I didn't think you'd entertained any thoughts at all for my well-being or comfort."

In spite of the anger that stirred through him at her response, Ryder did not know how to answer her. There had been reproach in that soft voice, an almost childish rebuff that he had not expected from someone who had earlier lied so convincingly. Again, curiosity about his traveling companion pricked Bingham, and he wished that he could penetrate the mourning veil and see this woman's face. How old was she? he wondered. Was she experienced enough, worldly enough, to be traveling on her own? If he swept the heavy fabric aside, would he read fear, defiance, or guile in her eyes? And more important, could he expect compliance or betrayal if another chance to expose him arose? He only knew that for all her earlier acquiescence, this Jillian Walsh could be a damned prickly woman, and again he cursed the circumstances that had thrown them together.

In hostile silence the miles and hours ticked away. The verdant hills across the river gave way to more rolling landscape, and as the sun rose higher in the sky, it brought lazy summer warmth to the interior of the passenger car. In time the stuffiness began to take its toll on the woman at Bingham's side. She slipped into an uneasy doze, and Ryder fought the weariness that threatened to overwhelm him, too. He had caught only a few hours' sleep at the Smitherses' and none in the three previous nights as he had worked to tunnel out of the prison. Still, he knew he could not rest and risk either discovery or this woman's defection. His shoulder had begun to hurt, too, growing stiff and feverish beneath the constricting bandage, but the pain helped to keep him alert.

The train's rhythmic swaying eventually brought Jillian's head to rest against his arm, and though it intensified the ache from his wound, he did not disturb her. While he had been shut away in Fort Lafayette, he had missed the closeness a man found with a woman. And while he had no idea of this woman's age or looks, he enjoyed her softness nestled beside him. Though he knew he should, he felt no urge to push her away, and he found her presence beside him somehow both pleasant and unsettling.

"Jillian." A soft voice intruded on her sleep. "Jillian, wake up."

Jill mumbled and shook her head, stubbornly keeping her eyelids closed.

There was a momentary pause, and when it spoke again, the voice had lost its softness. "Jillian!"

Her eyes snapped open at the gruff command, and all at once she realized that the train was no longer moving and that the other carriage passengers were filing toward the door.

"Where are we?" she asked, looking around at the man beside her. As she did, recognition came and with it a jolt of fear. She abruptly remembered who this stranger was and why she was with him; she remembered the threats he had made on her life and the feel of his gun in her ribs. Without thinking, she shrank back toward the window, stunned by the ruthlessness in his face, the menace in his eyes.

"This is East Albany," he told her, seeming satisfied by her reaction. "In order to continue to Niagara we have to take a ferry across the Hudson River to the Albany station on the other side."

The ticket agent had told her about the change of trains when she bought passage, Jillian remembered. Rising and ducking beneath the overhead rack, Jill came to stand in the aisle beside the rebel. He was even taller than she had supposed he would be, and half again as broad. In spite of her more than average height, his presence seemed malevolent and overwhelming.

"Do you have any baggage?" he demanded.

Jillian shook her head. "I had it all checked through to the Niagara Falls station."

"Very well," he muttered and swung his own valise out of the rack, grimacing with the effort.

His pained expression was not lost on Jillian, but she made no mention of it and started down the aisle toward the back of the car. She had taken no more than two steps when the man's hand tightened on her arm, pulling her to a stop.

"Stay beside me," he ordered. "I don't intend to let you turn me in to some overeager conductor, now that I've managed to get this far."

At his high-handed words, some contrary part of Jill began to stir, battling the feelings of intimidation the Confederate had done his best to foster. Something unfamiliar and very much like defiance seeped through her, and unconscious that she was doing so, Jillian squared her shoulders. She was fully prepared to do what she could to see the man apprehended.

Together the rebel and his hostage left the passenger coach and saw that the train had pulled onto a siding just above the ferry. The other passengers were making their way down the slight slope to the river, and the two of them took places behind the pretty young mother and her five small children. The group ahead fell into line with the pair of older girls walking together and the woman following them, holding one child by the hand and balancing a baby on her hip. Teddy ran some distance ahead, totally deaf to his mother's admonitions to stop and wait for the rest of them.

As they walked, Jill cast about feverishly for some way to slip away from her captor. If she could get him to turn his back, even for a moment, it might be possible to arrange her own escape or to let someone know his true identity. But under his close scrutiny, she had no idea how she might manage that. Then she noticed a privy set back behind the ferry office and, before she could lose her nerve, motioned to it with her free hand.

"I—I need to make a stop," she told the rebel, wondering if he would hear the catch in her voice and know how frightened and humiliated she was to have to make mention of her needs.

With suspicion masking his features, Bingham paused to glare down at her, as if weighing her sincerity.

Jillian held her breath. Would he let her go to the backhouse alone? Would he guess that she intended to do more than use the facilities once she was out of his sight?

Abruptly, he sidestepped the line of passengers. "All right, go ahead if you must," he conceded, "but be quick about it. We don't want to miss the ferry. I'll wait for you here."

Jill hurried toward the privy and fastened the rough wooden door behind her once she was inside. Handling her wide hoops in the enclosed space was difficult, but she managed, and she slipped a small foolscap tablet and a pencil out of her reticule when she was done. She scribbled a frantic message, then fastened it to a nail protruding from the outhouse wall. The note read simply: "There is an escaped Confederate prisoner on the westbound train."

Praying that her captor would have no reason to go inside, Jillian smoothed down her skirts and joined Bingham in front of the privy. He seemed impatient to be off and hustled her down the slope to the small steam-driven tug that waited at the ferry slip. Ryder guided Jillian toward a place in the bow and stood facing into the breeze as if glad for the open air after the stuffiness of the railroad car. There was color in his face now, two blotches of red high on his cheekbones. Freedom seemed to agree with the man, Jill noted irritably, and pulled the light woolen shawl more tightly around her. In spite of the sunshine and the bright blue sky, the storm the night before had put a fall-like bite in the wind.

With a creak of timbers and a groan of engines, the ferry left the slip and made its way into the channel. The Hudson was not all that wide at this point, and Jill could clearly see the city of Albany spread out along the opposite bank. Judging from the Dutch architecture near the waterfront, the fine new buildings farther inland, and the streets crowded with carts and people, Jillian surmised that Albany was both an old town and a prosperous one.

Just as the ferry was reaching the center of the channel, a commotion arose from somewhere along the port side. Jill and Ryder turned in the direction of the noise and saw the young mother and four of her children clinging frantically to the rail.

"Teddy!" The terror in the mother's cry reached them in spite of the wind and the noise of the steamboat's engines. "Oh, please! Somebody help me! My son's fallen overboard!"

Ryder raced to where the frightened family stood. After casting aside his frock coat and tugging off his boots, he leaped to the top of the rail and paused a moment to survey the situation before diving into the river.

The steam barge engines idled as Jill reached the rail, and her grip tightened around the balustrade as she saw that Teddy was being pulled under by the boiling river current. With fear for the child pounding in her veins, she watched Bingham fight his way toward where the boy had disappeared. When he reached the spot, he drew a breath and knifed down through the water in search of the child.

For what seemed like an aeon there was no sign of life on the surface of the river. The water lay a dark, unfathomable blue-gray, broken only by the ripples of the current and the wake the steam barge had sent ruffling back toward the eastern bank. Time seemed frozen, suspended, as they waited. Jillian found that her own breath was trapped in her lungs as she scanned the water for any sign of the man or the child. A tense silence enveloped the crowd of passengers who had begun to gather, a devastating, echoing silence broken only by the pitiful sound of Teddy's mother's weeping. Long seconds ticked by, and Jill's grip on the railing tightened, driving the mesh of her cotton gloves deep into her palms. Surely neither man nor child would survive if they did not surface soon. As Jill stood praying for their safety, bitter irony enveloped her: An escaped Confederate prisoner might well die in the attempt to save a Yankee soldier's son.

Finally, Ryder's head broke the surface, and at that same moment Jill could see a struggling child clutched tightly in his arms.

"He's all right!" she heard Bingham gasp as he fought to keep them both afloat, and a moment later the child's frightened wail echoed across the water. The boy had been rescued in time.

Jillian's limbs turned liquid with relief at the sight of the two of them, and she hugged Ryder's discarded clothes tight against her chest as a deafening cheer was raised by a score of other passengers. Ryder towed Teddy toward the side of the steamer, and several men rushed to the rail to pull the boy on board. Once he was safe, they hauled Ryder out of the river to stand shivering on the deck. From somewhere blankets appeared, and they were wrapped around both Bingham and the child as the travelers clapped the stranger on the back with words of praise for his daring.

The young mother was simultaneously weeping and hugging Teddy to her breast, and her other children stood around them crying noisily and clinging to them both. Finally the woman lifted the boy in her arms and made her way through the crowd to where Ryder stood.

"I thank you, sir, for what you've done today," she said, her voice clotted with emotion. "Teddy is not the most docile of children or the most obedient, but he is dearer than life to me. I thank you with all my heart for rescuing him."

Deep color tinged Bingham's cheeks, and he nodded his head in acknowledgment. "You're welcome, ma'am. I did no more than any gentleman would do."

At his response, Jillian became abruptly aware of the softness of Bingham's voice, of his silky drawl, of the mellifluous way his words were strung together. He sounded like the Southerner he was, she realized suddenly. Surely someone else would notice and become suspicious.

As she listened to the simple exchange, fear filled her, and illogically it was fear for her captor's safety. Even as her concern grew, Jillian recognized her feelings as irrational and contradictory. She should be glad that the Confederate was exposing himself for what he was, she told herself, hastening to shore up the unaccountable breach of her defenses. Men of his ilk had killed her husband, and she knew she should hate him with the same undiluted hatred most women of the North felt for the rebels. She should be glad if, by his choice of words and the sound of his voice, Ryder Bingham was revealing his origins and his allegiance to the enemy.

Yet somehow the events of the last few minutes had changed the way Jillian felt about the man who had taken her hostage. He had proved himself brave and noble by risking his life to save a child. He had hinted at some stronger, kinder self beneath the frightening facade he had shown to her. For his sacrifice, for having saved the child from drowning, Jill wanted with all her heart for Bingham to reach Canada and safety. But now it seemed that his own words would prove to be his undoing.

But then the danger was past. The crowd was breaking up, shuffling off across the deck in twos and threes to leave Jillian weak with relief for the second time this afternoon. Pride made it impossible for her to voice praise for Bingham after the threats and hostility that had passed between them, and the silence grew long and strained between them.

The ferry had stirred to life again and gotten noisily under way before Ryder spoke, the words sharp and staccato, bitten off by his continued shivering. "Why didn't you expose me?" he demanded. "You had a perfect opportunity to tell them who I was, yet you held your tongue."

Jillian shrugged and stared past him toward the bank. Once he had gone into the river after Teddy, the thought of revealing his identity had honestly never occurred to her. She had been caught up in the drama of the rescue, her thoughts on the safety of the people in the water and not on her own predicament. And after the child was safe, she had discovered that she did not want to see this man retaken. But how could she explain that to him when she barely understood it herself?

"You'll catch pneumonia standing there like that," she murmured instead, turning to bundle the blanket more tightly around him. "Surely you have dry clothes in your valise. Why don't you put them on?"

Ryder stared at her with narrowed eyes as if he wished to understand more of her than he did.

"The only clothes in that bag are the remains of my uniform," he answered. "And I hardly think that would be appropriate to our circumstances here."

Jillian glanced up at him and read the truth in his eyes. "Well, put on your jacket and boots, at least. That will do a bit to keep you warm."

Without further comment, Ryder tugged his boots on. But when he took the blanket from his shoulders to don Jonah Smithers's jacket, Jillian saw a red stain spreading down his shirtsleeve.

"You *were* wounded trying to escape," she breathed, stunned and perversely fascinated by the sight of his blood darkening the rough white cotton.

Gritting his teeth against the pain of the movement, Ryder pulled on the jacket, praying that the stain would not soak through the heavy broadcloth. "It's only a scratch," he told her.

But Jillian continued to stare up at him, confusion and concern warring within her. Finally she glanced away. "Once we get on the train, I'll see to changing your bandage."

"See to it so I'll live to be recaptured?" Ryder snapped, unable to understand the reason for either her silence or her help.

"Perhaps."

Jillian turned back to the rail, afraid that he would sense the change in her and angry at the conflicting emotions that sudden change had caused.

The ferry docked on the Albany side of the river without further incident, and they walked toward the train. The other passengers climbed aboard and hunted for seats, but Ryder and Jillian deliberately hung back. They were the last people to reach the open platform at the rear of one of the passenger cars, and when they did, Jillian pulled Ryder to a stop.

"We'll wait here until the train gets under way, and I'll see to your wound before we go inside."

Ryder shrugged and nodded, knowing there would be no privacy once they entered the car. His heroics at the river had deprived him of his anonymity, and that boded ill for his chances of escape. In truth, his efforts to pull the boy from the river had badly sapped his strength as well, leaving him shaky and strangely gone at the knees. For the first time, he began to wonder if he would make it as far as the Canadian border.

Then the train was moving, and as they picked up speed, Jillian had him unbutton his clothes.

The combination of the wind and movement made the open platform less than an ideal place for nursing, but Jillian stripped off her gloves and then removed the bloodied bandage. She'd had no experience with gunshot wounds, but she had bandaged other kinds of hurts, and she was not pleased by the puffy, reddened flesh she saw around the two bullet holes high in the Confederate's left shoulder. Tearing a strip of cloth from the edge of her frilled black petticoat, Jillian prepared to replace the bandage. Then, in order to better see what she was doing, she swept the heavy mourning veil back over her hat, showing her face for the first time.

For a long moment Ryder stared down at her, feeling as if he had been waiting all his life to see the woman who stood before him. With scrupulous concentration his gaze moved over the curves and hollows of her features: the delicate line of her nose, the delicious fullness of her dusty-pink lips, the alabaster luminosity of her skin. The impression Jillian Walsh gave was one of total femininity, yet hers was a face with undeniable character and strength. There was something in her that was vital, yet serene, something about her that was shy and demure, though he could sense boldness in her, too. Unable to help himself, he let his eyes linger on the curling tendrils of caramel-colored hair that peeped from beneath the brim of her bonnet; the fine, arched eyebrows and the fluff of deep brown lashes lying in a curve beneath them. Sensing a sudden change in her patient, Jillian raised her gaze to meet his, and Bingham was enthralled by the unusual color of her eyes. Her irises were dark gray-green at the edges, a shade that turned gradually to gold as they approached the pupil. And as he stood mesmerized, he felt that he could stare into those gold and green eyes forever and never tire of their uniqueness, their complexity.

"Mr. Bingham?" Jillian asked, concerned. "Mr. Bingham, are you all right?"

It was a few seconds before he could answer her. "I was feeling light-headed for a moment," he admitted truthfully, "but it seems to be passing now. And the name is Walsh, not Bingham. Roger Walsh, your husband, don't you remember?"

Jillian scowled and went back to work, and though her touch was gentle, it stoked the smoldering pain he had been fighting all day long. Without warning, incandescent agony came to swamp his senses, and Ryder went weak and trembly with the shock of it. Breathing heavily, he closed his eyes and tried to think of something besides the fire in his shoulder, the debilitating weakness that ran along his limbs. Gradually the scent of Jillian's lily of the valley cologne detached itself from his other perceptions. He fixed it in his mind with desperate concentration, calling up the memory of an early-summer garden: the color of new grass seen through a veil of dew, the songs of the morning birds, the coolness of the breeze against his skin. The soothing images helped, but not enough.

When the ordeal was over, Jill buttoned up his clothes, murmuring reassurances that couldn't quite mask her concern. Bingham looked past her, only half listening. The last minutes had badly shaken him, and he tried desperately to focus his energies for the trials ahead. But at the periphery of his vision the fields seemed to spray backwards with the speed of the train, leaving him dizzy and disoriented, and as hard as he tried to shepherd his strength, his determination had ceased to have an effect on his exhausted body. Finally he let Jillian lead him to a seat at the rear of the coach, where he sank down gratefully. Weariness drifted over him, and though he knew it was dangerous to succumb, he found it impossible to remain alert.

Beside him, Jill was painfully aware of the change the last hour had wrought in her companion. She had seen the color leave his face as she worked to stop the bleeding, had seen the way he closed his eyes as if to deny the pain. What she had done for him was necessary but makeshift at best, and she knew that he would need further care if he meant to cross the border into Canada once they reached Niagara Falls.

Slowly she began to recognize that she was in no danger from the man whose actions had left her rigid with fear only this morning. Bingham, if that was who he was, no longer had the strength to stop her if she chose to leave, nor could he hope to fight off the men she could bring to subdue him.

Yet, in some odd way they were still bound inextricably together. They were held fast by his actions on the ferry and her sense of responsibility, by his will to escape and her sudden desire to see him succeed. These were unsettling realizations, realizations she tried not to examine too closely. Still, the questions circled in her mind: If she was committed to Ryder Bingham and his desperate bid for freedom, what would happen at the Niagara station? Was there any possibility that she could help him reach Canada, or would her presence place him in even graver danger? Would they part without a word when they reached the place where her uncertain future and his only hope of freedom converged? Jillian stared blankly out the window, knowing there were no easy answers to these new, unsettling questions.

Trying to wipe her concern for Bingham from her mind, she watched the towns slip past one by one: Amsterdam, Schenectady, Utica, Rome. As they did, Jillian glimpsed the history of the region in rough-hewn fieldstone buildings; in the hard, well-traveled roads that followed ancient Indian trails; and in the strong, determined faces of the people who lived in the villages and on the farms that had been wrestled from virgin forest nearly a century before.

Here at the east end of the New York Central line, the train tracks ran close to the swiftly flowing Mohawk River, and on its wind-pleated surface Jillian could see snippets of delicate lace foaming white against the stones. Wildflowers patterned the marsh on either bank with brilliant color: clumps of goldenrod and spikes of purple lithrum hovering just above the greenery; cattails, their velvety heads peeping through the leaves; Queen Anne's lace like bits of nature's tatting displayed high on delicate stems. Beyond the marshes at the edges of the river were farmers' fields with endless waves of heavy-headed grain and ripe corn, with rows of squat bean plants and round silvery cabbages nearly ready for the harvest. Off to the north were waves of rolling hills, turning faint and misty blue, like the image of an echo fading far into the distance.

But as diligently as Jillian had applied herself to watching the panorama beyond the window, she was at least equally aware of the man slumped by her side. He had given up the struggle to remain alert and sat with his head bobbing and his eyes closed, half in the real world and half in a world of his own. Nor did Jillian like the look of him. This morning he had been pale and almost sallow complexioned, but now he was flushed, probably with fever. With difficulty she stifled the urge to raise a diagnostic hand to his brow, certain of what the touch would confirm. When she had tended his shoulder, it had been evident that the wound was not healing properly, and now a fever was coming on. It was to be expected, but the knowledge of what lay ahead of him filled her with foreboding.

Jillian bit her lip and tried to fight down her concern. There was not a reason in the world why she should feel any sense of responsibility for this man. Surely he had shown his colors only hours before when he had stuck a gun into her ribs and threatened to kill her. After that she shouldn't care a whit what happened to him.

But even as she argued with herself, Jill knew exactly when things had changed for her. They had changed when Bingham had dived into the river, risked his life to save a child. Whoever this man was, there was something fine in him, something which demanded that she treat him with kindness. Because of the child he had rescued, she must show him her compassion.

When the train made a dinner stop at the Syracuse station, Jill woke Ryder gently to ask if he was hungry. With one hand on his coat sleeve, she could feel the heat radiating from his body, and though he said he didn't want anything to eat, Jillian was not sure she believed him. Still, it seemed both less dangerous and less wearing to remain on board and avoid the crowded dining hall. They took turns using the facilities at the end of the car, and when Ryder returned, it was evident he had splashed his face with water. That seemed to revive him, at least enough for him to argue when Jillian went to buy meat pies, peaches, and bottles of cider from a vendor at the edge of the platform.

As they sat in the gathering twilight waiting to resume their journey, Jillian tried to coax Ryder to eat, but only the cold sweet cider seemed to appeal to him. Weariness overwhelmed him again before he had finished it, and Jill was filled with concern. Did he seem hotter than before? she wondered, risking to touch his cheek. Was his breathing growing labored?

He looked so uncomfortable trying to sleep in the low-backed chair that she put his feet up on the facing seat, then guided his head down to her shoulder. He seemed to rest more peacefully after that, though sitting close beside him was like curling up with a well-stoked coal stove.

The chills started just after they pulled out of the Lyons station. They were gentle tremors at first, and would have passed unnoticed if Ryder had not been sprawled against her. But in twenty minutes he was shivering convulsively, and his teeth had begun to chatter. Jillian tucked her shawl around him, but it offered no real warmth. Just as she was wondering what more she could do, a conductor came through the car.

"Please, can you help me?" she asked, catching him by the arm. "I need some blankets if there are any on board."

"Man's sick, is he?" the conductor asked impatiently, stating the obvious. "I'll see what I can find when I get a chance. We just got word that there's an escaped Confederate prisoner on this train, and finding him takes first priority."

Jillian's stomach dipped sickeningly at his words. She could guess the source of the message; someone must have finally found the note she had left in the ferry office privy. It seemed like ages since she had written it, long enough at least for her to have had a change of heart.

Suddenly she became aware that the conductor was addressing her. "Ma'am, I'm sorry to vex you at a time like this, but I'll need your reassurance that this gentleman is traveling with you."

Jill took a long breath, realizing what the conductor was asking and what an affirmative answer might mean.

"Of course he's with me," she blustered, putting all the conviction she could muster behind her words. "He's my husband, and I don't take kindly to you wasting time with foolish questions when you should be more concerned with finding him some blankets."

At her answer, Bingham's eyes fluttered open, and for an instant Jillian was sure he was going to spoil the game for both of them. She waited helplessly while he gathered his wits. "Your husband," he slurred, smiling up at her. "Your husband, Roger Walsh."

Satisfied that the sick man and his wife were all they seemed, the conductor bustled away to continue his search. He returned crestfallen a few minutes later with two blankets but no Confederate to show for his efforts. The blankets were thin, none too clean, and smelled of horses. Jill tucked them around Ryder anyway.

"What's the matter with him?" the conductor asked, settling himself in a vacant seat across the aisle as if for an extended stay.

The question caught Jill by surprise, and she rejected smallpox, consumption, and plague before a satisfactory answer came to her. "Malaria," she finally told him.

"Malaria? Ain't that one of them tropical diseases?"

As the conductor waited for an answer, Jillian tried to dredge up everything she had ever heard or read about malaria. People who spent time in the tropics did indeed catch it, and she knew there could be years of recurrent fevers.

"Before the war, my husband sailed a merchant ship," Jillian began, forced into blatant fabrication. "He did a good deal of trading in—in South America and picked up the fever on one of his voyages."

That explanation seemed to satisfy the conductor, and he launched into a story about some distant relative who had contracted the disease. While he prattled on, Jill got a cup of cool water from the pail at the back of the car and began to sponge Ryder's face with her handkerchief.

She was too preoccupied to listen to most of what the conductor said, but his last words, "And he died of it in the end," filled Jill with concern.

Although Bingham did not have malaria, she had been forcefully reminded of what could happen if a fever raged unchecked.

As if sensing her distress, the conductor offered advice. "If I were you, ma'am, I'd get off at the next big stop and find your man a bed. He seems too sick to me to go on to the end of the line."

Jill stared at the conductor, stunned by his suggestion. She might have been willing to care for Bingham while they traveled. She might even claim him as her husband to save him from recapture, but she certainly couldn't take him off the train and nurse him back to health! Yet even as she dismissed the possibility, she knew that was exactly what was needed. By the time they reached Niagara Falls, Bingham might well be out of his head with fever. He couldn't make his way across the border in that condition, and she wouldn't be in a position to take him in.

"And where would the next stop be?" Jillian heard herself asking the trainman.

"It'd be Rochester."

"Rochester," she repeated.

"Yes, ma'am. And you know, you'd probably be able to put up at Mrs. Marshall's boarding house. It's a nice clean place, and she 'most always has rooms to let."

"Mrs. Marshall's."

"I could wire ahead and have a wagon waiting," he persisted.

Jillian took a long look out the window into the gathering night, then let her gaze drop to the semiconscious man sprawled in the seat beside her. What chance of surviving would he have if she abandoned him? How would he escape the Yankees if she turned away? Compassion warred with pragmatism as she considered what the conductor had proposed.

It was madness to think about taking Bingham off the train, Jill chided herself. The man was an escaped prisoner and would be safe only after he had crossed the border into Canada. Every moment he tarried on American soil placed him in graver danger. And if she helped him in any way, she would be betraying her country—the Union her own young husband had died to defend.

Practical considerations rose to the surface of her mind. Her father-in-law was expecting her to arrive in Niagara Falls later this evening. What would he think if she was not on the train? Yet if she refused to care for Bingham and left him to his own devices, he would be recaptured and would likely die in some Yankee prison. Could she bear to let that happen? Could she walk away and let Bingham face his fate alone? *How could she take care of a sick man when she couldn't take care of herself?*

Her mind began to work on the problems at hand. Perhaps she could wire Gerald Walsh that she had been detained. Perhaps she could find Bingham a bed for the night and be on her way tomorrow. Couldn't she do that much for a man who had risked his life to save a child from drowning? Didn't his bravery and selflessness deserve some kind of reward?

"Shall I do that, Mrs. Walsh?" the conductor prodded her. "Shall I wire ahead and have Mrs. Marshall prepare a room?"

The answer came hard, but Jillian knew it was inevitable. "Yes," she agreed, "yes, I suppose you should."

Chapter Two

THE ROOM IN the boarding house was large, clean, and cozy, and Jillian was filled with relief when they had made Ryder comfortable on the big double bed. He was still fully clothed, but she couldn't take Mrs. Marshall up on her offer to help undress him, for fear that his bandaged shoulder might be discovered. Jill had stuck to her story about Bingham having had a relapse of malaria, and the landlady and her servants gave every impression of believing her.

Before they left the train station, Jillian had sent a telegram to Gerald Walsh saying that she had been unavoidably detained in New York City. She had even paid the telegraph clerk fifty cents extra to make it appear that the wire had indeed come from New York instead of Rochester. Then she had rounded up her baggage and had it loaded into Mrs. Marshall's wagon. Though he tried to remain alert, Ryder had not been able to sustain the effort and had been put in the bed of the wagon beside the luggage.

Now he lay pale and inert, needing to be bathed and bandaged and put to bed. Jill sat beside him on the edge of the mattress and stroked a hand across his brow. "Roger," she murmured softly, using the name he had claimed for safety's sake. It made sense to get used to thinking of him as "Roger Walsh," since circumstances and her own sense of responsibility had forced her to claim him as her husband. "Roger," she repeated, "how are you feeling?"

Ryder's eyes opened. They were midnight dark and glazed with fever. "Never better," he assured her.

Jillian's mouth narrowed at the barefaced lie. "Since you're feeling so well," she continued waspishly, driven by her own weariness and uncertainty, "perhaps you can help a bit when I undress you."

"Only if I can render the same service to you at some time in the future."

His reply caught Jill up short, and she fumbled for an answer. Did the man have his wits about him or didn't he?

"You're a great fool!" she finally muttered under her breath and saw the corners of his lips curl upward. "Well, then, sit up and help me if you can."

He did try to help but with limited success, and finally Jill found that she could remove his coat and shirt only by taking his weight against her and slipping the garments down his arms. Once his chest was bare of all save the bandage, Jill worked the covers back and rolled him down against the pillows. The removal of his boots came next, but not easily.

"They must be three sizes too small," she gasped after wrestling off the second one.

"I had to take what I could get," he drawled without opening his eyes.

She was just as glad that his eyes were closed as she approached the next phase of preparing him for bed. Even though

Jill had briefly been a married woman, even though she had nursed her father, she had never seen a naked man. Her father had been too proud to let her see to his basest needs, and the few times that she and Jeff had been together, he had come to her wearing a voluminous nightshirt that covered him from neck to knees. Without bothering to look, she knew there was no nightshirt in Bingham's valise, and she doubted he would wear one even if there was.

As the hesitation lengthened, Ryder raised his head and looked at her. "What's the matter?" he murmured. "You won't offend my modesty if you take off the rest of my clothes."

Jillian's cheeks warmed, but his taunt nudged her into action. Placing her hands gingerly on the buckle that lay just below his navel, she drew the tongue of the belt from its loops and bent it back so she could unfasten the buttons that lay below it. She had exposed nearly four inches of smooth, warm flesh before she realized Ryder wasn't wearing underdrawers. Her hands froze where they were, and she was unbearably aware of him: of his long male form stretched out on the bed; of the springy, dark hair brushing her knuckles; of what must lay just hidden from her view. Her heart was beating so hard that she could barely get her breath, and a wash of rich embarrassment seared her skin. How could she continue undressing him, expose the intimate parts of a man who was a virtual stranger? It was impossible, unthinkable. How on earth could she go on?

Still, the man was ill, she told herself, and less than an hour before, she had committed herself to care for him. This was no time to have second thoughts, no time to turn reticent and shy. But even as she accepted the consequences, she was furious with herself for having made this decision, furious with him for somehow compelling her to care for him. The anger gave her courage to do what she had to do. She briskly finished with the buttons and eased the trousers downward.

Bingham was a brutally masculine male, she discovered as she bared his hips, and though she chided herself for looking, she could not seem to help herself. With an even deeper blush rising in her face, Jill took a moment to study him and the undeniable proof of his gender nestled between his thighs. Was this what Jeff had so determinedly kept hidden from her view? Was this what made one sex dominant and aggressive while the other was retiring and submissive? Jill pushed the thought aside. She had no time to ponder the question of men's and women's roles when Bingham was in such desperate need of care. She worked the pants down over his thighs in deliberate haste, knowing that if he commented on her blatant curiosity, she would be totally, utterly mortified. But Ryder seemed to have drifted away again, and that was all that made it possible for her to finish preparing him for bed.

Once Jillian had tucked the covers under his chin, she began to rummage through her trunk to see what she could use for bandages. Her clothes were the only possibility, and as she tore up her oldest nightdress, she remembered the small cache of medicines left over from her father's illness. Once the strips were torn and water to cleanse the wound was poured and waiting in a basin on the nightstand, she went through the bottles she had tucked away. The most useful was the laudanum, a nearly full bottle, and perhaps she could make a mixture from the powdered bromide to cleanse and purify Ryder's wound. She should try to get some quinine tomorrow, since that was the accepted treatment for malaria. Surely it wouldn't hurt Ryder to have some if he was still feverish in the morning.

She put away the other medicines and carefully stirred a few drops of laudanum into a glass of water. The tincture of opium was powerful, Jill knew, and it was important to be sure the patient didn't get too much. Finally she approached the bed. As she did, she could feel the heat radiating from the Confederate's body and felt a wave of renewed concern. He was going to be all right in the morning, wasn't he?

"Roger," she murmured, bending over him, "Roger, take a bit of this."

Ryder raised his eyelashes and looked up at her. "What is it?" he demanded.

"It's laudanum."

"Laudanum!" His eyes opened wider. "I'm not taking any laudanum."

"It will help you rest," she coaxed moving the glass a little closer to his mouth.

"It will put me to sleep so you can sneak away and get the provost marshal."

Jill's lips narrowed at the accusation. "You *are* a great fool if you think that! Since we left Albany, I've had half a dozen chances to turn you in. But instead, I've claimed you as my husband, taken you off the train, and seen you put to bed—all against my better judgment."

"And I appreciate—" he began meekly, but Jillian was undeterred.

"Right now you have two choices, Mr. Walsh, or whoever you are: One is to drink this laudanum and spare yourself some pain when I cleanse your wound; the other is to bear that pain as best you can."

Jillian surprised herself with the heat of her ultimatum. She had never spoken to any man the way she had spoken to this one, much less to a man who'd had the power of life and death over her only hours before. Yet somehow her assessment of their situation pleased her. Either he trusted her or he didn't.

Ryder took a moment to deliberate, watching her as if to weigh what she had said against the truth that lay openly revealed by her actions. "All right. I'll take the laudanum," he conceded.

Jillian smiled grimly and pressed the glass to his lips before he had a chance to say more or change his mind. She hung over him to be sure he drank every drop of the mixture.

"It was bitter," he complained when she took the glass away.

"Yes," Jillian returned, "but revenge is sweet."

Whether the dose had been strong or his resistance weak, Ryder quickly succumbed to the drug. As she watched, Jill could see the tension drain out of his body, see the lines of pain in his face smooth away, see his eyes grow cloudy and unfocused before they fluttered and slipped closed.

"Roger?" she whispered, to test if he had indeed drifted into drugged unconsciousness so that she could begin to bathe and bandage his wound. "Roger?"

His lashes lifted slightly. "It's Ryder," he corrected her. "It's Ryder, Ryder Bingham."

It was almost dawn. Through a film of summer fog, the sky was brightening, and in the thickly leafed trees outside the window the birds had begun to stir. This was not the first dawn Jillian had met alone after keeping an all-night vigil. She had spent weeks watching her father die, knowing then, as she had this night, that the man she cared for might not live to see the light of day. Behind her the escaped Confederate lay sleeping the heavy, fathomless sleep of the desperately ill. Since the evening before, he had been lost in unconsciousness, unaware of her ministrations, of her diligence, of her concern. And though she had tried to help him, he lay burning with unchecked fever.

Sighing, she moved to the nightstand and turned up the wick on the lamp beside the bed. She poured more water into the basin and, taking up a cloth, began to sponge her patient's body. With careful, measured strokes, she bathed his face and throat, his sinewy arms and torso. She flicked back the covers and, after moistening the cloth again, drew it over his hips and legs, heedless of his nakedness. She bathed him as she had more than a score of times in the desolate hours between midnight and dawn. But in spite of her best efforts, Bingham's condition had not changed. What Jill had imagined was a simple fever that would respond to rest, liquids, and clean bandages had turned into something terrifying and life-threatening. It had turned into something she did not know how to fight.

As the night advanced, the temptation to send for a doctor had grown strong within her, and Jill had weighed the chances for the Confederate's survival against the certainty of his recapture. Were the attentions of a doctor worth the inevitable loss of Bingham's freedom? If he was retaken, what were the chances that he would lie untended in a Yankee prison until the wounds and fever took his life? She wished with all her heart that she could ask Ryder what he would have her do, but he was far beyond answering her.

Jillian stared blankly at the Confederate sprawled unconscious on the bed. But even as she watched him with fear glowing at the back of her eyes, it was her dying father she seemed to see before her. She remembered how his features had grown stark and drawn with fever, how his face had been marked by lines of pain, just as Bingham's was now. She had wanted so badly to save Benjamin Chandler, to urge him to cling to life for her sake if not his own. But as hard as she had fought, there had been nothing she could do. For all her care, all her strength, all her devotion, she had not been able to make a difference.

She closed her eyes against the image of her father lying dead and steeled her heart against the debilitating pain of defeat. Could she make a difference with Ryder Bingham? she found herself wondering. Did she have the courage and resourcefulness to fight for his life, now that she knew the price of failure?

Gingerly she peeled the bandage back from the rebel's shoulder and frowned at what she saw. The flesh was redder and more swollen than ever, and yellowish matter had begun to gather at the edges of the wounds. Clearly something needed to be done, but she was at a loss as to how to proceed.

Frantically Jill drew on the bit of medical training she had received while helping in the private school's infirmary and from what she had gleaned in nursing her father. But nothing she'd done had prepared her to care for Bingham. If his had been another kind of wound, she might have treated the inflammation with a yeast and charcoal poultice. But would such a basic remedy help now?

Jillian sighed and began to bathe Ryder again, but as she worked over him, her mind was busy. A visit to the boarding-house kitchen would provide the yeast and charcoal she needed for the poultice. But she would have to secure the ingredients now, before the servants began to stir, or wait until they left the kitchen at the end of the day. One look at the rebel convinced her that he could not wait for nightfall, and that knowledge forced her into action.

Setting aside the cloth and tucking the blankets beneath her patient's chin, Jill moved toward the door. Once out in the hall, the glow of a small hanging lamp guided her down the carpeted stairs to the darkened entryway. In most city houses food was prepared in a basement kitchen, and Jillian set out to find the servants' stairs. Beneath the slope of the steps toward the back of the house, she found two identical doors. Jill reasoned that one of them must lead to the cellar, but when she pulled open the first, she was half buried by an avalanche of heavy winter clothing. With difficulty, she muffled her gasp of surprise as coats, hats, mittens, and scarves pelted down around her. For an instant she stood staring at the multicolored tangle, then frantically stuffed the clothes back inside the closet and threw her weight against the door to get it latched.

Beyond the second panel lay a curving, pitch-black stairwell. Clinging to the banister, Jill inched her way downward, aware of the smoothness of the wood beneath her fingers, the coolness of the passage, and the smell of herbs and spices drifting up to her. It was slow going in the darkness, and she stayed close to the wall, both for safety's sake and to avoid the creak of the well-worn stair treads. Finally her feet touched the uneven brick of the floor below, and she stood frozen, trying to get her bearings. Then to her left she began to discern the hulking shapes of a cast-iron stove and a huge free-standing pantry. To her right she saw a soapstone sink and a row of barrels. Taking a match from the iron holder on the wall at the foot of the steps, Jill lit the lamp that hung above the table in the center of the room. The harsh yellow light seemed startling and overbright after creeping around in the dark, and she shaded her eyes against the glare as she peered around at her surroundings.

She had no difficulty locating the yeast; it was in a sealed jar stored in the coolest corner of the pantry. She scooped a quantity of it into a bowl and then pulled out the grate beneath the stove's firebox in search of charcoal. But the stove must have been cleaned the night before and new wood laid for the fire this morning. There was no leftover charcoal to be had.

Panic leaped in Jill's chest as she cast around for another source. Without charcoal the poultice would be useless. Already the sky beyond the kitchen windows had taken on a purplish glow, but in spite of the need for haste, she was drawn to glance out into the yard. There by the back fence stood an old-fashioned country smokehouse. The minute she saw the building, she recognized its significance.

Blowing out the kitchen lamp and setting the bowl of yeast aside, Jill snapped the lock on the kitchen door and burst into the yard. As she ran toward the building where bacon and hams were cured, she felt the dew-soaked grass whisper against her skirts, wetting them to her knees. But as she approached the smokehouse, there was nothing in her mind but the fate of the man who lay in the room upstairs. The bolt on the smokehouse door worked hard, but with a jerk she wrestled it free, and against her fierce assault the door itself creaked wide. As she stood in the opening, she sensed the sting of hickory smoke in her eyes and nostrils, the sweet, ripe scent of curing meat. Falling to her knees, she grubbed in the firebox, scooping chunks of smoldering charcoal from the banked, low-burning fire. Heedless of the heat and flying sparks, Jill shoveled up pieces of charcoal and plunged them into the pail of water that stood beside the door. When she was sure the fire was out, she retrieved the charcoal, scooped it up in her skirt, and sprinted toward the house.

Once inside, she snatched up the bowl of yeast and headed for the stairs. With fear of discovery dogging her, she raced for the second floor, sacrificing silence and stealth for speed. Just as she closed the door to the rented room behind her, there was the sound of footsteps in the hall. Panting with relief, she leaned back against the panel.

"Jillian?" A hoarse whisper cut through the silence. "Jillian, is that you?"

Jill started at the sound of her name. Then, realizing who had spoken, she set aside her burdens and went to where the Confederate lay. "Yes, Ryder, what is it?"

"Jillian?" Bingham asked, confusion wrinkling his brow. "Is this Canada? Did we escape to Canada?"

Jill settled herself on the edge of the bed and took his hot hand in hers. Though she might have wished it otherwise, she had nothing to tell Bingham but the truth. "No, Ryder, I'm sorry.

This isn't Canada. A fever came upon you, and we were forced to leave the train. We're in Rochester, New York, about ninety miles from the border."

She saw disappointment and resignation in his eyes, and she swallowed hard around the knot of emotion that suddenly clogged her throat. There was nothing more to say to him, little hope she could give. And without offering him false assurances, she heard the silence grow long and strained between them.

"Are you in pain?" she finally asked.

Jillian could see that he wanted to deny it but couldn't give voice to a lie. "Yes," he conceded wearily and let his eyes slip closed.

She sat with Ryder a few moments more, stroking his brow with one sooty palm. Soon he seemed to sleep again, but when she gathered herself to rise, Ryder stirred

"Jillian," he murmured, "Jillian, I need to get to Canada."

Regret flooded through her at his words. It was regret laced with tenderness and compassion, regret touched with remorse and concern. More than life, Bingham wanted to escape, and Jillian could no longer deny him the reassurance he was seeking.

"I know, Ryder, and you will get to Canada. I promise you. When you're well, I'll help you cross the border. But we can't do anything now, not while you're so sick and need to rest."

She gave Ryder another dose of laudanum, then put water on to boil in the brass teakettle that was a fixture of the ornate fireplace furnishings. While she waited, Jillian mixed a bromide solution and cleaned away the putrefaction that had formed around the wounds. When the water was hot, she mixed it with yeast and ground charcoal to form a thick grayish paste. Ryder stirred fitfully as she packed the poultice against his wounds and bound it in place. He slept heavily between the applications, and Jill was glad.

Toward midmorning she took a few moments to see to her own attire and turn her mind to the problems before her. Since she could hardly leave Ryder in this condition, she would have to remain in Rochester. That meant sending her father-in-law another telegram, concocting another lie to explain her delay. There were other things she needed to do as well: get a bit of quinine for Ryder's "malaria," alcohol to bathe him, and willow bark for tea to reduce his fever. He should have a nightshirt to hide his wound, and if she was not to sacrifice any more of her clothes, she would have to get some clean, soft cotton for bandages. As she smoothed her hair and studied herself in the looking glass, she could not help but wonder what madness had possessed her to accept responsibility for the Confederate.

She was just finishing her toilette when there was a knock on the door. Pausing only long enough to pull up the sheets to hide Ryder's bandage, Jill went to answer it. Outside stood their landlady, bearing a covered tray.

"How is your husband, Mrs. Walsh?" she inquired as she bustled into the room. "When you didn't come down for breakfast, I was worried."

"He's no better, I fear, Mrs. Marshall," Jillian answered, glancing at Ryder with undisguised concern. "I couldn't bring myself to leave him."

"I thought as much." The landlady nodded and set the tray aside, sending a speculative glance in Jill's direction. "You haven't been married long, have you, Mrs. Walsh?"

The question startled Jillian, and she fumbled for a reply. "No, not long," she gulped. "This is the first time Roger has fallen ill since we've been together." Her words had the ring of truth, and Mrs. Marshall appeared to believe them.

Smiling with understanding, the older woman patted Jillian's hand. "Well, malaria's serious; that's a fact. But once you get some quinine into him, your husband will come around. Don't you forget, these men are tough. But while you're caring for him," she advised as she turned to go, "see to yourself as well. Eat and sleep to keep up your strength, or you'll end up in bed beside him."

"That hardly seems likely," Jill muttered under her breath as she closed and locked the door behind her visitor.

The breakfast Mrs. Marshall had brought was welcome, though, and Jillian managed to rouse Ryder enough to feed him farina and tea before he slipped back into unconsciousness. Reluctant to leave him that way, she hurried out to do her errands. When she returned, she began a regimen of willow tea, alcohol baths, and poultices that would continue until he was better.

As she worked over him, Jill noticed things about her patient that the anger and fear of the previous day had prevented her from acknowledging. She saw Bingham's wide, noble brow; the thick, black brows that rose like a breaking wave to trace the ridge above his eyes. She saw the straight, high-bridged nose that accentuated the symmetry of his features; the sable crescents of silky lashes that lay like smudges on his cheeks. There was something uncompromising about the angle of his jaw, even softened by a two-day growth of whiskers; something strong and indomitable about the turn of his chin. Though he lay lost in unconsciousness, his mouth was set with stark determination as if the fight they fought together was demanding all his energies.

As she watched him, she acknowledged that there was something compelling about the man. He was mysterious and multifaceted, with a hundred shadings to his nature that were yet to be explored. She had seen evidence of his ruthlessness, yet there was tenderness in him, too. He had shown courage and a resolution as strong as tempered steel. Still, he was a man of largely undetermined virtues, of foreign and uncompromising loyalties. In spite of it, she wanted desperately to save him, to succeed with this Confederate where she had failed her father.

Jill rose from the chair beside the bed and went to stare out the window to where rows of snowy sheets snapped in the summer wind. She was tired, Jillian told herself, tired and filled with foolish fancies. In her weariness she was weaving improbable dreams around someone she hardly knew, ascribing impossible attributes to a man who might be little more than a ruffian. Granted, there was something about Ryder Bingham that touched her, but perhaps it was seeing a strong man made vulnerable that stirred her sympathies and her imagination.

In the blaze of afternoon sunlight Jillian closed her eyes and breathed a plea for her patient's recovery. Dear God, how much she wanted this man to live! She wanted him to live because he seemed worthy of concern, because he had been willing to trade his life for that of a child. She wanted him to live because she had known too much of death, seen too much of loss to willingly lose again.

But as sunset faded into darkness, Ryder showed signs of rising fever, and as the evening advanced, he began to toss and mumble fitfully. In a haze of exhaustion Jill worked over him, soothing him with a stream of murmured endearments, moistening his lips with water and willow tea, smoothing alcohol-soaked cloths over his burning skin. She used the last of the charcoal and yeast to make fresh poultices and applied them to his wounds. But for a long time nothing helped: not the tender care she gave him, not the jumbled prayers she whispered, not the determination that rose up inside her that this man would not die.

Forty-eight hours ago she had not even known that Ryder Bingham existed. She had not known the contours of his body, now as familiar as her own, had not heard the velvety drawl that was scored into her memory. She had not realized that a chance meeting, a single moment out of time, could alter and change so much.

How long she had soothed Ryder's fevered mutterings and bathed his burning flesh, she did not know. She only knew that sometime in the lonely hours before dawn he grew still and cooler at last. And somehow at the moment of victory, Jill surrendered the rigid control she had forced on her emotions.

The tears she had not been able to shed for the loss of her new husband, the grief she had not been able to express at her beloved father's passing came pouring from her in the anonymity of a stranger's bedside. Her joy at Bingham's recovery became a surrogate for her grief, and she shook with soft but rending sobs.

She wept for her sheltered childhood, for the depth of her father's love, for the hours they had shared, and for the years she would spend missing him. She wept for the husband she would never see again, for the man she had married but hardly knew, for the barren future that stretched before her, and for the children she had been denied. She wept for pain and fear and loneliness, mourning things she could neither change nor rectify.

How long she wept she hardly knew, muffling the sounds of her long-held grief. But as she cried, tender hands came to soothe and comfort her, to stroke her face and hair. Whether the comfort the Confederate gave was conscious or unknowing, rational or instinctive, she neither knew nor cared. She accepted it gratefully and wordlessly complied when he pulled her down beside him. He petted her and held her until sleep claimed them both. Curled together they passed the night, at rest, at peace, at last.

The creak of a hinge intruded on his consciousness, like the screech of a tomcat in search of his mate or the scrape of a bow on an untuned violin. Ryder stirred and opened his eyes, coming slowly awake in the room where Jillian Walsh had brought him two nights before. After sleeping most of the day, he was feeling better, though his shoulder was uncomfortably stiff and his head still ached a bit with the residue of fever. But in spite of it, he was already anticipating the time when he could resume his journey and cross the border into Canada.

What he was doing here or why Jillian Walsh had taken him from the train and cared for him were things he could not fathom. His illness should have provided her with a perfect opportunity to turn him over to the Yankees or simply abandon him to his fate. But instead, she had claimed him as her husband and undoubtedly saved his life. And though he had tried to discern her reasons, Jillian didn't seem willing to discuss her unexpected altruism. He only knew that he was grateful to her: grateful for keeping his secrets, grateful for the care she had given him, grateful for her inexplicable generosity. But did her actions mean he was safe, that she would not betray him to the Yankees? Or was there some unexpected twist to the cunning game she played?

With an effort he forced the dark thought from his mind and for diversion turned his attention to his surroundings. The room he and Jillian shared was lavishly furnished for one in a boarding house. Flowered paper covered the walls, and there were burgundy carpets underfoot. The fireplace was of hand-carved limestone, and the ornate fender and andirons looked to be made of solid brass. In the gentle glow of the lamplight, the cherrywood bedroom suite took on a warm reddish hue, and his gaze drifted from the decorative scroll on the foot of his bed to one on the nearby nightstand and on to the tall armoire, standing now with its doors half open, forming a protective enclosure.

In the space between the floor and the bottom of the doors, Ryder could see the hem of a woman's flowing skirt. But as he took note of it, the skirt began to rise, revealing the scalloped lace flounce on a black muslin petticoat. Intrigued, he watched the hem ride higher and began to surmise that i.1 the private enclosure behind the half-open panels his self-appointed guardian was preparing herself for bed. The elevation of the skirt was like a theater curtain rising, and Ryder squirmed left and right, trying to improve his view of the proceedings. But try as he might, nothing helped, and to his frustration he saw that the first petticoat was being raised to reveal another beneath. He had begun to scowl darkly at his abominable luck when a movement in the mirror on the opposite wall caught his attention. He stretched and craned his neck and was rewarded by a glimpse of flesh as Jillian pulled the second petticoat free of her head and shoulders.

There was a leap in his pulse at the sight of her, an acceleration in his breathing that might have given a doctor cause for either concern or jubilation on his behalf. Tantalized by what he had seen already, Ryder eased himself higher on his pillows and prepared to enjoy the show. He had been wanting a chance to study the woman who had taken it upon herself to rescue him, anyway. Those minutes on the train when she had been tending his wound had given him scant opportunity to take her measure; yet, in spite of the distractions, his impressions were surprisingly clear. He could recall the gardenia-pale glow of her skin, the delicate cast of her features, the compassion and concern in her eyes.

With the memory came the same rush of response he had known then, only now he was not so willing to accept either its spontaneity or its strength. Instead, he wanted to rationalize what he felt, to explain away what seemed to come perilously close to magic. It had been the danger that had made his perceptions of her so sharp and delightful, he told himself. It had been the risk that had made those moments seem significant. Staring all the more intently at the mirror, he tried to ignore the unsettling effect this woman seemed to have on him, to deny the needs she stirred.

But even as he struggled to master his emotions, what he saw in the looking glass made objectivity impossible. Beneath his fascinated gaze, Jillian continued to disrobe, removing her wide cage hoops and sliding the final layer of petticoats slowly down her thighs. As she bent to retrieve them, she moved with unaffected grace, then turned her back to the glass and tucked the discarded petticoats into the depths of the armoire. Ryder's eyes swept over her as she put the clothes away, skimming from the neckline of her chemise, down the laces at the back of her corset, to the curves of her shapely behind, outlined enticingly by the cut of her pantalets.

Only by biting the tip of his tongue did Ryder manage to stifle the offer to help her with her stays. For there was a need to touch her growing inside him, a need to strip away the layers of feminine subterfuge and reveal all of her to him. At the mere prospect of seeing her bared before him, of feeling her flesh beneath his hands, his mouth went dry, his palms went wet, and he wondered rather dazedly if he was feverish again.

With great difficulty he dragged his eyes from the image in the mirror and tried to collect his thoughts. His continued staring invaded Jillian's privacy, he told himself severely, and what's more, she would be furious should she discover what he'd been doing. If he retained any remnant of his genteel upbringing, maintained any pretense of being a gentleman, he couldn't continue to spy on her. But try as he might, he couldn't keep his gaze from straying back to the dresser mirror.

While he was battling his conscience, Jillian dispatched her corset and pantalets. She now stood behind the embracing doors of the armoire dressed only in her shift. It was a modest enough garment, covering her from collarbone to knees, but in contrast to the sheer black lawn the skin visible beneath took on a pearly glow. The hint of flesh was distracting enough, but then, with graceful, sinuous movements, Jillian began to take down her hair. One by one, she plucked the hairpins free, letting tendrils of honey-gold fall loose around her shoulders.

Dressed only in her shift, with her hair flowing down her back, Jillian seemed both innocent and wanton, at once inviolate and touchable. The cadence of Ryder's breathing altered as he wondered what it would be like to strip her shift away. If given half a chance, he would slide his hands beneath the hem and nudge the fabric upward, bare her thighs and slender flanks, then the shape of her hips and belly. He would span her waist with a brush of his hands, expose the crests of her rose-tipped breasts as his palms came to cup and caress her. He went dizzy and hot at the thought of it. And then a vision took root in his imagination: of this woman stretched out on the bed, supple and willing beside him, of her arms reaching out to beckon him, of her lips whispering his name.

But even as the fantasy grew, he knew he could not act on what he felt. In the past three days, Jillian Walsh had become someone very special, so much more than a stranger on a train. He had sensed her fear of him, known her tenderness and concern, recognized weariness and pain in her eyes. He had learned that there was intelligence and courage in her, resourcefulness and determination, sweetness and serenity.

With that knowledge came the realization that Jillian was not and never had been a woman with whom he might share a brief, bright spate of passion. She was not a woman he could take to his bed, then blithely walk away from. She deserved more than a quick tumble in the sheets, more than a few hours of unencumbered bliss. Jillian was not the kind of woman who could share her body without sharing her emotions, who could give any part of herself without offering her all. Making love to Jillian would be poignant, sweet, and binding. It would necessitate declarations Ryder had no desire or right to make.

After his long deprivation, Bingham was eager for a woman's warmth, eager for the feel of a woman's flesh against his own. But even as he recognized his need for mindless physical union, he knew he could not find that kind of release with Jill. The realization had a bitter taste, but it was just as well that he had made the discovery before he acted out his fantasies, before he made the irrevocable mistake of claiming Jillian Walsh for his own.

He took a long breath and closed his eyes. Until now, watching this beautiful woman had been a harmless diversion, but all at once it was stirring desires he knew he should not entertain, arousing needs he could not satisfy. It was time to turn his eyes from the glass, time to allow Jillian her privacy.

He settled back against the pillows and tried to will the wanting from his blood. Minutes passed as he lay feigning sleep and fighting for control. Finally the need seeped away, and he sank down into the pillows as drowsiness claimed him.

In the quiet he could hear the ticking of the mantel clock, the splash of water as Jillian washed up for the night, the rustle of cloth against skin as she drew on her nightdress and wrapper. Then came the rumble of coal from the scuttle into the fireplace, the flare of a match and the quick, sharp scent of sulfur. Soon the crackle of flames singed the edges of the silence, and the small fire in the grate dispelled the hint of evening chill. It was the footsteps that came whispering in the direction of the bed a few minutes later that roused him, and Bingham opened his eyes to find Jillian beside him.

"Ryder," she inquired softly, indicating the cup in her hand, "can you take a bit of willow tea? I think it will rid you of your fever."

He stirred, stretched, and took the cup from her. "Yes, I think so," he agreed. But when she turned to go, his fingers closed around the skirt of her dressing gown. "Jillian, please, will you sit with me awhile?"

There was entreaty in his voice that was difficult to refuse, and Jill paused to tug the black cotton robe more closely around her. Surely there could be no harm in talking with him for a few minutes before he slept. After all, they had spent the last three days constantly in each other's company. Still, there was something disconcerting about finding him wide awake, totally aware and intently watching her. Stifling the feelings of unease, Jillian went to gather up a bit of needlework before settling herself on the far side of the bed.

"What are you making?" he asked absently, watching as she threaded her needle from a skein of parchment brown.

"It's going to be a mourning scene, though I've hardly begun it yet."

It was not an unusual enterprise for a woman in an early stage of grief. The pictures were formula pieces comprising a burial urn, a grove of willow trees, and a group of mourners embroidered on a background of hand-painted silk. From what he could see, her painting was skillfully done; on the left she had begun to stitch the trunk of a tree.

The mention of mourning pictures gave him an opportunity to ask a question that had been plaguing him since that day on the train. "Who is it for?" he inquired, hoping to draw her out.

There was a long pause before Jillian raised her head, and when she did, there were tears gilding the tips of her lashes. "I don't know," she said with deceptive simplicity. "I don't know who or what I'm grieving for."

Ryder frowned, confused by her words, chagrined and ashamed of his tactless curiosity. "I'm sorry—" he began, but Jillian cut him short.

"No, it's all right, Ryder. Really it is. It's just that I seem to have lost so much so suddenly."

A muffling, velvet silence descended, and they sat staring: he with a desire to console and comfort, she with a need to bare her secrets. Yet even as she considered accepting this one chance to speak the shocking words aloud, she knew that nothing he could say would assuage her guilt.

"Jillian, please tell me." His words were hardly more than a whisper, much less than a demand, but they offered her a chance for understanding, a chance to share her grief.

Who was he to judge her, after all? she found herself thinking. He was an escaped prisoner, a Confederate. He might well have whipped slaves, killed men, done things too bad for her to know. And even if she told him everything, in a few days they would part and her secrets would be safe.

The words she ached to speak rose in her chest, swelled in her throat with the sting of bile. Because she knew it would hurt to give them voice, she fought to hold them back, but they burst from her, propelled by her need to be free of them.

"My father died just a bit more than a month ago," she finally gasped, "and my husband preceded him by days. But the thing I'm mourning, the reason I grieve, is the loss of my security!" It was a shameful admission, the callous, selfish truth. And as much as she wished to deny it, the confusion and uncertainty had affected her more than either death.

Once she had spoken, Jillian could not bear to look at the man on the far side of the bed. She knew he must be shocked by her admission, appalled by her words. But then his hand was moving nearer, taking hers, clasping her trembling fingers. He was offering succor, understanding, sympathy, and something else, something she could not name.

Time might have ceased to be as they sat without speaking, united in a silent communication that far transcended words. The communication was soothing, genuine, unaffected, and for the first time since she left Harrisburg, Jillian was able to think rationally about her loss.

Ryder waited patiently as she sat deep in thought, and though he sensed the release of long-held tensions, he knew Jill needed to put her feelings into words before she could be free of them.

"Is that why you grieve, Jilly," he pressed her at last, "for the loss of stability, control of your life? Are you afraid of what the future will bring?"

She turned on him with fresh tears rising in her eyes. "Yes! Yes!" she cried, feeling at once misled and betrayed by the questions he was asking. "I thought you understood. I've lost everything: a father who was dearer than life to me, a man I married but hardly knew. I've lost my home, my security, and my hope of happiness."

For him they were not unfamiliar fears; Ryder had lost people, too. He knew better than she might suspect the guilt and devastating ambivalence that could overwhelm a person in the aftermath of death.

"Jillian," he began softly, "listen to me, please. What you feel is natural, and in an odd way right, considering what's been taken from you. When someone dies, it's asking more than any of us can give to grieve for that person without regretting all the other things that change. In any ending there is grief, but there can be loss and fear and anger in it, too. It's natural to feel disappointment for broken promises, fear at being left alone, and anger at what sometimes seems very much like desertion."

His eyes held hers, and in their mysterious sapphire depths she saw that he spoke the truth.

"That's just how I feel," she acknowledged tremulously.

He nodded once. "I know."

They fell silent again, but it was a silence filled with companionship and comfort, with burgeoning friendship and mutual respect. As they sat side by side on the coverlet, the evening coolness feathered the edges of the curtains; the fire in the grate sent out a lambent warmth. Their hands lay linked on the blanket between them, her sewing and her sadness willingly cast aside.

From the lack of demand she began to speak, spinning her history out before him like a skein of silken thread. "My father knew he was dying long before he stopped teaching, long before the war began, long before Jefferson Walsh came into our lives. I see now that it was his fate to try to circumvent his own mortal-

ity, mine to try to ease his pain, and Jeff's to be the solution that
brought peace to all but Father's final days."

She paused to stare past Ryder, as if seeing happier times.
"Jeff had been mustered at Camp Curtin outside of Harrisburg,
and my father met him one afternoon when a group of Union
officers had come in to have a drink at the National Hotel. He
brought Jeff home to dinner that night, and from the beginning I
knew what my father intended."

"He wanted you to marry Jeff."

"Yes, that's right. If I married a man like Jeff, Father wouldn't
have to worry that when he died he would leave me alone and
penniless."

Ryder acknowledged her words with a nod. "What was Jeff
like?"

"Oh, he was a good man, a kind man, from a well-connected
family."

"His father was a congressman, I understand," Ryder commented, though Jill did not catch the irony in his tone.

"Yes, a congressman," she confirmed. "But Father was impressed with Jeff as well. He had been reading the law before he
joined the army, and the fact that the Walshes were wealthy didn't
hurt his prospects, either."

"No, I suppose it didn't."

"Soon Jeff was coming to dinner several nights a week, and
whenever he was there, my father conspired to throw us together.
Sometimes he would insist that Jeff sit beside me on the piano
bench and turn the pages of my music when I played, or Father
would smoke his cigar on the veranda to give us time alone. If
Jeff knew what my father was about, he never let on, but it
wasn't long before he was in league with Father's plans."

"So Jeff was smitten by a Pennsylvania miss," Ryder observed
wryly. "It's not hard to see why."

Jillian was not a vain woman, but Ryder's words pleased her.
What this man thought had become important to her. That he
responded to her in ways that went beyond her role as nurse
seemed vital to her femininity and self-respect. For a moment
their eyes held, and she was unaccountably delighted to find admiration for her there. A flush of pleasure mounted to her cheeks,
and dropping her lashes she finally glanced away.

"We all knew that Jeff's stay at Camp Curtin was bound to be
a short one," she went on, picking up the thread of her story,
"and when he asked me to marry him, I did what Father wanted
and accepted him."

"Why did you agree to his proposal?" Ryder prodded her.

"Why?" Jill paused, perplexed. "I told you. It was what my father thought was best for me."

"But why did you want to marry Jeff?" Was it possible that she didn't understand what he was asking? Hadn't she questioned her own motives at such an important juncture in her life?

"Well, Jeff was a good man," she began, "and he was kind to me."

Ryder waited in silence, determined not to make the telling easier.

"I knew that my father wanted to see me settled, and after the panic back in 'fifty-seven there wasn't any money left. So I accepted Jeff's proposal, and on the first leave he could get we were married."

The next question came hard, but Ryder knew he must hear her answer, no matter how difficult it might be for either one of them. "Did you love Jeff?"

He could see the color in her cheeks intensify as she struggled to admit the truth. "I was fond of Jeff," Jill answered precisely, "very fond of him."

"And for the sake of security and obedience, you agreed to spend the rest of your life with a man of whom you were merely fond?" There was censure in his tone when there had been none before, and the sound of it confused her.

"It's not wrong to want security," she defended herself, reclaiming her fingers from his grip. "Nor is it wrong for a daughter to obey a father she loves. All he wanted was the best for me; that was all I wanted myself. And I don't see how my feelings for my husband are any concern of yours!"

He saw a flash of defiance in her eyes and somehow welcomed it, though he curbed his own anger with difficulty. It wasn't wrong in this day and age for a woman to marry for expediency. And it was true that her feelings for her dead husband weren't any concern of his. But somehow he needed to be reassured that she hadn't grown to love Jefferson Walsh in the months she had been his wife.

Controlling his feelings, Ryder continued to draw her out. "So you married Jeff and, while he was at the front, kept house for your ailing father."

"Father needed me. He was very ill, and I wanted to stay with him until the end. Mother died when I was ten, and Father and I had always been very close. If I had been a man, I would surely have had a teaching position at the private school to sustain me."

Jillian paused with an absent smile. "Father was always so proud of my ability at figures. We used to play games with numbers and symbols and codes."

"What happened then?"

Jill drew a long breath and released it slowly, her expression strained and somber. "My husband died in an assault on Petersburg. And after that, after the life my father had planned for me crumbled, he simply gave up. He died less than a week after we got the letter from Jeff's commanding officer."

Swift, unexpected anger speared Ryder. How could a man who loved this woman as much as her father had simply give up and desert her? "Damned selfish bastard!" Bingham mumbled under his breath.

"What did you say?"

"It was nothing, Jillian, nothing. Go on."

"Go on? There's nothing left to tell. I sold what I could to pay my father's debts. And when Gerald Walsh wired inviting me to come to Niagara Falls, I didn't have any choice but to accept."

There was despair in her words, hopelessness and finality. Sensing it, Ryder was silent. She had made her peace with what she'd done, and he had no right to question her decision. Still her bland acceptance galled him.

"What I don't understand," he said at last, "is why you didn't seek out a teaching position instead of taking an offer you clearly don't want to accept."

"If I had never been married, I might well have been able to teach at a ladies' seminary, but that's not something a married woman can do."

It was true enough. A woman who'd had carnal knowledge of a man might carry the taint of it to the precious, virginal daughters of the wealthy who patronized such institutions. In the abstract he had always approved of the policy, but now he understood its absurdity.

His eyes moved over Jill's sweet, pure face, lingering on her smooth, clear brow, the flush across her cheekbones. They dropped to the curves of her lips, the tender depths at the corners, the width at the bow. His gaze moved to the riot of taffy-gold curls tumbling down her back and then to the deep-set eyes that gave her face a serenity beyond her years. Yet for all the delicacy of her features, for all her fashionable fairness, there was something about her that spoke of strength and character. Desire and solicitude stirred in him as he watched her, but he knew he could offer her neither his passion nor his protection.

"Why didn't you try to find some other work?" he finally asked her.

"Oh, I do sew a straight seam, and I have done my share of laundry. There aren't many places for a respectable woman to earn her keep. But then, I don't want to be alone, and the war has left a dreadful shortage of men for women like me to marry." There was derision in her tone, and Bingham felt his share of the sting.

"I can no more take care of myself," she continued bitterly, "than I can hope to fly."

There was a pause, a moment of consideration before Ryder spoke. "And yet you have taken care of me."

Jillian did not want to consider the possibilities he was posing. She had made a very difficult decision nearly a month before, and she was not going to let this stranger undermine her resolve. Accepting Gerald Walsh's invitation made the most sense for a woman in her position. As much as she dreaded being beholden to a man she had never met, of becoming an unwelcome member of Walsh's household, it was what she meant to do.

No, Jillian thought as she picked up her sewing, she was not prepared to discuss her motives in deciding her future or for helping Ryder Bingham. The reasons in one case were clearer than she would have liked and in the other more obscure. These few days were an interlude out of time, a few brief moments when things were as they would never be again. And though she couldn't say why, it made Jillian uncomfortable to acknowledge it.

"I must be tiring you out," she apologized abruptly, rising to stand beside the bed. "It's getting late, and you need your rest."

"I'm fine, Jillian, really," Ryder tried to reassure her, although she was busy smoothing the covers and paid him no mind. But when she moved to draw the extra quilt from the bed, he gathered the corner in his fist.

"Just where do you think you're going with this?" he demanded.

"I'm going to put the quilt around me," she told him, "and curl up in the chair for the night."

"The hell you are!" Ryder's eyes narrowed threateningly, and suddenly Jillian was reminded of what an intimidating adversary he could be.

In spite of it, she gave a determined tug on her end of the quilt. "Ryder—"

"Damn it, Jillian! We slept in this bed together last night. I will not have you spend tonight in the chair."

"Things are hardly the same as they were last night."

"And just how are they different?"

"Well, I'm not fully dressed," she stammered, flushing.

"Yes, I'd noticed that."

"And you're not nearly as sick."

He nodded in acknowledgment. "Thanks to you. And what kind of gratitude would it be if I let you sleep in that uncomfortable chair when you might as well have the other side of the bed?"

"But, Ryder—"

"Jillian, we're supposed to be married. What on earth will the servants think if they find you sleeping in a chair?"

"I hardly think they'll know what sleeping arrangements we've made."

"My point exactly."

Still she stood her ground, pulling the quilt inexorably in her direction.

Finally he lost patience with the situation and let his corner go. "Damn it, Jillian, don't you realize I'm not feeling up to molesting you!"

Her mouth went perfectly round at the implication of his words, and a flush of pure mortification moved up her neck to her hairline.

Realizing he'd silenced her temporarily, Ryder pressed his advantage. "I'll sleep under the covers, and you can sleep on top with that quilt pulled over you. Listen, woman, don't be a fool. Nothing's going to happen between us tonight. And I'm far too weary to argue with you."

Jill hesitated, weighing concern for her patient against what he had proposed. It was indeed a big bed, and she had spent one night in it already.

"If you promise . . ." she wheedled.

He turned on his side and nestled down into the pillows. "Damn it, I promise!"

She was not sure she could trust his promises, but she blew out the oil lamp and came to the window side of the bed anyway. "You promised," she reiterated, as she gingerly placed a knee on the mattress.

"Yes, yes."

He felt the dip and sway as she climbed aboard, heard the bedboards creak as she settled in.

His voice came to her just as she was pulling up the quilt. "You can take it off now."

"What?"

"Your dressing gown."

Jillian hesitated a moment. She had indeed been wishing she could remove the restricting garment and settle herself more comfortably. It was not difficult for her to decide to heed his suggestion. Turning away, she slipped the sash at her waist and tugged the close-cut sleeves down her arms.

Clad only in her nightdress, Jillian curled up on the bed again and pulled the quilt up to her ears. It seemed very strange to lie beside a man. During her brief marriage, she and Jeff had been apart more often than they were together, and she had never become accustomed to sharing a bed. Because of it, she was acutely aware of Ryder's warmth at her back, of the barely perceptible sound of his breathing. A scent that was completely his own drifted to her nostrils, and his slightest movement made her go tense and still. Yet somehow it also seemed wrong for them simply to turn their backs and go to sleep after all they had been through together.

Jillian raised herself on one arm and glanced back over her shoulder. She could see that Ryder was staring at the ceiling, his good arm bent and tucked behind his head. At her movement he turned to face her, and she could see his eyes shine in the dark.

"Good night, Ryder," she said softly, her voice tremulous and thin. "Sleep well."

His smile flashed, and there was either amusement or tenderness in his tone. "Good night, sweet Jilly. Good night and thank you. Thank you for everything."

Chapter Three

"YOU'RE NOT SETTING one foot outside that bed until I say so!" Jillian Walsh stood in the center of their rented room, her hands on her hips and her face set stubbornly. "You need at least two more days of bed rest before you'll be fit for anything, much less a visit to Canada."

Ryder saw raw determination in her face and was torn between an equal stubbornness and an overwhelming admiration for the beauteous female before him. This morning Jillian was perfectly enchanting, with her gown half buttoned and her hair dancing around her shoulders in a flurry of caramel-colored curls.

Arguing was the last thing he wanted to do with such a woman, but Ryder meant to have his way. "I won't be very pleasant company if you don't let me get up," he told her, his mouth drawn narrow and grim.

"Your behavior has been anything but exemplary since the moment we met, Mr. Bingham, so your threats don't frighten me a bit!"

There were a few seconds of combative silence, and then Jillian saw the grin Bingham could not quite repress quivering at the corners of his lips. Relief surged through her as she took note of it, because she had not been sure what Ryder's response to such an outburst might be. He could have been angry at her attempts to order his life or appalled by her waspish candor. But instead he seemed to enjoy her pepper, her willingness to stand up to him even though bland cooperation might have done more to smooth his way.

Until that moment, Jillian had never in her life spoken to a man in such a manner. But somehow this salacious behavior was at once both shocking and exhilarating. During the few talks they'd had, she had enjoyed bandying words with this Confederate, enjoyed it far more than any words she'd ever spoken to a man. But then, with her father she had always been the dutiful daughter, acquiescing to his wishes because she knew he only wanted what was best for her. With Jeff, she had practiced obedience, since it had been among the vows she'd made. But the temerity of her response to Ryder Bingham tickled her, and equally scandalous words bubbled to her lips in answer to the mischief in his eyes.

"Besides," she challenged, teasing him openly, "as far as I can see, you haven't got a shirt to don in proper company, anyway!"

"And I imagine I'm still missing some other less noticeable articles of clothing as well," he countered, then waited for Jill to color up.

He wasn't disappointed as a bright flush streamed from her breastbone to her hairline. He'd been only marginally aware of her undressing him the other night, but he could imagine how stunned she must have been when she found he was bare beneath his trousers. His grin widened at the thought, and Jillian's flush deepened.

"When the time comes, I'll be more than willing to remedy that deficiency," she snapped with what grace she could muster. "But until I do, you are certainly lacking the necessary accoutrements to join polite society."

He found himself enjoying her embarrassment and the overly proper tone she had adopted in an attempt to put him in his place. But in a way, what she said was true. He could hardly wander around bare-chested, and neither the bloodstained shirt he had been wearing the other day on the train nor the ragged tunic in his carpetbag would be suitable attire for what lay ahead of him.

"All right, Jillian, you win this time," he conceded reluctantly. "But find me something to do besides lie here and stare at the ceiling!"

Jillian nodded, seeing his restlessness as a good sign. In spite of the difficulties it might present, she was glad to see such strong evidence that he was feeling better. "There's a volume of poetry in my trunk you could read," she offered hopefully.

Ryder frowned. "Don't get me wrong," he began. "I've read my share of Shelley and Keats, but that's not quite the kind of diversion I had in mind."

"Well, perhaps I could get you today's newspaper," she suggested.

"That's a step in the right direction, to be sure." He continued to watch her, awaiting her next suggestion, his eyebrows raised quizzically.

An expression of exasperation settled around her mouth. "Why don't you simply tell me what you want, Ryder, instead of making me guess?"

"And miss the fun when I've had so little diversion lately?" When Jill made no reply, he continued, "What I'd really like is a knife."

"A knife!" Jillian was appalled. "I can just imagine what you want with a knife!"

"And maybe you could get me a few pieces of wood, too."
"Wood?"

"So I can whittle. Certainly you've heard of whittling, Jillian. I've been making little things from wood since I was a boy. On a long voyage or laid up in bed, it can be a tolerable pastime."

Jillian was not sure whether to believe him or not, and the doubt she felt must have shown in her face.

"If you bring me my carpetbag, I can show you the kind of things I make," Ryder offered.

Filled with suspicion, Jillian took his valise from the floor of the armoire. What was there in his carpetbag that he wanted to show her?

Gingerly she handed the bag to her patient and watched as he unfastened the straps. After rummaging around inside for a moment, Ryder withdrew several small carvings and set them on the coverlet. Each was slightly larger than a thimble and made of wood. As he began to arrange the objects in rows, she saw that they were chessmen. Some of them had been left their natural color, and others were darkened with lampblack. Jillian picked up one of the pieces, a knight, and noted that the work was delicate and carefully done. She could see the tilt of the horse's head, the texture of his mane and forelock, the flare of his tiny nostrils. She put it down among the others and fingered a rook. It, too, had been carved with artistry and care.

"Why, these are wonderful!" she told him, delighted and awed by his skill.

He chuckled but did not reply as he let half a dozen finger rings slip from his hand into hers. Three of them were dark and plain except for inlays of shell; another two were white, their tiny incised designs darkened, as in scrimshaw. The last seemed to be made of ivory, carved to resemble a circlet of roses.

"How did you make them? What did you use?" Jillian asked, enchanted by the things he'd done.

"Three are of gutta-percha, and the rest are made from bone. I had an arrangement with the cook at the prison, since we used nearly all the wood we got for heat."

"Bone?" she asked examining the rose ring even more closely. "Beef bone?"

He nodded. "Beef or ham or mutton. Chicken bones are brittle and have a tendency to shatter. I filled my pockets with the things I'd made before I escaped from Fort Lafayette. I didn't want to leave them behind so some enterprising guard could take them into the city and sell them off as prison oddities. You can have that rose ring if you admire it."

She slipped the ring on the third finger of her right hand, then turned it this way and that to show off the craftsmanship and fit. "May I really have it, Ryder?"

"Of course, you may," he assured her. "My God, Jillian, it's damned small payment for all you've done for me."

The expression of thanks somehow altered the atmosphere between them and made them suddenly aware of the larger world outside the rented room. It was not a reminder either of them welcomed.

"So you want a knife, do you?" Jill asked him, dropping the other rings back into his bag. "Is there any kind you prefer?"

"A common folding knife would be fine, and I need some bits of wood, too, if you can get them."

Jillian nodded. "And is there anything else that you require?"

"Nothing you'd be willing to give me," Ryder answered with an audacious grin.

Jill was wise enough not to pursue the subject of what else he wanted. It was clear that he was baiting her, and she was wise enough to avoid his trap. Instead she puttered around the room putting things away and finishing her toilette. Subduing her unruly locks took several minutes more, but finally she put on her bonnet and arranged the mourning veil over her face.

When she approached the bed to say good-bye to Ryder, she found that he had dropped into a doze. She lingered for a moment watching him. By outward signs alone she could tell how much better he was: vitality and color glowed in his face, and the dark circles beneath his eyes had faded completely. He was still too thin, but with good food and rest she would be able to—

Jillian paused, stunned by the trend of her own thoughts. She had no right to plan a future with this man in it. He was an escaped prisoner, a Confederate who could be recaptured at any moment. She was not going to be around to see that he ate properly and got sufficient rest. She would probably never even know if he made it safely into Canada.

It would only be a matter of time before they boarded a westbound train, and after she reached Niagara Falls, she would never see Bingham again. With that realization came a swell of disappointment that surprised and unsettled her. She had grown fond of the rebel, she was forced to admit. Once he had stopped being a threat to her, she had learned to enjoy his wry humor and his company. Now that they were no longer adversaries, she was able to talk with him openly, unfettered by expectations about what she should do or think or feel. And she realized with a shock that what she felt when she was able to share her feelings was very much like freedom.

She stood watching him for a very long time, tracing the determined cut of his features, noting the inky darkness of his hair and lashes, seeing the surprisingly gentle turn of his lips. She wanted to remember Ryder as he was now—handsome, tender, manly, napping in the midmorning sun.

An uncomfortable knot rose in her throat, and she turned away from the bed in haste. She should not let herself feel this softening for a man who was her enemy, a man who four days before had used threats to win his way. But in spite of her desire to subdue them, tender thoughts of Ryder Bingham lingered, and the regret and confusion she felt cast a pall on the promise of the bright, warm day.

Her errands in the city center were relatively few. First she went to the telegraph office to send another wire to her father-in-law; then she made a stop at the apothecary for a bottle of Dr. Flaherty's Enervating Tonic. If she was going to send Ryder off into the world before his health was fully restored, she would prepare him as best she could.

The longest stop was at the dry goods store where it took several minutes to gather her purchases. But when the clerk added up the cost of the things she had bought, Jillian was shocked by the amount.

"Seven dollars and thirty-five cents!" she exclaimed. "Are you certain you figured that correctly?"

"I surely did, ma'am," the shopkeeper assured her. "If'n you don't believe me, add it up yourself."

Jillian did and found a fifteen cent error in her favor, but fifteen cents really didn't help when she had less than ten dollars in her reticule. As she stood staring down at the column of figures, she knew her choices well. She could either put back some of her purchases or pay the bill in full.

"You might take out those men's handkerchiefs, or perhaps that extra pair of underdrawers," the storekeeper suggested, sensing her dilemma.

Jillian could feel the color mount to her cheeks and was thankful for the screen of her mourning veil. Ryder Bingham's lack of essentials had been embarrassment enough already, and she intended him to have everything he needed.

"No, no," she conceded. "I'll pay what you ask."

But as she made her way back to the boarding house, Jillian was forced to consider the depleted state of her finances. She had left New York on Friday with her ticket and a twenty dollar gold piece in her reticule. That gold piece had been the whole of her father's estate once his debts were paid, and after all she had been through with his solicitor, she had been happy to receive anything at all. Twenty dollars had seemed more than enough for her immediate needs, but now on Monday with the unexpected stop in Rochester, her funds were running low. She hadn't exactly squandered the money, but paying upkeep for an invalid Confederate was beginning to tax her budget. She had bought dinner that first night on the train and the things she had needed to nurse Ryder through his illness. Then, too, there was the expense of the telegrams she had sent Gerald Walsh, and now Ryder's clothes. She owed Mrs. Marshall for their stay, and after her many kindnesses Jill hated to cheat the woman.

When she returned to the room, Ryder seemed to sense her uneasiness and asked about it. But he was soon diverted by the knife and the little blocks of wood she had hunted up in the woodpile, and she was just as glad to keep her worries to herself.

Spreading the day-old newspaper across his lap, Ryder set to work. Though Jillian sat nearby with her sewing in her lap, she watched him covertly. She saw the way he scrutinized each piece of wood before he selected one to use and how he twisted and turned that block as if its contours held a compelling secret. Then as if he had solved the puzzle, he began to carve at last. With curls of wood falling away from beneath the blade, he worked for the best part of an hour, pausing now and then to flex his injured arm as if it pained him. But finally he folded the knife away and put a tiny sculpture on the edge of the mattress closest to where Jillian sat.

"You've carved a giraffe," she exclaimed delightedly, "just like the one Father showed me at the Philadelphia zoo when I was little!"

"Do you like it?"

She picked up the long-necked animal and stood it on her palm. "Oh, yes. You've done a wonderful job. He looks so gangly, yet somehow dignified and graceful."

"It's yours then."

She paused, raising her eyes from the sculpture to the now familiar lines of Ryder's face. "Like the ring, you mean?"

He leaned across the coverlet to close her fingers around the wooden giraffe. "Jillian, don't you realize this is all I have to give you?"

Her gaze met his, and there was something warm and tender in the midnight blue of his eyes. It was not friendship; it was not gratitude. It was something else: something sweet and nourishing, something that seemed to draw her closer, though she knew by some vague instinct it would be best to stay away.

But before she could do more than recognize the strange attraction, there was a knock on the door, and Ryder's noon meal arrived on a tray. It was Jillian's signal to wash up and tidy her hair before she joined the rest of the boarders in the dining room.

Though the last few days had been cool, the afternoon brought more seasonable warmth, and Ryder soon grew bored and restive.

"I'd give a lot to be out of this room," he complained. "What's this town like, anyway?"

Jillian drew her chair toward the bed. "Well, Rochester seems pleasant enough. We're only about four blocks from the center of town, the post office, and the city hall. Beyond that is the arcade of shops where I bought your things this morning. A river runs through the center of the city, and they say there are rapids and some falls. And not a block from where we're sitting is the Erie Canal."

Ryder nodded in genuine interest, but the description of the town beyond the windows seemed to deepen his restlessness rather than assuage it.

"Perhaps if you're feeling well enough tomorrow, we can walk down to the canal," she offered as encouragement.

A scowl darkened his features. "Damn it, Jillian, I'm perfectly capable of—"

"Of beating me at chess?" she interrupted, unwilling to resume the argument they had resolved to her satisfaction that morning. "Oh, I really doubt that, Ryder. I was trained by one of the best players I've ever seen."

He was perfectly aware of her ploy, of her attempt to both entertain him and keep him quiet. Still, he was not a man who could ignore a challenge. "So you think you're too good for me, do you? Well, go fetch a board, and we'll just see if you're as clever as you claim."

Within twenty minutes they were at war, and Jillian quickly discovered that Ryder had an extensive grasp of military tactics. He must have played often in the past, she decided as he defused her opening gambit, and with opponents who had tested his skill. She was clearly going to have to keep her wits about her if she intended to live up to her boasts. As they analyzed each other's strategies, she realized that there was a flair to the way Bingham maneuvered his miniature army, a style that spoke of the same boldness and determination she had seen in him that day on the ferry. Then he had risked both his freedom and his life to save a child, and he was willing to commit his chessmen with the same uncompromising courage. And even as she plotted the moves that would be his undoing, she envied him his daring.

Ryder had always enjoyed matching wits with his opponents, whether he did so by running the blockade at Wilmington or by meeting a challenge across a chessboard, and as they sat pitted against each other, Ryder studied Jillian with fierce concentration. That she played expertly was no surprise to him, nor was the conservatism of her moves. She handled her troops with a judiciousness that might well have been practiced in the war their nations were waging, as if she saw the pawns and knights as more than bits of colored wood. It was midway through the first match that he began to see the depth at which she played. Only after an hour and a half was he beginning to discover the plans she had been laying from the first moves. It was both intriguing and frustrating to watch his men being taken one by one, caught up in traps she had devised long before he had even sensed the danger. Jillian won that match and the one that followed, but before his dinner arrived, Ryder had learned a great deal about his opponent.

It was early evening when Jillian began to gather up her belongings in preparation for a bath. Ryder watched with interest as she took scented oil and soap from her trunk, then added clean clothes and towels to the pile.

"When do I get my chance to bathe?" he demanded as she moved toward the door.

She paused and looked across the room at him. It had been a humid day, and his skin shone with perspiration while his hair lay lank across his brow. In spite of the several bed baths she had given him, she knew he must not feel either fresh or clean.

"You're hardly up to a trip to the bathroom," she pointed out gently, "but I'll see what else I can arrange."

She returned to the room some time later, followed by a servant carrying a copper tub. Ferrying water down the hall, they prepared a bath for Ryder.

"Well, go on," he growled when the tub was full. "Get out of here."

"You don't want me to stay and help?" Jillian asked as he stripped off the nightshirt she had forced on him while he was too sick to protest.

If there had been even a hint of provocation in her tone, Ryder might have taken her up on the offer. "I've been bathing myself since before you were born," he told her, swinging his long legs over the side of the bed, "and I assure you, I'm quite capable of handling the task. Just go and leave me in peace."

As Jill neared the door, Ryder hauled himself upright. But when he came to his feet, his skin went cold and tingly and the room began to spin. Before he realized what was happening, Jillian was beside him, settling him on the edge of the bed and pushing his head between his knees.

"Breathe deeply!" she commanded, and Ryder did his best to comply, sucking long, deep drafts of air into his lungs.

"Good God! This is ridiculous!" he muttered between breaths. "My bones have turned to jelly!"

Jillian held his head down even after the giddiness had passed. When she finally eased the pressure on the back of his neck, he sat up gingerly and pulled the sheet across his lap.

"I don't know what came over me," he finally muttered, feeling foolish.

If he hadn't scared her so badly, Jillian might have been able to let the incident pass.

"And you thought you were ready to set off for Canada!" she scolded. "I have half a mind to pour you back into bed and leave you there until the middle of next week!"

Ryder didn't like the sound of that. "Look, maybe if you helped me . . ."

She heard the entreaty in his tone and saw that color was returning to his face. Perhaps with her help he could have his bath, and that alone would raise his spirits.

"All right," she agreed. "Let's try."

Working together they got Ryder to his feet, and Jill wrapped an arm around his waist for support. He seemed tall as an oak standing beside her, though he was trembling like a willow in the wind.

Ryder twined one arm around Jill, too, and as he did, caught the floral scent of her still-damp hair. Her flesh was soft and pliant beneath his hands, and he realized that beneath her gown she was wearing nothing more substantial than a chemise. The shock of that discovery and the subsequent trend of his thoughts didn't do a thing to allay his dizziness. But finally his head stopped spinning, and once he was steady, they started toward the tub.

Halfway there, Jillian paused. "Ryder," she began, her voice tinged with both exasperation and laughter, "you've got to let go of that sheet you're clutching around your middle, or we're not going any farther."

A bright red flush rose along his cheekbones.

"If I do that," he admitted sheepishly, "you'll have me at an even greater disadvantage than you do already."

She saw instantly that the roles were reversed from the ones they had played a few nights before, for now it was Ryder who was embarrassed by his nakedness while Jillian was at ease with it. It was Ryder who was clinging to propriety while she was concerned only with expediency. It seemed a delicious irony that it should be so, but she was wise enough to hold her peace, and bit by bit he gave up his hold on the sheet that was shielding his body from her view. They completed the journey satisfactorily and got Ryder settled in the tub.

"If you feel faint again, just put your head between your knees," she instructed as she took up the soap.

"That shouldn't be too difficult," he grumbled, shifting in the water. "This damned tub is so small that my knees are tucked up underneath my chin already."

"Perhaps by tomorrow you will be able to make your way to the larger one at the end of the hall," she said, "but for now this will have to do."

Not pausing to ask permission a second time, Jill began to help him with his bath. She started by wetting and working lather into his hair, turning his thick, dark locks into a fluffy cap of bubbles. She smoothed the soap this way and that, enjoying the surge of the foam between her fingers, the fullness of his sudsy hair. As she worked, lather oozed along his temples and frothed around his ears, spilled in rivulets down his spine and clustered in the hair on his chest. When she was done, he dropped his head forward, and with the clean water in the ewer, Jillian rinsed the soap away.

While he sat with elbows on knees, she began to soap his back. She worked down his neck and shoulders and felt the coils of muscle relax. Moving stroke by tender stroke toward the swell of his arms, she spanned the impressive breadth of him, finding pleasure and reassurance in his undeniable solidity. As Jill worked over him, she became aware of the vitality and smoothness of his flesh, of the boundless energy that seemed to flow beneath his skin. She liked the feel of him, the smell of him, the sight of his strength lying acquiescent beneath her hands. She liked the wondrous sense of intimacy this simple touching gave, and she knew she was bound to the man before her by more than his hard-won trust and the depth of her own compassion.

Gently stripping the bandage from his shoulder, Jillian cleansed the area around his wounds, then guided the soap across his back and along the valley of his spine. Using petal-soft swipes of her palms, she traced his rugged symmetry: the broad yoke of his shoulders, the ripple of his ribs, the narrowing of his waist where it disappeared into the water.

As she bathed him, Jillian made her way around the tub, swaying gracefully as if following the flow and rhythm of some elusive melody. She guided the cake of soap along his side, then followed the contours of his arm. She washed his hand, brushing her palm across his broader one, tracing the roughened whorls of his knuckles and the shape of his callused fingers.

She saw his Adam's apple waver as she soaped the stubbly skin beneath his chin, saw him narrow his lips and close his eyes as she rubbed a damp cloth over his face. Wringing out the square, she continued washing him: slipping her hands downward from his collarbones, spreading silky, translucent veils of soap across his chest. A spectrum of sensation flowed beneath her fingertips as she worked: the inviting roughness of the hair that overlaid the breadth of his rock-hard chest, the delicate smoothness of his paps hidden beneath it, the rhythmic ripple of his ribs.

The body she had nursed and come to know so well seemed suddenly strange and unexpectedly wonderful, enticing her to explore terrain she only thought she knew. And as she explored his impressive brawn, she became aware of the delicious disparity between male and female. He was broad where she was narrow, angular where she was curved, sinewy where she was soft. The difference fascinated and frightened her. How could two such profoundly different creatures find unity or resolution? What could a man and a woman possibly have in common that would enable them to share their bodies and their lives?

A host of emotions filled her that she could find no way to reconcile. Surely these unresolved conflicts should have warned her off, but something Jill could not explain compelled her to continue bathing him.

Ryder was even more aware than Jillian of the potent alchemy that flowed between them, and he was far more overwhelmed and unsettled than she. He was experienced enough to recognize that what was happening beneath the pretense of his bath could be the prelude to something wonderful. Yet he did not want to succumb to the desires Jillian sent rippling through his blood or the emotions she evoked in him. To feel such things for a woman he could never hope to attain was frustrating, pointless, and dangerous. He had already taken all the chances one man could safely take.

Determinedly, he tried to concentrate on something besides the effect Jillian's nearness was having on him. But she was on her knees before him, too close to be ignored. The gold and green glow of her eyes was warm and alluring; her full pink lips were mere inches from his own. He drew a breath and tried to keep his gaze from gliding to the hollow at the base of her throat and the alabaster flesh that lay exposed where her dress was open at the neck. He found he wanted to explore that satiny vee of skin with gentle hands, touch and taste her warmth with the tip of his tongue. The urge to act on his growing ardor was almost more than he could bear, and he didn't know how to ignore her.

Then, as she shifted to wash his other arm, a pendant swung free of the dusky opening. It flashed in the lamplight, its smooth, bright surface reflecting the golden glow.

Seizing on the tiny object as a diversion for his errant thoughts, Ryder focused on what looked to be a tiny silver flask suspended on a twisted chain. "What's that?" he asked a little breathlessly.

Jill sat back on her heels and glanced down at the sleek flagon that had come to rest on the bodice between her breasts. With a narrow neck and rounded bottom, the smooth, elongated bottle was a graceful piece, and against the dark cloth the patina of its old silver shone rich and mellow.

"It's a vinaigrette," she answered, fingering the necklace, "a container for perfume or smelling salts. It belonged to my mother and to her mother before her. Father gave it to me the day that Mother died; I've worn it ever since."

Ryder carefully took the pendant in his palm, noting the delicate teardrop shape, the shine only years of wear could impart. "It's lovely," he observed, "probably worth a pretty penny, too."

"To me it's priceless," Jill conceded softly. "This pendant and the shawl Father bought her on their wedding trip are the only things I have left of my mother."

Ryder nodded solemnly, knowing how much simple keepsakes could mean. He only wished he had something as tangible from each of the people he had lost.

"Then you'll have to keep the necklace always."

As he spoke, his hand fell away, and Jillian took up the soap to continue bathing him. But Ryder was no longer feeling cooperative. Everything above the water had been washed, and he had no intention of letting Jillian handle what remained. She might have seen to his most basic needs while he was sick, but he was better now and his natural reactions could embarrass them both.

He swallowed hard and inched backward in the tub.

"Jillian," he began uneasily, "I think I can manage the rest."

She glanced up in surprise. "But, Ryder—" she began and then suddenly caught his meaning. Flustered, she flushed, not knowing how to proceed.

"Why don't you see to straightening the bedclothes while I finish here?" he suggested. "I'll call you when I'm ready to get out of the tub."

Unaccountably relieved, Jill jumped to her feet and turned to the bed, flipping back the sheet and blanket with a vengeance. She worked until the bed was made to her satisfaction, with the sheets smooth and the pillows fluffed. By then Ryder had finished his bath. Teamwork and sheer determination got him from the tub to the edge of the bed, and while he sat wrapped in a towel, Jillian brushed his hair dry and rebandaged his shoulder.

Leaving him to his own devices, she slipped behind the open doors of the armoire to change into her nightclothes. When she was finished, she found that Ryder had climbed into bed and was nestled back against the pillows looking contented, fresh, and satisfied. His discarded nightshirt still lay crumpled beside the bed, and an impressive expanse of chest was revealed above the fold of the sheet.

It seemed suddenly as if their roles had been reversed again, and disconcerted by the thought of sleeping beside a naked man, Jillian hesitated, torn between trepidation and nervousness. But why should she feel so ill at ease at the sight of Ryder's body? she chided herself. She had been nursing this man for days, seeing to his most intimate needs. It made no sense to feel embarrassment now. Yet she could not deny that her palms were suddenly dewy and her mouth seemed lined with flannel. Something had been changed by the intimacy of his bath, and she didn't like what had happened at all.

But before she had time to consider how she should respond to the altered status between them, Ryder was addressing her. "If you're ready to come to bed, I'll put out the lamp."

Her first impulse was to gather up the quilt and sleep in the chair, but Jillian knew that would only cause an argument and draw attention to her discomfiture. Instead she moved toward the far side of the mattress, and when she was perched on the edge, Ryder plunged the room into darkness.

Warily Jill removed her wrapper and eased herself down onto the bed. She had slept beside this man last night and the night before, she reminded herself, and nothing untoward had happened between them. She should have felt better knowing that, but her uneasiness persisted.

"Jillian"—Ryder's voice flowed over her in the dark—"I want to thank you for helping me with my bath."

His comment was ordinary and mundane; she took a stabilizing breath. "You're welcome, Ryder."

"It feels very good to be clean."

She smiled as her tension sifted away. "I thought it might."

There was a moment of silence, and outside the open window a night bird began to sing.

"Jillian?" Ryder's voice came again, softer than before.

Feeling more at ease than she had for some minutes, Jill rolled in his direction. As she completed the turn, she could see that he was facing her, see that his deep blue eyes were shining in the dark.

"Jillian." The shading of her name had subtly altered, and as he spoke, one arm came around her shoulders to gather her close.

Jill's heart lurched as Ryder drew her against him, and after a moment's hesitation, she raised her hands to his chest in an attempt to push him away. Instead, she stared into his face, feeling breathless, compromised, confused.

Then his mouth was inching lower, covering hers, tender and whisper-soft. A murmur of protest rose in her throat, but before she could give it voice, a sense of approbation swelled through her. His nearness, the feel of his hands in her hair, the taste of his mouth on hers, was an insidious thing, and without volition her own mouth softened beneath the sweep of his. The kiss was slow, languid, and all the more potent for its lack of urgency. His lips brushed and hovered over hers; he shared her breath. Something exultant and bright ran along her limbs at the unexpected intimacy, bringing incipient joy and a melting euphoria. And just when she feared he would lift his mouth from hers, there was the thrill of renewed contact, sending a shimmer of delight simmering through her blood.

Jillian gasped at the sensation, and Ryder absorbed the sound of her pleasure, letting it feed his own. He felt her fingers curl around his arms as his tongue brushed the inner surface of her lips, tracing the contours of her mouth, absorbing her taste and texture.

She's so sweet, so damned sweet, he thought dazedly as his hand slipped downward toward her waist, urging her closer. Through the fabric of the quilt and the nightdress, he could feel her trembling and discovered he was as shaken by the magic as she. Things between them were as he had feared: sweet and incredibly tender, exciting and overwhelmingly right. What he felt with Jillian was different from anything he had known before; it was far more intense, far more mystical. Even these simple intimacies sent something powerful and heady bubbling up between them, something strong and elemental enough to change a man's perception of his life. But this was the wrong time to find what every man was seeking. He was in the land of his enemies, at a juncture in his life when freedom and revenge should be his only concerns.

Still there was no way to deny what was happening between them. As the kisses deepened and their lips clung, as their hands clasped and their bodies nestled close, an undeniable spark ignited their world. It was volatile and exciting, compelling and dazzling, tender and true. What they felt was more than either of them wanted to feel, but the kisses had loosed something wondrously unique that would be difficult to deny.

"Ryder?" Jillian whispered when he finally raised his mouth from hers. Her voice was strained and tremulous; her eyes were open wide. "Ryder?"

He pulled her close and held her, resting his cheek against her hair. He no more knew how to answer her unspoken questions than he knew how to still the tumult their innocent kisses had stirred.

He murmured her name instead, caressing it like the lover he longed to become. "Jillian." His voice was as soft as the summer night. "Oh, Jillian."

When Jillian returned to their rented room after breakfast, the air was nearly as blue as Ryder Bingham's eyes. As she opened the door, a string of surprisingly eloquent curses assaulted her and made her surmise that Ryder's day had not begun as pleasantly as her own.

After what had transpired the night before, Jill had purposely risen early and had gone downstairs before Bingham was awake. She had needed time to sort out the feelings his attentions had aroused, time to consider the unexpected haven she had found in Ryder's arms. In truth she was still stunned by her uninhibited response to him, overwhelmed by her delight at the simple intimacies they had shared. Jill had never guessed that a few chaste kisses could afford such stultifying pleasure or leave her trembling in anticipation of something more. Not even when Jeff had kissed her, caressed her, and made her his wife had she experienced the dizzying wonder she had felt with this man. And she knew more than a twinge of disloyalty to her dead husband at the thought.

Rational consideration of the encounter had been difficult for Jillian, but a walk to the canal at the foot of Fitzhugh Street had given her a chance to put everything into perspective, to decide what she should do and say when she faced the Confederate again. During those private moments, she had done her best to resolve her changing feelings for the man she had taken from the train five days before. Sharing a room and a bed had put them in an extremely provocative situation, she conceded, and caring for Ryder during his illness had led to far greater intimacy than they would normally have known. It had given them both a false sense of familiarity that had led him to take, and her to allow, the liberties he had claimed the previous evening. The recognition of the reasons for their behavior gave Jillian a feeling of resolution. She had only to avoid intimacy with Ryder Bingham to regain control of the situation. It was as simple as that.

Standing on the bank of the canal watching the packet boats get under way, Jill had known a certain calm, a modicum of confidence about her own motives and how she would behave when she saw Bingham again. But now, at the moment when she had to confront Ryder's uncertain temper and her own inconsistent emotions, her resolve melted away and she entertained thoughts of retreat.

Before she could slip back into the hall, however, Ryder caught sight of her in the mirror. "Where have you been?" he demanded, rounding on her. "You were gone when I woke up this morning."

Now that escape was impossible, Jill closed the door behind her and faced him resolutely, trying not to notice the expanse of his broad bare chest. "I was up early," she told him with a shrug. "And I found it pleasant to linger over breakfast, chatting with our landlady. What have you been doing while I was gone?"

From Ryder's half-clad body and the soap slathered on his face, the answer was patently obvious.

"I've been getting washed and dressed, and now I'm trying to shave," he answered, adjusting the straight razor in his hand. "Though with only one arm working properly, it's not certain if I'll end up cutting my whiskers or my throat."

Jill watched as he attempted to clear a spot below his ear. But without use of the other hand to hold the skin taut, the blade wavered and caught. A few seconds later a spot of red blossomed through the lather, and Ryder responded with a fresh burst of cursing.

"Cut yourself?" Jillian inquired, stepping closer.

"Damn it! Yes, I did. How's a man supposed to shave laid up like this?"

"Well, you could give it up altogether and let your beard grow," she suggested. "Or you could let me give you a hand, since that's what you seem to be lacking."

"And just what do you know about shaving a man?"

"I'm not without experience," Jillian offered quietly. "I shaved my father while he was ill."

Ryder hesitated, and she could see how much he wanted to do this on his own. If she had learned anything about the man before her, it was that he was proud and fiercely independent. She knew how much it rankled him to be less than sound, especially when he was in danger. Yet he was practical enough to accept her help if he needed it, as he had the night before.

With a disgusted huff, Ryder relinquished the razor.

"Will you sit, please?" Jill requested, hauling a high-backed chair a foot or two closer to the washstand.

"I'm perfectly capable of standing."

Jillian drew a long breath and exhaled slowly. "I don't doubt that, Ryder," she answered, conceding to his pride, "but unless you're sitting down, you're too tall for me to shave."

Muttering, Ryder sat.

Once he was settled back against the headrest, Jillian wet the razor and bent above him, pulling his skin taut as she drew the blade upward from the base of his throat.

"Careful," Ryder cautioned. But the waver the warning caused made her nick his tender skin.

"Just keep quiet, Ryder," she ordered sharply, as the cut began to bleed. "Your comments are more hindrance than help right now."

Once the bleeding was stopped, she continued with her task, leaving a swath of smooth, clean-shaven skin with each swipe of the blade. She paused often to swish the razor in the basin to dislodge the inky flecks of whiskers, and the soap was gradually scraped away from his neck and chin.

Jillian did seem to know what she was doing, Ryder finally conceded, and instead of worrying about her cutting him, he found himself taking note of her nearness. Her lily-of-the-valley scent surrounded him, and as Jill leaned closer to shave the far side of his face, he could feel her warmth along his body. There was the brush of her cotton gown against his skin, the pressure of her fingertips on his face in a touch that was sure, gentle, and subtly provocative.

The memory of the previous night's encounter swam toward the surface of his mind, and he recalled the taste of Jillian's lips, now a mere hand's breadth from his own. Last night they had been caught up in the inexplicable magic of mutual attraction. If only he'd felt better, he might have done more to explore what was happening between them. He would have liked to taste the tender flesh along the curve of her throat, to slide his hands beneath her nightdress and explore the texture of her skin. He might even have aroused and seduced her, wooed her with his passion until their trembling bodies melted into one. The hint of a smile touched his lips at the thought of claiming that final intimacy, and delicious anticipation flooded his loins.

There was something infinitely delightful about the prospect of making love to Jill, something so right about the thought of claiming her as his own. Her responses had made him suspect that she possessed a natural sensuality coupled with a generosity that would lead her to give as good as she got. Yet her attempts at returning pleasure for pleasure had been shy and almost innocent. If he had not known better, Bingham might have thought Jillian a green girl, unaware of the things a man and a woman did in the search for mutual satisfaction. She had seemed genuinely surprised at what had passed between them, at her own response to his kisses. Was it possible that her husband had never shown her the delicious possibilities of married life? Had Jefferson Walsh been a selfish boor who denied Jill her pleasure, or had he simply been unskilled in the ways of the world? No matter which, Ryder would have bet his last cargo that with the proper encouragement, Jillian could become a passionate woman indeed. At the thought of what he might teach her to help with the transformation, Ryder was forced to draw a long, unsteady breath.

Jillian heard it and raised the razor from his cheek. "Ryder, have I hurt you?" she asked, her voice filled with concern.

"It's all right," he assured her gruffly. "Just get done with this business, will you?"

It only took a few more swipes of the razor to complete the job, and when Jillian returned from disposing of the shaving water, Bingham was buttoning his shirt.

"Do you have plans for the day?" she inquired, looking away from the broad bare chest disappearing above the shirt placket.

He nodded. "I want to get out of this wretched room. Being shut up here has been nearly as bad as prison."

Jillian, who had not thought the past days were so terrible, was affronted. After all, she had done her best to make him comfortable. But then she noticed a desperation beneath his restlessness and realized that his feelings had nothing to do with the confinement his illness had forced upon him.

"How long were you held at Fort Lafayette?"

"Too long," he answered, struggling to knot his tie. "But then, a single day in a place like that is a day too long."

Sensing his rising frustration, she brushed his hands aside and made short work of knotting the necktie.

"Damn it all!" he muttered.

"You're welcome, I'm sure."

He glanced down at her with contrition in his eyes. "I'm sorry, Jillian," he began. "I didn't mean—"

"It's all right, Ryder. I didn't realize how much being cooped up here has bothered you. Let me help you downstairs. But if we meet anyone on the way, don't comment on anything more than the state of your health."

Jillian's proved to be a valid warning. They had just reached the landing when one of the older men who boarded with Mrs. Marshall passed them.

"Damned malaria can really take it out of a fellow, eh, Walsh?" he commented. "Serves a person right, though, sailing off to those heathen parts of the world."

Ryder nodded wide-eyed.

At the foot of the stairs, a maid commented on how nice it was to see Mr. Walsh up and about. And before they could leave the entry, Mrs. Marshall came bustling toward them.

"Taking our invalid for some air?" she inquired. "Well, it's good to see you out of bed, Mr. Walsh. The way Mrs. Walsh was hovering over you, I half expected her to take sick, too."

"Yes, Mrs. Walsh has been quite diligent in her care of me," Bingham agreed, eyeing Jillian. "You'd think she was anxious to get me well and out from under her feet."

Jillian laughed uncomfortably and tightened her grip on Ryder's arm, urging him toward the door. "Darling, how you talk!" she admonished.

"If you're looking for a place to take the air," Mrs. Marshall called after them. "There's an arbor in the side yard that offers a pleasant place to sit."

Jill took the woman at her word and maneuvered Ryder toward the shady trellised enclosure. He sat down heavily when they reached the wide bench inside the tunnel of vines.

"I feel so foolish," he mumbled after a moment, "that a little walk like this should tax me so."

"You ran a very high fever, Ryder, and that takes quite a toll. Be patient; give yourself time to regain your strength."

He shook his head. "I don't have time, Jillian. You know that as well as I do."

It was not necessary for him to tell her what would happen if he was arrested, yet she knew that his chances of surviving recapture were greater for every day that passed.

"I believe you'll make it into Canada," she reassured him. "But you need to rest until you're strong enough to cross the border."

"And you think I'm safe here in the meantime?"

"Yes, of course. These people think you're my husband. That charade should keep you safe unless you do something to arouse suspicion."

"Like singing 'Dixie' at the top of my voice or defending states' rights over dinner?"

Jillian sent him a contemptuous look. "This isn't a laughing matter, Ryder."

"Dear God, Jillian! You mean you haven't discovered yet that everything in this life is a laughing matter?"

Then, seeing the concern in her face, he sobered.

"Suppose you tell me what story you concocted to explain my illness so I won't unwittingly contradict you. It had something to do with malaria and 'heathen lands,' I take it."

"I told these people the same thing I told the conductor on the train: that before the war you were a sea captain and had contracted malaria while you were trading in South America."

He nodded in acknowledgment. "That's closer to the truth than you could possibly know. I was a captain before the war, though I traded in Europe, mostly."

In all the time they had spent together it was the first hint he had given of his past, and she pressed him for more information. "Were you sailing your own ship or working for a trading company? Have you been to Paris and London? Are they as wonderful as people say?"

Bingham frowned at her curiosity. "The less you know about me, Jillian, the safer you'll be when I'm gone. Don't you realize the chance you've taken in befriending me? If anyone finds out what you've done, you'll go to prison, too."

Jill preferred not to consider the consequences of her actions. She had done what she had to do to save Ryder Bingham's life; it was as simple as that. Looking back, it seemed that from the moment Ryder sat down beside her on the train, from the moment he had dived into the river to save little Teddy's life, she had been meant to aid him. In a way her actions, and his, seemed almost preordained. She had been raised as too much a pragmatist to believe in fate, and yet the way they had come together and what had transpired since seemed somehow to have been destined to happen.

"I don't care about the risks," she told him. "I'm glad I've helped you, and I'll do whatever else you ask."

Ryder looked across at Jillian and saw the conviction in her eyes. Did she know what she was saying? he wondered. Did she understand what dangers she was courting by helping him? She didn't really know what kind of man he was, yet she was willing to risk her reputation, her safety, and perhaps even her life. For reasons he could not fully comprehend, she trusted him, and he went light-headed with the responsibility. But why did she trust him? What had made her decide to take this chance?

Ryder studied the woman before him, seeing no hint of uncertainty in her face. Yet he knew Jillian was afraid for the future, that she dreaded the prospect of being dependent on her father-in-law. Was she offering to help him in order to forestall her fate? Did she think he could help her escape what lay ahead? Familiar bitterness rose inside him; once again he was powerless to change the inevitable.

Yet even as he considered what he would say to bring Jillian to her senses, he felt the lure of what she proposed. He knew the reality of his own weakness, the chance of recapture, and the danger of crossing a border that must be carefully guarded. It was certain that Jillian could do much to protect him. Why not allow her to go on helping him, to enjoy the few moments the two of them could share? In the depths of her green eyes, he saw a promise not only of cooperation and freedom, but of tenderness and succor as well. After the loneliness and hardship of the prison, after the things he'd risked to escape, he craved the ease that only Jillian's warmth could offer him. Surely it could not be wrong to accept what she was giving, to allow himself to enjoy their time together.

In the shade of the leafy bower, Ryder gave himself over to that promise of surcease. He stretched out on the bench beside her and willingly succumbed to the delight of Jillian's nearness and the languor of the summer day. This was only a respite from the savagery and bitterness of war, he told himself. This could offer him nothing but transient repose. Still it was infinitely pleasant to lie with his head pillowed in Jill's lap, to feel her fingers weaving patterns in his hair.

Vague half-memories of childhood filtered through his mind, of lying trusting and secure in his mother's lap. He could almost hear her crooning lullabies, hear the lilt of her voice as she repeated the songs her own Scottish nanny had sung to her. His mother would have approved of Jillian, he found himself thinking as his eyes drifted closed. Alysse would have liked Jillian very much indeed.

Ryder had no idea how long he slept, but when he awoke, there was a tray on the small table before them. Seeing it, he sat up quickly, bleary-eyed and disoriented.

Jillian gave him a moment to get his bearings. "Are you ready for a bite to eat? Mrs. Marshall was kind enough to send us luncheon on a tray."

Ryder nodded. "Yes, I think so. But why did you let me sleep so long?"

"I thought you needed it," she answered simply before handing him his lunch.

Mrs. Marshall had provided them with cold meat pies, vinegary cabbage salad, and slices of garden-fresh tomatoes arranged on flowered china plates. There was a pot of sweetened ginger tea for them to share, and peach tarts for dessert.

They ate their meal at a leisurely pace, enjoying each other's company and the solace of a summer afternoon. The gold and green light that filtered into the bower was muted and diffused; the sounds from the world outside were hushed and far away. The arbor seemed a haven from the too-demanding world, and both Ryder and Jillian reveled in the fleeting serenity they found together.

When the dishes were empty, Jillian took the tray into the house and returned with Ryder's knife, some bits of wood, and a volume of poetry. For a time she read aloud while Ryder whittled, but as the afternoon advanced, Jillian grew restless and took a turn around the garden. When she returned, she could see that the wood in Ryder's hands was taking on the shape of a ship.

"You told me you used to trade in Europe," she began, watching him, absorbed by his skill, "but that's all you've divulged about your past."

Ryder glanced up warily as if to discourage her curiosity.

"Please, Ryder," she continued. "I don't know anything more about you than your name: not where you're from, nothing about your life before the war. You can tell me that much, at least."

He drew a long breath as if considering her request, then shrugged resignedly. "My family owns a plantation on the Cape Fear River," he began. "They were some of the first settlers in that part of North Carolina."

"What kind of plantation is it?"

"We grow cotton and tobacco, mostly."

"And what's plantation life like?"

Ryder hesitated, and when he spoke, his voice was low and defensive. "Not at all what Mrs. Stowe and her histrionic novel would have you think."

Jillian sat beside him saying nothing, and it was several minutes before he realized that she wanted, not to judge, but to understand.

"The Binghams do own slaves," he finally conceded. "It would be impossible to grow cotton and tobacco without them, but no slave at Riverview has ever been mistreated. We take care of our own. Mother always made certain that the workers were sheltered and clothed and that no one went hungry. She used to sit up with our people when they were sick, just as she did when one of her children was ailing."

"Your mother sounds like a very compassionate woman," Jill observed.

Ryder lowered his head in assent. "And she was the driving force behind Riverview's success."

"How?"

"In order for a plantation to succeed, it must be self-sufficient, able to provide its own food supply and services. In addition to overseeing our cash crops, Mother supervised the vegetable gardens, berry patches, and orchards. We raised our own cows, chickens, and pigs for slaughter, and my father always saw to it that some of our men were taught trades. He even gave them the chance to buy their freedom with the profits they earned making barrels, producing furniture, or blacksmithing."

Ryder paused as he pared away slivers of wood to refine the tiny ship's bow.

"But instead of staying on the plantation, you went to sea," Jillian observed.

He nodded again. "While the men on one side of the Bingham family have always been content to be gentlemen farmers, those on the other side wanted more adventure. Before the war, the

Binghams owned a large fleet of merchant ships and a number of warehouses in Wilmington."

"Is that how you became a ship's captain?"

"I'd been sailing off Cape Fear since I was a boy, and as soon as I completed my education, I began shipping out on Bingham-owned vessels. I learned the intricacies of sailing just like any other seaman and earned my master's papers fair and square." There was pride in his voice and subtle longing that made her next question inevitable.

"And were you happy at sea?"

He turned to her gravely, his voice reverent and low. "It's the one place on earth where a man can be truly free."

She saw the intensity in his face and suddenly realized that for a man who harbored this passionate need for freedom, prison must have been a death by inches.

"I'd been captain of my own ship nearly three years when the war broke out," he went on, "and it seemed only natural that I should continue in war what I had done so successfully in peace. Many of the companies we traded with in Europe were outfitting blockaders and setting up depots of goods in Nassau or Bermuda. They could see that there were huge profits to be made in selling out the South."

His jaw hardened, and there was contempt in his tone. But as he went on, that contempt turned angry and defensive.

"I won't deny that I made my fortune running the blockade, and lost it just as fast. But at least I was patriotic enough to carry guns and medicines into the Confederacy instead of filling my ship with corsets, wine, and hoop skirts. And while there's no doubt that it was dangerous business, after a dozen successful trips, the money became secondary. At the last, running into Wilmington was nothing so much as a game."

The admission startled Jillian. "A game?"

"It was a challenge to outwit the Yankees, to sneak past their cruisers in the dark." His expression became intent as he remembered. "We burned anthracite coal to eliminate the engine smoke, built ships fast and low to the water, and painted them gray to blend into the fog. We would tamp down all the lights on board and run by the dark of the moon. And, too, we had the element of surprise in our favor.

"It became a game, a battle of wits. It was easy to lose sight of all that was at stake when slipping past the Yankees became a test of wills and strategy."

Jillian hesitated before whispering the question. "How were you caught?"

She knew instantly that she had asked something that should have remained unspoken, pried into things that were none of her concern.

Suddenly he was standing over her, his eyes as dark as lapis and every bit as impenetrable. "You're too damned curious, Jillian. I can't imagine what good that knowledge could do you."

She should have held her peace, but the words were on her lips before she could stop them. "Please, Ryder, I want to know, I want to understand."

"Understand what?" he demanded. "How an arrogant block-ader was brought to his knees? How overconfidence and bad judgment cost men's lives?"

"No, I—"

"We're on opposite sides in this war, Jillian; that's something neither of us can forget. In spite of what you've done for me, in spite of the fact that you've saved my miserable life, I can't help but remember that men like your husband are brutalizing the South. And if it takes me the rest of my days, I intend to make the Yankees pay for what they've done.

"With your husband dead at Southern hands, with all the South has lost, I don't think there can ever be any real under-standing between us, Jillian. As much as I hate to admit that, I'm very sure it's true."

She caught a glimpse of his set face as he spun on his heel and stormed toward the house, and though Jillian rose to follow, she knew there was nothing more to say. The sentiments he had ex-pressed were probably more real and rational than what she thought or felt. Perhaps she had been wrong to press him to tell her things he did not want to divulge, to try to gain some insight into his life. Perhaps she had been so insistent because with his improving health she felt that she was losing him. Still, she knew she needed to let go, not bind Ryder closer. She needed to send him on to Canada, submit to her own fate, though the thought of it depressed her.

She sank back to the bench and opened the volume of poetry in her lap, but as she tried to read, she was bedeviled by Ryder's words. She had not realized there was such anger in him, such a need for revenge burning in his heart. Though they had spent a great deal of time together in the past few days, she was begin-ning to realize how little she really knew of him.

Sighing, Jillian turned her attention to the volume of poetry again. Ryder needed time to himself, she decided, much as she had needed it this morning. She would allow him the privacy of their room and a respite from her questions. But even as she tried to attend to the page before her, the words blurred and the complexities of Ryder Bingham's personality filled her errant thoughts.

For the first time, Ryder took his dinner in the dining room, and though the other boarders tried to hide it, they could not help their curiosity about a man who had been shut up in his room for days. As they ate a hearty meal of vegetable soup, leg of lamb with mint sauce, boiled potatoes, and beans, Ryder skillfully parried the questions the other diners asked of him, relying on Jillian's fabrications and devising a few of his own. But as the raspberry shrub was being served for dessert, talk turned as it inevitably did these days to the progress of the war.

"Well, we're stalemated again," one of the bewhiskered men at the end of the table was saying, "with Sherman outside Atlanta and the Army of the Potomac dug in at Petersburg."

"At least Sheridan is clearing the rebs out of the Shenandoah Valley," another commented. "I hope he burns it from rim to rim and doesn't leave a single cornstalk standing."

Jillian felt Ryder's body stiffen beside her and impulsively jumped into the fray. "That seems like a very uncharitable attitude, Mr. Wilmot. There are women and children on those farms—"

"And they're giving aid to the Southern raiders, just as they have throughout the war."

"Still, sir," she countered, "it seems unnecessarily cruel—"

Ryder interrupted her protest, clearly unwilling to let her fight his battles for him. "By that line of reasoning," he argued, "Lee should have set all Pennsylvania ablaze when he paid his visit last summer."

Wilmot glared at Ryder, and Jill wondered if he had noticed the Confederate's silky drawl, the slower cadence of his speech. Panic rose within her chest as she waited for his reply.

"Have you served in the war, Mr. Walsh?" Wilmot asked instead. "Or are you one of the able-bodied men who bought out of Lincoln's draft?"

Jillian held her breath, waiting for Ryder to respond. Wilmot was as much as accusing him of cowardice.

"I served shipboard off Wilmington," he answered, carefully skirting the truth, "until circumstances conspired to do me in."

"The malaria, you mean, don't you, darling?" Jillian added

quickly. "It was a recurrence of malaria that sent him north."

She saw a spark of recklessness in Ryder's eyes and, for an instant, was afraid he might say something they would both regret.

"Malaria, to be sure," he finally conceded.

"Had malaria myself," put in one of the older men. "Got it back in 'forty-seven when I was in Mexico with Scott. Malaria takes it out of a man, I must say that. Why, I remember one trooper after Churubusco . . ."

Silently Jillian blessed the man at the far end of the table for defusing the situation at the crucial moment. What Ryder might have said or done if the conversation had continued, Jill could not say. Still, it had been evident from the flush in Ryder's cheeks and the sparkle in his eyes that he had enjoyed walking within a hair's breadth of disaster. The discovery unnerved her even though, after having seen him face down the detectives on the train, she should have known how capable he was of deception.

As soon as possible after the meal, Jillian pleaded a headache and, making sure that Ryder would accompany her, retired to their room. The scene in the dining room had terrified her, and she was reminded once again of how little she really knew about the rebel. Had it been madness to help a stranger on a train, no matter how deserving he had seemed? Before he escaped across the border, would he expose both of them and be recaptured? They were questions that chilled Jillian to the marrow of her bones.

When Bingham set up the chessboard and challenged her to a game, she accepted, hoping the intricacies of play would take her mind off her doubts. But Ryder played cunningly and well, winning both the first and the second match. And as she unwillingly succumbed to his daring tactics and her own inattention, Jillian sensed that she had somehow lost control of a far more crucial game.

Finally the evening drew to a close, and they prepared themselves for bed. They lay as they had for the last two nights with Jillian on top of the covers and Ryder beneath them. But tonight no words of good night were spoken. Instead they lay in silence, staring at the ceiling. Could it have been only the night before that Ryder had reached across and drawn her into his arms? Jillian found herself wondering. How could they have been so much of one mind then and so opposed to each other tonight? While she had no desire for more of Ryder's unsettling kisses, she missed the closeness, the communication. Unresolved anger and fear for the future mingled in her chest, and she wanted nothing so much as to be reassured and comforted.

For a time, she tossed restlessly, turning first toward the windows, then to where Ryder lay. As she did, she saw that he wasn't sleeping either. Instead, he was watching her with resignation in his eyes. They studied each other closely as they lay a dozen inches apart, their eyes holding, their breath mingling.

Suddenly there was the sting of tears at the back of her eyes, and Jillian knew that she could not allow things to go on as they were.

There was uncertainty in her voice as she spoke, but the apology was necessary. "I'm sorry about the questions I asked this afternoon."

There was the space of several heartbeats before she saw him shrug. "A little curiosity is natural, I suppose."

"I can't say that you're very forthcoming."

"No, Jillian, but I have reason not to be."

Another moment passed.

"Ryder?"

"Mmmm?"

It took all her courage to make the request. "Would you mind holding me?"

She could sense his surprise, but he did not ask for explanations. He only unfolded the arm that had been tucked behind his head and curled it around her shoulders. She crept closer until her head came to rest in the crook of his neck, until her hand lay on the sheet that covered his chest. They said nothing, did nothing more. But twined together in the darkness, they slept.

Chapter Four

"I'M GOING TO take the evening train to Canada on Friday."

Ryder's announcement came without warning or preamble, and Jillian turned from watching the packet boats on the Rochester branch of the Erie Canal to stare at the man beside her. She had known the Confederate was growing restless now that his health was so much improved. She had known that leaving the relative safety of the boarding house was inevitable, but somehow she had not been able to resign herself to a definite time for their departure. Foreboding curled deep inside her with the knowledge that Ryder had made the decision for both of them, and at that moment, she did not know if her apprehension was for the dangers he would face in crossing the border or for herself.

She took a long breath, trying to subdue her uneasiness. "But, Ryder, isn't it too soon? Are you strong enough to chance the crossing into Canada?"

He turned to her, and she could see determination in his eyes. "I've got to go," he told her softly. "You know that as well as I do. If I leave on Friday, I'll reach the border late that evening, and I'm gambling that the guards won't be as alert then as they might be at other times. It makes sense, Jillian, and there's nothing to be gained by waiting."

What he said was true, but somehow she could not resign herself to what he was proposing, nor could she accept that the future to which she had committed herself was at hand.

"You can go on ahead if you want," he continued. "You needn't wait to accompany me. If you leave on an earlier train, what you've done to help me won't be so evident."

She sat numbly, trying to weigh the possible ramifications of his decision. "Oh, Ryder," she finally breathed, "I'm afraid."

His hand crept across to cover hers. "I know you are," he acknowledged, as if sensing that her fear was deep and multifaceted.

"We've had so little time together." Where the words came from, Jillian did not know, yet they vividly expressed the feelings she had been unable to admit, even to herself.

At her words of regret, surprise registered on Ryder's face and in the depths of his flame-bright eyes, but it was a surprise that seemed tempered by recognition and incipient understanding. Did he feel the same painful reluctance to be parted from her? she wondered suddenly. In spite of the fact that he was in constant danger of recapture, had he found the time they'd shared precious and too brief?

"Then stay on until Friday," he urged her.

Even as he issued the invitation, Bingham knew there was no future for them together. He was a rebel in the hostile North bent on returning to the Confederacy to fight battles of hatred and vengeance that went far beyond the political differences that had embroiled their two countries in war. And Jillian had a life of her own laid out before her. Further contact between them was impossible. Yet they could have today and tomorrow if Jillian chose to remain in Rochester.

Ryder's gaze was intent as he tried to gauge her response to all he was asking. Was Jillian as aware as he of the strong attraction between them? Did she sense that what they felt might happen only once in a lifetime? Ryder's instincts urged him to take Jill in his arms and convince her with actions rather than words that she should grant them these last, precious hours together. But he knew she must make the decision to stay when it would be far wiser for her to go.

For herself, Jillian was overwhelmingly aware of what Ryder wanted. He was asking for far more than her physical presence in their room and in their bed. He was asking her to acknowledge the closeness that had been developing since he had begun to recover from his illness, the myriad of feelings they had only begun to explore. If she chose to remain, there would be no more chaste kisses, no more platonic tenderness. She would have to acknowledge the very real attraction between them.

There was no question that these last days had been something special, a time out of time. Jillian's old life had ended with the settlement of her father's debts, and her new life with Gerald Walsh had not yet begun. Ryder was in limbo, too, caught between the enforced idleness of prison and the need to act on his loyalties. Since last Friday they had inhabited a place apart, and though that place was safe and nurturing, it had no basis in reality.

Nothing could change the future for either of them. But was it wrong to want a respite from the struggles that raged around them, the destinies to which they were committed already? How could anything but good come from whatever fleeting happiness they could find together? Once they left the sanctuary of the rooming house and boarded the westbound train, their safe, separate world would be irrevocably destroyed. And Jillian had seen too many worlds, too many hopes, destroyed to be a party to more destruction.

Her voice was both eager and tremulous as she gave him her reply. "I think I'll stay," she told him. "I think I'll stay until Friday."

Ryder's fingers clasped hers more tightly, and something sweet and tender flowed between them as if to confirm the decision she had made. It was a warmth, an excitement, that they could not acknowledge in so public a place, and instead they made do with the simple touching of hands, the simple pleasure of being together.

Initially they had wandered down Fitzhugh Street to assuage Ryder's continuing restlessness, but when they reached the bank of the Erie Canal, they realized that they had come upon one of the greatest feats of engineering ever attempted in America. The canal did not look very revolutionary, with teams of mules plodding along the dusty trace at the edge of the waterway, towing heavily loaded packet boats. But this narrow, stone-lined ditch had been responsible for opening the heartland of America to settlement. Even now, with the advent of the railroads, it was the primary means of transportation for produce from the western farms to markets in Albany and New York and of manufactured goods to cities in the West.

They sat together on the grassy slope, watching the traffic on the canal, smelling the dust stirred by the mules' hooves, seeing the sunlight dance on the water, hearing the good-natured challenges that passed between the boatmen and the hostlers. It should have been a peaceful scene, but what they saw before them stirred an unexpected bitterness in Jillian.

"In a way we're like those packet boats, aren't we?" she observed after a moment. "We have our courses laid out before us and nowhere else to go."

"And where is it, Jillian, that you want to go?" Ryder asked her. "You had a chance to set your own course in life, and you refused it."

Jillian turned to him, stunned by the unexpected attack. But even as resentment seethed within her, she could not deny that what Ryder said was true. She had forfeited her chance to determine her fate by accepting Gerald Walsh's invitation. For the first time since her father's death, Jill wondered if she could have made her own way in the world. At the time when she had made the decision to live with Gerald Walsh she had been sure that she could not, but somehow these past days had changed her, encouraged a burgeoning independence she had not known she possessed. It was an unsettling discovery.

Ryder seemed to sense her confusion and tried to recant his accusation. "But your future's not something you need to ponder now; there will be plenty of time to consider it in the months ahead. We have today and tomorrow, Jilly, and I hope to make the most of them."

"And I," she agreed, forcing everything but the day ahead

from her mind. "And I." There would be plenty of time to think when Ryder and these precious hours were gone.

As noon approached, Ryder came to his feet, and with exaggerated gallantry he helped Jillian to hers. As he did so, his hand rested at her waist, and now that she had decided to stay, that contact seemed intimidating and overwhelming. Without thinking, she jerked away, confused by what she was feeling. But again Ryder seemed to understand more about her than she understood herself, and he allowed her some moments of privacy.

They spent the afternoon much as they had the previous day, holed up in the shady bower in the side yard of the boarding house. Jillian read and stitched on her mourning picture, while Ryder added a cat and a comical cow to the growing collection of tiny wooden carvings. After returning to their room, Jill won two games of chess, though in the second Ryder came very near to defeating her. It was another pleasant day to add to their store of memories. Dinner passed in a haze of anticipation, and as soon as it was proper, they excused themselves and went upstairs to bathe before what they both knew would be a very early bedtime.

When Ryder returned from his bath, Jillian was already dressed in her nightclothes. But at the sight of him with his face flushed and his eyes shining, she suddenly wondered about the wisdom of her decision to remain with him. Wasn't she courting disaster to spend another night in his bed? When she elected to remain in Rochester, she had made a tacit commitment to something more than nursing him back to health, and now that the time was at hand to fulfill her part of the bargain, she was overwhelmed by uncertainty. What if someone found out that she had given herself to an escaped Confederate, a man who was not her husband? What if Ryder brought the ruthless side of his personality to their coupling rather than the tenderness of which he was capable? What if she became pregnant with Ryder's child? What if . . . ?

Hectic color mounted to her cheeks as she made her way to the far side of the bedstead, and her flush intensified as Ryder began to open the buttons on his shirt. The cotton fabric clung close to his still-damp skin, and she could see the darkness of his flesh, the classical mold of his arms and shoulders. She swallowed hard as she watched his hands skim along the shirt placket, revealing a wider and wider view of his chest to her. As she nursed Ryder, she had seen every part of him, but until now she had not truly appreciated the rugged cast of his body, the latent power evident in every line of his torso. Each loosened button revealed more of him to her, and she watched mesmerized as he stripped the tails of his shirt from the waistband of his trousers and slid the garment down his arms. He hung the shirt on the scroll at the foot of the bed and lowered his hands to the front of his pants.

Jillian shrank back on her side of the bed in the hope that the distance would protect her from him, but staring across the wide expanse of bedclothes, she was more aware than ever of his flagrant masculinity. Still Ryder continued to disrobe, proceeding in spite of her evident unease. As he slipped the buttons on his pants from their holes, she could see the white of his underdrawers in the widening opening. When he reached the last button, he skimmed the trousers down his legs and laid them beside his shirt at the foot of the bed. She followed the progress of his hands, watching as his fingers slid inside the underdrawers that rode low on his hips. Slowly he worked the garment down his body, and when he straightened, he stood strong and bared before her.

Jillian tried to refuse herself the ultimate decadence of studying him unclothed and quickly looked away. But her eyes strayed back to where he stood, and she found it impossible to deny his magnificence. His shoulders were broad, and the planes of his wide chest were clearly delineated by the glow from the low-burning lamp on the nightstand. The curling hair that made a narrowing pattern from his paps down his lean, hard body seemed to trap the lamplight, giving the dark curls a reddish glow. She noted the swell of the muscles in his arms, the high arc of his ribs, the way his body narrowed at the waist and hips, the cabled muscles that ran down his flanks, and the proof of his gender stirring against the hair between his legs. Nature and hard work had given Ryder Bingham a body to be proud of, and though she should have known it well, Jillian could not seem to get her fill of watching him.

The level of the tension in the room seemed to increase with the lengthening silence, and finally Ryder spoke. "Take off your dressing gown, Jillian."

She started at the quiet command but made no move to obey it. How could she bare herself to Ryder when she had never been unclothed before any man?

"Jillian, please."

Though his eyes were blazing with emotion, his voice was low and persuasive. Somehow she raised her hands to the ruffle at her throat.

"You haven't slept in your dressing gown yet," he reminded

her. "I'm not asking you to do anything you haven't done already."

But tonight is different, she wanted to cry. Tonight you are watching me, wanting me. A self-conscious tremor ran through her as she sought the first button in the thicket of midnight-dark lace beneath her chin. She worked the fastener clumsily and then went on to the next. By the time she had loosened the sash at her waist and undone the buttons all the way to the hem, she was shaking, afraid of what more he might ask of her.

"Now put the gown at the foot of the bed."

She did as he bade her, moving slowly, not to tease or arouse but with genuine reluctance.

When she stood clad only in the black lawn nightdress, he bent to flick the bedclothes back, exposing the sheets. They lay open before her, a crisp, white challenge for her to overcome. She had not slept between the sheets before, and the idea of lying on them now seemed intimate and scandalous. But the unspoken invitation of the opened bed was between them, pristine, beckoning, just as Ryder had intended it to be. She gathered the shreds of her courage and sat on the edge of the mattress.

On his side, Ryder did the same.

"Are you afraid?" he inquired softly. "Surely you know I won't do anything to hurt you."

"I know," she whispered, extending one arm, leaning ever so slightly nearer. "It's just—"

"Hush, Jilly, hush. I think I understand."

Reaching across, he let his fingers brush up her arm to her shoulder, his warmth penetrating the fabric of the filmy sleeve. It was a soothing, not a seductive touch, but her response seemed to make it one. Her muscles knotted. Her thighs tightened. Shivers washed down her spine.

I want this, Jillian thought shocked and terrified. *I want this so much.*

Ryder seemed to sense her conflict, her irresolute emotions, and his hand rose from her shoulder to stroke her cheek.

"Trust me, Jilly," he whispered as he leaned close to kiss her. His mouth brushed hers once, twice. "Trust me. I don't want to do anything but give you pleasure."

His lips came to fasten over hers, and with that long, searching kiss came the rush of sweet sensation, the acknowledgment that being together was somehow magical and right. Without either of them knowing how it had happened, they were lying side by side in the center of the mattress. For an instant they merely gazed into each other's eyes. His were sapphire dark and shining with tenderness; hers were wide, green, and filled with uncertainty. Gently his arms came around her, urging her into the sheltering curve of his body. The insistent pressure of his hand at her waist should have been intimidating, but instead the closeness he was offering seemed a haven, a place apart. Jillian arched her back to press more intimately against him, and as she turned to give him freer access to her mouth, one arm crept around his neck to hold him, too. With the contact some vital force arced between them, making her realize how much she wanted him, needed him. *How could something this special be anything but right?*

But there was no room for doubts in what was passing between them. Ryder's lips caressed hers, brushing soft and light as if burnishing her mouth. His lips clung and then retreated, leaving her gasping at the loss. For the space of a heartbeat they lay with their gazes locked, their bodies tangled close, as if they were poised at the brink of some marvelous discovery. It was as if they had suddenly realized that this joining could be tenderness and succor, renewal and consolation, cloaked in passion's guise. And as Ryder lowered his mouth to hers, it was with a sense of approbation.

Pleasure washed over them as his tongue slid into her mouth, probing the contours of her half-parted lips, brushing the sensitive inner surface before tasting her more deeply. There was deft tenderness as he plundered the welcoming void of her, the taste of mint and passion and growing abandon. The kisses seemed endless, provocative, merging one into the next with nothing to separate them but tremulous sighs and the sweet-scented exchange of breath.

They curled tighter, Ryder's hands clutching in the tumbled softness of her honey hair, Jillian's clinging to the reassuring breadth of him. How well he filled her arms. How aware she was of his power and masculinity. How strong and sure the contact with Ryder made her feel.

Jillian willingly succumbed to the sense of belonging she had found in Ryder's arms, found with this man who by rights should have been her enemy. In spite of the differences between them, or perhaps because of them, she relinquished all control, all resistance. For indeed, she did not want to resist. She wanted to trust to Ryder's consideration and expertise, to discover the reaches of the mystical bond that had sprung up between them.

When Ryder sensed her surrender, his kisses became deeper

still, and as delight seeped through her, she felt the need to reciprocate all Ryder was giving her. The encroachment of her tongue was tentative and shy at first, but when she felt the tremors passing through him, Jillian became bolder, learning the delicious texture of his mouth. His teeth were slick and even, his lips, for all their chiseled contours, surprisingly soft as they pillowed her advance, the depths of him warm and moist and welcoming. Their tongues touched, circled, and at last Ryder lay back, pulling her down on top of him.

They sprawled on the virgin sheets length to length, her softer contours pressed to his, the proof of his passion nestled to the haven of her femininity. And while they kissed, their mouths were fused, as if they meant by that simple intimacy to find the unity they were seeking.

Jillian stirred against him, her lawn-covered breast teasing his chest, her hips instinctively fitting themselves to his. At the contact, Ryder laughed breathlessly. "Oh God, Jilly! You're so much sweeter than I ever dreamed."

He had recognized instantly her ingenuous sensuality, her instinctive understanding of the delight her body could give. Yet from her untutored response and inexperienced caresses, he knew that Jefferson Walsh had not shown Jillian the more pleasant realities of married life. While it infuriated Bingham to know that her husband had been so thoughtless, so brutish that he had not pleased Jillian as he had sought to please himself, a part of Ryder was glad for her innocence. It meant that he would be the one to introduce her to the delight of physical love; he would be the one to make her truly a woman.

When she moved against him again with tantalizing abandon, he rolled her onto her back and draped a restraining thigh across her hips. She was so lovely as she lay there, her hair shimmering against the pillow, her lips dark with the fervor of his kisses, her eyes flecked with gold and fierce with passion. With her pinioned beneath him, he kissed her into willing submission, until she lay quiescent and dazed.

It was only then that he began to open the buttons at the front of the long black gown, his fingers brushing over the tiny fasteners. As the filmy cloth fell open, the fragrance of a spring garden enfolded him, and he grew light-headed with the scent. Still, he remained at his task, stopping only when he reached the place where the fabric lay beneath his thigh.

From there his hand skimmed upward along the midline of her body until it reached the spot where the heirloom flagon lay. He closed his palm around the tiny silver bottle, seeing the patina, feeling the warmth her skin had imparted to the metal. He knew what the necklace meant to Jillian and brushed it gently aside, then bent to kiss the spot where it had lain, the hollow between her breasts. His tongue swirled over the vulnerable spot, marking it with his moisture, his heat.

He heard Jillian draw a rasping breath when he nuzzled the fabric of her nightdress aside and heard her expel it on a sigh as he took her nipple in his mouth. It was ripe and stiff even before he touched it with his tongue, and beneath the spiral of his kiss the bud grew tighter still.

Her skin was as pale as alabaster, the texture of rose petals, and unbearably sweet. She was so beautiful, so soft, so responsive to his touch. She was more than any man could expect a mortal woman to be. She was the sum of all his fancies, and he wanted to learn her body with a thoroughness that would linger in his memory from this day on. And though his body urged him to take her swiftly, succumb to the long months of deprivation and accumulated desire, he willed himself to savor the bounteous reality fate had seen fit to bestow on him.

As he continued to kiss her breast, his free hand traveled downward. It skimmed the rise of her ribs, the slimness of her waist, the curve of her belly, until he encountered the mound of golden curls at the juncture of her thighs. He heard her gasp at the contact, but before she could gainsay him, her words melted into a moan of mounting pleasure. As he explored her, he was unrelenting in his tenderness, probing deep, feeling her femininity unfurling beneath his hand. She was hot, wet, welcoming.

Her excitement fed his own, and he fought the overwhelming urge to seek his haven between her thighs. He wanted her. Oh, God, how he wanted her! But he wanted to share the world of wonder with this woman, not succumb to it alone. If he was to introduce her to the realm of unaccounted delight, he would have to hold back his desires, but after the months in prison, delay tested the boundaries of his will.

For herself, Jillian was lost in the sensual world Ryder was creating, and she moved through it with helpless, languorous abandon. She struggled within the confines of her nightdress until it was somehow borne away. She arched and trembled and whispered his name, and found that his efforts to please her were willingly renewed. There was a slow, spiraling ache building deep within her body, an inexplicable wanting that took her breath. She had no way to know what it was she sought, no way to guess that this sweet chaos was a prelude to something more. She had offered herself to this man in a way she had never offered herself to her husband, freely, joyously, without restraint. And she suddenly understood that giving was a part of receiving, that offering everything was a part of having it all.

"Ryder," she murmured, her voice slurred and breathlessly light. "Oh, Ryder, I've never felt like this before."

Smiling, he redoubled his efforts to please her, stroking until the essence of her need filled the air around them, kissing until she was consumed by a desperate, unnamed wanting. As he heightened her pleasure and his own, Ryder knew he was taking them toward a plane where pain and pleasure merged. And just before it became sweet torture to deny her, he moved above her, absorbing the heat beneath her skin, making her urgency his own.

"I want to please you, Jillian," he murmured, "if only you will let me. I want to teach you a world of wondrous things you've never had a chance to know."

His words of provocation eddied in her mind, and her answer was eager, devoid of fear. "Yes, Ryder, please me, teach me everything."

She shivered as she spread her legs to grant him access, feeling the roughness of his thighs against her own. There was his weight against her hips, the brush of his manhood at the entrance to her body, then a slow, surging stroke that came tenderly and deep. His flesh was hot, like a flame driving deep within her, kindling a world of sensations she had never known.

It was intense, wondrous, unexpected bliss. It was intimacy beyond imagining, tenderness wild and sweet. She felt whole for the first time in her life, whole and strong and free. *Now I understand*, Jill thought in breathless awe. *Now I know how it should be*.

"Jillian." Ryder whispered her name as if he had come home, as if he felt the oneness, too. He was lying above her, as close as people could be, his eyes meeting hers, his hands in her hair, his body joined to hers.

"Oh, Jilly, this is heaven," he whispered and lowered his head to kiss her.

His tongue probed deep, as if in keeping with that more intimate penetration, as if he wanted to bring them closer, closer still. They stroked and touched and pressed, meeting tongue to tongue and loin to loin. Jill was totally possessed, yet totally at ease with his possession. She understood, even as the maelstrom of sensation swelled around her, that somehow, on a different plane, she had possessed him, too.

When at length the kissing ended, they began to move together. He was pressing, stroking deep, his body searching the depths of her. In response her hips rose to meet his thrusts, to absorb his growing frenzy, and with each sweet, deliberate stroke her own passion and frenzy grew. Her thighs hugged the contours of his body, feeling the friction of skin to skin. Her fingers curled around his arms, clinging with wild abandon. Her breathing became labored and shallow; she tried to fit herself closer than before. Jillian gasped as an involuntary tightening coiled along her limbs, moaned with soaring pleasure as tension danced along her spine.

"Come with me, Jilly." Ryder's words were a demand, not an invitation. "Come with me, Jilly. Come with me now."

She turned her head against the pillow, her eyes wide, staring into his. "Yes, Ryder, yes," she breathed. "I'll come with you anywhere, anywhere."

Something strange and inexplicable ignited deep inside her as a wave of unspeakable delight spread through her blood. It was tension and release, resistance and surrender. As she gave herself to the sensation, she felt Ryder writhe and shudder, heard him gasp her name. His voice was rough with an ardor that was mirrored in her soul. It was hushed with awe and breathless with fiery resolution. She had never known a deeper communion with any human being. It was as if she could glimpse the world through Ryder's eyes, feel what he felt from inside his skin. It was as if they were mystically one, joined mind to mind and heart to heart. The tumult went on, leaping effortlessly into ecstasy, offering them pleasure, love, forgetfulness. Taking them to a world apart.

Tears gathered on her cheeks and lashes as the tumult of their loving ebbed, fell with unconscious abandon as their passion crept away. They had known the exultation of perfect unity, of two bodies and two lives joined inseparably. The experience was overwhelming, wondrous, and for all its intensity, far too brief. As they curled together, her tears were blotted on his skin, the litany of his murmured name muffled against his chest. His arms curled around her, comforting her, claiming her in a far different way than he had claimed her only moments before.

How long they lay tangled together, Jill hardly knew, but for a time the sense of oneness, of perfect communion, remained. They lay as close as people could be, with his breath upon her skin, her heart beating in time with his. They seemed to share a perfect understanding, without benefit of words. She grasped his masculine need for possessiveness, for dominion over her, and felt no resentment. He seemed to understand that she was spent but strangely elated, satisfied but somehow painfully aware. His tenderness was communicated through his touch, through his murmured endearments, through the way he sheltered her body with his own.

The security of the room enfolded them, the rhythmic ticking of the mantel clock a soothing counterpoint to their sighs, the breath of the summer breeze wafting between the curtains to wash across their skin. Here there was no war, no danger, no tomorrow. There was only the lingering contentment of two lives merged fleetingly into one.

At length, Jillian stirred and looked up into his eyes. They were calm, tender, dark, as blue as blue could be. "Why didn't you tell me it could be so wonderful?"

Ryder smiled. "Why didn't you tell me what a passionate woman you are?"

They were questions that had no simple answers, questions that defied the scope of words alone. They expressed a contentment that went beyond their ability to tell, a closeness that had no need of explanations. Each of them knew all that could not be said aloud, and even though they might have spoken, they kept their silence as if by mutual vow.

And it was enough. They had found comfort, communion, resolution. They had found peace, tenderness, delight. They had found in this union far more than either of them had dared to dream.

August 18, 1864

Mr. Walsh,

My business in New York is concluded. I will arrive in Niagara Falls Friday evening on the 9:15 train. I look forward to meeting you then.

JILLIAN CHANDLER WALSH

Jill turned away from the sound of the clattering telegraph key as if she could not bear to hear the operator transmit the message he was sending to her father-in-law. It was a message that sealed her fate, her fate and Ryder's. They were leaving. The time they'd had together was over; the magic they had found in each other's arms was at an end.

She made her way through the railroad station to the street outside, but as she stood on the walk, she was hardly aware of the carriages and wagons waiting at the curb or of the travelers brushing past her. She only knew that amid this bustle of activity she felt cold and terribly alone, shaken by the knowledge that sending the telegram had brought her one step closer to her inevitable parting from Ryder Bingham. She swallowed around the knot of unwelcome emotion that rose in her throat and made an effort to summon her strength. A full day and more lay before them, Jillian told herself, and she must do what she could to make each moment count. With that thought in mind, she turned in the direction of the boarding house.

As she walked, she became slowly aware of the beautiful summer day. The sky above was a clear, cloudless blue that seemed almost as deep and intense as Ryder's eyes. The sun was as mellow and warm as his arm around her shoulders, the breeze as gentle and tender as his kiss against her skin. She drew a long, deep breath, letting the crispness of the air invigorate her just as Ryder's presence did. And it seemed almost as if they had been granted this one last perfect day to spend together.

Jillian had risen early, as was her custom, leaving Ryder peacefully asleep in the bed they had finally truly shared. After she was washed and dressed, she had come to stand over him, letting her gaze drift down to where the blanket had fallen away from his shoulders and back, baring the magnificence of his body. Once she had relinquished her claim to the bed, one sinewy arm had usurped her place beside him, and Ryder had sprawled across its width with his face half buried in the pillow and his night-black hair dark against the sheets. He was so handsome as he lay before her, so unexpectedly vulnerable, that Jillian was forced to admit how incredibly dear he had become to her.

As she stood over him, temptation had teased the edges of her imagination, urging her to kiss Ryder awake and chance whatever fate might bring. But even as she considered it, the memory of the previous night's indulgences brought the heat of modesty to her cheeks. She could not forget the sweeping intensity of Ryder's kisses, the delight of his caress, the wonder of their union, or the inevitability of good-bye.

At last, Jillian had turned from the bed. There were things to be done while Ryder slept, and she had reluctantly left her lover, her Confederate, sleeping in their bed. Even as she went about her errands, her feelings for Ryder had filled her with warmth and happiness.

But those feelings of overwhelming contentment could not resolve the problem at hand: Jillian was out of money. Seeing to Ryder's upkeep and buying the things he had needed while he was sick had drained her resources, and the additional sums she had given the telegraph operator to make it appear that the wires she was sending Gerald Walsh had originated in New York had wiped out the last of her funds. What if there was an additional charge on Friday when she and Ryder boarded the train for Niagara Falls? she fretted. What if the railroad would not honor the tickets they had bought already? She had wanted to give Ryder money with which to bribe the guards at the border and additional money to use until he made contact with the Confederates in Canada. But most important and most distressing was the sum Jillian owed Mrs. Marshall. The woman had offered them far more than her hospitality, and it was a debt Jill felt duty bound to pay.

She paused on the curb as a curricle came down the street, its molded black body polished to a dazzling shine and two high-stepping roans between the traces. With the top down, she could see a handsome young man and a pretty woman snuggled together on the red plush seat, and Jillian watched them enviously. How wonderful it would be to escape the confines of the boarding house and spend the day exploring the city with Ryder. She had heard about the impressive falls on the Genesee River, the magnificent homes that lined the more fashionable streets, and the acres of plants and fruit trees in nurseries south of town that had given Rochester its reputation as the Flower City. She would have liked to explore the place with Ryder, to spend time ambling through the downtown area, chatting and window-shopping. She would have liked to eat in one of the hotel dining rooms, to pretend that they were nothing more than ordinary people free to enjoy their time together. Instead they were a truant widow and an escaped Confederate, without money for the most basic necessities. Jillian twisted her black-gloved hands together. She needed money for Mrs. Marshall, for Ryder, for herself. But short of robbing the bank up the street, there seemed to be nothing she could do.

Then as if in answer to her dilemma, Jillian noticed a sign in the window of a store across the street. "We Buy Gold and Silver," it proclaimed. That seemed a promising offer, though the only jewelry of any value she possessed was her mother's silver necklace and her diamond-studded wedding ring. There was no question that, of the two, she would prefer to give up the ring, but she would be seeing Gerald Walsh in two days' time and could not sell it. And in spite of her reluctance to part with something that had belonged to her mother, Jill found herself wondering how much the heirloom necklace might bring. Beneath her gown, she could feel the weight of the vinaigrette between her breasts, the warmth of the metal against her skin. It was one of the few things she had to remind her of happier days, and despite her need for funds, parting with the necklace seemed impossible. Still, the sign in the window tempted her. Perhaps if she went in, she could at least learn how much the piece was worth.

Drawing a deep, uneven breath, Jillian crossed the street and lifted the latch on the tall glass door that led into the shop. It was different from any jeweler's she had ever seen. Instead of elegant velvet-lined cases displaying gold cigar holders, glittering rings, and heavy necklaces, this shop was stacked high with all kinds of goods. There were clothes, silverware, musical instruments, weapons, and coins as well as jewelry of every imaginable kind. She approached the counter slowly, noting that the proprietor sat behind it at an overflowing desk.

He glanced up. "Can I help you, ma'am?"

Jillian cleared her throat twice before speaking. "I would like to know how much you'll give me for my necklace," she said, reaching beneath her mourning veil and the neckline of her gown to unfasten the chain of the vinaigrette. The clasp worked hard, and the smooth silver teardrop clung to her skin as she sought to withdraw it from her bodice. It felt as if she were wrenching out her heart as she pulled it free, but necessity forced her to lay the heirloom pendant on the counter.

The shopkeeper was old and heavy, and he wheezed as he came toward her. Without a word, he picked up the necklace and hefted it in his hand. He turned it over twice, examined the chain, and then smoothed his thumb over the surface of the flacon.

"An old piece," he commented.

"It was my mother's and her mother's before her." Jillian wondered if the man could hear the catch in her voice as she said the words.

"This is an outright sale, then?" he inquired, raising one grizzled brow.

"Is there any other kind?"

"You could pawn the necklace," the man suggested, "if it means so much to you."

"Pawn it?"

"I could advance you a loan and keep the necklace as collateral," he explained. "It would net you less money than a sale, but you would have ninety days to pay back the loan and the accumulated interest before I sell the necklace to someone else. Or at the end of the ninety days, you could pay the interest and extend the loan."

Jillian had never heard of such an arrangement but immediately realized that this might offer a solution to her problems. If she chose to pawn the necklace, she could have the money she needed now without losing the necklace permanently.

"Is there more to this than you're telling me?" she asked warily.

The proprietor shook his head. "Only that most people never come back to claim their things."

The thought of giving up the necklace forever left Jillian cold. "Oh, I'll be back," she assured him. "I could never let this necklace go."

"Then, if you mean to pawn it, I'll give you eighteen dollars," he offered, watching her.

"Eighteen dollars?" she echoed in surprise. The sum seemed like a fortune and the arrangement too good to be true.

"It's a fair price," the proprietor said encouragingly.

She nodded. "I'll take it."

As the man wrote out a claim check, Jillian's mind was busy. The eighteen dollars would give Jill enough to pay her debt to Mrs. Marshall, rent a horse and gig for the day, and pay for dinner at one of Rochester's finer hotels. She would have money to give to Ryder and to cover whatever other expenses might arise. This was proving to be a wonderful arrangement, and she was pleased at having discovered it.

With the claim check and the bills tucked safely away in her reticule, she began to look for a livery stable. As she hurried along, she was filled with plans for how she and Ryder would spend the day and night ahead of them. She would ask Mrs. Marshall's cook to pack a picnic lunch, then get directions to the nurseries and the falls. She would find out which hotel had the best food and make plans to take the evening meal in the dining room. Jill meant to do everything in her power to make the last day she and Ryder had together special, knowing even as she made her plans that it would make their parting more difficult. But for the first time in her life, Jillian felt sure and strong, in control and unafraid. She wanted the few hours she and Ryder had together to be sweet and tender and magical. She wanted to make today so wonderful that tomorrow wouldn't matter.

Bingham was sitting on the steps of the boarding house when Jillian drove up in front an hour later. At the sight of her, a welcoming grin blossomed across his face, and Jillian waved in response.

"Going somewhere this afternoon?" he asked, coming down the walk to offer his assistance as she clambered from the buggy.

"If you're up to going with me," she invited. As he clasped her hand to help her down, a shimmer of heat moved up her arm. Ryder seemed to feel it, too, and his fingers closed more tightly around hers.

"I feel as if I'm up to almost anything," he drawled, smiling lecherously. "Just what do you have in mind?"

As they secured the horse and walked in the direction of the house, Jillian laid out her plans for the day. But even as she spoke and Ryder answered, they seemed to share a vocabulary that went far beyond their words.

"I was disappointed to wake up and find you gone." *I wish you had been beside me this morning. I woke up wanting to make love to you.*

Jillian shrugged and looked away. "I had a few errands to do." *After last night, I wasn't sure how to face you and needed time to myself.*

"Well, I'm glad you got things resolved. I think a picnic sounds like a marvelous idea." *I want to have the day with you, away from anything that might intrude.*

"A picnic sounded like a good way to spend our last day in Rochester." *We have so little time to be together.*

Half an hour later, Ryder and Jillian pulled away from the boarding house with a hamper of food, a blanket to sit on, and directions to Rochester's points of interest. They had been told that the nurseries across the bridge on Mount Hope Avenue were a pleasure to behold, and as they approached the rolling hills just south of the city, the landscape seemed ablaze with yellow and orange, with crimson and purple. Rows of rosebushes striped the hillside, and spikes of gladioli jutted from nests of emerald leaves, filling the scene with hectic color. The orchards that nestled in the hollows between the hills were heavy with peaches and ripening apples in a delicious display of nature's bounty.

Jillian and Ryder left the carriage to better enjoy the spectacle of the late summer flowers, holding hands as they walked between the carefully tended beds. Half a hundred hues flowed like a sampling from nature's palette, creating shapes and patterns, a multitude of textures and colors brilliant in the midday sun. The flowers were as exquisite as each precious moment together seemed to be, and they wandered through the nursery for almost an hour before climbing into the buggy and heading back along the river.

After a time they came to a grassy expanse known as Falls Field. Tethering the horse, they took their belongings and walked across the grass toward the river. Both to the north and the south, the Genesee was flat and wide, but here a narrow limestone gorge turned the water dark and turbulent and sent it plunging down an escarpment into the chasm below. The falls was impressive with its veiled cascades of water, though not as mighty as the falls of the Niagara were reputed to be. Still, the grandeur awed and enchanted them. But in spite of the innate beauty of the cataract, the Genesee was a working river, and they could see the mills that lined the water above the falls, the outlet of a millrace, and the railroad trestle that straddled the upper river channel. A cluster of industrial buildings clung to the opposite riverbank like snails on the sheer rock wall. But the industrialization did not detract from the beauty of the falls, and Ryder and Jillian spread their blanket where they could enjoy the view.

Once they were settled, they unpacked their meal, finding cold chicken and fluffy biscuits in the hamper. There were grapes and peaches, too, as well as a corked bottle of lemonade and a tin of oatmeal cookies. Hungry and thirsty from the open air, they feasted and lay back to enjoy the afternoon and each other's company.

Jillian had removed her hat and mourning veil before they ate, and as she sat on the quilt beside him, Ryder's gaze came to rest on her. The sunlight that filtered through the trees above them caught in her caramel-colored hair, turning the thickly waving strands a brilliant honey gold. It gilded her brows and lashes and brought out the amber flecks in her eyes. In contrast to those mellow highlights, Jillian's skin was parchment pale except where the flush of heat and pleasure had crept into her cheeks. Watching her, Ryder was willingly enchanted by her delicate but compelling features, the opulence of her dusky-pink mouth, the tenderness in her eyes.

From the moment he had seen her face that day on the train, he had been half in love with her, and now, for a few brief hours, he could call her his. With the realization came the renewed need to hold her, touch her, please her. They had so little time that he wanted to do everything, see everything, experience everything with Jillian Walsh that a man and woman could feel.

There was something so wonderful and right about making love to her, something that verged on necessity about claiming her forever. He had always sensed that Jill embodied something deeper than beauty, something more lasting than desire, and now he understood what had drawn him to her. She was the kind of woman who could be everything to a man. She could share his happiness and grief, accept the challenges and defeats fate dealt them. She would stand beside him in his darkest hours and be there to cheer his victories. Jillian was the kind of woman his mother had been, the kind of woman he had been seeking all his life.

The notion jarred and taunted Ryder, and he drew a deep, uneven breath. Surely his feelings for this woman could not have grown so deep and profound in the few days they had been together. After thirty years of solitude, how could he have so suddenly discovered unity? Yet Jillian Walsh seemed to be everything Ryder wanted, and he was frightened by the scope and tenor of his need for her.

They spent most of the afternoon in the park overlooking the falls, talking of nothing, thinking of nothing. It was as if there were too many things to think about, to talk about, to let them spoil the time that remained. Yet even as they passed the pleasant hours, a tension was growing between them. It was fueled by the unexpected brush of hands, the way their gazes held, the need to express things they dared not say. It grew subtly until it became a compulsion in their blood, a need to come together that overshadowed everything.

Eagerly they left the park and when Jillian returned to the boarding house from the livery stable, Ryder met her at the door of their room. Wordlessly, he stripped off her bonnet and veil and took her in his arms. His lips covered hers, settling his claim on her, and they came together half dressed, half on and half off the bed because they could not hold their passion at bay. What passed between them then was desperate, urgent, primitive. And when it was over, they lay silent, awed by the strange perfection, the intensity of what had passed between them.

As Jillian had planned, they dressed and went to the Waverly Hotel on State Street for dinner, and while the food was excellent, neither of them tasted anything set before them. When the meal was over, they went directly back to the boarding house, passing up the confections at the Candy Works on Main Street and the show at the Varieties Theater. By mutual consent, they sought the sanctuary of their room, and when the door was closed and locked behind them, they faced each other, staring.

"Oh, Ryder, I didn't know it was going to be like this."

He shook his head. "No, Jillian, neither did I."

Without another word, they came close and began to undress each other. She loosened the knot in his tie. He unfastened the onyx mourning brooch at her throat. She opened the front of his shirt. He slipped the buttons of her bodice from their holes.

Their fingers explored the newly exposed flesh, hers grazing the dark hair that sprang up between the buttons and the placket of his shirt, his tracing the dipping neckline of her chemise. Heat rose up between them.

With a shrug, Ryder dropped his coat and shirt to the floor. Jill let slip the sleeves and bodice of her gown. He stroked his hands to the inward swoop of her waist and loosened the tapes that secured her petticoats. She moved away and pushed the fabric free.

"You're beautiful," Ryder breathed, as he stood watching her, "more beautiful than any woman I've ever seen."

Caught up in the whispered compliment, Jillian ventured closer, bending her head so he could strip the hairpins from her hair. With the release of her tightly held chignon, there was a sense of liberation that was heightened as the golden tendrils cascaded down her back. She could feel the weight of the silken mass against her neck, feel the tumbled hair pool against her shoulders. Then his fingers were delving into her loosened tresses, and she was aware of the potent sensuality of having a man's hands in her hair. She succumbed to the soothing strength of his thumbs against her temples, the heat of his caressing fingertips against her scalp.

"Beautiful," he murmured. "Beautiful. In the lamplight your hair shines like filaments of gold, shimmering, soft, all tumbled together." He held her close and pressed his face into the luxuriant mass, crushing the length of it between his fingers, crushing her body to his.

It was then she felt him trembling.

"Oh, Ryder," she breathed and raised her head to seek his kiss. "Oh, Ryder."

The brush of her mouth against his was sweet and warm, and the tongue she ran along the seam of his lips unlocked the tender barrier. He gave her free access to the treasure beyond: his warmth, his moisture, his taste. She teased him, merging her mouth with his and then withdrawing, using the probe and flick of her tongue to arouse his passions as he had aroused hers the night before. She pressed the length of her half-clad body to his and with the jolt of contact, felt the full, fiery force of his need.

With what seemed like barely leashed impatience, he worked the fasteners of her stays, easing the constriction, opening her to him. His hands swept over her lawn-covered flesh as the corset fell away, and Jillian knew how gently and how cherishingly a man could touch a woman, how urgent and demanding even those gentle strokes could be. Everywhere he touched, her flesh began to quiver; every brush of his hands seemed to ignite sensations she had only begun to know. He kissed her again, and she seemed to drift against him, overwhelmed by his tenderness, stultified by the potency of her own desire.

Ryder half carried, half dragged Jillian to the bed and tumbled down beside her. Bending above her, he kissed her, wanting her, needing her as he had never wanted or needed another woman. He charted the contours of her face, her curving shell-shaped ear, traced his lips along her throat, making sure he could never forget her.

"Ah, God, Jilly. You're so sweet," he mumbled against her shoulder, marking the place with a swirl of his tongue. "I want to love you, love you, love you . . ."

Jillian's hands tangled in his soot-black hair, traced the breadth of his shoulders and his back. She clung to him fiercely, possessively, knowing with an ache of bittersweet longing that nothing could alter their fate. Still she fluttered kisses along his throat and chest, buried her lips in the mat of dark hair. She held him, never wanting to let him go, never wanting the magic to end.

At length she found the belt buckle that lay between them and slipped the barrier free. She loosened the buttons on his pants and waited while he stripped them away. His underdrawers were no impediment, and she delved down deep inside, finding the proof of a wanting as overwhelming as her own. With a smile on her lips, she set herself to please him, and though her first attempts were tentative, she discovered the meter of the stroke that brought him close to ecstasy. Beneath her stroking palm, Ryder was hot and hard. As she bent above him, she saw that his eyes had grown heavy-lidded and lambent, and she lost herself in their blueness. She heard his breath catch as she touched him, felt him stir and arch against her. Still she caressed him unrelentingly, giving back measure for generous measure the satisfaction he had given her.

But in response to her ingenuous seduction, Ryder demanded

a more active role and, turning her on her back, stripped the last of her clothes away. When she lay bared before him, he feasted on her loveliness: the billow of her ample breasts, the narrow sweep of her waist, the rounded hips and slender flanks that made her irresistible.

His fingers trailed slowly down her body, following his gaze, complimenting her, teasing her, singeing her with his desire. His hands explored the recess of her femininity as he dropped his mouth to her breast. The sensation was exquisite, evoking wild delight, and she curled and pressed against him, caught in mounting frenzy. As he touched deep inside her, his mouth moved down her body, along her chest, across her midriff, past her navel, setting his lips at the apex of her thighs.

Jillian gasped at the intimacy, but he set his claim on her anew, tasting the essence of her femininity and sending her senses reeling. He searched out the central island of her desire and plied it with his tongue, tasting, stroking, drawing her against him. All the while he urged her onward, taking her, showing her, expanding her understanding of rapture until his accomplished sexuality sent her spinning into the realm of pure sensation. Desire seemed to flare around her like a blinding light, wash over her with the force of a wild spring tide. Reality seemed to shatter as she spun beyond control into a world of energy and life made more beautiful by this man's selfless generosity. She pulsed with the unexpected pleasure he had evoked, writhed with the tremors that moved along her limbs, gasped with the intensity of her satisfaction. And through it all she clung to him, whispering his name.

When her passion had ebbed, he moved up along her body, wrapped his arms around her to hold her near. But she was tingling with excitement, newly alive and overwhelmingly aware, and when she opened her legs to him in blatant invitation, Ryder sheathed himself within her.

As they lay together on the bed, each sought to shelter the other: Ryder's body curling around hers to offer a haven, Jillian's arms and legs closing over him to bind him close. For a time, each merely sought to absorb the essence of the other, the tenderness, the care, the uniqueness. For long moments they were totally aware, of their weaknesses, their strengths, their joys, their sorrows. It hardly seemed fair that they had been granted so brief a time together, such a short span of days to last a lifetime. And to hold the threat of melancholy at bay they kissed, sweetly, fervently, willing those kisses to express all they could not say. The kisses were meant to be communication, comfort, succor, but they soon became something more. They became passion, pleasure; they became desire, delight.

Ryder and Jillian tried to remain motionless though intimately joined, tried to prolong each precious moment though their needs were surging higher. There was eagerness in their blood, excitement racing along their nerves, inspiring them to a more ardent coupling, inciting their increasingly feverish movements. They tried to hold back, but tumult swept through them, frenzy and elation, furor and forgetfulness. They were dissolving in bliss, their bodies and their souls flowing into one, their hearts and their lives inextricably merged. Though neither would speak the name of the emotion that had grown up so unexpectedly between them, they both knew what it was, and both felt they were surely damned for knowing.

For a long time, they lay drifting in the hazy aftermath of love, sighing tender sighs, stroking tender strokes. They were too full of joy and contentment, too full of languor and forgetfulness to stir, so they lay listening to the fitful swishing of the trees outside the window and the chirp of crickets in the summer night.

But there was a limit to how long they could keep reality at bay, and at last Jillian turned to Ryder with tears rising in her eyes. "Oh, Ryder," she whispered. "Now that we've had this, how can we possibly part?"

It was a question Bingham had hoped he'd never have to answer, and he was silent for a time as he did battle with his conscience. He cared for Jillian as he had never cared for any other woman. But it was the wrong time in his life for him to find a woman he could love. He was in the land of his enemies with a dangerous, uncertain future laid out before him. As much as he might have wished it otherwise, he had nothing at all to offer her. For Jillian's sake as well as his own he gave the only answer he could give.

"We haven't any choice, Jillian," he told her, trying to hide his own disappointment. "You know as well as I do that there's no future for us together."

"But there could be, Ryder. You could take me with you," she suggested tremulously. "I could help—"

He shook his head. "No, Jillian, no. I don't have anything to offer you. I might not even make it safely into Canada."

"Don't say that!" she admonished in a whisper, covering his lips with her fingers.

"Why shouldn't I say it?" he challenged, brushing her silencing fingers aside. "We both know it's the truth."

"Please, Ryder, don't refuse me. Let me come with you."

He shook his head again, his mouth drawn almost angrily. "If I refuse you, Jillian, it is for your own sake. What would happen if I were recaptured? What would happen if I were killed? What would become of you?"

Her eyes were bright, her passion clear as she rose on an elbow above him. "It's a chance I'm willing to take."

"Is it?" he demanded, determined to deter her. "Five nights ago you were weeping for your loss of security because your husband and your father had left you without protection. I can't offer you either protection or security. I can't offer you anything at all!"

His words were heavy with bitterness and derision, and tempering that derision was the kind of resignation that could rob a man of his soul.

"I'd chance it all to be with you," she insisted.

"But *I* won't. I won't chance anything at all where you're concerned." He took a long breath and tried to make her understand his reasons for refusing her. "If it were only as simple as getting across the border, I might consider—"

"But what more is there to it than that?"

He faced her in the darkness, and he could see the stubborn set of her jaw. "There's a war on, Jillian," he began brutally, "or had you forgotten. And you're on the other side. Don't you realize that once I reach Canada, I'm going to get back into the fight?"

The thought of him going back to war terrified her anew. Even if he did manage to cross the border safely, there were battles yet to come, dangers he would face that she could not even know about or comprehend.

"Go back to war as a blockade-runner?" she gasped. "But why? The Union fleet is constantly patrolling the Carolina coast. Grant has Lee bottled up in Petersburg. The South is all but defeated. Ryder, what can you do?"

"I don't know. Something. I have to do something!"

"Ryder—"

"You can't come with me, Jilly, and that's final. You have a future with your father-in-law. I know it's not the future you wished for or the one that seems most exciting to you now, but it will be safe and secure. It would be madness for me to let you jeopardize it."

"But, Ryder, I've made my choice."

"No, Jilly, no," he whispered rolling over her, changing his tactics with a suddenness that took her breath. "Go live your life with Gerald Walsh," he whispered, dropping his head to kiss her seductively. "Do it for me, because it's the only way I can be sure you're safe."

"No—" she protested, but he stopped the word with a kiss, slanting his lips across hers, tracing the contours of her mouth with his tongue.

There was a humming in her head, a weakness creeping down her arms that had nothing to do with conceding the argument. She tried to fight the feelings Ryder was ruthlessly evoking to defeat her.

"Unfair," she breathed against his mouth. "So unfair."

Still, she was helpless to resist him, and as the kisses deepened, he became helpless, too. The sensual veils closed around them, and they succumbed once more to the magic that their bodies wove together. They were two made one, with every hint of discord dispelled between them. And for a few minutes nothing intruded on their world, the only world they could ever share. They drifted for a while, half awake and half dreaming, clinging close as if mere closeness could dispel the reality that daybreak would bring.

They slept, and the house was dark and silent when Ryder finally stirred. For a moment he lay cherishing Jillian's nearness, the wondrous thing they had shared. Then abruptly he became aware that the ticking of the mantel clock was hustling away the last hours of their time together, and he sat up at the edge of the bed. There was so little of the night left to them, so little time to watch her, touch her, commit every facet of her perfect face and body to his memory. He bent to kiss her mouth, leisurely savoring the taste of her. He twined his fingers in her hair, caressing its silkiness and vitality one last time.

Jill opened her eyes and smiled at him.

He smiled, too, tracing her chin and jaw, down the hollow of her throat, along her collarbone to the dusky valley between her breasts. It was then, as his hand lay above her breastbone, that Ryder realized that something was missing, that something very precious to Jillian was inexplicably gone. There was no silver pendant lying warm against her skin or tangled in her hair, and though he searched, there was no twisted chain around her neck.

"Jilly?" he whispered, knowing even before he voiced the question how she would reply. "Where's the necklace?"

"What necklace?" she murmured, smiling seductively, running her hand through the hair on his chest.

"Don't distract me, Jillian. What have you done with your mother's necklace?"

"I've taken it off."

"You told me you never took it off. You've sold it, haven't you? You sold it so you'd have money to keep me while I was ill." The accusation was cutting, venomous, but it was directed more at himself than at her.

Jillian reached up to catch his wrist, hoping for a chance to explain. "No, Ryder, I didn't sell it, honestly. I pawned it at a shop over by the station."

"You did it so there would be money to pay our bill here, to care for me while I was sick, and to keep me in medicine, shirts, and underdrawers!" he accused.

Jillian shrugged, all pretense falling away. "I also used the money to rent a horse and carriage and to take us out to dinner in the hotel. I wanted to make today special and wonderful. I don't understand why you're angry. They were all things I wanted to do."

"They were things you did because of me!" Ryder blustered. "And to do them you gave up your mother's priceless necklace!"

"But I'll get it back."

"Will you? How?"

"As the proprietor explained it, all I have to do is send him eighteen dollars and the interest due, and I'll get the necklace back. I'm sure I can bear to be without it for three months' time."

"But how will you get that money?"

Uncertainty flickered in her eyes before determination took its place. "I'll get it; don't worry," she assured him. "I can always pay the interest if I don't have all the money."

"Oh, God, Jilly. Don't you know you've risked your most prized possession?"

"Yes, I know," she agreed with a tender smile. "But then, to hear you tell it, I've risked far more than that already."

Ryder sighed in defeat, realizing the deed was done, beyond his ability to rectify. "Indeed you have," he admitted. "You've saved me from the Yankees, nursed me back to health, taken risks I had no right to ask you to take. Now you've sold a valuable keepsake, with no guarantee that it isn't gone for good."

"I did those things because I wanted to, Ryder, not for any other reason."

His hands tightened on her arms, and he pulled her close. "You've done far too much for me already, more than any man would have a right to expect. But I promise, Jilly, someday I'll make this up to you."

She smiled into his eyes and tangled her fingers in his hair. "Oh, Ryder, don't you know? You've more than made it up to me already."

Chapter Five

"LAST STOP, NIAGARA Falls station. Niagara Falls station in five minutes," the conductor's deep voice rang out as he came down the aisle of the passenger coach.

At the trainman's words, Jillian's heart leaped in her chest, and though she knew the danger, she peered over her shoulder to where Ryder Bingham was seated toward the rear of the car. Even as she allowed herself a fleeting glimpse of him, she knew she must not let on that they were more than strangers. Still, she ached for contact with the man, the reassurance only an exchange of glances could impart. But Ryder was studiously ignoring her, staring out the window into the night, and while she understood the reason for his caution, she felt a stab of disappointment.

With a sigh, she faced forward again and began to assemble her possessions. Since her trunk and her larger valise had been stowed in the baggage car, she had only to gather up her reticule and the tapestry bag that held her sewing. Fumbling in the depths of the latter, Jillian produced two brass tags she would need to claim her luggage and gripped them tightly in one gloved hand. She swallowed hard, trying to quell her rising panic. It would have been difficult enough to leave the train and meet Gerald Walsh for the first time even if things were as they should have been. But with the stories she had fabricated to extend her stay in Rochester and with Ryder a passenger on the train, Jill did not know how she was going to get through the next minutes.

Jillian had truly intended to ignore Ryder's presence in the railroad car as he had instructed her. But with the memory of their good-bye bright as a beacon in her mind, with the knowledge that when they reached the Niagara Falls station they would part forever, indifference was impossible. She could not forget how they had awakened early this morning and made love with a frenzy that had surprised them both. Nor could she dismiss the way they had lain together once it was over, clinging close, knowing that the time they had together was infinitely precious and far too brief. They had said very little, for there was little left to say. There were no promises to make, no dreams to discuss, no future to plan. Instead they had curled close, their physical proximity, the tenderness of their embrace expressing far deeper emotions than they had shared even during the intense communion of their physical joining.

By sheer will, Jill had kept her emotions in check until they stood dressed and ready to leave for the station. But when she realized that these were the last private moments they would ever have, her control had begun to melt. With ferocious concentration, she had looked up into Ryder's face, wanting to impress his features on her mind, wishing that she could always remember him as clearly as she saw him today. But if her memories of Jeff had dimmed in the scant three months since he had left Harrisburg, then surely Ryder's image would fade as well. Someday she would be left with nothing to remember him by but filmy daydreams and insubstantial memories. That realization devastated and terrified Jill. She wanted so much more of Ryder than what fate had seen fit to give her.

As Ryder had bent his head to kiss her one last time, Jill had begun to weep, her tears wetting both their faces.

"Jilly, sweet Jilly," Ryder had whispered as his mouth moved over hers, "I have never been as happy as I've been these last days, nor have I ever known such pain at parting. Whatever happens, Jilly, whatever the future brings, you'll always have a place in my heart."

"Oh, Ryder," she had begun in a voice dimmed and choked with tears, but he had not let her finish. Instead he had tightened his arms to bind her close, and kissed her a second time. As they kissed, their lips had flowed together, mingling tenderness and regret, sweetness and sorrow. When he finally raised his head, he had stood for a full minute watching her before he lowered the thick black curtain of her mourning veil.

Jillian shivered with the memory. *Ryder, Ryder,* she wondered, *how can I live without you?*

While she was lost in thought, the train had begun to thread its way through the outskirts of Niagara Falls. Fenced backyards flickered past the window; trees ran together in a blur. Brick factory buildings skimmed by as bit by bit the speed of the engine slowed. Then with the clanging of the bell and the screech of the iron wheels, the train gasped, wheezed, and ground to a halt.

Beyond the window lay the platform of the busy Niagara Falls station, its roof supported by towering iron pillars, a milling crowd gathered to greet the incoming passengers, horse-drawn coaches and hacks lining the street beyond. Jillian stared at the scene before her, filled with dread. Beyond the glass lay her future, the course she had chosen for her life, and her uncertainty about the decision she had made seemed overwhelming. She had never wanted things to change; she would have been more than happy to live out her life in her father's house or under Jeff's protection. That was the future she had planned. What had she done that it should be denied her?

Acknowledging that there was no answer to the question and no way to change her fate, Jill rose from her seat and fell in with the other departing passengers. As she shuffled down the aisle behind them, her gaze was riveted on Ryder. If only he would give her some sign, some last gesture of farewell. But Bingham continued to stare out the window, his face blank, his expression carefully remote.

He's so much stronger than I am, Jill reflected as she moved nearer. Ryder was going to honor the pact they had made in Rochester: to have no further contact once they boarded the train. That he could live up to the bargain when she could not seemed to reinforce Jillian's belief that she was cowardly and weak to want more than what they had been granted already.

But just when she had given up all hope of acknowledgment, Bingham turned, and she saw in his face the pain, regret, and despair that were tearing her apart. There were shadows in the blue of his eyes, shadows of terrible loss, thwarted desire, and incipient loneliness. Tears singed her eyelids and spilled down her cheeks, but Jillian made no move to wipe them away. She could not let Ryder sense her grief, could not let him see that the parting was destroying her. It would make it more difficult for him to do what he must, to do what his life depended on, and she was glad the thick black mourning veil kept the secret of her grief.

A dozen steps took her past Ryder to the end of the railroad car and down the stairs to the platform. She was instantly engulfed by the crowd. Around her were tourists boisterous with holiday merriment, families being joyously reunited, and businessmen who elbowed their way toward the looming station building. Yet in this throng of strangers no one approached her, and Jill knew a moment of mingled hope and panic. Wasn't her father-in-law coming to meet her? Hadn't he received her message? Was she to be left on her own, free to do as she chose?

Then as the group on the platform thinned, a slight, gray-haired man came forward. He was wearing dark green livery and a black-peaked cap. "Are you Mrs. Walsh?" he inquired.

Jillian nodded, studying the man before her. There was no trace of resemblance between this man and her dead husband. "Yes, I'm Mrs. Walsh. Are you Jeff's father?"

The question brought a smile to the man's lips and made his cheeks go round and rosy. "No, ma'am, I'm not, though I'd have been proud to claim Master Jefferson as my own. I'm Noble, the coachman. The master sent me 'round to collect you at the station."

The master. Those two simple words brought home the dramatic change her life was about to undergo. The coachman's words gave evidence that Gerald Walsh was a man of wealth, with a place in society, and powerful political connections. There would be a tremendous disparity between the simple life she had known with her father and the one of luxury she would be living in Walsh's house. A feeling of inadequacy rose up in her. How was she to succeed in the multitude of unfamiliar tasks that would be expected of her?

"Are those your baggage checks?" the coachman asked, taking the numbered tags from her nerveless fingers. He seemed to understand that Jill was frightened, overwhelmed, and he gently took her elbow. "If you'll come with me, ma'am, I'll show you to the carriage."

He led her across the platform to a fine closed coach, settled her inside, and went off in search of her luggage.

As she waited, Jillian peeked out the window, seeking some sign of Ryder. She soon realized that, while she had been talking to Noble, Bingham had left the train and now stood braced against one of the iron pillars, watching her.

Leave! she wanted to shout when she saw him. *Don't wait there on my account!* Irritation and panic joined the score of emotions already clogging her chest. Why was he standing there chancing recapture when he should have been on his way to Canada?

But even as the question took shape in her mind, Jillian knew why Ryder had stayed. He wanted to discharge his final responsibility, to see her settled, to bid her one last good-bye. And though she knew it was not wise, she was glad he was waiting. She wanted to use each second to set his image more firmly in her mind, wanted to cling to the inexplicable magic they had so briefly shared. There was comfort in the knowledge that Ryder was remaining at the station because he was as reluctant as she to give up the wondrous thing they had known together.

All too quickly Noble returned with her baggage and loaded it into the boot. The well-sprung carriage dipped slightly as the coachman climbed into the driver's box; there was the sound of his whistle and the jingling of harnesses as they got under way. Jill slid across the leather seat to the opposite window to catch a last glimpse of Ryder. He was standing as he had been for some time, so still he hardly seemed to be breathing, his face stark and his eyes as intense as leaping flames. She tried to cling to that scene, that vision of the man she loved. But the carriage rounded the corner and Ryder was gone.

Jillian sagged back against the dark leather cushions, shocked, stunned, trembling. The dreaded moment of parting had come and gone; she would never see Ryder again.

He watched the carriage leave, saw the matched pair of blacks draw it away from the station platform and around the corner, taking Jillian out of his life forever. He immediately felt the void, the bleak hollow in his chest, the vast numbness that preceded terrible pain. It echoed through his body, stealing his strength, his will, his purpose. Ryder stood staring across the train yard, incapable of movement, feeling his loss of Jillian with an intensity that he had never known in a lifetime of losing those he'd loved. He felt empty, bereft, betrayed. In that moment he knew that being without Jillian was and always would be like being without a vital part of himself.

How long he stood leaning against the tall iron column he hardly knew, but at length one of the railroad guards approached him.

"Something the matter, mister?" the uniformed man asked. "You feeling sick?"

Necessity forced Ryder to straighten and shake his head. "No, just tired. I've been on the train since early morning."

The man nodded and moved on, but the guard's questions had made Ryder realize how foolish he was being. He was drawing attention to himself when his only chance for survival and escape lay in anonymity. With an effort, he hoisted his battered carpetbag and made his way into the station. He asked directions to the stage that would take him to the Suspension Bridge depot, then wandered outside to wait. It was from another railroad station, two miles downriver, that he would catch the train into Canada. He had refused the chance to take a branching line from Rochester directly to Suspension Bridge because he wanted to travel with Jillian and see her safely in her father-in-law's hands before he attempted to cross the border. It bothered him more than a little that the man had not seen fit to meet Jill himself, but Walsh had sent his carriage and driver, proof that Jillian would be provided for monetarily, at least.

Ryder boarded the nearly empty horsecar and paid his fare, silently blessing Jillian for the cache of funds she'd forced upon him. He'd been angry when he learned that she had pawned her necklace, but he now realized that she had seen reality much more clearly than he. The money she had received for the heirloom was proving to be a necessity, and he was glad she had been so farsighted. Without volition, Jillian's image rose up before him: lovely, caring, tender. Dear God, he hoped she'd find some measure of contentment here in Niagara Falls.

Beyond the window of the horsecar, the darkened streets of the village slipped past. There were luxury hotels built for the visitors who came to see the wonders of the Falls; clusters of stores along the main street, closed and shuttered for the night; houses, large and small, screened from view by ornamental plantings and high wrought-iron fences. Jillian would walk these streets, shop in these stores, perhaps even visit in these homes. She would be absorbed by the life in this thriving town, and he wanted to be able to think of her in a setting that he had experienced and seen. In his mind at least, he wanted to maintain some connection with the woman who had become so quickly and so completely a presence in his life.

As the horsecar plodded onward, the buildings began to thin. There were more vacant lots, more patches of untended greenery, older looming trees. They had reached the edge of town. With that realization, Ryder settled back and let his eyes drift closed. He was tired and still feeling the effects of his illness. But there was no time for weakness when the most difficult part of his escape lay ahead of him. If only he knew what would be expected of him as he made the crossing into Canada. Would he need some kind of pass to cross the bridge? Would he be questioned about his reasons for going into Canada? Had posters bearing his likeness been circulated to the customs agents? Was he wrong to believe that an escaped Confederate could elude the Yankees and pass across the frontier of the United States unchallenged? Weariness had robbed him of his optimism, leaving him the dregs of determination and the dawning conviction that he would not be taken alive. After all, how precious could life be when he had lost everyone and everything he'd ever loved? Somehow revenge seemed a poor excuse for living another day.

Outside the window the density of the buildings was increasing; more houses and stores lined the shadowy streets. Blocks of business buildings slid past the windows of the streetcar. The settlement known as Niagara City was clustered at the edges of the road.

They moved northward through the center of town, across a washboard of railroad tracks, turned right onto a drive that led directly to the station. When the stage came to a halt, Ryder took up his bag and disembarked. Cinders crunched beneath his boots as he walked toward the depot, crossing a brace of uneven tracks, climbing a flight of stone steps that led to the northbound platform. On all sides of the brick and stone station, tracks lay like double lengths of rope. There was a freight yard to the east with stripes of iron rails gleaming in the moonlight and loaded boxcars linked together like strings of butchers' sausages. To the south another pair of tracks looped back toward the station at Niagara Falls, and somewhere to the west was the famed Roebling Suspension Bridge, the bridge that Ryder prayed would carry him to safety.

The platform that skirted the depot appeared to be deserted except for a ragged drunk sprawled on one of the wooden benches. His sonorous snores were a counterpoint to the rhythmic clang of a hammer meeting metal, which came from the engine house, and the melodious plink of a tinny piano, which drifted from one of the saloons across the street.

Drawing a long, deep breath, Ryder made his way toward the central door that led into the station building. In spite of the bank of arched windows at one end, the high-ceilinged hall was stuffy, dimly lit, and occupied by no more than a dozen weary-looking travelers. They were huddled on the wooden benches singly or in pairs, smoking, reading, or trying to catch a nap between trains. Bingham took a turn around the place to get his bearings, then paused to consult the schedule posted on a board above the ticket window. The train he wanted—the one that would go to Niagara Falls, Canada, and then on to Hamilton—would arrive at 12:05

and leave half an hour later. Consulting the station clock, he saw it was not quite eleven.

Ryder faced the wait before him with rising trepidation. Would he be better served to stay here at the depot keeping his eyes open for trouble, or should he search out some other place to pass the time? As he considered his options, Bingham prowled the length of the room and back before he realized he was pacing. On shipboard it had been one of the ways he had worked off his nervous energy while waiting to run the blockade. Since the war had begun, he must have walked a hundred miles in ship-long increments. But here the pacing might draw unwanted attention and make his restlessness too obvious. He slipped out the door onto the platform and began a slow circuit of the building. He had almost convinced himself that the depot was unguarded when he came upon a contingent of soldiers gathered around a vacant baggage cart. In the warm night air Bingham could hear the murmur of their voices. Two of them were nasal and sharp; one was booming and deep. Another voice carried the unmistakable twang of a displaced Iowan, and though the last man never spoke, he laughed at everything the others said. The guards were relaxing between trains, enjoying their smokes, passing a bottle, and swapping stories of the war.

"An' outside of Murfreesboro we come upon the prettiest little Southern gal anyone ever saw," one intoned. "She had skin like fresh cream and breasts as round and firm as . . ."

Ryder slid back into the shadows and stood there with his heartbeat volleying against the wall of his chest. He lowered his satchel to the platform and felt for the derringer in his pocket. The way it nestled in his palm gave him some feeling of security, but not as much as he had hoped. He wouldn't stand a chance against five armed men if it came to a fight, and he contemplated taking the derringer's single bullet himself rather than letting them recapture him.

The notion was foreign and disillusioning, but it was still nibbling at the edges of his mind when the door to the depot snapped open and a man of diminutive proportions stepped out into the night. Ryder started at his sudden appearance and half drew the derringer from his pocket as his instinct for survival outweighed everything else.

The tiny man paused just beyond the doorway to light a cheroot, and the movement in the shadows alerted him to Ryder's presence. He turned sharply, his narrowed eyes sweeping over the taller man, assessing him in a glance. If he sensed imminent danger, he gave no sign of it and brought the match closer to the end of the cigar, inhaling to draw the flame. Once the cigar caught, he flicked the lighted match out into the murky blackness and exhaled a plume of smoke.

"Nice night," he observed. "You waiting for the train to Canada?"

Bingham nodded. Jillian had warned him about his drawl, and he deemed it better not to reply to this man's questions directly.

"They tell me it's right on schedule."

Ryder said nothing.

"You have the time?" The stranger seemed to take no offense at the lack of response on the part of his companion.

In response Ryder shook his head and ventured a single syllable. "No."

"S'pose we got a wait of an hour or so."

As they stood less than a yard apart on the platform, Bingham tried to make out the other man's features. In the flare of the match they had seemed rounded, soft, and almost pretty. As his eyes grew more accustomed to the dimness, Ryder could see that beneath his low-crowned hat, the stranger's hair was long on his collar, as fair and soft as a girl's.

"Can I offer you a chaw of tobacco?" the smaller man continued. "It's a filthy habit, tobacco, but I just can't seem to shake it."

With the words, the fellow took a wad from his jacket pocket and extended it in Ryder's direction. Alysse had not approved of chewing tobacco, and Ryder had never tried it. He was about to refuse the offer when he noticed that the man was handing him plug, not short-cut, tobacco; plug was the kind Confederates used. Ryder raised questioning eyes to the other man's face and found him staring intently.

"I was watching you in the station," he commented offhandedly. "You walk like a man whose boots are too tight, like they once belonged to someone else."

It was common knowledge that this late in the war many in the Southern army wore boots of Union issue. Only scavengers stripped bodies on the battlefield of their personal effects, but it was considered perfectly acceptable to take a pair of boots from a bluecoat who had no more need of them.

It took Bingham no more than a second to grasp the man's insinuation, and it chilled him to the marrow. Even with the rush of fear that raced along his nerves, the irony of being discovered through something as innocent as a borrowed pair of boots did not escape Ryder. Still, his accuser seemed to pose no threat, and that confused him.

"Shall we go somewhere and get a drink?" The stranger's voice dropped as he made the offer. "I think I might be able to give you something you very badly need."

Without waiting for Ryder's reply, the smaller man tossed the cheroot aside and made his way across the tracks as if convinced that Ryder would follow him. There were several hotels fronting on the street beside the rail yards, and he entered the largest one, Attwood's Western Hotel. Still in the lead, he traversed the lobby, entered the saloon, and took a table by the wall. Ryder sat down across from him. A signal brought a waiter with a bottle and two glasses; the stranger paid in gold. With a flourish, he poured three fingers of whiskey for each of them.

"To your health, sir," he toasted and tossed off the contents.

Ryder did the same and had to fight down a hiss as the whiskey seared its way to his belly. Since he hadn't had spirits of any kind in nearly a year, the liquor went right to his head and sent caressing tendrils of warmth curling along his limbs. It was a totally pleasurable sensation.

When the other man moved to fill his glass again, Ryder placed his palm across the rim. "Not just yet," he murmured. There was a warning in his tone, and the fair-haired man took note of it.

Instead he refilled his own glass and took out another smoke. "Cigar?" he offered.

Ryder was tempted but refused.

The man made a show of lighting his own cheroot, then bent nearer. "I have a story to tell you, just to pass the time," he began, "a story that might be false but might just as well be true. It's a story about an escape, an escape from military prison."

The smaller man's words sent ice water through Bingham's veins, instantly diluting the pleasant effect the liquor had had on him. It took an effort to meet the stranger's eyes, but Ryder managed, wondering at the approach the other man was taking.

"Where did this prison escape take place?" Ryder parried, sitting back in his chair, willing to play his part in the game, at least temporarily.

"Oh, I don't know." The stranger blew a puff of smoke. "On an island maybe, perhaps in New York Harbor."

Ryder was stunned by the man's perceptiveness and chilled by the realization that only a Yankee agent would be privy to such information. Had this man recognized him from a wanted poster?

Did the stranger know his secret? Would it be necessary to kill the fellow to ensure his silence?

Ryder looked at the man more closely, taking advantage of the lamp that hung directly above the table. With the glow of the light falling full on his face, the fellow looked guileless and cherubic. He was a small man, a foot shorter than Ryder and easily sixty pounds lighter, but for all his tiny stature the man's shoulders were broad, his arms sinewy and muscular beneath his jacket. He seemed wiry and strong, a fine specimen of a man in miniature. He was very blond, both his hair and his eyelashes, though the latter made an impressive feathery fringe around eyes of translucent gray. His face was open, boyish, and clean-shaven, his features delicate and rounded. But there was something in his presence that belied the look of innocence.

He confused Bingham with his questions and his cordiality when it seemed likely that the fellow was a Yankee. But if he was, why hadn't he simply taken Ryder prisoner instead of letting him sit here with a derringer in his pocket, affording him a chance to escape? What did the man want, anyway?

Conversation returned to the prison escape. "But how would a man get out of such a place as you describe, a prison in New York Harbor?" Ryder asked.

"There's no question that the prisoner would have to be daring and shrewd." The smaller man's eyes narrowed as he speculated. "First, he'd have to get outside the walls of the prison itself, on a pass, maybe, or with a work detail or by bribing a guard."

Ryder raised his brows with genuine interest and said nothing.

"Then, the fellow'd have to find a way to get from the island to the land."

"But how might he do that?"

The smaller man watched him consideringly. "How would you do it?" he baited Ryder.

Bingham shook his head. "How should I know? I'm neither daring nor shrewd."

A glance filled with skepticism flashed across the table, but the stranger continued. "Well, the prisoner might steal a boat or put together a makeshift raft."

The story was becoming more fiction than fact. Perhaps this fellow knew less than he let on. That thought gave Bingham courage. "Or a man might swim."

"Swim? Brave the waters of New York Harbor? That hardly seems likely."

"Perhaps the fellow was a strong swimmer," Ryder continued,

"and maybe he was desperate enough not to care if he lived or died."

Gray eyes met blue as the two men stared across the table, assessing, considering, each taking the measure of the other.

"Who the hell are you?" Ryder finally asked.

The stranger's round face broke into a grin. "My name is Jamieson Bradford, but most of my friends call me Jamie."

Bingham hesitated, studying the other man. "And are we going to be friends?"

Bradford's grin broadened. "Fast friends, I think. Fast friends."

Ryder watched him speculatively until the silence forced Bradford to continue.

"Unless I miss my guess, you won't be willing to help me complete this story until you cross the border. And right now I'd wager half my worth that you'd like to know what to expect."

Bingham acknowledged the other man's observation with a lift of one brow and the quirk of his mouth.

"An invalid corps and a Negro regiment have been given the responsibility of guarding the border, and you should be prepared to answer a few questions before you board the train."

"What might they ask?" To Ryder it seemed a safe enough question.

"They'll likely ask your name, though I don't plan to give my real one. They'll want to know where you're from and what your business is in Canada. You might have a problem with your drawl, so tell them you're from Maryland."

"Will that convince them?"

"Most likely. These troops guarding the border aren't known for their perceptiveness, and it sounded as if they'd been drinking."

There was contempt in Bradford's tone, as if it was no fun for him to play this game against men who had not achieved full mastery. It was an attitude Ryder recognized and could readily understand. It was also an attitude that could lead to disaster, as Ryder also knew.

"What else?" he prodded.

"Perhaps they'll ask your business or if you were in the war."

"And how would a man answer them?"

"Why, with the truth, if possible."

"And if not?"

"Then it might help to have some papers to establish another identity." Bradford dipped into the breast pocket of his jacket and withdrew a long white envelope. He slid it across the table, then sat back in his chair.

After a brief hesitation, Ryder took the packet and opened it. For several minutes he studied the documents he had been given, then returned them to the center of the table.

"Would it be easier to cross the bridge on foot?"

Jamie shook his head. "On foot or in a wagon, you need a pass from the provost marshal. The train is by far the easiest route. It's something you should remember if you come this way again."

"By the grace of God I won't," Ryder murmured fervently, "at least not while there's a war on."

"I wouldn't be so sure of that if I were you."

Silence fell between them, and Ryder's mind was busy. Just who was Jamieson Bradford, and why was he befriending him? Was he another Confederate headed for Canada? Or was he a clever imposter, a Union agent, trying to gain his confidence? Ryder tried to assess the other man rationally and failed.

Silently, Ryder fingered the envelope. Was it safe to take the documents the other man was offering him, or should he return the packet to Bradford? Were they a ruse, a trick to identify him to the border guards without involving the other man in his recapture, or would the papers help him pass safely into Canada?

As he pondered the questions, the noise of the approaching train reached them, the distant roar, the wailing whistle. The sound of it carried well in the heavy evening air. It came louder, nearer. The lamps swayed; the floor began to quake. Liquor sloshed in its bottle.

Jamieson consulted the clock above the bar. "It's the five after twelve. Right on time, just as I told you. We have time for one more drink before we go. Perhaps you'd like a little Dutch courage to help you through what's ahead?"

All at once Ryder didn't care who the other man was, didn't care if the papers were bogus or genuine. The next few minutes would decide his fate, and he knew he had no choice but to accept whatever came. He would live or he would die; he would escape or be recaptured. He had done his very best to reach Canada and safety, but he had long ago recognized that there were forces in the universe over which he had no control.

He picked up the papers Jamieson had offered him and moved his glass a little closer to the bottle. "I think I'll have a bit of your liquid courage, though I doubt courage, liquid or otherwise, is of any particular nationality."

"Not Dutch, hum?" Bradford asked with a grin as he refilled Ryder's glass.

"Not Dutch," Bingham confirmed, and downed the whiskey in a single swallow. "Now I think it's time to head for the station. I don't want to miss my train."

Beyond the window of General Walsh's carriage lay the village of Niagara Falls, but Jillian felt no curiosity about the place that was to be her new home. She did not care to look at the tree-lined streets, the impressive buildings along the main thoroughfare, or the stores and businesses they were passing. She did not peer out at the homes where the people of Niagara Falls lived, did not try to catch a glimpse of the lives revealed by the scores of open windows. All she could think about was Ryder Bingham and how desperately she missed him already. How was she going to live the years that stretched before her, knowing he would have no part of them? Yet live them she must, in a new and totally unfamiliar environment apart from everyone she had ever loved. The realization brought fresh tears to her eyes, and now that there was no reason to hide them, she wept freely, filling the coach with the muffled sounds of her grief. She felt helpless, hopeless, overwhelmed. Could she possibly find happiness in so foreign a place?

It was the jolt of the carriage turning from the street into a brick-paved driveway several minutes later that roused Jillian from her dark thoughts, and she hastily dried her eyes. But her doubts about the future were redoubled as the coach rolled to a stop before an impressive gray stone house. Built in the fashionable Grecian style, Gerald Walsh's home stood strong, sturdy, and palatial, with four Ionic columns guarding the portico at the front. To the right, a two-story wing of the same gray stone nestled close, united to the main building by a deep, dentiled cornice. Jillian gaped at the size of the place; it was nothing less than a mansion.

With Noble's help, she alighted from the carriage and made her way up several steps to the veranda and the wide fanlighted door. The panel, adorned with a huge black mourning wreath, loomed before her, solid and impregnable, hemmed by beveled sidelights and crowned by the sweep of a bow window. A golden light spilled through the glass, though somehow Jill sensed no welcome in its glow. She stood before the portal for a moment to gather her courage, but just as she raised her hand to knock, the door swung wide and a grim-faced woman stared across the threshold.

"Good evening, Mrs. Walsh," she said after a moment. "I'm Elvira Pryor, Congressman Walsh's housekeeper."

"Good evening, Mrs. Pryor," Jillian answered, stepping through the open door into the entryway. A hanging lamp illuminated the impressive space, the high ceiling, the wide hall, the graceful staircase that rose to the second floor, a shimmering multipaned window at the landing. Straight-backed chairs flanked the walnut pocket doors that closed off rooms to the left and right, and an ornate cherrywood hall tree stood nearby, its gleaming circular mirror draped with mourning gauze.

After Jillian's gaze had swept the foyer, it came to rest on the housekeeper. The woman stood every inch Jill's equal in height but was shaped like a block of granite, solid and compact, starched straight by the confines of her corset. Mrs. Pryor's thick iron-gray hair was reined in tight beneath a starched black cap, though the plainness of the face beneath made the unadorned cloth seem a bit of frippery. With a long, thin nose that dropped from her forehead like a plumb and a mouth as pursed and narrow as a puckered seam, Mrs. Pryor was an imposing figure and, Jill sensed, a hostile one.

Mrs. Pryor had been studying Jill, too, but the modest cut of her gown and the thick gauze of her mourning veil must have made accurate judgments impossible. Huffing with apparent disgust, Mrs. Pryor turned and swished toward the carpeted stairs. "I'll show you to your room," the housekeeper offered gruffly.

The chamber Mrs. Pryor indicated was the first at the top of the stairs, and she went ahead to light the way. A moment later the room sprang to vibrant life, and as Jillian stepped inside, she could see that it was larger and more luxurious than any bedroom she had ever seen. Above the cream-colored wainscoting, the walls were covered with a delicate ivy-patterned wallpaper that matched the thick Brussels carpet of subtle mossy green. The sheer white muslin curtains on the windows matched the ones draped around the bedstead, and the suite of heavy walnut furniture was both simple and exquisite. Jillian tried not to stare at the unaccustomed opulence but could not seem to help herself.

"The room is beautiful," she breathed after a moment, "so restful and serene. I'm sure I shall pass many pleasant hours here. Can you tell me what's beyond the windows?"

Mrs. Pryor shrugged and gestured with one hand. "There's a woodlot to the east and the river to the south."

"And are we very far from the Falls?"

"No, not far. A mile or so."

Jillian stepped to the open window and stared out into the night. Beyond a fringe of trees she could see the intermittent gleam of moonlight on the water and hear a faraway roar.

"Is that them?" she asked, turning away from the glass. "Can I hear the Falls?"

"Might be," Mrs. Pryor answered. "I expect you'll want to freshen up before you meet the congressman."

"Mr. Walsh wants to see me tonight?" Jillian could not quite hide her nervousness; she had been hoping for a reprieve.

"Those were his orders."

"Then I'd like time to wash and change my dress, if you don't think Mr. Walsh will mind the delay."

"As you wish." The woman turned away. "I'll send one of the men up with your bags."

As she waited, Jillian puzzled over her first impressions of her new home. On one hand it was far grander than she had been led to expect. Jeff had never given her any hint that he had lived with such magnificence. If the rest of the rooms were as sumptuously furnished as this one, the house would be a showplace of elegance and style.

On the other hand, there had been no word of welcome either from Mr. Noble at the station or from Mrs. Pryor here. But then, what had she expected? She had known from the outset that Gerald Walsh's invitation had been extended out of duty, not genuine concern. His servants probably knew that, too. Still, she had been given a fine room, and she should feel gratitude at Walsh's concern for her comfort.

Jillian had removed her hat and mourning veil when a man arrived with her baggage.

"Is there anything else, mistress?" he asked before he turned to go.

"No, nothing, thank you," she told him.

He bobbed his head and left, closing the door behind him.

Alone in the room, Jillian set herself to opening her trunk and finding a dress that was not too wrinkled from the trip. Her new black bombazine had fared the best, and after she had washed, she slipped it on. The wide, draped skirt, with its rows of fashionable ruching, and the snug-fitting bodice were flattering. Ryder had expressed his approval of the gown only the night before. Still, she fussed nervously with the lay of the collar and the buttons at the cuffs of the wrist-length sleeves, then pinned a crepe stone brooch at the neckline. She took down and brushed her hair, but returning the obstinate tresses to some semblance of order took longer than she had expected. By the time she had succeeded, Jillian was even more edgy than she had been before. Clutching a black lace handkerchief, she returned to the hall, where Mrs. Pryor was waiting.

The woman's cool black eyes swept over Jill, taking in the creamy complexion, the curly caramel hair, the full, but slender lines of the younger woman's body. Snorting her opinion of what she saw, the housekeeper rose from one of the straight-backed chairs and led Jillian to a door behind the slope of the stairs.

"Go right in, Mrs. Walsh. The congressman is waiting for you in his study," she instructed.

Jill opened the door timorously and stepped into the large book-lined room. It was furnished richly, as befitted a man of the congressman's stature, with thick tapestried carpets and heavy leather furniture. There were carefully draped lambrequins above the mahogany-shuttered windows, and a door that led directly outside so clients could come to the study without tracking through the house. An oil portrait of Jeff and his father was mounted above the fireplace, and on the marble mantel was a sword that Jill recognized as the one her husband had carried into battle. In the center of the room was a wide partner's desk, but one look at the proprietary air of the man who sat behind it convinced Jill that he had never willingly shared the desk or anything else in his life.

As she entered, Gerald Walsh looked up from his papers and studied her with the dispassionate thoroughness of a man who was very sure of his position and contemptuous of hers. Jill felt hot blood course to her cheeks at her father-in-law's appraisal, and she stood frozen, clinging to the doorknob.

Silence stretched interminably between them before Walsh rose from his chair and spoke. "Come in, Jillian; take a chair. I have been waiting a long time to meet the woman who managed to entrap my son."

Jillian caught her breath at the stinging insult, unsure whether to turn and go or to advance as Walsh had bidden her. It seemed unwise to disobey him at this juncture in their relationship, and she moved forward, drawn against her will by the command in his dark eyes.

"Have a chair," he continued, "here by the light where I can get a better look at you."

She did as she was told and sat down gratefully, not sure that her quaking knees would have carried her any farther. As she arranged her skirts, Walsh came around the desk and, with a finger beneath her chin, tipped her face to his. For several minutes he studied her in silence, and Jill was as much aware of his scrutiny as she was of his disdain. The only thing that saved her from descending into panic was that in those moments she was watching her father-in-law every bit as closely as he was watching her.

She was struck first by the sheer power of the man, the menacing breadth of his body, the ruthlessness in his face. At first she was sure that there had been nothing of him in Jeff, but slowly she began to see the similarities. They were similarities that in Gerald Walsh had been transformed by age and personality, but there was no question that there had been some of his father in her husband. The shape of the face was the same, square and heavily boned; and the nose had the same aggressive bend an inch below the brow line. Gerald's eyes were of a similar color, too, a mix of hazel and brown, but Jeff's had twinkled with life while his father's were murky and impenetrable. Gerald was heavier and more ruddy than his son had been, and instead of wavy and brown, Gerald's hair was thick and snowy white. But there was a sensual curve to his mouth that he had not passed on to his son and a certain inbred arrogance that Jeff had totally lacked.

As she stared up at her father-in-law, she sensed other things about him: that he was a man who got his way, that he would be a formidable enemy. The curl of his lips made him seem ruthless beyond all reason and revealed that he thought of her as nothing but grasping and contemptible. Anger flared inside her at his wholesale condemnation of her, and the tenor of her feelings must have been evident in her eyes. Abruptly he loosed his hold on her chin and returned to the far side of the desk. He picked up the stub of the cigar that had been trailing noxious vapors from the ashtray and drew a long stream of smoke into his mouth.

"I suppose I can see why Jefferson was so smitten with you. You have a fair face and a figure to match, though no sense of style, that's certain. Are all your clothes as outmoded as that gown?"

Jillian's mouth narrowed. It was the only new dress she had; she had finished sewing it the night before she left for New York. If he found fault with her best, she had no idea what he would think of her other twice-turned dresses or the gowns that had been hastily dyed when the household was plunged into mourning.

"We hadn't much money to spend on clothes," she said softly.

"And I'm sure both you and your father saw Jefferson as the vehicle to a more affluent life."

There was a gram of truth in Walsh's accusation, as much as Jillian hated to make the admission, and she dropped her eyes to her hands, clutched tightly in her lap. Her father had wanted her to marry Jeff for the financial security he could provide, but there had been none of the cunning behind her marriage that this man seemed to imply. She had married for security, not for money, and there was a fine distinction between the two that Walsh would never be able to discern.

"Now that you've become my responsibility, I suppose you think you got what you've been scheming for. Well, I may have been forced to take you into my home, and I suppose I'll have to pay to dress you properly, but you'll receive little more than that from me."

He took another pull on his cigar. "And I suppose there's no chance you're carrying a baby and will repay my kindness with a grandchild."

At the question, Jillian's cheeks flamed anew, and she was glad that Walsh could not see the sudden panic in her eyes. Perhaps she was carrying a child, but if she was, it would not be this man's grandchild. And suddenly she was glad she would bear no kin of his. If she was pregnant, it would be with Ryder's child, Ryder Bingham's and hers. Yet with the uncertainty of her situation, she did not know how to answer her father-in-law. If she told him there was no baby and then discovered she was pregnant, how would she explain her condition? But then it had been three months and more since she had lain with Jeff, and she could not plead uncertainty either.

"Well, speak up, girl. Am I to be a grandfather?"

Jillian decided to gamble on the truth. "No, I haven't conceived Jeff's baby."

His frown deepened. "Well, that's too bad, too bad. If you're not with child now, there won't be anyone to carry on the name or inherit the Walsh fortune either."

There was a genuine note of regret in the man's tone, and Jillian glanced up hoping to see some touch of humanity in his eyes. But though she searched his face, there seemed to be no tenderness or grief in his imposing features.

"I'm sorry," she added for his benefit.

"As well you should be," he replied.

It was not the response Jillian had expected, and if there had been a momentary vulnerability to Gerald Walsh, it was gone so quickly it might never have been there at all.

"Since I'm not breeding you an heir," she began with an uncharacteristic flash of resentment, "what is to be my role in your household?"

"Your role, girl?"

"I am quite capable of earning my keep," Jillian offered defensively. "I have seen to the duties in my father's house since I was ten."

His response was curt. "Mrs. Pryor's housekeeping suits me very well. Nor will she tolerate any interference."

"But then what am I to do here?"

"Do?" He appeared to be surprised by the question. "Do? I suppose you'll do what most pretty women do, be decorative and obedient."

Frustration rose in Jill. She had accepted this man's invitation because she truly had no choice, but she had also been certain that she would be given duties that would be of service to her father-in-law.

"But I thought—"

"I don't care what you thought," Walsh interrupted sharply. "You're here because I could hardly have my son's wife cast out on the streets, but you're of no earthly good to me. The irony is that you took from me the one thing I can never replace and have given me nothing in return. Since you're not breeding me a grandson, you have little purpose here. But you're my daughter-in-law, my responsibility, and I'll look after you because honor demands it of me. But I warn you, girl, don't cross me or expect more than food and lodging. And if you'd planned to worm your way into my affections to get your hands on my money, you can put that out of your mind. I'm not as easily taken in as my son; you'll never see a penny of my fortune."

Jillian sat back in her chair, stunned by the venom of Walsh's outburst. Was that really what he thought of her? Did he really hate her so? And how could he think so little of his son as to believe she would have married Jeff only for his wealth?

Confusion and anger mingled in her chest, and Jill came to her feet in a rush. But before she could turn away, Gerald Walsh had come around the desk to catch her arm.

"Where do you think you're going?" he demanded. "I haven't dismissed you yet!"

She shook free and turned to face him, her anger quelling her doubts and uncertainties. "I'm not without resources," she told

him. "I write a fair hand and sew a straight seam. I'm well edu-
cated, and perhaps I can find a teaching position, though it would
be a good deal easier if I were a maiden."

"And no one wishes you a maiden more than I," he snapped.
"Still, I won't have it said that Gerald Walsh shirks his duty.
You'll live here with me and do as I say, or I promise you you'll
wish that you had."

His words and the malice in his eyes chilled Jillian; there was
no question that his threats were real. At his words, Jill's defiance drained away, and she stood trembling, knowing Walsh
had defeated her.

That defeat must have been clear to Walsh as well, because his
voice, when he spoke, was thick with condescension. "Now,
there's a good girl. You go off to your room and think on what
I've said. You're my son's wife, and it's up to me to see to your
needs. If you reconsider your options, you'll see you have no
choice but to do as I say. You must have known that all along, or
you'd not have come this far."

Without another word Jillian turned to go, but as she reached
the door, Walsh's voice followed her. "I'll have Mrs. Pryor see to
your clothes. We can't have you accepting calls from some of the
town's most prominent women looking like some poor relation."

Pointing out her true role in the household was the final insult,
the final humiliation. How Jillian made it out the door of the
study and into the hall she never quite knew. For a moment she
stood beneath the slope of the stairs trembling with the shock of
the interview. She had not expected her father-in-law to welcome
her with open arms, but she hadn't been prepared for the extent
of his enmity. Why did he hate her so? How could she live with
such hostility?

Slowly Jill became aware that Mrs. Pryor was still sitting in
one of the straight-backed chairs, watching her. There was the
hint of a smile at the corners of the woman's narrow lips, a gleam
of satisfaction in her eyes. Did she know what had transpired
behind the closed door of the study, or had she merely guessed?
Either way, Jillian preferred to keep her own counsel. Pride stiffened her spine and enabled her to glide to the foot of the stairs.

"I'm quite exhausted after my trip," she announced to no one
in particular, "and I think I'll go directly to bed."

With her head high and her shoulders squared, Jillian made
her way to her room, but once locked behind the heavy door, the
enormity of the disaster swelled over her. In agreeing to accept
her father-in-law's invitation, she had gravely erred. She should

have done whatever she had to do to make her own way in the world. In the last hour, Walsh had made his contempt for her unequivocal. She had no future here except the one Gerald Walsh saw fit to allow her. But where else could she go? Walsh had made it clear that he would tolerate neither her disobedience nor her defection.

Dazedly she stood at the open window and stared out into the night. In these last minutes she had learned the tragic truth of her situation She was not a daughter; she was not a wife. She was nothing. No, she was less than nothing; she was a responsibility, a thing beneath contempt. Nor could she see any means of escape. She had nowhere to go, no money, no friends. All the people she loved were dead or gone to a future even more uncertain than her own.

Tears washed down her cheeks, and she wept for the men she had lost: one to illness, one to war, and one to the cruelties of fate.

Sobs clotted in her throat, and she twisted the delicate bone ring she wore on her right hand as if by doing so she could conjure up its maker. She wanted Ryder here beside her to offer the tenderness and comfort only he seemed capable of giving, and though she knew it was a fruitless plea, she whispered the words as if they were a litany. "Oh, Ryder, help me. Help me, Ryder, please."

"Name?"

"Justin Mathews."

"Occupation?"

"I work for a lumbering concern."

Ryder stood before the gaunt captain who was checking passengers' identification on the northbound platform of the Suspension Bridge depot. Less than a dozen feet away stood the train to Canada, and it was all Bingham could do to keep from bolting past the guards and into the nearest passenger car. He was trembling inside like a thoroughbred before a race, his head clear, his senses sharp, his heart thundering like hoofbeats driving into the final turn. But to anyone observing him, he would have seemed totally composed, deathly calm.

"Have you any identification?" the captain asked.

Ryder produced the letter of credit from a Montreal bank that Jamieson Bradford had given him. If the document was false or a signal to the Union guards to arrest him, he would learn of it now. Cold sweat crawled down his ribs and gathered in the valley of his spine. His pulse was quick and erratic; his mouth was desert-dry. He would far rather run the blockade, he thought fleetingly, than confront the enemy face to face.

Was the captain suspicious of his papers? Was he going to be arrested? Bingham's fingers itched to delve into his pocket and touch the reassuring shape of the derringer, but he fought down the impulse, just as he subdued the urge to turn and look back at Bradford. Had he been a fool to trust the man?

The officer handed the paper back to Ryder without comment. "Your home, Mr. Mathews?"

"Carroll County, Maryland."

Ryder could almost read the captain's thoughts in the expressions that crossed his face. He was suspicious of Ryder's drawl, though many Marylanders spoke with a similar pronunciation and cadence.

The officer chose to question him more closely. "Have you served in the war, sir?" he wanted to know.

Ryder nodded. "Off Wilmington, I did."

"And was there a reason for your dismissal?"

"A recurrence of malaria."

"Malaria?" There was a moment of disbelief. "Contracted on the blockade fleet?"

"No, sir," Ryder went on to explain, blessing Jillian for the plausibility of her lies. "I contracted malaria before the war, while I was trading in South America."

"I see." The captain's words were slow, considering, drawn out. Ryder held his breath, and at length the officer nodded. "Very well, Mr. Mathews. Have a pleasant trip."

"Thank you, sir," Ryder replied, then picked up his carpetbag and strode toward the train. He found a seat in the nearest passenger car and sank into it gratefully as his knees turned rubbery beneath him. Did he dare to hope that the danger was past? It was tempting to believe that, but it seemed premature to let down his guard.

Moments later Bradford joined him. "You see; it worked!" he whispered, grinning triumphantly as he took the seat beside the blockade-runner.

"We aren't across the border yet," Ryder answered in an undertone.

"Then be skeptical if you choose, but the worst is over. There will be only a few quick questions from the customs officers in Canada, and then—"

Bradford's words were cut short by the blast of a whistle, and

the train began to roll. They made a jerky start, inching forward
and hesitating, lurching forward again. The engine slowly picked
up speed, laboring as they began their approach to the famed
Suspension Bridge. It had been built nearly a decade before by
John Roebling, a renowned Union engineer, and had been the
first suspension bridge in the world to be used for railroad travel.

As the train moved forward, Ryder took note of the heavy
stays anchoring the tall stone pylons that were the apex of the
maze of cables. From them a weave of interconnected wires
slanted, twined, and spiraled to support the two decks of the
bridge itself and a single set of railroad tracks. Though some of
the cables were as thick as a man's leg, they shone silvery in the
moonlight and gave the appearance of a graceful gossamer web.

Ryder watched out the open window as the train moved onto
the narrow span stretching high above the river that marked the
boundary between the United States and Canada. Lights from the
deck below, where carriages and pedestrians made their crossing,
illuminated the rough stone walls of the Niagara River gorge,
casting wavering shadows on the scarred rock face. The trees that
overhung the bank deepened the menace of the scene. But for
Bingham, the most disconcerting discovery was that the brightness of the bridge lights did not reach the bottom of the chasm.
As the train crept toward the center of the bridge, it seemed that
they were suspended above the nightmare blackness of a yawning
abyss. Fathomless darkness lay below them, an emptiness as
deep and vast as death, as threatening and infinite as aeons of
endless eternity. Ryder strained his eyes, trying to penetrate the
depths, to probe the midnight shadows for a hint of reassurance
that the bridge would hold their weight. But the blackness below
them was unbroken and impenetrable. The sight chilled
Bingham's bones.

Then Bradford's words washed over him, chasing away the
demons, bringing reality and light to his dark and fanciful
thoughts.

"If it were day," he noted with the air of a guide, "we could
see the Falls from here. They're quite beautiful, you know—ma-
jestic, almost mystical with the sunlight playing on the surface of
the water, giving birth to a score of rainbows."

"You sound like a poet, Mr. Bradford," Ryder observed with a
curl of his lips.

Jamieson laughed. "Hardly a poet, I assure you. Though there
is something about the sight of the cataracts that could stir the
finer part of any man. Up close they're even more impressive.

And if you want a truly thrilling perspective, you can don a slicker and go into a cave at the base of the Falls. It's an impressive sight, I'll tell you. You must make a point to go there, Mr. Mathews, should you pass this way again."

Ryder hardly heard the other man's words, for his thoughts had strayed to the day he and Jillian had picnicked beside another falls, in Rochester. Though not as dramatic as the ones at Niagara were reputed to be, there had been something stirring about the veiled cascades of white. Watching them had brought him a wondrous sense of peace, a feeling of belonging, of being one with God and man. Or had it been Jillian's presence that had made him feel so contented and serene? And how long, he found himself wondering, would it be before he found that kind of contentment again?

To Ryder's relief, they soon reached the Canadian end of the bridge and passed the twin towers that marked the return to solid ground. A feeling of satisfaction began to seep along his limbs at the passage into Canada, and though he knew he had one more gauntlet to run before he could consider his escape successful, he was suddenly sure that all would be well. Clearing Canadian customs proved to be no more difficult than Bradford had promised. Ryder merely repeated the name and business he had given the American authorities, and the customs officer let him pass.

Soon the train got under way again, struggling forward, gaining speed. As it swept off into the night, Ryder felt the tensions and fears of the last week drain away. He was leaving the dangers of the beleaguered United States behind him, leaving the hell of prison behind him, leaving Jillian behind him. His relief was tinged with regret. Here in Canada he might be safe, but he had left behind much of importance. Still, the future lay ahead, and he knew that he could face whatever it brought now that he was his own man once again.

Chapter Six

OUTSIDE THE WINDOW of the train lay Lake Ontario, a vast stretch of cerulean blue mirroring the clear and cloudless sky. In the freshness of early morning, the lake sparkled as if sprinkled with diamonds, the sunlight skipping across the water, setting sparks of light dancing on the waves. On the opposite side of the railroad car lay the countryside of Canada West, verdant, pastoral, studded with farms, villas, and groves of ancient trees. At a different juncture in his life Ryder would have found this new country exciting and compelling, but now he was anxious to reach Toronto, anxious to discover what future fate had planned.

He and Jamieson Bradford had arrived at Hamilton in the dead of night and had caught what sleep they could on benches in the station. The train for Toronto had left at six forty-five this morning, and they were the first aboard. Though it was still early, Ryder could see that the countryside was awake. There were fishing boats riding the swells on the lake, farmers turning their livestock out to pasture, pickers headed into the peach and apple orchards that flourished along the lakeshore. But in spite of the bucolic splendor, the landscape was subtly changing, and Ryder sensed that they were approaching the city. Would he find Holcombe, the Confederate whom Smithers had told him about, once he reached Toronto? Could Holcombe indeed arrange for his passage south?

As the train began to wend its way through the outskirts of the city, Bradford roused from a doze and glanced around. "Almost there," he offered. "'Nother ten minutes or so and we should be arriving at the station."

Once they crossed the border, Bradford's speech had subtly altered, the vowels growing more slurred and lazy, the cadence slowing and softening. He sounded more and more like the Southerner he claimed to be, but Ryder was not sure he should take the man at his word. And though Jamie had pressed him,

Ryder had not revealed how he had come to be in the Suspension Bridge depot seeking passage into Canada.

All at once, the city of Toronto enfolded them with warehouses and train sheds on one side, grain silos and docks on the other. Streets lined with stores and commercial buildings ran off to the north; steamers and sailing ships bobbed on the water of the bay. In a glance, Ryder recognized the vitality of the city, and it filled him with mingled trepidation and curiosity.

When the train finally rolled to a stop, Bingham took his carpetbag from the overhead rack and followed Bradford onto the platform. "Is there anything more I can do to help you?" Jamieson offered, squinting up at his rangy companion.

Ryder hesitated, wondering how he would go about locating one man in so large a place, wondering if he could trust Bradford to help him find the fellow he was seeking. He drew a long breath as he made the decision. "I was told to look up someone called Holcombe if I got this far," he finally conceded.

"Holcombe?" Bradford repeated with the hint of a smile. "You know any more about the fellow than his name?"

Ryder shook his head.

"As I recall, I ran into a man name of Holcombe at the Queen's Hotel the last time I was in town. He might be the fellow you're looking for; then again, he might not. I'm headed that way myself, if you want to tag along."

It was an open-ended offer, and Ryder took him up on it.

Together the two men left the Great Western Railroad depot and made their way along Front Street, past the gray stone Customs House and the Bank of Montreal, along the quays that rimmed the harbor, through the oldest part of the city. The streets were busy, filled with carriages and drays, barrels and crates, stevedores and businessmen. Toronto was obviously a flourishing city, its prosperity fed by these several tightly packed blocks of commercial establishments grown up along the harbor.

"How big is Toronto?" Ryder wanted to know.

"'Bout thirty or thirty-five thousand souls, I should think. And it's a fine town, too," Jamie answered. "There are some real good restaurants and plenty of places for a man to quench his thirst. There's the Terrapin Saloon and Digby's Cork and Cleaver. The Apollo up on King Street has a minstrel show some nights; I'll take you there if you like."

"I'm not sure just how long I'll be in the city," Ryder hedged.

"Well, suit yourself," Bradford conceded with a shrug as he came to a halt on the sidewalk. "That's the Queen's Hotel over there."

With a nod, Jamieson indicated a large building across the street from the harbor. The hotel was three stories tall and appeared to be composed of four attached town houses with newer wings added at either end. Of neatly painted brick, the Queen's Hotel looked pleasant and inviting, with its graceful crested lintels and arched doorways, lace-curtained windows, and pots of geraniums out front. Following Jamieson's lead, Ryder crossed the street and went inside. The two men traversed the paneled lobby and went directly to the entrance to the bar. As they stood in the doorway of the smoky room, a man at a table in the corner hailed Bradford, and as Jamie moved toward the stranger, it seemed natural for Ryder to follow.

"Jacob, it's good to see you looking so well," the smaller man greeted his friend.

"And you, Jamieson. I'm glad to see you made it back to Toronto safely."

As Bradford's friend spoke, Ryder took note of his deep Mississippi drawl and the inbred good manners that marked him as a Southern gentleman. The fellow was well into middle age, and his face was broad, open, and half covered with the curly, shovel-shaped beard. On closer observation, Ryder thought he seemed particularly deliberate and earnest in his actions and speech, an impression that was reinforced by his close-cut hair and conservative clothing.

"I brought a new friend with me, Jacob," Jamie continued, indicating Ryder. "I found him at the Suspension Bridge station, awaiting passage to Toronto. He's looking for Mr. Holcombe."

The older man's passive but inquiring gaze moved to Ryder's face. "Mr. Holcombe, is it? Well, I'm sorry to say you missed him by several days. He's gone off to England on a matter of some importance, but as an associate of Mr. Holcombe's, perhaps I can be of service."

Ryder hesitated, alarmed by the news of Holcombe's departure. If the man he was seeking had indeed left Canada, he was totally without aid in this foreign country.

"Is there something I can do to help you, Mr. . . . ?"

"Bingham, Ryder Bingham."

The older man reached out to shake Ryder's hand. "I'm Jacob

Thompson, chief Confederate commissioner in Canada."

Ryder stared openly, trying to make some sense of the other man's words. He'd had no idea that the Confederates had commissioners in Canada. It had been surprising enough to learn of Holcombe's presence here. What on earth were these men doing for the Confederacy in Toronto?

"I'd very much like your help in a matter of some importance," Ryder finally said, deciding to take his chances with this man.

"Speak up, then," Thompson urged. "Tell me what you want."

Ryder glanced around the crowded bar. Could so many have gathered at this time in the morning simply because the hotel sold good whiskey, or was there another purpose to their presence? Either way, Ryder was not prepared to reveal himself.

"Is it wise to talk in so public a place, Mr. Thompson?" Ryder returned quietly.

Thompson's eyebrows drew together. "No, Mr. Bingham, it's not. I was quite wrong to encourage you. It's said that there are so many Union detectives and informers here in Toronto that three Confederates can hardly talk together without someone reporting the conversation. Since that's undoubtedly so, perhaps you gentlemen will accompany me to my suite where we can speak privately."

Thompson's rooms were on the third floor of the hotel, and a few minutes later they entered a spacious sitting room. Once they were settled in a cluster of chairs that overlooked Front Street and the harbor, Thompson turned to Ryder. "Perhaps now, Mr. Bingham, you can tell us what business you had with Mr. Holcombe."

Ryder glanced at Bradford and received a nod of reassurance.

"I was hoping that Mr. Holcombe would help me return to the Confederacy," Ryder told them. "I was captured last October, and I have a hankering to get back into the fight."

"And just where were you captured, sir?" Thompson wanted to know.

"It was off Cape Fear. I was running the blockade."

"On what ship?"

"On my ship, *The Wraith*."

Thompson's arched brows rose higher. "So you're Captain Bingham." Thompson seemed impressed. "May I say that word of your exploits has preceded you. Your service to the South has been touted everywhere."

Ryder acknowledged his comments with a narrow smile.

"And since your capture, Captain Bingham, where have you been imprisoned?"

"At Fort Lafayette in New York Harbor."

Surprise at his answer registered on both men's faces, though there was a gleam of quick intelligence in Jamieson Bradford's eyes.

"And you escaped?" Thompson demanded in surprise. "Why, no one has ever escaped from Fort Lafayette!"

Ryder enjoyed their incredulity. "No, sir, no one has ever escaped. Till now."

"And just how did you manage it?"

There was skepticism in the older man's tone, a hint of disbelief that made Ryder realize it was reasonable for them to doubt he was who and what he claimed. Theirs was natural caution, he supposed, but somehow it irritated him when he had come so far.

"I tunneled up from a second-story casemate to the roof of the prison," he answered coldly, "then swam the channel to Long Island."

He could sense that Bradford instinctively accepted his claims, though it was obvious that Thompson did not.

"Swam the channel, indeed! I'm sure that's quite impossible!"

The memory came clear in Ryder's mind: of the fury of the storm, of his swim in the raging water, of the cold that numbed his limbs and stole his reason, of the determination that had driven him on. In retrospect, swimming the channel did seem impossible, but he had done it. His presence here proved that unequivocally.

"As I told Mr. Bradford last night, nothing is impossible if a man doesn't care if he lives or dies."

"And you lived."

Ryder nodded. "As you say."

Jamieson sat forward in his chair. "But how did you get to the Suspension Bridge station?"

"I had help," Ryder explained. "There was a woman in the town of New Utrecht, a Mrs. Gelston, who gave aid to those at the prison. When I went to her home for help, her husband sent me on to a couple who are loyal to the Southern cause. They gave me clothes, a ticket to Toronto, and Mr. Holcombe's name." It seemed both dangerous and useless to mention Jillian's aid. She was safe now, unscathed by the risks she had taken to see that he escaped. It was better for them both if he kept her help a secret, if he put the episode from his mind.

"Bingham's story is just fantastic enough to be true," Jamie mused. "And who in his right mind would make up such an implausible lie?"

"Yes," Thompson agreed after a moment. "And I've heard of Mrs. Gelston's kindness."

"Then you believe me?" Ryder demanded. "You'll send me back to the Confederacy?"

"Is that what you want, Captain Bingham?" the older man inquired. "To get back into the fight?"

"Yes, sir. I have a score to settle with the Yankees."

"This late in the war so do we all, sir." Thompson's face was grim. "So do we all."

There was a reticence in the older man's words that seemed to indicate that they might not do as Ryder asked, and the prospect of failure put words into his mouth. "My brother died at Fort Lafayette," he stated baldly. "I want to see his death avenged!"

Silence hung between them as Jacob Thompson rubbed a hand across his eyes. "You have to understand, Captain Bingham, shipping men into Wilmington has become much more difficult these last months."

With an effort, Ryder kept his tone reasonable. "Then get me as far as Nassau. I have friends there who will get me through the blockade."

"I will have to take it under consideration," Thompson answered. "Yours is certainly not the only request for passage we've received."

"But I have to get back into the fight. I want to make the Yankees pay for what they did!"

"For your brother's death, you mean," Jamieson put in sympathetically.

Ryder fought to stem the flow of words rising in his throat. They were words of grief and anger, words of guilt and responsibility. They were truth and pain and sorrow, words that quite suddenly could not be denied.

"Don't you understand?" he demanded, going on with uncharacteristic candor. "I saw my brother waste away, and there was nothing I could do. Mitch had never been very strong, and the cold and dampness of winter in that godforsaken place brought on consumption. I watched him die, slowly, painfully, coughing incessantly, his strength drained away by the unremitting fevers."

"And the Yankees gave him no medical attention?" Thompson queried, shaking his head.

"Not after my money was gone. I didn't know anyone in New

York to write to for additional funds, and we couldn't get help from the South. Those men who got packages shared their food and liquor, but Mitchell never rallied." Ryder's throat worked as he fought to suppress his grief. "It was horrible, being helpless, watching him die."

"And still you want to go back to war, Captain Bingham?" Thompson asked after a moment. "After enduring what you've been through, many men would say they'd done their part."

"I told you I have a score to settle. I won't be content until I've made those bastards pay for what they've done!"

Thompson was quiet for a moment, and it was Jamieson Bradford who broke the silence. "Bingham might be just the kind of man Hines needs for the things he's planning."

The older man nodded thoughtfully. "Captain Hines is in Chicago at the moment, but there's something else brewing that might take advantage of Captain Bingham's talents."

He turned to Ryder consideringly. "Perhaps before you go, there's something you could do to help us," he suggested.

"But I want to get back on board a ship—"

"And this mission might well give you the chance you're looking for. I can't give you the details yet, but within the month we're going to need men who want to fight the Yankees and have seamen's skills. Are you willing to entertain our proposition?"

Ryder paused to weigh the man's offer. If he refused, he might well forfeit the help these men could give him.

"I'd like to know what you're proposing," he negotiated.

"And we'll tell you, in time. Meanwhile, you need a place to stay and a change of clothes, I should imagine."

Thompson's reticence irritated him, but Ryder understood the reason for his caution.

"There's probably a place at my boarding house for him," Bradford offered.

"Is that agreeable to you, Captain Bingham?" Thompson inquired. "Are you willing to stay here in Toronto for a few weeks and see if you can be of service to the Confederacy?"

"I'll stay for the time being."

"Very well, then." Thompson rose to shake Ryder's hand. "Now, if you wouldn't mind waiting downstairs, Jamieson and I have some business to conduct."

Dismissed, Ryder let himself out of the suite of rooms and descended to the bar. While he nursed a single glass of ale, Bingham began to take note of the saloon's other occupants.

Whether it was by their attire or from some less tangible link, Ryder surmised that there were other escaped prisoners here. The most obvious ones wore the remnants of their tattered gray uniforms, while others were thin and gaunt or had skin stained dark by the unrelenting sun in the treeless prison yards. And almost all the men he suspected of being prisoners shared a certain cowed demeanor, as if they were waiting for the next order, the next cruelty to be visited upon them. Was he as obviously one of them? Ryder found himself wondering. Was that how Jamieson Bradford had recognized him for what he was when he had seen him in the depot the night before? He hoped he did not wear that same mantle of despair and degradation evident in so many of the others, but he was not sure he had escaped it. The notion of being marked in such a way troubled him no small bit. After all, he was a Bingham, and the Binghams had their pride.

When Jamieson Bradford came into the saloon nearly an hour later, he was smiling his disarming lazy grin. "Shall we go find you a place to lay your head, Captain Bingham? After waiting all night for trains, I could surely use some rest."

"I am a bit weary at that, Mr. Bradford," Ryder readily conceded as he followed Jamie out onto the street.

They stopped at a place Jamieson knew to get a bite to eat and then proceeded to the house on St. Ann Street where Bradford had a room. It was a narrow frame structure that ran deep into the lot, with a warren of additions tacked on to the back and sides. As they entered, the landlady came bustling toward them.

"Well, Mr. Bradford, home from your travels, are you?" the woman inquired, her voice warmed and softened with a charming Scottish burr. "You've some letters waiting for you. And there's one among them from your lass, unless I miss my guess." After rummaging through a desk just inside the parlor, she handed Jamie a packet of envelopes. "I've been keeping them safe, Mr. Bradford, keeping them safe just like you said."

"Ah, Mrs. Moire, you're a treasure," he said, mimicking her lilting speech almost perfectly. "But I've no other lass but you. How could you think such a thing?"

"Ah, go on with you!" she answered, rolling her eyes at Ryder. "Have you ever seen such a bounder?"

"Have mercy on me, darlin'. Your coquettish ways are enough to break my heart." Jamie winked at her before turning to the business at hand.

"I've brought you another boarder, if you have a place for Mr. Bingham." Jamie had deliberately dropped the "Captain" from his name, and Ryder took note of it.

"Aye, I do," she agreed. "Mr. Murray moved out of the big room upstairs. And by the looks of you," she went on, eyeing the taller Confederate, "you can use the three full meals a day that are part of the price I'm asking."

"Mrs. Moire is the best cook in Canada West," Jamie confided. "You should taste her roast beef and Yorkshire pudding, though I fear I'll never develop a taste for steak and kidney pie."

"Sacrilege!" she exclaimed. "Sacrilege! Why Mr. Moire is probably rolling in his grave to hear you say so. But then, we've hardly the time to stand here, Mr. Bradford, when your friend looks tired out. Now, then, the room is ten dollars a month," she calculated carefully, "payable in advance."

Ryder hesitated, knowing he had nothing near ten dollars in his pocket.

Instead it was Bradford who was pressing the money into the landlady's palm. "Wasn't Mr. Murray paying eight?" he teased her.

"Nine, but it's a fine room, and the bed is very comfortable."

"A bargain." Jamie grinned and, taking the key from the woman, led Ryder up the stairs.

"Breakfast is at seven," he instructed as they climbed, "though they usually serve until eight. Dinner is at noon. Supper is promptly at seven, and God help you if you're late."

He unlocked a narrow door at the head of the hall and led Ryder into a clean, well-appointed room. There was certainly nothing luxurious about the accommodations, though the iron bed was covered with a colorful quilt and there were bright rag rugs on the floor. Translucent muslin curtains veiled a bank of windows looking west. A wooden washstand, two sagging armchairs, and a humpbacked chest were the only other furnishings.

Ryder put down his valise and turned to Bradford. "I haven't any money to repay you for this," he began, "and while the room's very pleasant, I can't accept—"

"Thompson gave me fifty dollars for you to use," Jamieson interrupted, digging into his pocket for the rest. "For now, consider yourself in the employ of the Confederate commissioners."

Ryder opened his mouth to object, but the other man waved

him to silence. "Go ahead; take the money. You'll have need of it before we're able to get you passage home, and you may be able to do something to help us in return.

"But for now, I'm going next door to get some sleep. If you need anything, that's where you'll find me."

With a last quick grin, Jamie closed the door, leaving Ryder alone to ponder the morning's happenings.

Groaning with the effort, Bingham removed his coat and tie. He was tired from the long hours on the train, from the tension and uncertainty. But his mind was troubled by the things he had heard and seen.

What was going on here in Toronto? Thompson seemed to be doing far more than helping escaped prisoners return to the South. He must be running some kind of mission, but what could he hope to accomplish? The war was being fought in Georgia and Virginia, not here along the border. And how did the Canadians and the English, to whom the provinces belonged, feel about Thompson's presence and about the Confederacy itself?

Earlier in the war, when English mills had been starved for Southern cotton, there had been talk that Great Britain might enter the war on the Confederate side. But for all the fine oratory in the South, for all the maneuvering that was said to be going on behind the scenes, the talk had come to naught. The Confederate States were left without alliances and were in grave danger of losing the war. Was there new hope that England might finally intercede? Was that why these men were here?

Ryder removed his boots and stretched out on the bed. It was every bit as comfortable as Mrs. Moire had claimed, soft as a cloud beneath him. He closed his eyes and willed himself to relax. He was exhausted, hollow with weariness, but somehow sleep eluded him. His shoulder ached, and he rolled to one side, then the other, seeking a more agreeable position. He turned on his back and frowned up at the ceiling, not knowing what was wrong with him.

He felt as if something was missing, something he needed to lull him to sleep. He felt empty, unsettled, incomplete. Then all at once he realized what was wrong. He had grown used to having Jillian beside him as he slept, her well-rounded form both a comfort and a distraction. He missed her warmth, missed the feel of her body nestled beside him, missed the closeness they had shared. It seemed impossible that in so short a time she could have become essential to him.

He lay for a time staring at the ceiling with unseeing eyes, reliving the few wondrous days he and Jillian had shared. He remembered their words and their passion, their tenderness and their companionship. He needed Jilly, needed her with him always, bringing serenity and contentment, tenderness and rest. Yet he knew she had a path of her own to follow in the world, a life of her own to live without his sharing it.

The pain of parting swept over him again, just as it had when her carriage pulled away from the railroad station. He ached with the loneliness, the emptiness, the futility of his life. His need for her was something Ryder did not know how to assuage, and it was only when exhaustion finally overwhelmed him that he found a modicum of peace.

"Bingham, you in there? Bingham, you awake?"

Ryder jerked upright in bed and stared around him in confusion. The room where he had been sleeping was warm, hazy with the last rosy glow of afternoon sun. And for the life of him, he couldn't remember where he was. Acting on instinct, he came to his feet, snatching the derringer from the pocket of his jacket as he staggered toward the door. With a curse, he threw open the heavy wooden panel, cocking and leveling the gun at his unexpected visitor.

"God damn it, Bingham!" the man in the hallway exclaimed as he lurched backwards. "Who the hell were you expecting?"

Who indeed? Ryder wondered as his surroundings came into a clearer focus. Had he been expecting prison guards, soldiers sent to see to his recapture?

Ryder lowered his pistol and sagged against the doorjamb, awash with relief that there were neither soldiers nor guards in the hall outside his room. Instead, it was Jamieson Bradford who had awakened him. Bradford's stance was loosening, too, as he realized the moment of crisis was past.

"I'd forgotten how it was," Jamie said apologetically, "how jumpy and uncertain you are right after you escape."

Ryder shook his head as much to clear his thoughts as in response to Bradford's words. "It's all right. It just took me a minute to realize where I was."

After the fears and tensions of the past few days, it was difficult for Ryder to accept that he was finally in Toronto, finally safe, finally free. It would take time for him to readjust his thinking, to realize that there was no longer a threat in each unfamiliar sound, an enemy in every stranger's face.

"It's all right," he reiterated softly.

Jamie nodded and straightened, anxious to put the incident behind them. "I stopped by to see if you were awake and getting ready for supper. I've only been up long enough myself to have a bath and shave."

Ryder noticed the towel draped around Bradford's shoulders; his long blond hair was damp and curling on his neck.

"I suppose I could do with a bath myself," he admitted with a self-conscious grin.

"There's still hot water in the reservoir," Jamie offered. "Unless you decide to soak, you should be through by suppertime."

Turning, Bradford made his way toward his room, and Ryder closed the door behind him, just managing to reach the edge of the bed before his knees gave way. He hung his head and tried to stabilize his breathing, realizing suddenly how frightened he'd really been. For a few seconds, he had been so sure his freedom was a dream, an illusion that had shattered upon awakening.

He drew a long breath and let it out slowly, aware that his hands were shaking and his heart was still drumming in his ears. He was safe, he told himself, well beyond the reach of Yankee soldiers. He was free, in control of his life once more. But even those reassurances could not quite dispel the lingering panic.

He tried to turn his mind to other things, but there was nothing reassuring on which Ryder could concentrate, nothing grounded and secure to which he could cling. Reaching Toronto had been a watershed, but mere safety did not resolve the uncertainties that plagued him. The future was a labyrinth, a void so vast and terrifying that he wondered how he would find the courage to face what lay ahead. And before he could take solace in his memories, there were the mistakes of the past to live down.

So much had happened in the war that he was loath to confront: his father's death in battle, the loss of his mother's love, the exile from his home, and the loss of the ship that had been his livelihood. If he looked back, he would have to accept the blame for Mitchell's death and examine the lapse of judgment that had sent *The Wraith* floundering into Yankee hands. He would have to find a way to live with the knowledge that men had lost their lives for his mistakes, that others had paid the ultimate price for the gambles he had taken. Someday he would have to find a way to live with all that, but not today, not now, not yet.

With an effort he made his mind a blank. He could not think about what was past or dwell on the prospects for the future. Only the present mattered; it was the only reality he could trust.

Ryder's bath did a great deal to revive him, and when Bradford knocked again half an hour later, Ryder had nearly finished shaving.

"You didn't say you had been wounded," the smaller man observed as he took note of the bulky bandage that bound Ryder's naked chest.

"I ran into some troopers once I reached Long Island," he answered as he returned to the tiny mirror above the basin and maneuvered the razor beneath his lip.

"They shot you during the escape, and you got away from the Yankees, anyway?" Jamie's tone was low and subtly shaded with awe.

Ryder shrugged and tested the freshly shaved area with the tips of his fingers. "The wound was nothing much, and the Smitherers bandaged me up before they put me on the train."

"But were you able to travel?"

"I didn't have much choice."

It was the truth, but necessity was not the only thing that had driven him. He had also been spurred onward by grief and frustration, anger and fear. Through the armor of those emotions, the pain of his wound had very little effect, not when the other things he'd felt had hurt him so much more. When Jeb Smithers put him on the train, Ryder had been filled with determination and fully expected to make it into Canada.

"But weren't you weak from loss of blood?" Jamieson persisted. "Didn't you run a fever?"

Bingham hesitated, remembering, knowing he could not answer Jamie's questions. It would be dangerous to reveal Jillian's involvement in his escape, dangerous for him but more dangerous for her. She could be accused, ostracized, imprisoned for what she'd done, and for the sake of the new life she had begun in Niagara Falls, he had to keep her help a secret.

"I'm done shaving, Bradford," Ryder returned evasively, wiping the last of the soap from his face. "We have no time to waste talking if we mean to be on time for supper."

Bradford recognized Bingham's ploy and was instantly suspicious. The newcomer was quite obviously hiding something, protecting someone, though his purpose was not clear. But even as that conviction grew, Jamieson surmised there was a reason for Ryder's secrecy, and he was willing to wait for explanations, for a little while, at least.

"All right, Bingham," Jamie conceded. "Have it your way. Let's get on down to supper."

When they reached the dining room, they saw that seven other people had already gathered for the evening meal. There were two young men who seemed to be colleagues of Bradford's, one rough-hewn older man who worked in the flour mills on the waterfront, and another with a pencil-thin mustache and the oddly precise ways of a lifelong bachelor. A garrulous middle-aged woman named Mrs. Claremont sat at the far end of the table. Beside her was her sober, whey-faced niece, and it was evident immediately why the niece sat silent as a stone. Mrs. Moire was also part of the group and was clearly enjoying her role as hostess.

As two Irish maids bustled to serve the brisket of beef, boiled potatoes, and cabbage, the boarders expressed a certain curiosity about the stranger in their midst. But when Ryder politely turned aside their questions, they were well mannered enough not to pry. It was clear that Jamie felt none of Ryder's reticence, for he regaled the group with stories of his recent travels in the North. His good-natured tales and friendly manner were pleasant and entertaining, but as Ryder listened, he wondered if it was wise for Jamie to be so outspoken about his activities.

Few of the other Confederates seemed to share his concern, however. When Jamie, Ryder, and the two young men from the boarding house adjourned to the Queen's Hotel after dinner, they found Jacob Thompson holding court at one of the tables in the bar. The four men took seats nearby, and though Ryder found it pleasant to drink and joke and recall happier days before the war, he also felt apprehensive to hear the Confederates talk so freely. Perhaps he was overly sensitive and reading more than he should into the gathering, but even Thompson had admitted that the Confederate presence in the city had not gone unnoticed by those who were friendly to the Union cause. Knowing that, Ryder thought it seemed foolhardy for them to talk and meet so openly.

As they made their way back through the streets of Toronto at the end of the evening, Ryder said as much to Jamieson.

"Perhaps we should act with greater discretion," Bradford answered, lagging behind the two other men, "since the town is full of Union spies, all trying to find out what the commissioners are up to in Canada."

"And just what are they doing here?" It was a question Ryder had been longing to ask since morning.

Jamieson stopped in his tracks and gave Bingham a hard look. "Now, how do I know you're not the kind of fellow you've been warning me about, one of those Yankees out to learn my secrets?" he challenged wryly.

Ryder did not find his words amusing. "You don't. You haven't asked me for credentials. You don't know where I came from or who the hell I am. But then, I didn't approach you in the station last night, either. Surely that proves something."

"Perhaps that I'm a softhearted fool."

"Perhaps," Bingham answered, smiling.

Though their conversation had become companionable, Jamie knew that what Bingham said was true. He had no proof of Ryder's loyalties. He had befriended the other man on nothing more substantial than the fit of his boots and a few minutes' observation. Since then, though, half a dozen little things had convinced him Ryder was all he claimed. He was cool, single-minded, self-contained. He had admitted to acts of courage and determination, acts of ruthlessness and daring. But in spite of all that, it was Jamie's instincts that confirmed, when logic could not, that Ryder Bingham was loyal to the cause. Bradford was equally sure the newcomer would be an asset to the Confederates in Canada, and if he was to recruit Bingham for the missions they were planning, he would have to entice him with a few of the commissioners' secrets.

"There have been Confederate refugees in Canada since the early days of the war," Jamieson began, taking a fresh cigar from his pocket, "and there has been talk of sending an official delegation to Toronto off and on since then. The Canadian provinces have always expressed a certain sympathy with our cause, but the British have been adamant about maintaining their neutrality."

"But why were the commissioners sent now? Has the English position changed?"

Jamie shook his head. "Holcombe was sent first as a vanguard to see that the Southern boys who'd escaped the Yankees had a way to get back home. And, of course, his role has become more and more important since Grant stopped the prisoner exchange."

"Because the South is running short of defenders."

Jamieson nodded and paused to light his smoke. "Since the English did not complain about Holcombe's presence, Jeff Davis ordered two more commissioners, Jacob Thompson and Clement Clay, to Canada this spring. And preceding them was Thomas Hines, a young captain from Morgan's Raiders, sent to oversee the military aspects of our mission here."

"Military aspects?" Ryder's head snapped around, and he stared at Bradford in surprise.

Jamie blew a long plume of smoke before he replied. "Because the Federal armies are attempting to close a vise around the Confederates, President Davis and his advisers decided it was time to give the Yankees something else to think about."

"You mean there's to be military action launched from Canada?" Ryder was incredulous.

"Not a military action, precisely." Jamie grinned. "We're to stir up trouble along the Great Lakes and promote ferment from within."

"Within the United States?" This was getting more and more preposterous. Bingham shot Bradford a long glance, trying to discern if he was joking. Yet Jamie seemed perfectly serious.

"There have been many facets to the plan," he went on, talking around the stub of his cigar. "We have made an effort to buy up Union gold and ship it out of the country so as to upset the Northern economy. We have bought certain newspapers in order to influence editorial content."

There had been a subtle change in at least one of the New York dailies that had been smuggled into Fort Lafayette: More criticism of the draft, stronger calls for peace, and greater condemnation of Lincoln's policies had begun to appear in its pages. It was common knowledge that the people of the North were growing tired of war, tired of the disruption of daily life, tired of the endless casualty lists and loss of life. But were Confederate-controlled papers creating dissent, Ryder suddenly wondered, or were they merely giving it a louder voice? Could this kind of control lead to the defeat of Lincoln in the forthcoming Union election and, with that defeat, to a negotiated peace?

"What else are you about?" Ryder wanted to know.

There was a hint of a satisfied smile on his lips as Jamie

continued. "We're making alliances with the Copperhead organizations, those in the North who supported the Confederate cause. Tom Hines is in Chicago now trying to disrupt the Democratic convention and break the Confederate prisoners out of Camp Douglas. With an army from the prison at his back and the support of the Copperhead organizations, he hopes to march south to Indianapolis and free the men imprisoned there, firing towns, capturing munitions, disrupting the railroads and telegraph lines as he goes."

Ryder listened, stunned; he'd had no idea that anything like this was happening. "Who's helping Hines carry out his plans?"

"The men he took to Chicago are men like you, men who managed to escape from Yankee prisons and make their way to Canada. They're men who wanted another chance at the Yankees."

It was a desire Ryder could readily understand.

"Somehow I always imagined going back to sea," he admitted thoughtfully. "That's where I've always been most effective, on the bridge of my own ship. I know that raiders have been built in England for the Confederate Navy, and somehow I figured I'd manage to get one."

Bradford did not tell him how difficult it was to garner such a command. He did not say that there were Confederate captains cooling their heels in Liverpool who had been waiting months for their ships.

Jamie didn't need to tell him; Ryder already knew how it was. But in spite of that, he had harbored the hope of getting a ship of his own, a command where he could do as he saw fit, where he could wreak merciless revenge on the Yankees.

"Bingham, before you go off to England, consider what we can offer you here. We can give you a chance to get back into the fight, a chance to do something important for your country." Jamie's voice was charged with energy. "You're smart and you're determined. You don't let circumstances get in your way. Consider how much of a difference you can make right here, right along the border. Soon we'll have something tangible to offer you, and when we do, I hope you'll join us in this fight."

Ryder said nothing as he listened to Jamie's words, but they were juxtaposed against the jumble of images that were always in his mind: Mitchell's face as he lay dying, the strangely empty house at Riverview, *The Wraith* burning to the waterline, the brownstone prison wall. Was this his opportunity to pay the Yankees back for all they had done, his turn to bring the horror of war to the people of the North? He wanted vengeance to set aside his pain, action to relieve the feeling of helplessness. Had he been led to the Confederates in Canada to serve this purpose, to exorcise his guilt?

He stared down the darkened street, wondering about his place in the Confederacy's future.

"Will you come in with us, Bingham? Will you help us affect the outcome of the war?"

Jamieson Bradford was a very persuasive man, but Ryder was not ready to commit himself. "When the time comes, Bradford, we'll see. We'll just have to see what comes."

Chapter Seven

JILLIAN CHANDLER WALSH hadn't made many mistakes in her life. Sheltered by her father's love, she hadn't been given the opportunity. But after the interview in the congressman's study that first night, Jill had begun to realize that coming to live in Niagara Falls was a mistake, a mistake she did not know how to rectify. She had faced the discovery with characteristic pragmatism, weighing her options and deciding on a course of action.

It was the decision to find a place for herself in the congressman's home that had made her venture into the basement kitchen a few days after her arrival. She had always been a good housekeeper, and it seemed the one place in the household where she might have something to offer. Her appearance at the foot of the servants' stairs had caused a stir, and the moment she stepped into the room, Mrs. Pryor advanced on her like a lioness defending her domain.

"May I help you?" the woman had demanded as she approached. "Have you somehow lost your way?"

The hostility in the housekeeper's face made Jillian want to retreat, but instead she stood her ground, drawing on her courage.

"I kept house for my father for some years," she began hesitantly, "and I hoped to find a way to be of some service here."

By Mrs. Pryor's response, it was evident that she had never expected Jillian to offer help with the household duties. While the older woman struggled to accept the idea, Jill took advantage of her silence.

"I bake quite well," she said, then went on to enumerate her accomplishments, noticing how the other servants gathered from all corners of the room to listen to the exchange. "I'm a fair hand with an iron. I have been putting up food for the winter since I was ten, and at this busy time of year I thought an extra pair of hands—"

Mrs. Pryor seemed suddenly to recover herself and interrupted brusquely. "Edna is the cook and does all her own baking," she informed the interloper, indicating a red-cheeked woman poised above a half-completed pie. "And Lydia does the ironing. This is a very well-staffed household, Mrs. Walsh. We hardly need your assistance."

Jillian felt the color rise in her cheeks at the tone of the rebuke, and though her immediate impulse was to turn and run, she decided to try again. "Well, perhaps I could consult with you on the menus or review the household accounts."

Mrs. Pryor swelled with indignation. "I can't see how you could advise me on menus, since you're not aware of Congressman Walsh's preferences. And as for the household accounts, I've kept them for nearly twenty years, and no one has ever questioned me."

The woman's deep-set eyes had swept over Jillian, measuring the exact extent of her daring. "But then, if you wish to discuss assuming those duties with Congressman Walsh, I certainly cannot stop you."

Jillian had no intention of speaking to her father-in-law. He had made her position in his home very clear.

When Jill did not answer her challenge, the housekeeper haughtily ushered her toward the stairs. After that, Jillian had kept to herself, feeling angry and humiliated by the scene in the kitchen, feeling frustrated and resentful at Gerald Walsh's attitude. Certainly his contempt for her was a factor in making her situation untenable, and as time passed, her disillusionment had become intense and far-reaching.

Until she discovered the summerhouse at the river's edge, Jill had felt shut in, confined. Shrouded by a bank of looming lilacs and a fringe of willow trees, the gazebo was not visible from the mansion, and she had come upon it accidentally a week after she arrived. It was a pretty retreat, too, with its graceful, dome-shaped roof and lacy trellises overrun with roses. She had liked the place immediately: the graceful feminine lines of the structure, the seclusion, and the peace engendered by the river's ceaseless flow. It had become her habit to visit the gazebo every afternoon, just as Jefferson's mother must have done during summers long ago.

Usually the beauty of the river and the solitude of the setting satisfied Jillian, but on this sultry Wednesday the heat had made her restless. She sighed, stretched, and set aside the book she had been reading. She had taken it from the library shelves only that morning, a tome on the textile industry in the mill towns of New England, and she knew that in spite of its ponderous subject, she would finish it by bedtime. But then, there were plenty more books in Gerald Walsh's library, and she wondered how long it would take her to read them all.

Nothing in her life had prepared Jill for the role of a pampered lady in the home of an influential man. She was not used to endless empty days when the most useful thing she did was read or sew a few stitches on her embroidery. Nor was she used to the constant monitoring of her movements. Walsh's instructions to her were very strict: She was not to leave the property except to go to Sunday services, was not to visit with the servants, was not to interfere with Mrs. Pryor's authority in any way. The strictures necessitated an idleness and isolation Jillian found depressing.

Coming to her feet, she smoothed the skirt of her rich new gown and moved down the steps of the gazebo to the riverbank. The dress was eminently fashionable, as were all the clothes General Walsh had bought for her. It was made of cotton nankeen with a full, box-pleated skirt; a high-necked, tight-fitting bodice; and wide pagoda sleeves. Lacy undersleeves of embroidered lawn peeped enticingly from beneath the flaring oversleeves. It seemed odd to Jill that her father-in-law should be so concerned with the state of her wardrobe when she was in virtual seclusion. She had not even been allowed to see her callers, the women who had come and left their cards when word got out that Congressman Gerald Walsh had recently acquired a pretty daughter-in-law. Jill knew that they had come out of curiosity, and perhaps that was why Walsh had forbidden her to greet them. But still, he wanted her dressed and coiffed as if she were expecting visitors.

As she made her way to the river, Jillian noted how the water's blue-gray surface swirled and sparkled in the sun. Here, just a mile above the Falls, the current was swift and treacherous, the river turbulent and choppy, too fast for even steam-powered boats to brave. And on the far side of the water was Canada. Jillian had often stared across to that verdant strip of land, wondering about Ryder, wondering if he was safe.

In the days after she had left him at the railroad station, she had pored over the local papers, looking for and yet loath to find some mention of his name. She wanted reassurance that Ryder had reached Canada and freedom, reassurance that could not be found in the fine black type of the *Niagara Falls Gazette*. Though she knew silence was the best she could hope for, she had wished for something more. But her search for word of Bingham had been fruitless until now.

She had been a member of the household several days when she noticed that in addition to newspapers from Niagara Falls and Buffalo, Walsh subscribed to those from New York and Washington as well. After that she scanned them all, reading the *New York Tribune* closely, remembering Ryder had said that Confederate soldiers sometimes bought space in the personals column to herald the success of their escape. She had waited nearly three weeks for news of the man she loved, and this morning a message had magically appeared: "Dearest Jilly: 'Stone walls do not a prison make, Nor iron bars a cage'—R.B."

She had carried the paper to her room and wept for joy, then tucked it safely away in the depths of her sewing bag.

Now she stared across at Canada, knowing Ryder was safe, knowing she wanted nothing more than to be with him. It was an idle thought, one Ryder would not entertain even now, especially when these last days had proved she was not carrying his child.

Yet she knew there were reasons why he had refused to take her with him. Even that last night, when they had been twined as close as a man and woman could be, she had sensed there was much Ryder was keeping from her. It was as if he had a resolution he would not share, something to accomplish she could not help him do. And now, safe and free, he might well be headed back to the Confederacy, back into the fray to seek his destiny.

Still, she yearned for him, remembered the shelter of his arms and the sense of security his presence gave her. Tears of loneliness and frustration rose in her eyes, and she fought to force the memories away. They were hurtful and served no purpose. They were pointless and unwelcome. They were fragments of a wondrous closeness she would never know again.

This travesty of usefulness was to be her life forever after, and she saw with stinging irony that she had chosen it for herself. She would forever be confined to a house with people she was coming to loathe, made to feel useless because her abilities were not being utilized. She hated this feeling of hopelessness; self-pity always made her angry.

She wandered farther up the bank, pondering a solution to her problems. Though she had been preoccupied with her father's illness when she lived in Harrisburg, she had known women from genteel homes who were banding together to help the Union. They rolled bandages, scraped lint to pack in battle wounds, sewed shirts, and knitted socks for the soldiers at the front. Only this morning she had seen a notice from just such a group in the Niagara Falls paper, and she felt sure that even her father-in-law could not forbid her participation in such a worthy enterprise. If he agreed to let her join, she might be able to make some friends in Niagara Falls, offer skills that would otherwise go unused. If only Gerald Walsh would let her, she might rediscover the purpose in her life.

It would take courage to approach him, but she meant to broach the idea at dinner. Wouldn't it reflect well on him if his daughter-in-law was involved in such a cause? Couldn't he be convinced of the advantages in allowing her this bit of freedom? Jillian slowly returned to the gazebo, rehearsing her arguments, feeling more energetic and hopeful than she had for many days.

But Gerald Walsh did not put in an appearance at the dinner table. Several political meetings would keep him away until late tonight, Mrs. Pryor informed her. Jillian ate her meal in silence and, when she finished, went into the parlor seeking diversion.

The room was the most formal in Gerald Walsh's home and was papered with an intricate floral-patterned wall covering that matched the burgundy brocade lambrequins and the elegant suite of tufted furniture. Jillian wandered to the grand piano in the corner and turned up the light beside the music stand. She had taken lessons as a girl and could have given a fair accounting of herself at any of the amateur musicals that were so popular throughout the North. The songs that ran from beneath her fingers this evening were slow, melancholy ballads, songs about men gone off and lost to war, songs about sweethearts waiting for lovers who would never return.

After a time Jillian lifted her hands from the keys, thinking that the stories the selections told seemed too much like her own. She had a sweetheart lost to war, a lover who would never return. The music was not providing solace but reinforcing her loneliness.

As she sat staring, the photographs on top of the piano came into focus. There were some in ornate iron frames, others hemmed with inlaid rosewood. A few of the pictures were displayed on bamboo easels while others remained in the small hinged cases photographers provided. The photographs showed the lives of the Walsh family encapsulated. There was one of Gerald Walsh in his judge's robes and another of him standing with Abraham Lincoln beneath a drape of patriotic bunting. A third daguerreotype showed a bride and groom, and as she looked at it more closely, she recognized a younger Gerald and the woman who had been his bride. Serena Walsh had been a lovely woman with a high brow, wide-set eyes, and a rosebud mouth. Beside that photograph were several others, including one of Serena alone with a rose in her hand and another with a baby in her lap.

Jillian picked it up and studied the picture of the man who had been her husband, seeking in that child the germ of the man she had married. There were other pictures of him as well: Jeff as a chubby toddler with a stuffed-toy dog clutched to his chest, Jeff in short pants and a school tie, Jeff dressed as a soldier ready for war. She looked at all the pictures, trying to see how Jeff had changed from one to the other, how he had grown taller, broader, progressively more handsome. She found to her dismay that she had forgotten about the single misplaced dimple in his left cheek, the higher quirk of his right brow. She tried to remember how he had looked the first time he came home to dinner with her father, how he had behaved when he took her for a buggy ride. She tried to remember a great many things about her husband and found that all the memories had grown sepia-toned and dim.

That she had forgotten him seemed the worst kind of betrayal, and Jill wished with all her heart that she could live those times again. If she had known how briefly she and Jeff would be together, she would have savored every hour, treasured their time together just as she had treasured every moment with Ryder. Perhaps the intensity of what she felt for the Confederate was a reflection of the urgency of their joining, while the passivity of her love for her dead husband was a result of the lifetime they had planned to share.

Jillian sighed, hoping that she had stumbled on the answer to the thing she had been trying for weeks to resolve. Her life was here in Niagara Falls, and she would be so much more at peace with her decision if she could explain why she cared more for Ryder after a few short days than she had ever cared for Jeff. She wanted to belong here, in this house and in this gallery of photographs. She longed to think of this as home, to prove that she deserved a place at Jefferson's side. She had not been able to feel worthy of that when her mind was filled with thoughts of Ryder, but now that she understood the reason for her preoccupation with the Confederate, she could feel less guilty for wanting all the things she felt she had not earned.

As Jillian sat looking at Jeff's photograph, she suddenly remembered the pictures they'd had made the day they were married. There was one of both of them with her father and one of the two of them alone. Suddenly she wanted a place on the top of this piano at her husband's side. Without taking time to reconsider her decision, Jillian mounted the stairs to her room to get the wedding photograph. In it Jeff seemed proud, rakish, fearless in his uniform of blue, and beside him she stood cradling her bouquet of early roses, looking innocent and shy. The photograph seemed suddenly to reveal so much: her naiveté and reticence, the bravery and determination that had cost Jeff his life. It seemed odd that she had been unable to see the future in the picture when it had been so clearly revealed by the lens of a gifted photographer.

Jillian returned to the parlor and set the photograph carefully on the lid of the piano. It seemed right there somehow, as if it belonged, and it made her hope that perhaps one day she would belong in this household, too.

It was midafternoon the next day when Jillian was summoned to Gerald Walsh's office. She entered cautiously, though she was pleased by the opportunity to speak with him alone. It seemed a good time to discuss her need for greater freedom, her desire to join one of the women's groups here in Niagara Falls. But as Gerald rose to greet her, she saw the scowl on his mouth and the picture in his hands.

"Mrs. Pryor found this on the piano when she was dusting,"

Walsh began as she approached him. "Do you have any idea how this came to be with the rest of the family photographs?"

His anger was palpable and malevolent, his fury barely controlled, and Jillian clung to the back of one of the chairs as if to shield herself.

"It's a picture of Jeff and me," she offered timorously. "I thought you wouldn't mind if I put it with the others."

"Wouldn't mind?" he echoed. "Of course I mind. You stole my only son from me!"

Somewhere inside her a tiny spark of anger flared to flame. It stiffened her spine and renewed the pride that had lain dormant since her arrival in the Falls. "I stole nothing from you, Mr. Walsh." Her voice was cold. "I did nothing more than marry Jeff."

"No, you did nothing more than that. You married my son for his fortune and sent him off to battle. And when he was dead, you descended on me like a plague, wanting shelter, a place in my home—"

"I wanted nothing from you, Mr. Walsh, nothing more than what you freely offered. But if that's the way you feel, I'll pack my bags and leave today!"

Jillian swung around as if to carry out her threat, but Walsh was suddenly beside her, catching her arm.

"You'd like that, wouldn't you?" he demanded. "You'd like a chance to humiliate me before the whole town, now that they know you're here. You'd like them to say that Gerald Walsh shirks his responsibilities, that I can't hold on to all that's mine."

She was stunned by her father-in-law's ravings, frightened by the feral light behind his eyes.

"No, you'll stay, girl. You'll stay because you have nowhere else to go. And by all that's holy, you'll do as I say."

Jill snatched her arm from her father-in-law's grasp and faced him fiercely. "No, Mr. Walsh, I won't stay another moment as things are now. I'm not happy here, not useful, not—"

"You spoiled, ungrateful girl!" he flared. "No one will raise a hand to support you if you leave. No one else will give you the things I've given you."

"Then I'll make my own way in the world. I'll make a living on my own."

Walsh hesitated in the face of her determination, and Jillian could almost see him weighing his options. Would it be worse to have his daughter-in-law stay or to face the humiliation of losing her? Would it be worse to have her remain in this household or to slip beyond his control?

"What would you need to be happy here?" he asked her suddenly. "I thought I'd provided everything a woman could want—a lovely home, fancy clothes, servants."

Jillian paused, confused by his question. What had made him so conciliatory, so willing to make concessions? Why was he giving her this unhoped-for opportunity to dictate terms?

Though she did not understand why Walsh was willing to listen, she meant to make the most of his capitulation. What did she want? She had to ask for everything now, while she had her chance.

"I need something to do with my days," she began. "I'm not used to sitting idle. I'd like your permission to join one of the women's organizations here in the city; they are working so hard to offer relief to the soldiers."

"And what else?" the congressman negotiated, giving no sign that he was willing to agree to her demands.

"I'd like the freedom to leave the house on my own. I want to be able to go out for an afternoon carriage ride, to go shopping, visit friends."

"Is that all?"

Possessed of a new boldness, Jillian voiced the feelings she'd harbored for weeks. "I'd like to feel that I belong here: in the gallery of photographs on the piano, as a participant in the household, as your hostess when you begin to entertain again."

Walsh's eyes were narrowed as he considered her terms, and she could read no hint of a response in the planes of his dour countenance. She waited, holding her breath. Was he going to give in to her demands or punish her for having had the temerity to make them? Was he going to agree to what she was proposing or refuse and force her hand?

And where would she go if he told her to leave? What would she do without money or friends? How could she make a life for herself now when that possibility had seemed so bleak before? Thoughts of Ryder flitted through her mind, but she knew there was no future for her with him. She had no idea where Ryder had gone, nor was it likely he would welcome her if she somehow managed to find him.

It was clear that her father-in-law liked her no better now than he had before, that he still thought her an avaricious tramp who had married his son for money. Yet he seemed reluctant to sever the relationship between them, and Jillian could not fathom his motives.

Walsh drew a long breath and pinioned her with his eyes. "I'm aware of the good work the women of the Falls are doing," he conceded with evident difficulty. "And I don't see any reason why you can't join them in their efforts. As for the rest, your visits and your shopping must be carefully chaperoned. Your father may have let you wander like a hoyden, but I won't tolerate any scandal."

His capitulation was so unexpected that it took Jillian a moment to respond. "I shan't behave scandalously, I assure you. But I want your word that once I've agreed to stay, you won't renege on what you've promised."

"Done," he told her with finality that seemed tinged with both resignation and relief. "I'll inform Mrs. Pryor and Noble of the change in your status here."

Jillian was not sure why, but she found it necessary to thank him. She was demanding nothing more than her due, she told herself, but she was grateful nonetheless. These concessions would not change the way Gerald Walsh felt about her, but they had changed the way she felt about herself. She had faced down her father-in-law, and she had won.

She had turned to go when she remembered the wedding photograph and slowly retraced her steps to where Walsh had discarded it on his desk.

She glanced down at the picture, seeing the eager young man and the lovely girl in the frame. She had changed since the photograph was taken, and she wondered if her husband would even recognize the woman she was today.

"I'm going to put this photograph back on the piano," she said quietly. "If I'm to stay in this house, I've earned the right to have it there."

Chapter Eight

THE MAP OF Lake Erie lay spread on the table in the home of one of Jacob Thompson's contacts in Windsor, Canada West. Around the map were gathered more than half a dozen men, each of whom ran his fingers along the horizontal length of the oval-shaped lake and murmured about the possibilities that lay before them. As the men speculated, they nodded consideringly and sipped from glasses of fine Kentucky bourbon as they waited for the meeting to begin.

Commissioner Thompson stood at the head of the table looking thoughtful and grim, as well he might have at this juncture in the war. Grant still held Lee captive within the earthworks at Petersburg, Sheridan was running amok in the Shenandoah Valley, and only this morning news had come through that Sherman had taken Atlanta. Thompson was flanked by two of his aides: his efficient secretary, William Cleary, and a quiet, well-dressed man named Phillip Sheppard, who had recently joined the commissioner's entourage. At the opposite end of the table sat Captain Thomas Hines. Though only twenty-six, Hines had been appointed by Jefferson Davis himself as the military commander of the Confederates in Canada. A handsome man of intelligence and daring, Hines had ridden with John Hunt Morgan earlier in the war and had helped his illustrious commander escape from the Ohio Penitentiary at Columbus. He was a man the Yankees considered wily and dangerous, an infamous man with a price on his head.

On either side of Hines were the two men who would spearhead the mission they had gathered to discuss. One was fair and good-looking, with a jaunty, carefree air. His name was Charles Cole, and on Thompson's authority he had recently completed a reconnaissance of the cities along the American shores of the Great Lakes. The other man was John Yates Beall, who had already served in the war as a cavalry man, a privateer, and a battlefield engineer. He was spare and dark, with a long cadaverous face and a beard that seemed to underline his quiet intensity. Ryder Bingham had met both men for the first time tonight and liked them immediately. Oh, yes, he liked them, just as he liked the prospect of the mission they had proposed. It was not a new idea, Ryder had learned when Jamie recruited him for the enterprise, but it was an idea the Confederacy was finally prepared to implement.

"Gentlemen," Thompson began, his words cutting across the murmur of speculative voices and half-formed plans. "As you know, we have gathered here tonight to discuss the capture of the *Michigan*, the only Federal gunboat on the Great Lakes, and to decide how we can use it to free our men from the prison at Johnson's Island. With those objectives in mind, Captain Cole has just returned from making a study of Sandusky, Ohio, where the prison is located and of the other cities along the American lakeshores. Captain Cole, if you would, please tell us what you've learned."

Cole cleared his throat and pointed to an inlet near the southwest corner of Lake Erie. "The U.S.S. *Michigan* is stationed here, in Sandusky Bay, guarding the military prison. She is here from early spring to late fall, returning to her anchorage at Erie, Pennsylvania, during the winter. The ship is a steamer with a capacity for sail and can bring fourteen guns to bear on the prison, the city, or any approaching vessel. She is captained by a man named Carter, a rough and unpolished sort, who is at odds with the navy over the post they've seen fit to assign him. He feels his talents are being wasted patrolling Lake Erie when he might be better assigned to the blockade fleet or to shelling Southern harbors."

"Do you think Captain Carter can be bought?" Hines asked intently, cutting to the heart of the matter. It was rumored in Toronto that the Confederate commissioners had unlimited funds to spend in the hope of bringing the North to a negotiated peace, and from what Ryder had seen in the past weeks, he believed the tale was true.

"In spite of his disenchantment with the navy, I doubt Carter can be bribed," Cole answered after a moment's consideration. "But he's not an incorruptible man, and I think there are other ways to influence him."

Thompson leaned closer to the table. "Such as?"

Cole smiled, suave and sure of himself. "A sailor who would turn down silver might respond to other favors: favors like imported cigars and whiskey, good food and pretty women. A man willing to offer such boons could easily ingratiate himself with the good captain. And who knows what advantages that might give us?"

There were whispers around the table, but Beall was the first to give voice to the possibilities. "Do you suppose your friendship with Carter could lead to an evening when the captain and his officers were absent from the gunboat?" he asked thoughtfully.

"Perhaps," Cole replied. "What did you have in mind?"

Beall shrugged. "The *Michigan* cannot be on full alert when we approach her. There is no other vessel on the Great Lakes as well armed as the *Michigan*, and if she is prepared for an attack, we will not be able to capture her. It will be fruitless to even try unless we find a way to even the odds."

"Do you think you can win the confidence of Captain Carter?" Thompson asked Cole.

"I made his acquaintance while I was in Sandusky on this last trip. He seems the kind of man who would welcome a free-spending friend, someone willing to buy him drinks and listen to his frustrations. The Copperheads in town might well be able to afford us some useful introductions."

"The Copperheads," Hines muttered in disgust. "Don't rely too heavily on what they promise." His advice was well taken, especially in light of Hines's recent debacle in Chicago. He and fifty of his men had gone there to unite with the Illinois Copperhead organization and disrupt the Democratic national convention. There had been plans to release the Confederates held at Camp Douglas, too, but the aid the Copperheads promised had failed to materialize, and Hines's plans had been discovered. Whether that betrayal had come from spies among the Copperheads or from his own men, it was not clear, but additional Union military units had been sent to Chicago, and the Confederates had been forced to flee. In the days that followed, a dozen or more of their number had been arrested, including Captain Breck Castleman, Hines's close friend and second in command. It was easy to understand why the young captain was suspicious of help from the Copperheads. Still, everyone in the room knew the importance of the secret society in offering money, support, and a loud dissenting voice in American politics.

"I think they can be counted on to provide introductions, at least," Thompson put in.

"But what about after the prisoners at Johnson's Island are

freed?" Hines persisted. "Will the Copperheads live up to their agreement to supply arms to the men as they march south? And will the Copperheads help us free the Southerners being held in Columbus and Indianapolis?"

"We have to believe they will," Thompson argued. "Besides, freeing those other prisoners is not our first priority. We want to capture the *Michigan*. That's the problem we've come here to discuss."

Tension crackled between the two men like an arcing charge, giving evidence of a disconcerting breach between the political and military factions of the Confederacy in Canada. It was evidence of a dissension that made Ryder very nervous indeed.

Then Beall's voice cut through the air, his words spoken softly but with undeniable authority. "I have a plan that I've been considering for some time, but to succeed it would need the kind of diversion only Cole or the Copperheads could devise."

"Go on, then," Thompson invited. "Tell us what you have in mind."

"Well," the dark-haired man began, "since we hope to avoid compromising Great Britain's neutrality, everything we plan must be executed on American ships and in American waters."

There were understanding nods around the table before Beall continued.

"Several American ships call at Canadian ports before setting off for Sandusky. I propose that we board one of these vessels and take control of it as soon as it enters American waters."

"And you do know a bit about capturing enemy ships, don't you, Captain Beall?" Thompson asked with a twist of his lips. It was common knowledge that the months Beall and two comrades had spent privateering on the Chesapeake were advantageous ones for the Confederacy.

An acknowledging smile curved the thin man's mouth. "I might just know a thing or two about capturing enemy ships, Colonel Thompson. Yes, indeed, I just might."

"But any ship that Beall might capture could not be armed to go against a Union gunboat," Ryder observed, speaking for the first time.

"You're quite right, Captain Bingham," Beall agreed. "Nor is there any way for us to arm ourselves properly on such short notice. But the element of surprise is in our favor, and perhaps we could do some other things to turn the situation to our advantage."

"And I suppose that's where I come in," Cole responded. "It

will be up to me to provide a diversion while you approach and take the ship."

Beall's smile deepened at Cole's words, at the confidence in the other man's tone. "Exactly," Beall confirmed.

"But what form should that diversion take?" Thompson mused. "And how will you get word to the prisoners at Johnson's Island that their release is at hand?"

"Could the diversion be in the form of a Copperhead attack from the shore?" Cole suggested. "And isn't it possible they could help me make contact with the men in the prison?"

"They might be able to help you get in touch with the men in Johnson's Island, but I wouldn't count on that kind of overt support from the Copperheads," Hines reiterated.

"Captain Cole, what if you were to invite the *Michigan*'s officers to a party at your hotel?" William Cleary offered. "If they were away from the ship for an evening, perhaps we could mount our attack."

"That idea has some merit," Cole agreed, "but I doubt that they would all be off duty at the same time."

"What if a fancy dinner were to be served in the wardroom of the gunboat?" suggested Thompson's other aide, Phillip Sheppard. "Then they could all attend."

Cole was silent for a moment as he considered the plan. "But how would I keep the officers below deck once the lookouts spotted Beall's approach? They could be at their battle stations in a matter of minutes."

"They could do very little if you had the foresight to drug the wine you served them."

There was a pause around the table as Sheppard's second suggestion sank in.

"That might work," Thompson breathed.

"It just might," Cole answered, nodding. "And while they're asleep, I could sneak out and capture the ship's armory so that even if the crew tried to drive Beall off, they wouldn't have access to the weapons and powder they'd need to defend the ship."

"But could you do that, Cole?" Thompson asked. "Could you become friendly enough with the captain and his officers to receive permission for such a dinner?"

" 'The shortest way to a man's heart is through his stomach,' " Cole quipped, grinning. "Until now I had always considered that advice for old maids, but it might apply to our plans as well."

The murmurs among the men gathered around the table slowly became nods of agreement and approval.

"Then do I have permission, sir, to make my way to Sandusky and begin courting the Yankee captain?"

"Yes, Cole, you do," Thompson agreed. "It seems a good beginning to our plan. What about you, Beall? Do you concur with what's been suggested? And how soon will you be able to get a force of men together for your part in the capture?"

Beall pulled thoughtfully at his beard. "I won't dare gather a force of more than fifteen or twenty men; any larger group would raise suspicions. And perhaps I could have them board the American steamer we select for the initial capture at several ports instead of one. Captain Bingham, you're to be one of the men involved. What do you think of what we've proposed?"

Ryder hesitated for a moment before putting his thoughts into words. "I think the plan is fine as far as it goes, but our men surely won't be able to come aboard that steamer armed for battle. Perhaps some of us could bring on luggage packed with weapons, or we could have the guns we'll need loaded on as cargo."

"A good observation, Bingham," Thompson complimented the newcomer.

"That sounds fine to me," Beall agreed.

"Well, then, are there any more concerns?"

"Only about how Cole is going to keep me abreast of the developments in Sandusky."

Again Charles Cole smiled with what seemed like overwhelming confidence. "I have a man called Robinson who can pass freely across the border. He's by all appearances a half-wit and not subject to suspicion."

"But can we trust him with such important messages?" Beall looked skeptical.

"Implicitly," Cole assured him. "I'll sew the messages into the lining of his coat sleeve."

"Then it's set," Beall murmured, staring down at the map.

"Yes, it's set," Cole confirmed as if the success of the plan could never be in doubt.

"Then let's drink to the capture of the *Michigan*," Thompson toasted, raising his glass of bourbon.

"To the capture of the *Michigan*," the other men replied as one.

* * *

Turning up his collar against the morning wind that slashed across the water of the Detroit River, Ryder watched the gusts raise whitecaps on the gray-blue surface of the channel. He would never get used to this damnable northern weather, he thought irritably, drawing his frock coat more closely around him. Why did people live way up here where summer was as cold and fleeting as a virgin's kiss? It was only mid-September, and already there was the bite of fall in the air.

Beside him on the dock at the small Canadian town of Sandwich were John Yates Beall, the commander of the mission to capture the *Michigan*, and a man named Tate. They looked no warmer than he was, Ryder conceded, as they waited for the packet boat. The *Philo Parsons* was the steamer they would board and capture as a means of taking a bigger prize, and it did nothing to ease his mind that the *Parsons* was running late. Since that first meeting more than two weeks before, the plans for the mission had moved forward smoothly until now the three men stood poised and ready to take their part in making history.

It was a heady thought, but Bingham did not dwell on the prospect of glory. Partly because he knew that the best laid plans could go awry and partly because he possessed a fatalistic bent in his nature, Ryder had spent most of the previous night settling his affairs and penning a letter to his elder brother. It had been a difficult letter to write, not only because of the unspoken animosity between them but also because, in forming the painful words, Ryder had been forced to acknowledge the finality of Mitchell's death. He had been with his younger brother the day he died, had held Mitch in his arms to his last breath. But somehow Ryder had not accepted what had happened as irrevocable. Writing to Wade had forced him to recognize the depth of his loss and the scope of his responsibility. It had brought home his terrible guilt and crystallized his helplessness.

He should have been able to circumvent the capture of *The Wraith*. After having sailed the waters around Cape Fear most of his life, he should have known the channels well enough to have kept the ship from running aground where the Yankees could shell and burn her. He should have been able to secure proper medical attention for Mitchell while they were in prison, should have been able to prevent his brother's death. His mother had given Mitch into his care, and he was eternally damned for having failed her. Owning up to his own deficiencies and writing Wade of Mitchell's death had been one of the hardest things he'd ever done. It had left him sleepless until almost dawn as he lay pondering the allegiances and jealousies that had kept Wade and him from being all that brothers should be. Since they were the only Binghams left, writing the letter should have strengthened the bond between them, but instead, Ryder had never felt farther from his stalwart older brother. What Wade's reaction to the letter would be, Ryder could only guess, but none of the scenes he imagined could make his eventual homecoming easier.

"Here she is," Tate suddenly murmured from beside him, and Ryder welcomed the chance to turn his thoughts from his failures to the vengeance he would wreak on the Yankees. He was looking forward to his revenge, looking forward to being back in action. With a grim smile on his lips, he watched the lake steamer plodding toward them. She was a typical wooden paddleboat of medium size, unremarkable in every way except for the use the Confederates meant to make of her.

In order to avoid the formality of customs, the *Philo Parsons* would not stop at Sandwich and they would have to jump aboard as she approached the dock. They tensed expectantly as the boat slowed, coasted nearer, and just as the pilot reversed his engines, the three men leaped aboard. As soon as they landed on the deck, the man Beall had sent ahead to Detroit came forward to greet them.

The introductions were made quickly. "Ryder Bingham, Ambrose Tate, this is my old friend, Bennett Burley."

They shook hands all around, and when Burley turned to confer with Beall, Ryder stared after them. He knew the younger man had been Beall's partner in his exploits on the Chesapeake, knew that the compact Scotsman had proved himself clever and resourceful. Watching him, Ryder saw in the clear boyish face an unwavering loyalty to his soft-spoken commander, and since it mirrored Bingham's own feelings, he trusted Burley implicitly. With his mind at rest, Ryder sauntered along the deck, enjoying the feeling of a ship beneath his feet. It had been too long since he'd put to sea, too long since he'd had his own command, and merely being aboard a ship renewed his faith in the future.

As they steamed up the Detroit River, the United States and Canada lay on either hand, their heavily treed banks separated by nothing but their loyalties and this shimmering ribbon of water. As he contemplated the Confederates' role in days ahead, Ryder wondered if they all would be caught as they were now, between two opposing powers. What they were doing would not be sanctioned by Great Britain, and he could not help but wonder if they would become pawns in the greater game of politics. Still, he would not have wished to be any place but here, and he was willing to accept the consequences of his actions.

Since the meeting with Jacob Thompson, Ryder had learned a great deal more about the *Michigan* and the plans the Southerners had for her. The iron-hulled gunboat had been assembled at Erie, Pennsylvania, in the mid-1840s to patrol the American waters of the Great Lakes. Originally it had been outfitted with a single eighteen-pound gun, but now it carried far heavier ordnance. At the beginning of the war, the ship had been ordered to the Atlantic, but after it had proved too large to pass up the St. Lawrence River, it had returned to its anchorage on Lake Erie. The *Michigan* had been a Union embarrassment from start to finish, and if the Confederates had their way, it would prove to be even more so. According to what Beall had told him, once the vessel was in their hands, the rebels meant to free the men at Johnson's Island, then turn her guns on the American cities along the lakeshore. Beall planned to capture the arsenal at Buffalo and destroy the munitions plants at Cleveland. And if given the chance, he would enter Lake Michigan and free the Confederates in Camp Douglas near Chicago.

Somehow the scope of what Beall was proposing filled Ryder with satisfaction. For the loved ones he had lost, for the devastation he had seen, he wanted the war visited on Northern families, wanted those safe, smug Yankees to taste the bitterness Southerners knew so well.

As they approached Amherstburg at the head of the lake, the *Philo Parsons* nudged once more toward the Canadian shore. Just down from old Fort Malden there was a cluster of passengers waiting to come aboard. There were women, a handful of children, and nearly twenty men, two of whom were carrying a heavy trunk, which was locked and bound with rope. Ryder recognized a number of the men he'd met in the bar at the Queen's Hotel. He smiled as he watched them board. Then, knowing there was nothing to do but wait, he found a place at the poker game in the ship's commodious lounge.

At four o'clock they reached Kelley's Island, and once the *Parsons* had discharged its passengers and gotten under way, Beall took over the ship. With Ryder, Burley, and several other men at his back, Beall burst into the steamer's wheelhouse and drew his navy Colt.

"This is a prize ship of the Confederacy!" he announced to the startled helmsman, mate, and clerk.

There was a moment of stunned silence before anyone spoke.

"Are you men rebels?" one of them finally demanded, raising his hands above his head.

"We are, sir," Beall responded, and with little more in the way of discussion the helmsman surrendered the wheel.

Leaving two men in charge of the pilothouse, Beall, Bingham, and Burley returned to the main deck and found the other Confederates herding the passengers into the main salon. Armed with knives, guns, and hatchets from the trunk, the Confederates looked to be ruthless brigands. Fear simmered in the long, narrow room, evident in the tearful children's faces and the women's widened eyes. The men aboard stood tensed but helpless, clearly frustrated by their impotence. As Ryder watched them, he knew their emotions well.

"You have nothing to fear from us," Beall said, trying to console the passengers. "We are Confederate soldiers and will not harm you. We require nothing but the use of this ship."

But neither his words nor the courteous way they were ushered into the hold reassured the passengers.

"You won't hurt my children, will you?" one weeping woman pleaded as she brushed past Ryder. "You can do what you want with me, as long as my girls are safe."

He tried his best to calm her, but his words had little effect.

A few men resisted their confinement and were hustled down the companionway, though some of the crew remained free to run the ship. But once the majority were secured, Beall gathered his men together. They had overcome the ship so efficiently that it was still too early to set out for their rendezvous with the *Michigan*, and besides, one of the Confederates reported, they were running low on wood. Beall decided to return to Middle Bass Island to replenish their supply, and under the control of the *Parsons*'s pilot, they returned the way they had come.

An hour later they were tied up at the Middle Bass Island quay where, under the supervision of two armed guards, the dockhands were loading wood. But as the *Parsons* wooded up, another steamer appeared on the horizon. At first it seemed as if it would bypass the island, but instead it came about and made its way toward the dock. The Confederates were armed and ready. They swarmed over the side of the unsuspecting *Island Queen* the moment it pulled in beside them.

Ryder was among the first aboard, and he had no more than scrambled onto the deck when he heard gunfire. The shots seemed to come from the direction of the wheelhouse, and a moment later one of the crew staggered through the door, bleeding from a neck wound. Screams and shouts erupted at the sound of the firing, and with the help of several other men, Ryder moved to subdue the passengers. On this ship was the usual complement of travelers, but in addition there were twenty-five or thirty soldiers from an Ohio regiment. For one tense moment the Yankees resisted, but seeing themselves outgunned, they had no choice but to surrender. While the *Island Queen*'s passengers were herded into the *Parsons*'s hold, Beall held a hurried conference with his men. The appearance of the second ship was an unexpected complication, and Beall was not sure how to proceed.

"Let's put everyone aboard the *Island Queen* and set her adrift," one of the Confederates proposed.

"Let's scuttle her with everyone aboard."

"Maybe we'd be better off attacking the *Michigan* with two vessels instead of one," someone else suggested.

Beall frowned, considering what a change of plans might mean to those waiting in Sandusky. Since they were critically short of Confederates to man the boats, using the *Island Queen* seemed a risky choice at best. Finally he ordered the passengers and crews ashore, and the *Parsons* pulled away from Middle Bass Island with the *Island Queen* in tow. Several miles from the island, Beall scuttled the second ship and gave orders for Sandusky.

As they steamed toward the *Michigan* and their fate, Ryder found a quiet place in the bow and stared out across the water. He watched the sinking sun spangle the crests of the waves, watched the sunlit path on the surface of the lake turn from peach to midnight blue. What lay ahead he could not know. It could be death; it could be dishonor. Or it could be a victory of the spirit that would grant him peace at last.

In the darkening twilight Mitchell seemed very close at hand. Ryder could almost see his brother's face, hear his infectious laugh. Mitch had always been the lighthearted one, sensitive, chivalrous, and gentle. He had brought light into every life he touched. Ryder ached with the memory of the boy who had tagged after him from the time he was old enough to toddle, who had enjoyed tales of Ryder's pranks and escapades, who had given his love unconditionally. Alysse had always depended on Ryder to look after her precious youngest son, and he had accepted the duty gladly. But he had failed in the end, failed both Mitch and his mother miserably. Now he would strike back, make the Yankees pay for what they'd done.

Yet beneath the need for revenge was fear. It was not the same fear that had made him sure and sharp as he'd faced the challenge of running the blockade. It was not the kind of fear that had made him calm and fierce in battle. This was a murky, oily fear that lay deep in his belly. It was a fear that this mission would be a failure, a fear of cowardice and recapture.

At Fort Lafayette he had been so preoccupied with seeing to Mitchell's needs that he had hardly realized what effect imprisonment had on him. But now the horror of it came clear again. He remembered the cold and dampness that penetrated his bones, the crush of humanity in the cells, the ceaseless murmur of voices, and the tedium that had threatened his sanity. During all those long months he had not felt the sun on his face or the wind in his hair, had not known the leap of a ship beneath him or been alone beneath the starlit sky. Those things that were most basic to his nature had been denied him, and he knew he could not endure prison life again.

Yet this mission lay before him, his chance for revenge and redemption. And in spite of the fear that lived in his heart, he would see Beall's plans fulfilled. It would take courage to do that, courage Bingham was not sure he still possessed. But as the ship steamed through the night, he was determined if not at peace.

The moon was high, the water clear and dark when the *Parsons* approached Sandusky Bay. Ryder and Burley had been in the bow for some time, scanning the deeply indented shoreline with night glasses. For a time they watched in vain, and then slowly the outline of the *Michigan* became visible through the shadows. It was lying tranquil in the water as if nothing were amiss. As the *Parsons* crept closer to its quarry, Beall came to stand beside them.

"Has there been any signal?" he asked quietly. There was concern in his voice, but it was edged with determination. "Have you seen flares either from the ship or from Johnson's Island?"

Ryder turned the glasses toward the hulking shape of the prison where fifteen hundred Confederates were captive. "There's been nothing," he reported.

"Wasn't there to be a message at Kelley's Island if all had gone as Cole planned?"

Beall gave a distracted nod to the Scotsman's words. "That's why I was hoping for a signal, some indication of how to proceed."

As they waited for some sign, the *Parsons* continued to stalk the gunboat, crawling nearer to its lair. In the quiet of the night, the steamer's engines droned like locusts.

It was cold on the water, and though Ryder shivered, his skin was clammy. Behind him on the decks the other men were sweating, too, caught in the same mixture of determination and doubt that afflicted Bingham. The waiting was intolerable.

"What are we to do?" Burley voiced the question for everyone aboard. "Shall we proceed without Cole's signal, or should we lie off here awhile?"

For the first time Ryder saw indecision in Beall's face, and reckless words sprang to his lips. "I could row ashore to see if there's any activity. If Cole has been discovered, the Yankees will have laid a trap, and there's bound to be some sign of it."

It took Beall a full minute to consider Bingham's offer, and then he nodded. "I don't believe there is a problem," he answered slowly, "but it would help us to be certain."

With that, Beall gave the order to lower a skiff, and taking a pair of field glasses and extra rounds of ammunition, Ryder climbed over the steamer's side. "I'll be back as soon as I have something to report," he called up to the cluster of men gathered along the rail. "It shouldn't take more than an hour to determine if something's wrong."

After settling himself in the open boat, Ryder set out across Sandusky Bay with sure and measured strokes. Something about the rhythm of rowing was soothing, and as he watched the outline of the *Philo Parsons* recede into the night, Bingham knew a quiet satisfaction. He was acting, moving to decide their fate, and after the months of inactivity it renewed his sense of power.

It took him nearly fifteen minutes to reach the dock at the edge of the bay, and fastening the boat to one of the pilings, he climbed the ladder to the top. All was quiet along the waterfront. Fishing boats were tied up to the wharfs; larger ships bobbed at their moorings out in the bay. But there was no sign of their crews about, no ships preparing for voyages. Light spilled from the windows and doorways of taverns along the water, but no sound of music or revelry drifted out into the night.

Screened by piles of crates and boxes, Ryder moved along a row of warehouses and shops until he stood opposite the *Michigan*'s anchorage. The lights on the gunboat shimmered across the surface of the bay. Nothing seemed amiss, nothing seemed to stir. Did that mean that the *Michigan*'s officers were sleeping off the effects of their drugged wine or that they were lying in wait for the Confederates?

A frisson of apprehension moved up his spine, and as he slipped along a smaller quay, Ryder drew his Colt from the waistband of his trousers. Still, he saw nothing to confirm his suspicions, no signs of a Yankee trap. Halyards clacked against their masts; waves lapped rhythmically against the pilings. Gulls squalled and sailed inland to nest for the night. The air felt and smelled as it should, moist and faintly fishy. Yet Ryder knew there was something wrong; the scene before him was unnaturally quiet.

Then a quickly muffled snicker came from the far side of the boxes where he had taken cover.

"Shut up, you damned fool!" a man whispered. "Want the rebs to hear you?"

"Rebs, shit! Ain't a reb within four hundred miles of here 'cept those over on the island. This is some crazy notion of Carter's meant to keep us up all night."

"Still, they arrested that Cole fellow who's been playing up to the officers."

"Yeah, and the story I heard was that he meant to drug everybody aboard the *Michigan* so he could take over the ship. Now, don't that sound like a smart Confederate plan, one man doing the work of a regiment?"

There was derision in the fellow's tone, and Ryder stiffened. The plan had been a good one, well thought out and simple. Though now that he knew it had been compromised, he had to give a warning.

He was just gathering himself to move away when one of the men demanded: "Where the hell are you going?"

Ryder's heart slammed against the wall of his ribs before he heard the second man's reply.

"I'm just gonna stand up and piss. I won't wet myself for ol' man Carter or nobody."

The sounds from the far side of the boxes confirmed the man's actions quite clearly.

"I don't know," his companion went on as the man returned to his hiding place. "I hear tell there are lots of Confederates in Canada, men who've escaped from the stockades, Southern sympathizers who live in the North. It's common knowledge that Copperhead, Vallandigham, was living up in Windsor, and I don't doubt that there are others there who'd like to see us beat."

The other man gave another snort of laughter. "Well, you can bet this is the most excitement we'll see in this war. I may have joined up to fight, but I haven't done a damned thing to tell my grandchildren!''

As the two unseen men chortled softly, Ryder slid deeper into the shadows. If he had harbored any hope for the success of Cole's mission in Sandusky, it had been erased by the sailors' words. He had to get back to Beall with this information before he attacked the *Michigan*. Beall was a valorous man, a man with no fear for himself, and Ryder had to warn him that a trap was set and ready to spring.

As he skulked along, Bingham began to see more evidence that the Yanks were lying in wait for the Confederates. He spotted an armed man at the side of a warehouse and another tucked into the doorway of a shopfront. He saw the flare of a match in the deep darkness between two buildings as someone lit a smoke, and he heard men shifting positions behind a bank of empty barrels.

His senses expanded with the danger, making him more alert, more cautious. It seemed to take hours to reach his boat, and instead of setting out across the bay where his movements might be revealed by the moonlight, he maneuvered beneath the dock, using his hands to propel the craft along. The pilings were slippery with moss, cold and rough beneath his palms. He ripped a gash in his thumb and bit back a violent curse as he edged the boat forward. Moving silently, carefully, he tried to avoid detection by the guards. When the dock gave way to lakeshore, he stayed beneath the fringe of trees that grew along the bank until he reached a point he judged to be beyond the range of rifle fire.

Only then did Ryder use the oars, pulling with all his might to drive the skiff through the open water. He rowed hard, panting with the effort, sweat running into his eyes. The boat darted along, moving swiftly to where the *Philo Parsons* awaited him. He rowed for almost half an hour, glancing over his shoulder, checking the shoreline to get his bearings. When he reached a point opposite the northernmost end of the bay, he stopped and looked around.

The *Parsons* should have been easily visible against the moonlit water, but neither with his naked eyes nor with the aid of the field glasses could he see any sign of her. The water was smooth, gilded by the moon, and totally empty. The *Philo Parsons* was gone.

Chapter Nine

JILLIAN WALSH ADJUSTED the black lace parasol to better screen herself from the bright fall sun and leaned back in the open carriage to enjoy her afternoon ride. It was a perfect day: the sky bright, clear cerulean, the sunshine warm on her shoulders, the rustling trees above just turning from green to gold. She breathed deep of the crisp, clear air and reveled in the freedom Gerald Walsh had seen fit to allow her. Even now, several weeks after the confrontation in Walsh's study, she was surprised that she had found the courage to face him and demand concessions. Where the gumption or the words she had used to argue her case had come from, she did not know. She only knew that her efforts at the women's relief organization were bringing her both friendship and satisfaction, and the daily carriage rides were worth every bit of the unpleasantness they had cost her. It was good to be back among the living, and this taste of freedom had given her peace of mind.

Today Noble, Walsh's coachman, had turned east along the river, and as they drove, Jillian found herself watching the sun glinting on the broad expanse of water. Beneath the shimmers of light the river looked smooth, calm, tranquil, but she was well aware that a swift, treacherous current lay beneath the surface. Was she a bit like the Niagara? she found herself wondering as she thought back on the scene with her father-in-law. Did her acquiescence hide a woman of passion and strength? Because they had both wanted only what was best for her, Jill had never opposed either Jeff or her father. But Gerald Walsh's demands were based in expediency not altruism, domination not concern. As she rejected the life to which her father-in-law would have her conform, she was discovering an unexpected stubbornness within her.

What other strengths lay beneath her placid facade? What else would she learn about herself in the months to come? The questions frightened her, and yet they piqued her curiosity. She had not courted change, and yet her world had been irrevocably altered. She had never dreamed that the difficulties of her new life in the Falls would open realms of self-discovery, never expected that in order to preserve her self-respect, she would need to learn to stand alone.

In retrospect she realized that taking Ryder from the train and nursing him back to health had been the beginning of the change. Seeing to his welfare had taken a determination and courage she had not known she possessed. Yet by that impulsive act she had tapped some inner reserve, had fostered new strength and independence. And she was reaping the fruit, both bitter and sweet, of that discovery.

In these past weeks, she had not allowed her thoughts to dwell on Ryder Bingham. Once she had discovered the item in the *New York Tribune* and assured herself of his safety, she had tried to put him out of her mind. But in spite of her best resolves, he was with her still. She could not help wondering where he was, if he was well, if he was safe. And the articles about the Confederate raiders terrorizing Lake Erie, which had appeared in this morning's papers, only deepened her concern. With fear in her heart, she had read the accounts of the rebels who had captured two American ships and approached the gunboat stationed at Sandusky Bay. The incident had set panic racing along the American border, and the mayor of Buffalo was sufficiently alarmed to arm two steamers to patrol the harbor. But as she read the accounts of the attack, her concern had been more that Ryder was involved than for her own safety. The news reports had brought thoughts of him to the fore and made her wonder if he had indeed gone south to fight.

In the weeks since she had come to Niagara Falls, she had begun to take a new interest in the war. When before she had been too concerned with her father's failing health to take much note of the world around her, now she had time to read the accounts of the battles in the newspapers. She heard Gerald Walsh discuss with passionate fervor the issues that had led to the breach in the Union, and she found herself agreeing with his views. States should not be allowed to secede from the Union. One race should not be able to hold another in bondage. Even as her understanding of the issues grew, she realized that the carnage on distant battlefields was being caused by little more than men's belief in "should." "Should" was such a little word, yet it wielded terrible power.

Still, there had to be a way to negotiate the differences between the factions in the United States. Surely the men who made these decisions understood that when divided by sectionalism and slavery, neither faction was as strong as the nation as a whole. Hadn't the United States been formed by compromise? Couldn't compromise unite that nation again?

She stared across the river to where Canada lay, thinking of Ryder, of the loyalties that were driving him to risk his life again. They were loyalties with which she could no longer agree, loyalties as foreign to her now as the country he was fighting to protect.

They turned inland from the river road, passing through the fertile farmland where fields of ripened grain and towering corn stood on either hand. Beneath the blazing sky she could see the farmers working, old men and very young ones laboring for their country and their livelihood. Only the men of military age were missing from the pastoral scene, the men who had taken up arms for their country, who were fighting and dying for its cause. Even here where life should have been peaceful and bucolic, it was impossible to escape the evidence of war.

But as they returned from the countryside to the main street of Niagara Falls, normalcy reasserted itself. There were women going about their marketing, older men lazing on the porches of the hotels, children hurrying home from school with packs of books on their backs. Here was evidence that life went on in spite of the nation's political upheaval, that there were things the war could never change. It was supremely reassuring.

As they passed down Falls Street, Jillian's gaze came to rest on a tall man who was making his way down the sidewalk. Why he snared her interest she could not say. Perhaps there was something she admired about the set of his shoulders or something familiar about the way he walked, and she watched, intrigued. But when he paused at the corner to let a wagon lumber past, she caught a glimpse of his profile, and her life abruptly changed. She knew the shape of that nose and the set of that chin, knew the contours of that mouth with an intimacy that made her flush. He was the man who had occupied her thoughts so much of the day. It was Ryder Bingham.

The realization so unsettled her that for a moment Jillian sat frozen, her hands clenched around the handle of the parasol and her heart volleying in her chest. Then before she could lose her nerve, she leaned forward in the buggy. "Stop here, Noble," she ordered. "I have some shopping to do."

Without waiting for the coachman to assist her, Jill climbed out of the buggy and hurried up the street after Ryder's retreating figure. After what she had read in the newspapers, Jillian was sure why he was here. He was a rebel agent come for some clandestine purpose. And as she brushed past the people on the walk, she knew she had to see and talk to him no matter what had brought him to the Falls.

She saw him pause to look in the window of a shop, and for an instant she thought he was waiting for her there. But before she could approach him, he moved on, his long-legged stride quickly outdistancing her. At the next corner, Ryder turned left, and she nearly lost sight of him in the crowd of people gathered before the elegant tiered porches of the Cataract House. Somehow she managed to wade through the crush in time to see him turn at Bridge Street, toward the arching spans that led to Goat Island and the Falls.

As she followed him across the walkway, she was scarcely aware of the turbulent river that poured beneath, hardly saw the violent swirls and eddies, the whirlpools and leaping spray in the shallow rocky channel. She was too intent on her quarry to give more than a glance to the beauty all around her, and when she paused at the tollhouse on Bath Island to pay and sign the register, she took note of the name written above her own. It was Justin Mathews. Though he claimed a different identity, she knew the man she sought quite well, and her need to overtake him grew with every step she took.

Goat Island was the largest in a chain that lay scattered at the crest of the Falls, and though roads and paths crisscrossed its length and breadth, the greenery was lush and verdant. Bushes crowded to the edges of the path, and trees arched above her, enfolding her in a world of green and gold. But Jillian was oblivious to her surroundings while she tried to keep Ryder in sight. As she rushed after him, Jill could not keep from wondering if he had come this way by chance, to glimpse the wonders of nature, or because he was trying to escape her.

At the westernmost end of the island the foliage fell away, and a grassy slope gave way to the dazzling panorama of sky and water. To her right was the narrower stream of the Bridal Veil Falls, and beyond it lay the vast, uneven brink of the American cataract. Icy green water streamed toward the edge of the abyss and tumbled over to meld with the towering column of spray that mounted skyward. The appearance of the spectacle took Jillian by surprise, and in the moments it took her to tear her eyes away Ryder disappeared. She scanned the open space around her and the screen of trees that grew at the edges of the clearing, but he was nowhere to be seen.

Just when she had given up any hope of finding him, a couple emerged from a footpath, midway along the cliff. "Where does that lead?" she demanded as she approached them.

With evident difficulty, they turned their gazes from each other to her. "It goes to the Biddle Stairs and the base of the Falls," the man finally answered her.

"And did you pass anyone on the way?"

The woman nodded. "A tall fellow wearing a black hat."

It was all the information Jillian needed, and without even pausing to thank them, she headed down the path. She found that the Biddle Stairs were a tall, thin column of steps encased in oak and bolted to the side of the cliff, and though she peered over the railing, she could see no sign of Ryder below her. The stairs spiraled downward, their treads worn smooth by the feet of countless visitors, and she moved along the narrow passage as quickly as she dared. When she reached the foot of the steps, the Niagara River sprawled before her like liquid jade, calm and smooth after its turbulent journey over the Falls, its surface graced with lacework swirls of foam. The smell of the river was strong in the air, and the coolness from the water stole around her like a cloak. The path she had been following branched at the base of the steps, the left fork marked to the Horseshoe Falls and the other to the Cave of the Winds. Moving on instinct, Jillian took the path to the right toward the base of the American Falls. As she walked, she was aware of the rock face looming high above her, dour and pale gray, as if issuing a warning not to proceed. The cries of the gulls that circled overhead were shrill and eerie, and in spite of the warmth of the sun, Jillian found that she was shivering.

What would she do or say if she found Ryder? she wondered. Since he had obviously meant his presence in the city to be a secret, would he be angry she had followed him? Would he think she meant to expose him as the enemy agent he must surely be? And how could she reconcile her new loyalties to her country with her feelings for the rebel?

Then she topped a rise and saw Ryder just below her. He seemed deep in conversation with a second man, and as she approached, this second man disappeared into a makeshift building and returned carrying what appeared to be a length of dun-gray cloth. As Ryder shrugged it on, she could see it was an oilcloth slicker, and though he did not turn when she reached them, he clearly knew she was there.

"You coming for a closer look at the Falls, ma'am?" the second man asked, rounding on her. "No visit to Niagara is complete without a trip to the Cave of the Winds. It only costs a dollar, and you'll carry the memory all your life."

Jillian fumbled in her reticule for the price the man was asking. "Yes, I'd like to see the cave. Must I put on one of those?"

"Yes, ma'am, and you'd best take off your hat and veil. It can get mighty damp once you're down inside."

While the guide returned to the wooden hut for a second slicker, Jillian stripped off her gloves, worked the ties to her bonnet, and pulled the heavy netting free. It was only then that Ryder turned to look at her, and she stared back with equal intensity, trying to read some message in his eyes.

"Put this on right over your dress," the man instructed as he handed her the full-length duster. "And mind you, put up the hood to keep from getting wet."

Jillian did as the man bade her, and when her coat was buttoned up, he reached for a slicker of his own.

"I don't think we need a guide," Ryder put in, as if suddenly realizing the man meant to accompany them. "If we just follow the path, won't we find everything we came for?"

The guide shrugged once and set his raincoat aside. "Suit yourself," he agreed. "Just mind the steps down into the cave. They get slick this time of year."

Without a word, Ryder offered Jill his hand, and though she felt uncertain, she reached out to take it with her own. His grip was warm and firm, but at that simple contact a tingle of response shot up her arm. Ryder must have felt it, too, for his fingers tightened reassuringly.

They followed the well-marked path without conversation, though questions clamored in Jillian's mind. But then they came around an outcropping of ragged rock and stopped short, awed by the sight of the Falls. There was a torrent cascading toward them, ribbons of shimmering white, translucent in the sun. The water lay like an undulating curtain along the face of the cliff, like banners of delicate lace streaming in the wind. Above them, at the brink, the water was an icy green that slowly thinned and paled, turning opalescent and silvery as it fell. The flood seemed to hang above them, suspended between the earth and sky in brilliant veils of alabaster that frothed down as if to envelop them.

There was magic here. Jillian felt it in an instant, and when Ryder's hand curled more tightly around hers, she knew he felt it, too. There was peace in the midst of the tumult, solitude, a world apart. The air seemed spangled with gossamer threads; rainbows arced and glowed around them. Then all at once, they were rushing down the path, their cries of joy and exclamations of wonder lost in the roar of the Falls.

A series of bridges led them closer to the cataract, and as they moved along the slick wooden surfaces, they were enveloped by the grandeur. Mist swirled to seal them off from the world. The air grew thick and hoary. The torrent billowed above their heads, thundering down around them. The driving spray lashed against them, pearling on their skins and clothes, frosting the rugged landscape with a glaze that shone like glass. The rocks gleamed iridescent in the sunlight, and delicate ferns flourished in the crevices, fed by the perpetual rain. Ivory foam lathered at the base of the rocks, and through the boards beneath their feet they could see the spent water tumbling, turbulent and milky white, over a field of broken stones.

Then they were at the top of the steps that led to the cave, and they followed them carefully, slipping beneath the edge of the Bridal Veil Falls into a world that was even more isolated and mystical. They clung together for a moment to catch their breath, overwhelmed and invigorated by the beauty all around them. Inside the cave the light was soft and diffused, the air thick with rebounding spray, the roar of the tumult so wild and intense it might have passed for silence.

Slowly Jillian turned to look up at Ryder, seeing the flush of color in his face, the droplets of spray caught in his night-dark hair, and as she looked into his eyes, she saw exhilaraton and tenderness. For an instant a rueful smile touched the corners of his mouth, and then he was pulling her against him, lowering his head to taste her lips.

He kissed her once, twice, before his mouth settled over hers, and with the contact, weakness trickled down Jill's spine, sapping her strength and melting her knees beneath her. As if sensing her response, he bound her close, crushing her against his slicker-clad body, fitting her pliant form to his. Whether because of the place, the separation, or her need for him, delight swelled in Jillian's chest, leaving her warm and strangely giddy, quaking in his arms.

Ryder kissed her tenderly and long, his lips moving over hers, his tongue seeking the familiar contours of her mouth. He explored the depths of her, touching her tongue with his, savoring both the sweetness of her mouth and the joy of their reunion. At the intimate contact, a low moan of pleasure rose in her throat, but the sound was lost and muffled by the tumult all around them. Still, her eagerness was evident in the way she touched him, brushing his face with trembling hands, tangling her fingers in his wind-blown hair. How long they clung together Jillian hardly knew, but finally Ryder raised his head.

"I wasn't sure who was following me," he breathed. "I hoped somehow it was you, but I couldn't take the chance."

But Jillian did not want to hear more, was not ready to let the war intrude on a moment of such enchantment, a moment so filled with unexpected wonder. Instead she stretched up and silenced him with a kiss. In her wish to keep reality at bay, she became the aggressor, claiming the solace of his lips, curving her body to the hardness of his. Knowing that their time together would be fleeting, she wanted to absorb all the warmth and tenderness he was capable of giving, to drive away all thoughts of their loyalties and the war. In the maelstrom of the falling water they kissed until they were breathless and dizzy from the contact, until their pulses throbbed and roared in their ears like the thundering Niagara. Passion tingled like the mist in her veins, renewing, intoxicating, vital. They clung together desperately, as if at any moment their tiny insular world would somehow come apart.

At length, with great reluctance, Ryder backed away, and Jillian saw the time had come to give up magic for reality. Now she would ask her accusing questions and hear his damning answers. It was not something she wanted to do, but she knew it was inevitable.

"What are you doing here?" she began, her tone concerned and almost scolding. "Why have you returned to the North when your safety is in jeopardy?"

He stood for a moment staring down into her eyes, seeing fear for him, confusion, and a vital lambent glow that might well have passed for love. He knew he should not tell her his reasons for being in Niagara Falls; it would reveal things she could not know, compromise too much. The choice that lay before him was a simple one: He could tell the truth or he could lie. There was no question that he could trust Jill with his life; she had proved her loyalty weeks before. But he could not bring himself to explain things that could expose the plans of his confederates and cost them both their lives.

"I had business to attend to," he finally hedged, "things I couldn't do in Canada."

His reply was shallow and evasive, and Jillian was not appeased. "You're connected to the Confederate raiders, aren't you? Or are you here scouting for the rebels?"

"No, Jilly, no," he murmured, trying to convince her.

But Jill stood her ground, shrugging his hand from her arm. "Don't lie to me, Ryder. I read the papers. You're one of the men who tried to capture the *Michigan* at Sandusky, or you're the vanguard of some vile attack the Southerners are planning."

He heard the change of allegiance in her words, the altering of attitudes that had been the basis for their personal truce. Apprehension assailed him at the expression of unexpected sentiments, and he had the unnerving feeling he did not know her anymore. Somehow during the intervening weeks Jill had changed, turned into a stranger. It made him wonder about her reasons for following him and if it was still possible to trust her with the truth.

Jillian took his silence for acquiescence, proof that her suspicions were well founded. She had hoped there would be another explanation for Ryder's presence in Niagara Falls: that he was heading home to Wilmington, that he had come for her at last. The latter had been a foolish hope, one she had dared not consider as she followed him. Now she wished that it were so, wished that he had come to rescue her. She wanted so much to leave all this behind, to escape her empty life and her overbearing father-in-law. Disappointment and anger mingled in her heart, and though she was not sure she wanted to hear what Ryder had to say, she pressed him for an answer.

"Well, which is it? Did you pirate the ships on Lake Erie, or shall we be entertaining rebel visitors?"

Ryder's jaw hardened at the bite in her words, and he chose to tell her the truth. "I was with the men at Sandusky Bay," he told her. "I was with them and glad to be. But all I want right now is to get safely back to Canada."

Though it was not quite rational, Jillian believed him. But as always his motives haunted her. "But why, Ryder, why were you with them? You've done your part in the war. Why did you deem it necessary to risk your life by capturing American ships?"

There was no time to explain his reasons; they were too complex for her to comprehend in the few minutes they had left to them. "I have a score to settle with the Yankees, Jillian. Can't we just leave it at that?"

"No, Ryder, please. I need to understand."

His expression became cold and impassive. "I don't know why you always try to understand things that are impossible to explain."

It was a sharp rebuke, but it fueled Jillian's determination. "Please, Ryder, I need to know. If you can't explain it now, come to me later. We could meet and be together."

It was a tempting offer, but he was suddenly in doubt of her loyalty when before he had been so sure.

"And if I agree to meet you, how do I know there won't be Yankees waiting for me instead?"

His unexpected cruelty took her breath, and before words of outrage could spring to her lips, she reached across and slapped him.

The sound of the blow seemed to reverberate above the roar of the Falls, and they both drew back, stunned by what she'd done. There was horror in her eyes and dawning contrition in his. For the space of a heartbeat neither spoke, but when they did, apologies spilled between them.

"I'm sorry, Ryder! I didn't mean to hit you."

"No, Jillian, I was wrong. I know you'd never betray me!"

Then she was in his arms, weeping wildly against the front of his oilcloth slicker, burrowing against the wall of his chest. He cradled her close, his lips against her temple, brushing the curl of honey hair that had escaped the hood of the raincoat.

"Oh, God, Jilly," he breathed, crushing her against him. "What's to become of us? We can't let either our loyalties or the war turn us into enemies."

She clung to him, frightened by what had happened, by the realization that the changes in her life had nearly destroyed something precious and wonderful.

She turned to him with brimming eyes, knowing by instinct the only thing that could mend the rift between them. "Then come to me tonight. Let me prove that you can trust me."

"I do trust you," he assured her. "I was wrong to say I doubted you."

"Then meet me at ten tonight," she persisted.

"No, Jilly, no. It would be mad to even consider it."

"And I suppose taking you from the train at Rochester was sane, nursing an escaped Confederate was infinitely wise and rational?"

It was true. She had taken terrible risks to see to his safety, to help him escape. Now she seemed willing to risk even more. Did the days they'd had together mean so much to her? Did they mean as much to her as they meant to him?

"It would put you in needless danger," he argued. "What if someone sees us together?"

Jill shook her head. "Believe me, no one will. There's a gazebo at the back of the Walsh property, down along the river. I go there all the time, and no one ever questions me."

She could sense the scope of Ryder's resistance and did her best to counter it.

"No one will see us, Ryder. I promise you. My father-in-law has a political meeting this evening, and he's often gone until quite late."

"And what about the servants?"

"They won't bother us, either. Most of them go home at suppertime, and the housekeeper is always in bed by nine o'clock."

Still Ryder was determined to refuse her. "Jilly, this is crazy. You're safe now; no one knows you helped me escape. Why would you want to meet when it can only lead to disaster?"

"You know, Ryder, as well as I. You know why it's necessary."

Indeed he knew; he understood her reasons for wanting to meet him. But he remained adamant, refusing for her sake.

"We can't part like this," she pleaded, "not after what we've done and said. Can you leave things as they are? Can you just walk away?"

He wished he could leave her; it would have been so much better for both of them. But he, too, was aware of the growing gulf between them. It was the same terrifying breach that had split their nation in two. He did want to hold her and cherish her, find a unity in fact as well as in words. Even though the anger and suspicion were gone, he was still aware of her nagging doubt and of his shame for how he'd treated her.

But she had suddenly begun to use an even more persuasive ploy to gain his acquiescence. While he was wrestling with the contradictions inside himself, she was trailing kisses down his throat, pressing her body into his, hinting at delight untold. It made him want the wondrous peace they'd found together, the kind of solace he'd never hoped to find again. In spite of his best resolves, he found his arms had tightened around her, clutching her, binding her close.

To agree to meet her tonight would be a disastrous mistake. Ryder knew it certainly. But Jill's body was so warm and vital against his own, and her lips were so accessible. He lowered his head almost grudgingly and took advantage of her nearness.

The temptation of what she was proposing eroded his will. How many nights had Jillian haunted his dreams? How many days had he taken refuge in his memories of her?

They did need the intimacy of loving to force the anger and suspicion from their minds, to erase from their hearts the words that had threatened everything. They needed to be together once more before he went away. It was madness, but necessity. His mouth closed over hers, and he was lost, lost to the devastating perfection of their passion, lost to the need to claim her as his just one more time.

There was nothing in his barren world as precious as the woman beside him. Without her he was empty, his life nothing but vengeance and fury. He needed Jillian to temper his anger and soothe his pain. He kissed her deeply, giving desire sway, letting the promise of sweetness and unity dispel his doubts and suspicions.

As they clung together in defiance of all that would keep them apart, a voice echoed above the roar of the Falls, shattering their solitude. "You all right down there? You comin' out soon?" The guide had ventured after them out of curiosity or concern.

"We'll be right along," Ryder shouted back.

"You will come tonight, won't you?" Jillian pleaded as he hustled her back over the bridges, through the shrouds of welling mist.

"I can't promise," Ryder hedged. As reality reasserted itself he knew he should refuse, but he could not bear to extinguish the hope in Jillian's eyes, could not bear to disappoint her, or himself.

"Ryder, please—" she began, but the guide was at the head of the trail to greet them.

"Ain't that the grandest sight you've ever seen? Nothing like it in all nature."

Ryder nodded, agreeing with the man. "It was everything we'd hoped and more."

"Then you tell your friends. Tell them what you saw at the Falls."

The man disappeared into the hut to get their things, returning to hand Jillian her bonnet and veil and Ryder his low-crowned Stetson.

"You from around here?" the guide asked, making conversation.

"Yes," Jillian answered.

"No," Ryder replied.

"The Falls brings all kinds of folks together," the guide continued, eyeing them. "It's a wellspring of romance."

Ryder obviously did not like the trend of the conversation and dredged up a question about the Falls to turn aside the fellow's curiosity. While the guide answered, Jillian tied her bonnet in place, then hesitated, hoping for one last chance to talk to Ryder. But he seemed totally intent on the information the guide was imparting.

Finally breaking in, she bade him good-bye. "Thank you, Mr. Mathews. Your company made my visit to the Falls far more stimulating than I ever imagined it could be."

She saw Ryder fight to suppress a grin. "It was my pleasure to escort you."

Realizing there would be no more chance for conversation, Jillian turned toward the Biddle Stairs. As Ryder watched her go, he prayed he'd have the strength to refuse her invitation. It would be wrong to meet her tonight; it was insanity to even consider it. Yet as he watched her move up the path, he did not know if he possessed the resolve it would take to stay away from the gazebo, the strength of will it would take to deny himself all Jillian had to give.

He could just barely make out her figure in the darkness, her flowing black clothes blending into the shadows at the foot of the garden. Only the light that seeped out into the night when she opened the door of the mansion had given him any hint that Jillian was on her way to meet him. As she drew closer, he could make out the paleness of her face and hands and the nimbus of her fair hair flowing down her back.

She passed within yards of where he stood hidden in the foliage, but his apprehension kept him from approaching her. Instead he watched as she mounted the steps to the gazebo, saw her silhouetted against the water as she descended on the far side and prowled along the riverbank. She retraced her steps more slowly, scanning the shadows that lay thick at this end of the yard.

"Ryder?" His name was little more than a whisper, but it seemed to echo in his ears. "Ryder?"

The time had come for him to make his presence known, but instead he waited, wondering if they were truly alone. He wanted to trust Jillian, wanted to believe that there was no trick in the meeting she had planned. But after the discovery of her new allegiances and the hours he'd had to brood on them, he was suspicious of her loyalties.

A few yards from his hiding place, Jillian paused to stare across the water, and Ryder could see the moonlight skim her exotic features, catch and shimmer in her hair. Then, with a barely audible sigh, she turned back toward the house, her shoulders drooping dejectedly, a bleak expression in her eyes. The sight of her disappointment struck him like a physical blow, and Ryder was angry and ashamed for having doubted her.

As she passed the bank of greenery, he reached out to catch her wrist and felt a jolt of fright run through her. But when she realized who it was, her arms came around his neck as she pressed close beside him.

"Oh, Ryder, you are here! I was so afraid you wouldn't come."

"I was just watching to be sure you weren't followed," he told her. "I wanted to make sure we were alone." The half-truths came all too fluently to his lips, but she did not seem to hear the contradictions in his tone or sense the self-loathing balled deep in his belly.

Instead she was smiling up at him, retreating to catch his hand. "Come into the gazebo," she invited. "It's so much more comfortable there."

Ryder let her lead him across the lawn and up the steps, smelling the sweetness of the roses that wreathed the summerhouse and the tang of her perfume. It was cool inside, darker than it had been on the riverbank, but he had no trouble seeing that joy had replaced the sadness in her eyes.

"I'm glad you came. I was so afraid you would think better of it once I left you at the Falls."

He had thought better of it—repeatedly. He had argued with himself while he bathed at one of the side-street bathhouses, while he was barbered in the shop at the International Hotel, and all through dinner in the dining room. He was sure he had rid himself of the preposterous notion of meeting her, but as he sat in the hotel saloon watching the hands of the clock creep toward the appointed hour, he had grown tense and restless. Biting back a livid curse, he had finally downed his drink and headed toward the river. He knew exactly what a fool he was in going to meet Jilly, knew exactly what he was risking. He was furious with himself for his lack of restraint, furious with Jillian for enticing him. But in spite of his best resolves, he found it impossible to stay away. Only his newly fostered caution had made him wait in the bushes in case Jillian had brought Yankees to their meeting. But instead she had come alone, and he was glad she had proved his suspicions wrong.

"It's so good to have you with me," she breathed, pulling him down to sit beside her on the wide cushioned bench that skirted the interior of the summerhouse. "When I left you that night at the station, I thought I'd never see you again."

He saw the hope and sadness mingled in her eyes and did his best to deny the answering emotions swelling in his chest.

"That's the way it should have been," he told her savagely, "the way that would have been best for both of us."

Before she could make him admit that he had felt the pain of that parting as deeply as she, Ryder lowered his mouth to hers, taking it with sudden ruthless abandon. Her lips curved beneath his own, soft and incredibly sweet, a refuge of delight or a trap for the unwary. As he held her, his hands roved the contours of her face, feeling the sheen of her flawless skin, the strength of the bones that lay beneath it. He caught the sheaf of tumbled hair in his hands, crushing the length in his fists. As he did, the heavy gilded strands curled around his wrists, like silken shackles binding him.

He continued to kiss her harshly, furiously, fighting emotions he preferred to deny. But Jill answered his touch with an acceptance that was devoid of apprehension, acquiesced willingly to the barely leashed violence in his caress. She met his fervor with a calm that was the antithesis of his turmoil, made his dark emotions her own, gave herself with a wordless understanding that seemed soul deep and infinite. Frustration, pain, and confusion seemed to flow from him to her, to be absorbed by the vast sweet peace he sensed inside her.

A moan of acknowledgment rose in his throat, and though he held her as tightly as before, the terrible need to disavow his feelings was ebbing away. Instead he took refuge in her tenderness, sought safety in her arms. She was a haven of enchantment and delight away from the life he was forced to live, an oasis of serenity and peace in a parched and hostile world. He drank deep, wanting her nearness to soothe him, wanting her compassion to assuage the bitterness in his heart. Jillian seemed to know what he needed when he himself did not. She stroked him until he felt reassured and comforted, held him until he was chastened and absolved.

"Oh, Jilly," Ryder admitted at last. "Oh, Jilly, I've missed you so."

At his words, she offered herself with wordless generosity, seeking the texture of his mouth with hers, threading her fingers through his hair. Her lips were moist, clinging, searching the contours of his own. Her touch was soothing, consoling, tender, and as he accepted all she had to give, the familiar magic swelled between them. It took them far from a country at war, far from the confusion of their conflicting allegiances, far from all that could keep them apart. The wonder of their closeness held reality at bay, and they were lost in the soft, sweet-scented darkness and each other.

As they kissed, Ryder sprawled back against the cushions and pulled her over him, liking the weight of her body above him, liking the way they fit together. Sensing the welcome he could not seem to express, Jillian stirred, pressing closer, sending a bolt of giddy desire sizzling through his blood.

With his fingers plowing furrows through her hair, he brought the lush curves of her mouth against the narrower planes of his. With infinite thoroughness, he tasted the deeply indented corners, traced the delicious width at the bow, drank deep of her womanly vulnerability. With the tip of his tongue, he stroked the opening of her lips, explored the place where the outer texture went even more smooth and satiny. He touched her tongue with his, feeling hers twine, circle, and surrender to his probe.

Pleasure grew within him, a spreading, sprouting ache in his chest; a warm, sweet wanting that sent roots deep into his belly. It crept along his limbs, leaving them heavy with exquisite anticipation, weighted with a curious billowing languor. He sighed and Jillian's sigh merged with his; he moaned and she drank in the proof of his longing.

Moving as if in a dream, his hand slid from her shoulder to the swell of her breast, feeling by its unencumbered softness that she was naked beneath her gown. A murmur of appreciation rose in his throat as he brushed aside the buttons and layers of lace to cup her warm soft flesh against his fingers, to contour her fullness to the curve of his palm. He heard Jill gasp in response to the intimacy of his touch, felt her body quiver in expectation of the pleasure he could give.

Murmuring breathless endearments, he thrust the screen of fabric aside, baring her shoulders, letting the moonlight fall unencumbered on the lustrous swell of her breasts. She was so beautiful as she lay above him: the pale pearly glow of her skin enhanced by the half-light, the sheaf of her honey hair tangling around them, the smoldering desire glowing like embers in her eyes. He wanted to crystallize the moment, seal it away, hold it safe forever in the recesses of his mind.

As he watched, entranced, she moved above him, her hands sliding over him, loosening his necktie, opening the buttons on his shirt. A whisper of night air drifted across his skin, and then her hands were skimming over him, deft and unfailingly gentle. They brushed the turn of his jaw, lingered in the hollow of his throat, raked through the coal-black hair that sprouted just below it. She brushed his paps with trailing fingers, and when Ryder gave a helpless gasp, she returned and dropped her head to take one nipple in her mouth. Her tongue swirled over the sensitive peak, slick and erotic, teasing and provocative. Delight ran through him like a tide.

Without breaking the contact for more than a few moments, Jillian reared back to remove his boots, to deftly work the fasteners of his trousers and push the fabric down his legs. In the tussling, her gown had fallen away, and they sprawled bare and elemental, entwined in the dark. Her smoothness came in contact with his hair-roughened skin, her curving contours molded to the angular hardness of him. Tangled together in the silence of the late-summer night, they were oblivious to everything but each other.

They kissed long and fervently, fierce and tenderly, sharing their bodies and emotions as they had never thought to share them again. As the ardor grew between them, Jillian offered him herself, the scope of her tender emotions, the moist sheath of her femininity. They came together slowly, their joining the poignant resolution of their two disparate lives. When she had fully taken the length of him, when the unity was complete, Jillian stretched back along his body to claim his lips in a kiss that was tender, shy, and sweet. He whispered love words into her mouth, reassuring her, inciting her. Then her tongue probed deep, seeking the cavern of his mouth in a way that was the antithesis of the more intimate penetration.

They lay tenderly fused, totally one, lost to everything around them. As they kissed, Ryder's breathing became shallow and fast. Tension gathered along his spine and ran prickling down his limbs. He was hovering, shuddering, filled with need, but Jillian would not be hurried. She played with his lips, stroked his face and hair, and he accepted the ministrations with a barely leashed eagerness, inching toward the point where pain and pleasure merged. He wanted to prolong the moment for the solace Jillian offered him, wanted to cling to this precious time when there was no world but theirs. Yet even as he tried to hold back, he felt the strain of desperation, the spreading, surging need to find satisfaction in her arms.

Only when she sensed he had moved beyond his ability to wait did Jillian urge him onward. His body rose with hers, arched and twisted in tandem with her sinuous movements. The pleasure built, swelled, soared, until it eclipsed reality. His world began to spin, heat spiraling, need swirling, the crisis gathering in a whirl of blind sensation. There was affirmation in the midst of the tumult, a renewal in the mute communication they had always known. Through waves of reeling ecstasy, he heard Jilly cry his name as her body tightened and convulsed, binding him deep, so deep inside her. She was with him as he reached the peak, united by the magic their bodies wove together. She held him close as sanity flew away, was part of him as they reveled in the welling bliss that nothing on earth could dispel.

When the rush of joy receded, they collapsed in each other's arms, hands clutching, breath pooling, bodies tangled close. Caught in the languorous aftermath, they drifted helplessly, and when Ryder finally roused, he found Jillian nestled in his arms, as if they had the night to spend together.

Smiling, he watched her as she dozed. Her features were soft and vulnerable in the half-light; the spill of honey hair seemed to snare the mist of moonbeams. He drew her nearer, thinking how precious this woman had become to him, how she had filled the void in his life when he was lost and empty. He slid gentle fingers across her shoulder, trailed them slowly down her arm. Until she had begun to give her body and her tenderness, he had not known the extent of his need. Until she had begun to share the whole of herself, he had not recognized his solitude.

Jillian was all the woman any man could want, the ideal mate it might take a lifetime to find.

She's good for me, he reflected hazily, *so very good. She's the other half that makes me whole.*

At another juncture in his life, that realization would have brought delight and comfort; it would have been a prelude to a brilliant future they would eagerly have planned. But their loyalties and the war had made that future impossible, and the knowledge brought the terrible sting of loneliness. Reluctantly Ryder stirred, knowing there was nothing to be gained by delaying the inevitable, knowing every moment he spent at Jillian's side would make their parting more difficult.

"Jilly," he breathed, "Jilly, it will do neither your reputation nor mine any good if someone finds us so blatantly compromised."

She stirred, stretched, and smiled at his words. "Did you know that you and my father are the only one's who've ever called be Jilly?" she asked sleepily, running a hand across his chest.

Only men who loved her had the right to call her that, Ryder found himself thinking, and in that unguarded moment the scope of his feelings for Jill came clear to him. He did not welcome the unexpected revelation, for it reaffirmed his need to go. It made him realize that every minute they spent together was fraught with danger, that being here was tempting fate to callously destroy the precious thing they found together. In that instant he knew he could not tell Jillian how he felt, not when he had no home, no life, no future to offer her. Nor should he allow himself the luxury of loving her when any day could be his last.

Filled with the need to escape, he disentangled himself from her and began to rummage for his clothing. His coat and shirt were bunched around his shoulders, and once he found his pants and boots, he rose to tug them on.

"Are you leaving?" Her voice was thick with disappointment.

He reached across to catch her hand, feeling the nubbly rosettes of the ring he had made and given her. "Jillian, you know I have to go. It was lunacy to come here in the first place."

It was only the tenderness of his touch that dispelled the hurt his words had caused. "But, Ryder, where are you going?"

"Back to Canada, I suppose."

"I don't even know why you're here, what brought you to Niagara Falls."

He knew her curiosity was natural, just as he knew it was impossible to tell her less than the truth.

"I was with the men who captured the steamers on Lake Erie as a means of attacking the *Michigan* and freeing our men from the prison on Johnson's Island. But as we approached the gunboat, the signal we expected from shore didn't come. Finally we decided to send someone to find out what was wrong."

"And that someone was you."

Ryder nodded as he fumbled with his tie.

"Had the Yankees found out about your plans?"

"Oh, yes. They'd prepared quite a welcome for us. It didn't take me long to discover the trap they'd laid, but when I rowed back to warn the ship, the *Philo Parsons* was gone."

"Gone?" Jillian gasped, sitting up as she struggled with the fasteners of her gown. "What happened?"

Bingham shook his head, returning to sit beside her. "I don't know. They must have gotten tired of waiting and given up the plan altogether."

"And they abandoned you?" Jillian was angry and incredulous. "They left you at Sandusky to take your chances with the Yankees?"

As difficult as it was to admit, his silence gave assent.

"But if they abandoned you, why are you going back to Canada? Surely what happened absolves you of any loyalty to their cause."

"It's not just the cause anymore. This war has become personal; I have a score to settle with the Yankees."

He had told her the same thing before, and she had no more reason to understand it now than then. "What score do you have to settle with the Yankees?"

Ryder sighed. He should have known she would not be appeased by simple answers and would demand more than he knew how to explain.

"I've lost a great deal in the war, Jilly," he admitted with difficulty, "more than my ship and my livelihood. My father was killed at Antietam, and after he was gone, my mother just wasted away. My younger brother died of consumption while we were in prison, and there wasn't a thing I could do to ease his pain."

She saw the anguish in his face and drew close in her need to assuage it. "I'm sorry, Ryder. Were you and your brother very close?"

He looked away and nodded. "Very close."

It seemed as if her persistence had finally breached that inner reserve, and he seemed ready to tell her his deepest feelings, to explain them to her at last.

"It's not just the losses, Jilly, it's the helplessness, the responsibility."

"What do you mean?"

"Men died because of my mistakes—not just Mitch but the men in my crew as well. Those deaths were my fault. They're on my conscience, and until I've done something to avenge them, I can never be really free."

His torment was so evident that it brought the sting of tears to her eyes. It would be useless to tell him that the men in his crew had known the risks, that his brother's death had come from things he had no way to rectify. But Ryder had long ago accepted the responsibility for what happened, and though words of denial sprang to her lips, she realized logic would have no sway.

"If I take part in raids, it's because I want to make the Yankees feel the things I've felt, know the hopelessness and anger I live with every day."

"And will having that revenge on the Yankees really make a difference? Destruction breeds destruction, Ryder. Bitterness breeds bitterness. Won't it hurt you even more to know that you've given others a reason for suffering?"

Jillian could feel Ryder's withdrawal the moment she spoke, sense the barriers between them being hastily reconstructed.

He rose and stood looking down at her with resignation in his eyes. "I knew you couldn't understand what I felt, wouldn't understand my reasons for continuing to fight."

"I do understand, Ryder. I understand your hurt, the responsibility you feel for what has happened. What I don't understand is how you can expect to make things better by trying to right one wrong with another. It's not the way life works, and in the end your need for vengeance will destroy you."

She came to stand beside him, reaching out to catch his arm. "Ryder, please, think about what I'm saying. You matter too much to me to see you eaten alive by something so useless and obsessive."

"This is what I've chosen to do, Jillian," he told her. "It's the only way I know to live with what has happened. My only hope for either revenge or absolution is to settle my score with the Yankees."

She could see the fallacy in his decision, but it was useless to argue when she could not change his mind. They had reached an impasse, as Jillian well knew. Nothing she could say would help Ryder change what he had accepted as truth; nothing she could do would ease his suffering. He had come to her as he was now —angry, grim, and bitter. And though they had found momentary solace together, she had forced the wedge of their disparate loyalties between them once again.

They stood motionless for a time: Ryder facing the river with his hands thrust in his pockets and his shoulders hunched protectively, Jillian staring at the expanse of his back, wanting to reach out and hold him. She wanted to tell him she loved him, to convince him that somehow he would find a way to resolve his guilt. But she could not say those things now, not when he had turned away from her. Instead she needed the silent reassurance just touching him would bring, needed it every bit as much as she sensed Ryder did.

It took every ounce of her courage to let her hands creep around his waist, took every bit of daring she could muster to press her cheek against him. She did it, though, knowing his rejection could hurt her more than anything else he'd ever done. But after a moment, she felt him lean into her embrace, felt his hands close over hers, holding them in place. They stood that way for a time, letting their closeness ease away the antagonism that had sprung up between them, letting it reestablish the understanding that seemed to flow between them so much more readily in silence.

Finally Ryder turned to her, looked down into her eyes. "Oh, God, Jilly," he breathed wearily. "Where will all this end?"

"We've come to this, Ryder. We've had more than either of us had ever hoped to have. Let's just try to trust in fate, in fate and in each other."

He shook his head in resignation but said nothing more. Instead he kissed her, slowly, sadly, as a means of saying good-bye. And though she did not want to let him go, she knew their parting was necessary. Tears were on her cheeks when he raised his head at last, and he brushed the silvery droplets aside before he turned away.

She watched him go, not knowing if he would cross the border safely, not knowing how she could live her life without him. He moved quickly but cautiously, the lithe unconscious grace of his long-legged stride taking him from her. She watched until he disappeared into the veil of willow trees along the bank of the river, watched until he was lost in the darkness and silence. When he was out of sight, she dropped her head to her hands and began to weep once more.

Chapter Ten

"A MUTINY! MY God, Jamie! A mutiny?" Ryder hurled the shirt he had just removed across the bedroom in disgust. "Is that why the *Philo Parsons* was gone when I rowed back to report?"

Ryder had spent most of the night on trains returning to Toronto, and his patience was worn thin. When he had entered the boarding house, he'd had nothing in mind except catching a little sleep, but Jamie had pounced on him the moment he came in the door. His friend's concern had been evident in the way he had trailed him up the stairs, in the questions he'd asked. But it was Ryder who had asked the more pressing questions and had been stunned by Bradford's answers.

"From what I hear, the men on the *Philo Parsons* pleaded with Beall to give up the attack on the *Michigan*," Jamie reported.

"And just as well, too," Ryder put in bitterly, "since the Yankees had laid a trap."

"When Beall refused to abort the mission, they banded together and told him they would not support him if he chose to continue his course into Sandusky Bay. Beall argued, as you might well imagine, then pleaded with them to wait until you came back with a report. But when they refused to listen, he drew up a statement of their cowardice, then dared them all to sign it."

"And they did, I suppose."

Bradford nodded. "I think he meant to shame them into attacking the *Michigan*, but the ploy failed. They signed the document to a man, except for Burley and Beall himself."

Ryder shook his head in regret. Even though he had meant to warn John Beall of the danger and counsel retreat, he could not believe that without proof of danger Confederate soldiers had refused to fight.

"Then what happened?"

"Beall had no choice but to leave. He did the only thing he could do: He gave orders to set off for Canada."

"Leaving me stranded," Ryder put in, "as if those damned shirkers cared."

"In the throes of panic, I doubt those men even considered your predicament. But if they did, I suppose they figured that since you'd outwitted the Yankees once, you'd be able to do it again."

"Well, I'm glad they didn't misplace their confidence," Bingham put in cuttingly. "Though it seemed like pretty long odds to use the papers you gave me again."

"Is that how you got across the border?"

Ryder sat down and pulled off his boots. "I used the papers just as I did before."

"Then thank God you had them with you!" Jamie breathed.

"Yes, I did." Ryder grinned for emphasis. "I thanked Him more than once for the papers and enough money to buy me passage."

"Did you go north and cross at Windsor?"

"No, I went back to Niagara City, since there I knew what to expect." That decision had not been tempered by his need to see Jillian, Ryder assured himself. Their meeting on the street had been by purest chance.

Though he did not tell Bradford, it had been ridiculously easy to use the papers as he had some weeks before. When he left Jill at the gazebo, he had simply walked up to the station on Falls Street, taken the stage to the Suspension Bridge depot, and waited for the 12:35 train to come rumbling down the tracks. There had been a new Union captain checking the passengers, and he had given Ryder's papers hardly more than a glance before allowing him to board the train.

"Since you know about the mutiny, I assume that the *Philo Parsons* reached Canada and safety."

Jamieson nodded. "They put in at Sandwich the next morning, then cut the injection pipes to sink the ship. Beall came directly to Toronto to report to Thompson. That's how I found out what had happened."

"And where is Beall now?" Ryder asked, wondering how the commander of the mission had dealt with such a devastating failure.

"Thompson suggested that Beall make himself scarce for a while since Toronto is full of Yankee spies. As far as I know, he went hunting up north somewhere."

Ryder sighed and looked longingly at the bed. "Well, the debacle is over now, at least," he concluded wearily.

"Not if I know Beall. He's already come up with another plan to buy and arm a ship. He means to have another try at the *Michigan*."

"Well, he'll do it without my help," Ryder murmured, thinking how differently the mission had turned out than what he'd hoped or expected. There was a bitter ache of failure deep inside him that came with the realization that his plans for revenge against the Yankees had been dashed by the failure to capture the gunboat. The things Jamie told him made him feel more hopeless than before, but at last the smaller man seemed to sense Bingham's exhaustion and shuffled toward the door.

"I'll let you get some sleep," he told Ryder. "Things will look brighter once you're rested."

Ryder doubted that, but he did not voice his pessimism.

When he heard the door to the room close behind his friend, Bingham stretched out on the bed and burrowed deep into the pillows.

"A mutiny," he muttered in disgust. "Who'd have expected a mutiny?"

There was no answer to his question, and though there was still much in his future to consider, he sighed and closed his eyes.

Jillian primped before the hall tree mirror, smoothing the curls against her neck, plucking at the frilly mourning cap the maid had pinned atop her head. She fussed with the lace that edged the deep décolleté and readjusted the pointed waist of her new black gown, never taking note of its flattering lines, not seeing how the night-dark silk complemented her tawny beauty. Instead she worried that her father-in-law would not approve of her appearance, tonight of all nights, when she would be acting as his hostess for the very first time.

She had driven herself and Mrs. Pryor to near distraction with the constant changes in the menu and arrangements for the intimate dinner party the congressman was hosting. It did not help that Mrs. Pryor had accepted the situation with poor grace and had been at first outspoken and critical, then silent and sullen about Jillian's new role in the household. As she stepped into the dining room, Jill prayed the housekeeper would not do anything out of spite to spoil the evening ahead.

The table laid before her was little short of spectacular. The ecru damask tablecloth pooled onto the floor at the corners of the table, its creamy color the perfect foil for the dark mahogany wainscoting and blue silk wallpaper that swathed the dining room walls. The cloth was laid with ten settings of fine gold-rimmed porcelain; gleaming silver flatware and an array of cut crystal glasses attended every place. The fluffy golden chrysanthemums at the center of the table burst from the huge hand-painted vase that matched the candlesticks on either side and the tiny china place cards Jill had lettered the night before. Everything was in readiness, and Jillian was terrified.

Perhaps it was foolish to be so nervous, she chided herself, laying a hand against her midriff as if it could quell the fluttering. This was to be a small dinner party by Walsh's usual standards. But he would be judging her abilities as a hostess tonight, and she was striving for perfection.

As she hovered over the table, she heard her father-in-law's footsteps on the stairs and rushed out into the hall to greet him. If he had reservations about the arrangements or her looks, he would surely voice them now.

Walsh was checking his watch against the tall grandfather clock at the foot of the stairs and looked quite handsome in a black faille suit, snowy shirt, and speckled tie. But the moment he turned to face Jillian, his expression became harsh and judgmental. She felt his eyes move over her, taking in the cut of her gown and the elaborate sweep of her hair. She waited for his verdict, steeling herself to bear his comments stoically. He only nodded and murmured, "You'll do, girl, you'll do."

It was not a compliment, but it was not criticism either, and Jillian had time to breathe a sigh of relief before the doorbell began to jangle.

The dinner guests were all Gerald's close friends, the only visitors appropriate to a house in mourning, and Jillian had met most of them at church or through the women's relief organization. That fact made her a little less nervous about how the evening would go, and as Walsh led his guests in to dinner, Jillian felt her apprehension begin to ease.

Though the meal was not an elaborate one, she had selected every course with care, serving her guests leek soup from a covered tureen, overseeing the arrival of the second course of lamb cutlets and green beans. Jill managed to converse cordially with the men who sat on either hand, while Gerald carved the huge baked ham that was to be served with an apricot glaze. The main course, the julienne potatoes, and the garden vegetables spiced with ginger were greeted with enthusiasm by her guests. She acknowledged their compliments with a satisfied smile, though she could eat very little herself. At last a compote of plums and apples was brought up from the kitchen, a tribute to the cook's artistry and skill. They finished the meal with petit fours decorated with swirls of icing, and as Jillian rose from the table to lead the ladies into the parlor, Gerald gave her an almost imperceptible nod. It was grudging approval for the evening she had planned, and Jillian was satisfied.

She felt utterly content as she settled herself in an ornate slipper chair by the fire. She had done her best to make the dinner pleasurable and had been duly acknowledged for her efforts. While the men had their brandy and cigars in the dining room, she presided over a few minutes of friendly feminine gossip. Gerald Walsh was acknowledging her abilities at last, and she hoped this was the beginning of a more equitable relationship between them.

The coffee service had just arrived when the men filed into the parlor, and once everyone had been served, Mrs. Mott took her place at the piano and ran through a repertoire of popular songs. As the music swelled through the elegant, well-appointed room, Jillian took note of her guests' enjoyment and slowly let down her guard. The dinner party had been a success, and she was finally able to revel in her accomplishments.

Once the entertainment was over, the guests broke into smaller groups. The women gathered near the fire to swap anecdotes about their children and discuss plans for the forthcoming bazaar to raise funds for the soldiers' relief, while the men's discussions turned to the progress of the war. As Jill made her rounds as hostess, offering another cup of coffee or a second sweet to those who seemed to want them, she paused by one particularly boisterous group standing near the door.

Her interest and her ire were unwillingly piqued by the sentiments one of the men was voicing.

"I hope Sherman burns Atlanta to the ground!" he espoused vehemently. "I hope he burns every barn and house just as Sheridan is doing in the Shenandoah Valley!"

Jillian understood the reason for the man's venom; he had lost a son at Vicksburg. Still his views brought angry color to her cheeks. Couldn't he see beyond his bitterness to the consequences of the acts he was endorsing? Didn't he realize that as a result of such atrocities, innocent people would die? Before she could censor her words or think how the others might receive them, Jill spoke up, giving an answer he had obviously not expected.

"That seems a rather uncharitable point of view, Mr. Melvin,"

she offered softly, "since there's nothing to be gained by despoil-
ing the South."

Melvin's florid face took on a darker hue as he rounded on his
hostess. "And just what would you suggest we do, Mrs. Walsh,
to put these rebs in their place?"

"If the nation is to be reunited as President Lincoln hopes,"
Jillian began reasonably, "what can possibly be gained by burning Southern farms and leaving rebel families homeless?"

That Jillian's views found no sympathy with the others was
immediately obvious. All conversation stilled, and her guests
turned to stare at her incredulously.

Across the room Gerald Walsh was glaring at his daughter-in-
law, expressing his disapproval with a threatening frown. Realizing his displeasure and the impending unpleasantness, Jillian
tried to demur and slip away. But the men closed ranks around
her, like hunting dogs snapping at the heels of a cornered doe.

"You condone conciliation, Mrs. Walsh?" one of the men
baited her. "You think we should simply forgive our Southern
brothers and let them go their way?"

Jillian straightened perceptibly as she tried to meet his challenge. "Destruction breeds destruction, sir. Bitterness breeds bitterness." Jillian's answer was precise; it was the same one she
had given Ryder nearly a month before, the argument much the
same as one they'd had over dinner at the boarding house in
Rochester.

"It will be difficult enough to bind the nation's wounds once
the war is over," she went on. "There is nothing to be gained by
inflicting additional hardships on the civilians."

"It's civilian support that keeps the Southern army in the
field," someone else put in. "Without the backing of the populace, the rebel troops would not be able to sustain their resistance."

Jillian shrugged and slowly shook her head. "Yes, but isn't
cutting the supply lines to the Confederates all that's really necessary?"

It did not set well that the whole of the Union Army had been
unable to accomplish that simple task.

"You seem to have taken a very peculiar position for a Northern widow," Melvin accused, attacking her anew, "particularly
when your husband was a casualty of this war."

Jillian drew a long breath, trying to control her anger. "Jeff
was killed in battle fighting rebel soldiers. He knew the risks he
was taking, as I did when I married him. Jeff was a gallant, noble

man, but I don't think there's anything gallant or noble about depriving women and children of their homes."

"Don't you think the Southerners would burn houses and farms here in the North if given half a chance?" he goaded her.

"Lee and his men did not burn and pillage Pennsylvania on their way to Gettysburg."

Jillian's was a powerful argument and all the more offensive for being irrefutable.

"But how will we bring the South to its knees, Mrs. Walsh, unless we deprive the army of its resources?" one of the men demanded. "Defeating the rebs in battle has proved a poor deterrent to their cause."

"I want to see the North victorious as much as you do," Jillian assured him. "I believe it is wrong for the South to divide the Union, wrong for one race to hold another race in bondage. All I'm saying is that there's no reason to treat the people in the captured areas so callously. In burning homes and farms, in destroying crops and livestock, in reducing their cities to rubble, the North may be losing far more than it can ever hope to gain."

By the time Jillian had made this pronouncement, Gerald Walsh had threaded his way through the guests and was at his daughter-in-law's side. He took her arm solicitously, though with an angry grip that sent unexpected pain jabbing up her arm.

"Jillian, you must not forget your duties as a hostess," he admonished her. "The ladies by the fire have been asking for your company."

It was a lie, evident in the slack-jawed expressions on the women's faces. It was equally easy to read the censure in their eyes. In that instant she realized what she'd done. She had debated politics with the menfolk, had expressed opinions of her own. She had broken one of the cardinal rules of polite society, but somehow she was not sorry she had spoken her mind.

She returned to the women with what grace she could muster, but in spite of Walsh's attempts to salvage the evening, it had been irreparably spoiled by the disagreement and Jillian's scandalous behavior. Almost immediately the guests began to take their leave, pleading other engagements or fatigue. When Jillian and her father-in-law had seen the last of their guests to the door, Gerald rounded on her furiously and struck her an open-handed blow that sent her staggering.

"You traitorous little bitch!" he raved, grabbing her arm as if to prevent her untimely escape. "What the hell were you thinking about, expressing views like those? The victors in any battle are entitled to the spoils. If the Northern generals choose to plunder every hamlet, set the whole Confederacy alight, what concern is it of yours?"

Though she knew it would have been the wiser course to hold her peace, Jillian blinked back the sting of tears and faced him defiantly. "Bitterness does breed bitterness, Gerald; hatred breeds hatred. I only want the Union to show compassion to the vanquished in the hope of securing a lasting peace."

"We'll secure a lasting peace by defeating our enemies, just as the victors always have. Those are the ways of war, girl, the way things are in the world."

"But can't you see those ways are wrong, that peace can be accomplished more humanely through compromise and—"

Walsh's hand slashed out again, striking a blow that sent her reeling back against the stairs.

"Your secessionist views dishonor your husband," he raged. "They dishonor me and your presence in this house. That Jefferson died for the likes of you is more than I can bear. Go upstairs! Get out of my sight, or I won't answer for my actions."

For an instant she thought he might drag her to her feet and hit her again.

Instead he whirled toward his study, as if the devil himself were at his heels. He slammed the door at the end of the hall, the sound echoing thunderously in the silence.

Jillian stared after the congressman with a shiver of dread. She was alone and helpless here, at the mercy of a man who clearly hated her. With that realization her anger and defiance fled, to be replaced by overwhelming fear. She was frightened not only by what had transpired, by the feelings that had been brought to the fore by this evening's violent confrontation. She had to leave this house now that the breach had been made, had to leave it quickly, before Walsh became even more brutish and abusive. But she was caught in a web of her own making, snared by her dependence on her father-in-law. She might well need to leave, but there was nowhere else to go.

Slowly Jillian pulled herself to her feet and staggered up the stairs. When she reached her room, she locked the door behind her but knew no security for doing so. Until she found a way to leave this house, Gerald Walsh owned her soul.

"But you've got to be part of this, Ryder. It's going to be the most important mission ever launched from Canada!" Jamie's voice was determinedly persuasive as the two men climbed the stairs toward Jacob Thompson's rooms in the Queen's Hotel.

"I told you I'd listen to what they're proposing, Jamie. I said I'd listen, nothing more." His friend's enthusiasm was infectious, and Bingham was trying to maintain some semblance of immunity.

A frown narrowed the corners of the smaller man's mouth. "You can't pass up the chance for such excitement, pass up the chance to confront the Yankees."

Ryder sighed, thinking that Jamieson was probably right. Since the failure of the mission to capture the *Michigan* and his subsequent return to Toronto, Bingham had been dissatisfied and restless. With every day that passed, it seemed less and less likely that he would be sent to Nassau or Bermuda, less and less possible for him to return to running the blockade. Nor was he any closer to settling his score with the Yankees, and the need for vengeance gnawed at his insides. In the past month, he had chafed under the enforced idleness, the dismal news from the front, a general disenchantment with the Confederate cause, and his own flagging self-respect.

Whatever Thompson and his cronies were planning was big, something more daring and complex than even Jamie could know. Ryder only hoped it would be something he could embrace wholeheartedly, a mission with skilled leaders and cohesive plans—something that had a good chance for success. Another failure so close on the heels of the last would seriously damage the morale of Southerners in Toronto. Yet as they waited to be admitted to Thompson's rooms, Bingham wondered if he would involve himself in whatever the Confederates proposed, if only to end the tedium of these last weeks.

Phillip Sheppard opened the door and ushered the two men inside. As he led them toward a table of decanters, Bingham reflected that there had always been something about Thompson's aide that set his teeth on edge. It wasn't anything he could pinpoint. Sheppard was the soul of efficiency and charm, but there was something not quite right about the man, something that made Ryder uneasy.

Once he had secured a drink, he forced thoughts of Sheppard from his mind and turned to see who else had come to hear Thompson's plans. On the far side of the room, he recognized Tom Hines and a grizzled Englishman named Grenfel, saw William Cleary scrabbling together the papers at his desk. Thompson was in the center of another group, conferring with three young men Ryder did not recognize. There were plenty of others he knew, men he had met in the bar downstairs and in other establishments he'd frequented throughout the city. At last his gaze came to rest on a much older man seated alone by the windows. He looked gray as day-old mush and profoundly ill at ease.

"I told you this was an important meeting," Jamie confided, coming up beside him. "Do you know who that is?"

Bingham shook his head, eyeing the man by the windows.

"It's Clement Clay, the third Confederate commissioner in Canada. He came from St. Catharines tonight just for Thompson's meeting."

Ryder studied the man, noting his sunken eyes and long white beard. It was rumored that he and Thompson had been at odds since the moment they arrived in Montreal; that because the commissioners did not get on, Clay had established his own headquarters in St. Catharines while Thompson had remained in Toronto. Bingham had also heard that the two men did not concur on what was to be done to forward the cause. Yet Clay was here tonight. Did that mean he sanctioned whatever Thompson was proposing?

Before Bingham could ask anything more, Thompson was gathering the Confederates together.

"Gentlemen," he began. "Gentlemen, I'd like to introduce you to some new recruits to our glorious cause here in Canada. This is Captain Robert Martin from Kentucky, Dr. Luke Blackburn, lately of Sterling Price's command, and Lieutenant John Headley, who rode with Morgan earlier in the war."

Martin was tall but stooped, sporting a spidery mustache and matching goatee. Blackburn was remarkable only in that he was totally unremarkable, a veritable everyman. Headley seemed very young, his face still round and boyish, his smile warm and eager to please. They were the newcomers Ryder had wondered about.

When the introductions were acknowledged, drinks replenished, and cigars lit, the Confederates found chairs and prepared to discuss the business at hand.

"William, if you please, read the editorial from the *Richmond Whig*," Thompson requested when they were settled.

Cleary took a crumpled newspaper from the pile beside his chair and began to read: " 'Sheridan reports to Grant that, in moving down the Valley to Woodstock, he had burned over two thousand barns filled with wheat, hay, and farming implements, and over seventy mills filled with flour and wheat. This is done by order of Grant himself, commander—' "

"No, William, farther down. Read the passage I have marked."

Cleary complied: " 'Now it is an idle waste of words to denounce this kind of war. We simply have to regard it as a practical matter, and ask ourselves how it should be met. There is one and only one that we know of, to arrest and prevent this and every other kind of atrocity—that is to burn one of the chief cities of the enemy, Boston, Philadelphia or Cincinnati.' "

The men sat nodding in agreement with the sentiments expressed in the editorial. There was no question that the passage was the best kind of Confederate rhetoric, and while it made for stirring prose, Ryder could not fathom why Thompson was quoting it.

It appeared that most of the other men shared his confusion until Thompson made his reasons clear.

"Gentlemen, what we mean to do for the glorification of the South is just what that editorial suggests. On November eighth, Election Day, we are going to burn selected Northern cities in retaliation for the destruction of houses and farms in the Shenandoah Valley."

It was an electrifying statement, and for an instant stunned silence was the only response. Then, as the import of what Thompson had declared rolled over them, a blur of excited voices erupted around the room.

"Is such a thing possible?"

"Does the government in Richmond sanction this plan?"

"Can we coordinate such an effort in the time we have left to us?"

"Gentlemen, gentlemen," Thompson called for order in spite of his evident pleasure with their response. "If you will listen, please. Already the groundwork has been laid. Richmond has long accepted that the most satisfactory way to end the war is through negotiated peace, an honorable peace that secures Confederate independence. For a time, it seemed the defeat of Abraham Lincoln's bid for reelection was the best way to make the Union bargain, but with Sherman's victories and the resurgence of the President's popularity, we can no longer count on the Democratic candidate carrying the day.

"Since those high in our government realized the need for some other kind of leverage to force the Yankees' hand, we have been empowered to make this bold move. It will force the Northerners to realize that the war is far from over and bring the agony of battle into Yankee homes. That is why we have been designated to burn Union cities, turn the tables on our enemies, and make the civilians of the United States pay for the hardships visited on our countrymen. We are honored that this difficult and important task has been entrusted to those of us in Canada, and we mean to fulfill and surpass Richmond's expectations."

As Thompson paused, Ryder took a breath, shaken by what was happening.

"The leaders of three of the coordinated missions are with us tonight," Thompson continued. "Captain Hines, with Colonel Grenfel as second in command, will take a group to Chicago. Dr. Blackburn will oversee our efforts in Boston, while Captain Martin and Lieutenant Headley will lead the group to fire New York."

"Are other cities slated for destruction?" someone asked when the response to Thompson's announcement had faded away.

"There are plans afoot in Cincinnati, as well as other cities across the North," Phillip Sheppard noted quietly.

Thompson stroked his beard and smiled with satisfaction. He was clearly pleased by the enthusiastic way his plans were being received.

"The most encouraging part of the plan," he went on, "is that our efforts will not stand alone. In Chicago and New York the Copperhead organizations are going to rise up beside us. While we are setting fires, paying the Yankees for torching the farms in Georgia and Virginia, the Sons of Liberty will be taking over their respective cities."

The men collectively caught their breath at this new dimension to the plan. A Copperhead revolt could break the North into several separate confederacies and make reunification impossible. At first the plan seemed unlikely to succeed, but on careful consideration Ryder saw that it did nothing more than consolidate ideas that had been discussed for years, since long before the war.

As the men mulled over Thompson's revelations, Ryder found himself watching Tom Hines. In planning the capture of the *Michigan*, Hines had been outspoken about his mistrust of the Copperheads. If he had doubted their loyalty then, why did he trust the Copperheads now? Had promises been secured? Were the dissenters in the North finally prepared to fight?

"Have the Copperheads guaranteed their role in such a plan?" Ryder felt compelled to ask, though he knew he risked censure by the others.

William Cleary did not seem surprised by the question. "Indeed they have, Captain Bingham. We've had correspondence from Dr. Edward Edwards in Chicago and James McMasters in

New York assuring us that their men are armed and prepared for battle.

"After the draft riots last July, New York is poised for revolution, anyway. With twenty thousand Sons of Liberty behind us and the governor of the state in sympathy with our cause, there are numerous possibilities. There are plans afoot to take over both city and government buildings, the police department, and the treasury. Another group is going to free the men from Fort Lafayette. . . ."

With that bit of news, Ryder's doubts about being part of the enterprise evaporated. He would give everything he had to help emancipate the prison where he'd been held captive, the prison where Mitchell had died. Perhaps this offered a new hope of avenging his brother's death. Perhaps he would resolve his responsibilities in a way he'd never anticipated.

A number of other questions were asked and answered, but Ryder hardly heard them. He was thinking about setting fires in New York, about seeing the city in Confederate hands, about liberating Fort Lafayette, about the possibilities of a negotiated peace.

Across the circle Jamie caught Bingham's eye and flashed a knowing grin. Bradford realized that the plans to liberate Fort Lafayette had committed Ryder to the mission as nothing else could.

"So you see, our efforts are well in hand," Thompson reassured them. "Success is ours for the taking. We only have to select the men who will carry out the mission and coordinate our plans."

Somehow the idea of burning Northern cities seemed feasible now, when minutes ago it had seemed unlikely at best. Convinced by Thompson's glib tongue, the determination in their leaders' faces, and the need to retaliate for Union atrocities, the Confederates believed not only in the practicality of the mission but in its chances of success as well.

Commissioner Clement Clay had said nothing during the meeting, but now he offered his blessing to the plans. He spoke softly but powerfully, offering a fiery benediction.

"This mission is as important to securing Southern sovereignty as any battle in this war. It is as daring as the raids of Stuart's Black Horse Cavalry, as tactically brilliant as Stonewall Jackson's march at Chancellorsville. It has the potential to change the outcome of this conflict, to force Northern participation in peace negotiations, to shore up the flagging spirits of our brothers in the field.

"We must implement this plan to turn the tide of battle. We must bring it to flaming fruition to influence Northern opinion. We must accept the charge given us by our leaders and execute it well. Though we abhor the tactics the Yankees have forced upon us, we must fire these Union strongholds, let the Federals taste the anger and frustration we Southerners know so well.

"As you go forward on Confederate business, think not of the Northern civilians who will suffer the results of your acts, think not of the homes and factories that will be set alight. Think instead of the people of the South who have suffered terrible hardships and indignities, of the thousands who are hungry and homeless because of Sherman's foraging and Sheridan's flaring torch. Think instead of the cause, the necessity of what you do to the survival of the South. Take pride in the sacred trust your country has given you. Live to honor it; die to honor it. Sanctify yourselves for the role you have been asked to play. The birth of a new nation is the greatest fulfillment we can hope to achieve. Pledge yourselves to your comrades and your country. Go forth and do her will."

Around the circle, faces were flushed, shoulders were squared, eyes were bright with determination. Patriotism beat in every heart, and duty molded every will.

In their midst, Thompson rose slowly to his feet and raised his glass.

"Tonight we stand together, united by the daring of the thing we propose to do. Let us drink to seeing New York in ashes, to watching Chicago's embers grow dim, to igniting a holocaust at Boston that will flare across our enemy's lands. Let's drink to the success of a new confederacy in the Northwest and to revolt along the Atlantic's shores, to the bravery of our brothers with the army and to the independence of the South."

Caught up in the fervor of Thompson's words, the men surged to their feet as one, lifting their glasses in a toast to success, to victory, to independence. The men glowed with fierce pride and love for the South, with the courage and defiance that had served its defenders so well. For those few moments the men in Thompson's rooms were bound together, forged inseparably by all they cherished and believed. Emotions were high as they reaffirmed their allegiance to the country they longed to call their own. They drank deep, a pledge of their fortitude and loyalty, a pledge to securing a homeland for themselves and their posterity.

At last the men resumed their seats, and Thompson closed the meeting by explaining the means by which their goal would be attained.

"The leaders of each contingent will meet with their subordinates in a few days' time to put the final touches on each phase of the plan," Thompson summarized. "There is daring in what we are proposing, but practicality, too. We will succeed in this. And with that success, we will prove to those in Washington that our cause is strong and viable, that our independence from the North is both inevitable and imminent. I thank you for your attendance tonight, and now we will adjourn to contemplate our victory."

The meeting was over, and while the men milled around the suite, pouring fresh drinks and sharing their enthusiasm for the plan, Ryder threaded his way through the crush to give his name to Robert Martin. He wanted to be part of the group going to New York, was more than willing to fire the city if it would lead to the liberation of the prisons in the harbor.

But once he had made the commitment, Ryder felt a compelling need to be alone. Quietly he left the room so filled with patriotism and camaraderie, making his solitary way down the stairs and out into the night.

It was cold on the street, the sky clear and the breeze stiff, but Ryder hardly felt the chill. Instead he was drawn toward the bay where ships rocked gently at their moorings, where the path of the moon was cut to shimmers by the waves.

The plan Thompson had proposed was the perfect antidote to the lethargy that had overcome him. Just thinking about the possibilities made him feel strong, bright, and purposeful for the first time in many weeks. This mission might even offer him a chance to even the score for Mitchell's death. But there was another dimension to the plan, and his need for vengeance was suddenly tempered by a deeper purpose. If burning New York brought the war to a negotiated peace, Ryder would be able to return to the home he loved, to gather up the remnants of his shattered life and forge a new future in the South. It would not be easy to regain all he had forfeited in the name of patriotism, but Ryder was willing to meet that challenge if he could share his life with the woman he loved.

Jillian. Her memory calmed and soothed him, even though he knew she would never approve of the things Thompson had proposed. She would rail against the destruction of Northern cities, argue against the loss of life and property that was inevitable if the plan was to succeed. But if one abhorrent act brought peace, wasn't it worth the condemnation? Wasn't it worth the suffering of a few to ensure the good of the many?

Jillian's feelings mattered to Ryder because he loved her, but they would not sway him from his course. He was struggling to forge a better world where freedom and peace would abound, fighting to maintain some semblance of the life he and his countrymen loved so well. He could look past the transient destruction, the fiery cataclysm that would lay waste to Northern cities, and embrace the vision of what could be. But could Jillian see the possibilities? Would she understand his need to have a life and a future to offer before he asked her to be his wife?

They had shared a few wondrous days and had tried to be content with what fate had seen fit to allow. But now Ryder had hope, a renewed belief in himself and in the life he could make for both of them.

From somewhere in the depths of memory came a prophesy his mother had made years before: "Someday you'll meet a woman worthy of you, Ryder, and when you find her, you'll make her the center of your world. You'll find your soul's mate and overcome any obstacle to ensure your life together."

Jilly was everything his mother could have wished her to be —understanding, wise, and gentle. But if he meant to have a life at Jillian's side, if he wanted to make Alysse's words come true, he had to do his part to bring Thompson's plan to fruition. He had to go to New York.

As he stood at the lee of the wide harbor, his mind was filled with thoughts of Jill. Alone in the darkness, he imagined her beside him, her heavy caramel hair tumbling down her back, her gold and green eyes alight with passion, the joy that would fill her face when he offered her the future they had never dared to contemplate. He remembered the way her touch sent ripples of delight along his nerves, recalled the understanding and compassion she had offered when last they'd been together. He wanted and needed Jillian, for now and all eternity. He would do whatever he had to do to turn the dreams of a future at her side into a reality.

"So there you are," Jamie's voice sounded from behind him, making Ryder start with the suddenness of his appearance.

Bingham turned as the smaller man came to stand beside him. "I needed to be alone. I needed time to think."

"And just what was it you were thinking about?"

Ryder shrugged. "About the mission, mostly."

"Oh? And just what do you think about the mission?"

Ryder drew a long breath, knowing it was safe to express his concerns to Jamie. "Well, I can't say I'm completely in agreement with what Thompson wants us to do. When I went with Beall to capture the *Michigan*, I knew that the men on board were sailors, that they'd accepted the risks of battle. I can't say I like the prospect of depriving civilians of their homes, of making war on women and children."

Jamie nodded. "I know how you feel, but the complexion of war has changed in these last four years. The actualities of battle have robbed war of its gentility, its honor. You know as well as I do that the Yankees have never shared our fine illusions or harbored compunctions where civilians are concerned."

"Still, it seems wrong to sink to their level, to reply to Union atrocities with atrocities of our own."

Jamie took a cigar from the inside pocket of his coat. "That's what separates gentlemen from barbarians, I guess. Still, there's a finer purpose in what we'll be doing. Setting these fires will be only a means to an end. We want independence for the South, and this may be the only way we'll ever achieve that goal."

Silence fell between them. It was not a silence of approval, but one of acceptance. It acknowledged the futility of questioning the moral implications of something they were both committed to do.

"And what else were you thinking, Ryder, standing out here alone in the dark? Were you thinking about a woman, perhaps, someone you'd like to see before you go off to sacrifice your life?"

Jamie's words were at odds with the optimism he had expressed earlier in the evening, a stark contrast to the hopes Bingham himself was harboring.

A frown knotted Ryder's brows. "Do you think that's what will happen, Jamie? Don't you think the plan will succeed?"

"Oh, we'll fire the Yankee cities, all right." There was confidence in Bradford's tone. "But there are thousands of them and dozens of us. I can't say I like the odds."

"But if you don't believe this mission will make a difference, why are you supporting it?"

"I think what Thompson has proposed could well force the Yankees to bargain with us. I wouldn't have agreed to go to New York if I didn't think that was true. It just seems foolish and imprudent to deny the danger we'll be facing."

The smaller man paused to light his smoke, and Ryder weighed what he knew of his friend. Traveling as courier between Toronto and Richmond, Bradford had risked so much so often that it seemed strange to hear him voice his fears or acknowledge his own mortality.

"I believe if I die firing New York," Jamieson continued, "my death will make a difference. Anyway, I've always thought I'd rather lose my life fighting for something finite and tangible than in some gallant, high-mettled charge meant to gain some insignificant plot of ground."

Ryder dismissed Jamie's jaundiced view of battle but was appalled by the resignation in the smaller man's tone. He could not fathom what dark scepter had eclipsed Jamie's usually sunny disposition or what had filled him with such pessimism. Besides, it seemed wrong to contemplate death when life beckoned with such beguiling promises. He had been so caught up in the possibilities of Southern independence, the hopes for a future with Jillian as his wife, that he had not considered the more dire consequences of their plans. Was he risking everything for a fleeting chance at happiness? Wasn't the gamble he was taking worth all he stood to gain?

Jamie exhaled a long plume of smoke and watched it drift on the breeze. "Don't pay me any mind," he warned. "I'm just feeling melancholy, wishing I could see my Laura before I go."

He took another long pull on his cigar and shook his head. "God, Ryder, Laura is so beautiful—small and pale and delicate, like a fragile porcelain doll. Her hair's as dark and thick as a sable's pelt, and her skin's like sweet fresh cream. She's a dream I long to possess, a miracle of tenderness and beauty I know I've done nothing to deserve."

"You love her very much, don't you, Jamie?"

Bradford nodded. "More than I can find words to express. And what about you, Ryder? Who's the woman you've been pining for?"

Ryder cast a glance at his friend, startled by his perceptiveness. His initial response to Jamie's questions was to deny there was a woman in his life, but it seemed wrong to hold back the admission when Jamie had bared so much of himself. Yet Ryder could not simply declare what he was feeling. Instead he shuffled his feet and stared out across the bay, forced to speak as much by Jamie's silence as by the need to share his secrets.

"She's a young widow living in Niagara Falls," he finally admitted. "She saved my life when I was trying to escape."

Jamie's eyebrows cocked with interest. "Tell me more," he urged.

Ryder propped a foot on one of the crates and rested an arm on his upraised knee. "Jillian was on the train when I left New York. At first I forced her to help me, forced her to tell the detectives searching the cars that I was her husband. But when the wound I'd received during the escape began to trouble me, she took me off the train. She nursed me back to health and gave me money to get to Canada."

"Imagine that," Jamie observed softly, "a Yankee widow risking everything to help a Confederate. And in return, you fell in love with her."

Ryder shook his head disparagingly. "It happened so quickly, so unexpectedly."

Jamie's mouth curved in an understanding smile. "And does she know how you feel? Have you told her that you love her?"

"It seemed futile until now."

"And now you have a reason to hope?"

Ryder turned to glance at Jamie, not quite able to hide the glow at the back of his eyes. "If what we do brings a negotiated peace, there will be a chance for a life with Jillian, a chance to take her home."

Jamie shook his head at the irony of his friend's words. "You see the mission to New York as a beginning while I see it as an end."

"Most things are what we make them, Jamie. This mission offers a chance to resolve old hatreds, a chance to start again."

"And if it's not all you hope, Ryder? If it's sacrifice and not renewal?"

"It's a gamble I'm willing to take, a bet I'm planning to win."

Ryder's determination lay between them, a challenge that Jamie seemed afraid to answer.

"You're risking so much," he observed.

"No more than you."

"Ah, yes, no more than I am risking."

The silence fell between them again, a test of courage and resolve. The curse of their mortality lay between them, spoken of not because they feared death but because they had accepted the possibility.

"Why don't you go to her, Ryder?" the smaller man urged, trapped by his own dark thoughts. "Why don't you tell her how you feel? Tell her that you love her, in case things don't turn out the way you plan."

"Now, Jamie? How could I go to her now?"

"We won't be meeting for a few days yet. Martin needs time

to gather recruits, to find other men he can trust."

Ryder shook his head in silent negation, but Jamie continued to press him.

"All I know is that I'd go. If I had the chance to be with Laura for just one night, I'd brave anything the Yankees might do. Go to Jillian, Ryder," Jamie urged. "Hold her. Tell her you love her."

Ryder knew what Jamie proposed was fed by his own uncertainty, yet the thought of visiting Jillian was as beguiling as the woman herself. The prospect of being with her, however briefly, spread through him like a balm, soothing him, calming him, offering him a respite from the knowledge of what he'd agreed to do. Jamie's words were persuasive, and Ryder spread the possibilities before him. In the light of rationality, what he was considering was madness, but when he looked at it through the eyes of love, he was blind to everything but Jillian's allure. He would go, not because he was afraid to die, but because he had acknowledged death. He would go, not because he wanted to share his burdens, but because he could finally offer Jillian hope.

A slow smile softened Bingham's features. "You know, Jamie, I do believe I'll go to Niagara Falls. There are all sorts of wonders there that draw me. But mark me well, Jamie. I'll be back, and then we'll take on this mission together."

He saw Bradford nod with satisfaction before he turned to go. But as Jamie's footsteps receded into the darkness, Ryder breathed a silent vow.

"We'll go to New York together, Jamie. And once we've done everything we must, I'll get us both out of this alive."

Chapter Eleven

Dearest Jilly,
    I must see you tonight. Meet me at the usual time and place.

                                          R.B.

JILLIAN'S EMBROIDERY LAY forgotten in her lap as she clutched the tersely worded note. Its tone of urgency frightened her. What had happened that made it imperative that Ryder see her? Why had he crossed the border when his presence in Niagara Falls was both foolhardy and dangerous?

Before she could discern an answer or even read the note a second time, a threat to his safety appeared in the guise of Congressman Walsh's housekeeper. Jillian stifled the urge to tuck the precious note into her pocket or up her sleeve, knowing that by doing so she would confirm any suspicions Mrs. Pryor might be harboring. Instead she carelessly tossed the paper into her sewing bag and glanced up at the woman approaching her.

"One of the maids said a boy brought a letter to the door," the housekeeper began coyly. "Is it anything I should know about? Will we be having guests for dinner?"

The woman's feigned concern could not mask her guile, and Jill answered the question calmly, with far more nonchalance than she felt. "It was only a message from Mrs. Mott. The meeting scheduled for this evening to discuss the charity bazaar has been canceled."

A sly smile drew the corners of Mrs. Pryor's mouth. "I didn't think you'd been seeing so much of those women lately, not since the night everyone came to dinner."

What the housekeeper said was true. Since Jillian had voiced her political opinions, the women at the relief organization had done everything but shun her.

"Well, they could hardly let me show up for a meeting if there wasn't one," Jill replied tartly. "Even if they don't agree with my views on the war, that would be an appalling breach of manners."

Seeming satisfied by the answer and the fact that she had been able to nettle her young mistress, Elvira Pryor nodded and returned to her duties, leaving Jillian to breathe a sigh of relief. As far as the housekeeper knew, the note was nothing more than what Jill claimed. Even if the woman told Gerald Walsh about the message, he could not make her reveal its contents, and the lie she had concocted was a plausible one.

To keep it safe from prying eyes, Jillian took the missive from the sewing bag and tucked it down inside her bodice. Later she would find a better hiding place, but for now she liked the feel of Ryder's words snug against her heart.

Though Jillian continued to stitch serenely on her mourning picture, her mind was busy. It was not rational to hope that Ryder was coming to take her back to Canada, but she wished with all her heart that it were so. Since the night Gerald Walsh had struck her, Jill had been determined to leave his home and had begun writing letters of application to schools in Pennsylvania and New York. She did not delude herself that it would be easy to secure a teaching position without either experience or references, but that course seemed to offer more hope than any of the others open to her. Now that she had the chance, she was tempted to tell Ryder what had happened and ask for his help, but she could not use Walsh's mistreatment to garner an invitation Ryder did not want to extend. He had reasons of his own for being in Toronto, things to resolve within himself of which she could have no part. But if by some miracle he should offer to take her with him, Jill would not refuse.

In spite of the things she found to fill her day, the hours crawled until Jillian was able to retire to her room and prepare for her meeting with Ryder. After she bathed, she slipped into a soft woolen gown and tied her hair with a wide black ribbon. Satisfied with her attire, she leaned close to the mirror and frowned at what she saw. The congressman's anger several nights before had left its mark, and she dusted a veil of powder over the bruises, hoping it would hide the evidence of how Walsh had mistreated her.

Just before ten o'clock, she drew a cloak around her shoulders and crept silently down the stairs. Mrs. Pryor had retired at nine as usual, and when Jillian passed the door of her father-in-law's study, she could hear the murmur of voices. It would have been better for her purposes if Gerald Walsh had gone out for the evening, but Jill took comfort in knowing he would be occupied with his client's legal problems while she was meeting Ryder.

Bingham was waiting when she reached the gazebo, his shoulders hunched against the wind and his collar turned up around his ears.

He looked cold, Jillian noticed with a twinge of concern, but when Ryder came down the steps to greet her, his eyes were bright and warm.

"Jilly!" he whispered, his face alight with pleasure. "Oh, Jilly love, I've missed you so!"

Those were not the words she had expected, and while the sincerity of his declaration soothed the cold, stark place inside her, she sensed a niggling inconsistency. Jill drew breath to ask him why he'd come, but before she could speak, his arms were coiling around her shoulders and his mouth was gliding over hers. With the soft, insistent brush of his lips came the sweet, compelling magic she had always found in his embrace. It

swelled in her chest, knotted in her throat, unfurled along her
limbs with a delicious, spreading ache. Jillian abandoned herself
to the sweeping intensity of his kiss, letting it quell her questions,
nullify her doubts, banish her uncertainties.

They clung together, shivering in the night, his hard strong
hands trailing over the curves and hollows of her body, his
fingers tangling in her free-flowing hair. His tongue stroked and
glazed the contours of her mouth as his lips drew on hers, tender
and arousing. Penetrating warmth spilled through Jillian and she
answered the ardor of his kiss with a welcome that was raw and
deep with longing, fierce and desperate with loneliness. She
strained against his body as if by the contact she could share his
strength. He obligingly bound her to him, shielding her, sheltering her, holding her as if he never meant to let her go.

When last they'd come together, Ryder had been the one in
need of all the understanding and comfort she could give, and
from the tenor of the note, Jillian had half expected to find that
same barely leashed desperation in the man. Instead, his kisses
were slow and lavish, his touch unhurried and cherishing. Suddenly it was Ryder who was offering ease, Ryder who was at
peace with himself when Jillian was frightened and unsure. The
inexplicable change in him gave her pause, but her disillusionment rose up to absorb his tenderness, her desperation homing to
the succor he was offering.

Ryder sensed a change in Jillian, too. He could feel her need
for closeness in the way she nestled against him, feel her need for
consolation in the way her mouth opened and molded its contours
to the shape of his. She was not a small woman, yet she seemed
suddenly frail and delicate in his arms. It was as if he held something as fragile as a butterfly within his cupped hands, as if she
were trusting him to protect her from a wide and hostile world.
With that realization, a sense of power swept through him, making him feel vital, potent, confident, and alive. But at the same
time, her reticence made him temper his strength with tenderness, forced control over his more primitive and strident emotions.

As his mouth moved over hers, he was glad he had come, glad
he had accepted Jamie's counsel. He loved this woman, and he
wanted to tell her so. She meant all the world to him, and he
wanted to prove the depth of his commitment with words as well
as with actions. His arms tightened, the pressure of his lips in-
creased, and though he was relentlessly tender in his wooing,

Ryder allowed Jilly to feel his power surrounding and protecting her.

Jillian accepted what he was offering and took refuge in his embrace, letting his presence soothe and reassure her. Held against the planes of Ryder's body, she felt as secure as a child tucked snug in her bed on a snowy night, as safe as she had when her father enfolded her tiny child's hand in his all-encompassing larger one. It was not a feeling she was eager to forfeit, though at length she willed herself to draw away, and the questions that had plagued her through the day returned to haunt her.

"Ryder, what has happened to bring you here?" she whispered. "Why have you risked recapture to come to me?"

Instead of answering her, Bingham lowered his mouth again, as if he sought to drown her curiosity in a tide of pleasure, subdue her questions with a sweeping sensual awe. His hands against her back were compelling, strong, cajoling, and as she accepted the insistent pressure of his lips, his tongue slipped deep inside. He stroked the interior of her cheeks, the vaulted roof of her mouth. His kisses tasted of brandy and mint and of himself, an intoxicating mixture that made Jill's heart thud hard against her ribs and her blood run fast. Shivers swept down her spine in a wash of pure sensation. Weakness welled through her like a tide. It was a weakness of sweeping languor, a rush of incipient surrender. He was overpowering her deliberately, yet in the sweetest way she knew, wiping all fears, all concerns, all reality from her mind.

Then Ryder was sweeping her up in his arms, carrying her into the gazebo, settling her on the bench where they had made love once before. But before he could take his place beside her, Jill tugged two blankets from beneath the bench.

An appreciative grin lit his face when he realized she must have smuggled them to the summerhouse earlier in the day, and he was still smiling as they spread one of the quilts over the thick pallet of leaves on the floor.

"Your resourcefulness never ceases to amaze me," she heard him murmur as he bore her down to their makeshift bed, pulling the second blanket over them.

"It's gotten rather cool for this kind of endeavor—" Jilly began, but Ryder was kissing her again, and the comment melted into a sigh.

As they tussled under the cover of the second quilt, he brushed aside her cloak and sought the buttons on her bodice.

"You wore fewer clothes the last time we made love," he complained, nuzzling against her neck.

"I could have come dressed for the Arctic, and I doubt that it would have hampered you."

He laughed again and covered her mouth with his, letting his caress affirm the truth of the accusation. His fingers moved deftly over the row of fasteners, stripping the buttons from their holes, slipping the bow at the front of her chemise, and parting the fabric below it. As he freed her from the confines of fashion, Ryder brushed her lips with indolent kisses that compelled her to respond in kind. He tugged the ribbon from her hair and gathered the skein of caramel tresses in one hand.

Jillian curled sinuously against him, both drawn and inundated by his presence. His blatant masculinity and the power of his body seemed at once overwhelming and protective. His determination and his tenderness seemed to sap her will and strength. The tenor of his endearments soothed and gentled her while the flutter of his lips against her ear was tickling and provocative. The contradictions in him were puzzling, but she did not want to explore the mystery of his arrival now. Instead she wanted to share her wonder with him, to revel in his eagerness, to seek the mindless delight he alone could give.

As her senses sharpened and her need for Ryder grew, she wanted the same accessibility he had to her. Murmuring softly, she pushed the nubbly fabric of his frock coat down his arms, struggled with his silky tie and the small cold studs at the front of his shirt. As she loosed the fasteners, he shrugged out of the encumbering garments and tossed them aside, then bared her torso with hands that scaled her creamy shoulders and stroked the newly accessible flesh as if it were a treasure.

"Jilly," he whispered into her mouth. "Oh, Jilly, sweet Jilly, you're even more beautiful than I remembered." His voice quivered as he spoke, the words intent, serious, flowing over her like his caress.

His trousers and underwear soon joined the rest of their discarded clothes, and he sprawled above her, spare and elemental, strong and unencumbered. She reveled in the feel of his long-limbed body against her own, the weight of him crushing her into the fragrant rustling nest of fallen leaves. He was heavy, but his bulk felt good. With his arms trapping the width of her shoulders and his hands tangling in her hair, she was subdued and overwhelmed, sheltered and secure.

A quivering awareness moved through her as he feathered

kisses down her throat, paused to swirl his tongue in the delicate hollow at its base. A flush melted against her skin wherever his kisses strayed, a rich internal heat that only Ryder could arouse. He moved lower, and at the narrow plain between her breasts, he detoured right, then left, his head disappearing beneath the blanket as he laved one pale soft globe and then the other. Her flesh contracted, shrank, and tightened when his mouth moved away, but the chill of the night air fed Jillian's excitement, enhanced her need. He moved downward again, pushing the rest of her clothes aside as he trailed kisses to her navel, down across her belly.

She moaned as he approached the apex of her thighs, stirred with welling desire as his tongue probed the nest of red-golden hair. Brilliant heat shot up the midline of her body as his mouth closed over the intimate core of her. She twisted helplessly in response to his delicate probe, her toes curling, her back arching, a tightening straining need spiraling up from the lower reaches of her body. She gave herself over to the thrill of sensual magic, shuddered with the potency of what was to come. But it was too delicious a thing to be borne alone, and she reached for him in a flurry of impatience.

"I want you," she demanded. "I want you, Ryder, please. Come to me, come to me now."

Hearing the breathy desperation in her tone, he moved upward in one smooth stroke to seek his haven between her thighs. She gasped with new and remembered rapture as he gave her all of himself, and she twined her legs around his hips, holding him deep inside her.

"It's wonderful like this," she murmured, reveling in the security she found in his arms.

"Yes, Jilly," he agreed. "It is wonderful."

"Oh, Ryder, please. I want this to go on forever!"

He knew unequivocally what she meant and felt a stitch of bittersweet irony tighten around his heart. He wanted that unity as fiercely as she, felt a need to meld their souls and lives, a need that went far beyond the transient merging of their bodies. He saw her demand for what it was, a perilous desire born of their long separations, an enduring desire that went beyond the physical expression of their tenderness. But as things stood now, it was dangerous to want something that might well be unattainable— dangerous for him but more dangerous for her.

He tore his eyes away and sought to deny what she was asking by deliberately misunderstanding her. "Ah, my darling, yes. If only it *could* go on forever."

They began to move together, and the masterful way he took her seemed to belie the veracity of his words. His strokes were strong and constant, his tenderness infinite and all-encompassing. He thrust and she moved with him; he paused and she hung trembling at the brink. They gasped in mounting wonder as a sweet dark tide came welling up between them, catching them in its flow, pulling them in its current. It swept them along as helplessly as a skiff on the crest of a wave, a leaf in the midst of a whirlwind. They were drowning in elation, borne away by ecstasy. They spun, swirling in a maelstrom of their own making, succumbing to the thing that separated men from gods. When it was over, they were cast adrift, clinging together, trembling in the latent waves of the bliss they had shared so selflessly.

Sanity returned by slow degrees. There was the seep of cold stealing through the blankets, the crackle of leaves beneath their makeshift bed, the crisp, tart scent of fall ripe in the air around them. They roused, shifted, snuggled together.

"Are you warm enough?" Ryder asked against her ear.

"You know this is hardly proper weather for an outdoor assignation."

"You're right, of course. We should be lying on a rug before a blazing fire or bundled together in a creaky old bed beneath half a dozen quilts."

"We'll catch our death of cold, at the very least," Jillian protested pessimistically.

"And I'll think of you with every sneeze."

His grin flashed in the darkness, and to press her point Jill twined her feet around his legs.

"You are cold!" he exclaimed, a chuckle rumbling in his chest as he bound her closer still.

But the moment of teasing passed, and Jillian went suddenly quiet, suddenly pensive, suddenly solemn.

"Ryder, why are you here?" she whispered.

He paused, frowned, smoothed a curl back from her brow. "I came because I was so tired of being alone, because I needed to see you, hold you, and make love to you."

She read the truth in his eyes, saw emotions in the indigo blueness that gave undeniable proof of his needs. He was no longer trying to deny what he felt, no longer holding back his trust and vulnerability. Her heart ached with the words they had not said, for the tangible proof of the bond between them that neither had given the other.

The declaration was on her lips before she knew she had

decided to give it voice. "I love you, Ryder," she whispered. "Oh, Ryder, I love you so."

Tears shimmered on her cheeks in spite of the valiant effort she made to smile.

Jillian's words offered Ryder the chance to express his own emotions, to tell her he loved her and offer her hope for a future they had never dared to contemplate.

"Oh, Jilly," he murmured, brushing the tears away. "You must know I—"

But at the touch of his fingers against her cheek, she flinched away, and the words he had been about to speak went dry and brittle on his lips. He withdrew and studied her closely, seeing for the first time the faint discoloration visible through the veil of powder.

"What's that?" he demanded.

"It's nothing, Ryder. Nothing."

But he was not appeased by her evasions and caught her chin, turning her face into the faint light that filtered into the gazebo.

"It's a bruise," he burst out. "A bruise. But how did you . . ."

She shrank back as if she expected some new cruelty to be visited upon her, and the source of the injury came clear to him. For an instant, his heart jarred to a stop inside his chest, and he went light-headed with the implications.

"He hit you, didn't he?" Ryder asked on a hissing breath. "Your father-in-law hit you!"

She shook her head and tried to lie. "No, Ryder, I—"

"God, I'll kill him!" Ryder snatched her pliant body against his own as primitive protectiveness and mindless fury warred inside him. Gerald Walsh had struck Jillian, treated her cruelly, barbarously. Hatred clouded Bingham's mind, and he was not sure which he wanted more, to keep Jillian safe in his embrace or to avenge himself on Gerald Walsh. It did not matter why Walsh had struck Jillian. No man had the right to use his strength on someone weaker than he.

"Is Walsh there now?" he demanded, stirring against her. "Is he in the house tonight?"

Jillian's arms tightened around Ryder, binding him close. In spite of what he meant to do, Jillian found she could not lie to him.

"Yes, he's there. But he's not alone. Ryder, please! It would be madness to confront him!"

He hardly seemed to hear her warning and began to disentangle himself from her arms. "He can't treat you so callously and expect to remain unscathed. He can't turn his strength against you without some retribution."

Jillian clung closer still, desperation giving her strength. "Ryder, please! I'm making plans to leave here, making plans to get away. If you go to him tonight, what I'm trying to do may well be forfeit."

For an instant, her plea made no difference. But then either the logic in her words or the entreaty in her voice reached him, and Ryder went still beside her.

"Just where are you going? How do you plan to leave?"

Sensing that he was going to give her a chance to explain, Jillian spoke quickly, persuasively. "I have written to several schools asking for a teaching position. It's what I should have done in the first place, but I was afraid to be on my own. In a few weeks, I hope to have an answer, and as soon as I do, I'll pack my bags and go."

Ryder's face was set, his muscles like skeins of knotted rope. "Will Walsh let you leave? Will he abuse you in the meantime?"

Jillian managed to counterfeit an assurance she did not feel. "I don't intend to give him any choice about my leaving. And no, I won't let him hit me. He caught me unprepared once, but that won't happen again."

Now was the time for Ryder to tell her of the future he had begun to plan, to speak the words of love he had come here to say. But the declaration stuck in his throat, silenced by the constraint Walsh's actions had forced upon him. How could he tell Jillian that he loved her, weave fantasies of the future they would one day share, and then leave her at the mercy of a man who had so callously mistreated her? Speaking of those things would demand that he act on what he felt, commit him to things he could not do, offer her solutions to her problems he was not yet able to provide. Uncertainty fluttered in his chest. No matter how much he loved Jillian, he wasn't ready to turn the promises he had come here to make into reality.

If I was any kind of a man, Ryder chided himself, *I would take Jillian to Toronto anyway, just to make sure she's safe from Walsh's bullying.*

But even if Jilly agreed to go with him, Ryder had nothing to offer her in Canada. In a matter of days he would leave on a mission from which he might never return. It would be callous and uncaring to take Jilly north, then abandon her to a world of strangers. She would be frightened and alone, and he could not disavow what he'd pledged, even for her sake. He had a mission to accomplish, a duty to discharge before he could offer her even so trifling a thing as himself, and he had to acknowledge that his taking her with him tonight might compromise the plans she had been making for her future.

He looked into her tear-streaked face and longed to tell her how he felt, if only for the transient comfort it could give. He wanted to whisper love words and solidify the pledge she had made to him. But how could he say those things, then leave her here in Walsh's home? How could he tell her he loved her and then ask her to wait while he resolved conflicts he could not even explain to her? How could he ask her to put aside the solutions she was seeking for herself when he had nothing tangible to offer?

He wanted this woman, had dreamed of making her his wife, but when she needed him most, when she was in the most desperate kind of trouble, he was incapable of offering her his help. The irony of his quandary and the knowledge of his impotence burned in Ryder with the bitter sting of gall.

He sank back beneath the blankets and wrapped his arms around her. Jillian was right; there was nothing to be gained by confronting Gerald Walsh. It would expose too much, risk both her safety and the plans she had finally found the courage to make. He was proud that she had taken the responsibility for her future into her own hands, glad she was discovering her independence, and he could not undercut her efforts by offering her something that was so tentative, so nebulous. At this moment he could give her nothing but his support in the path she had chosen for herself, nothing but his approval for the solution she was seeking on her own. He silently cursed the war, his duty to his comrades, his sense of responsibility.

Since he could not take her with him, he could not tell her where he was going or why he could not offer her safety in Toronto. He had to keep his hopes for the future a secret for a few weeks more, had to continue to hold his peace instead of saying the things he had come here to say. He had to let her make her way alone until he could offer her something tangible.

As his trembling hands brushed her face, her hair, her shoulders, he hated Gerald Walsh and himself with the passionate impatience of blighted hope.

"Oh, Jilly," he breathed, his voice ragged with regret. "Oh Jilly, I only wish I could do something to help you. Perhaps in time..."

Jillian closed her ears to his excuses. Ryder was not going to offer her sanctuary in Toronto, she realized with a stab of disillusionment. He was not going to offer her the chance to be with him, if only for a little while. Disappointment welled up within her, but it was disappointment shaded with understanding. She had known for weeks that there were things Ryder felt bound to do, demands he had made on himself that had nothing to do with his feelings for her. The predominance of these other concerns wounded her, but even through the pain she knew she would never again allow herself to become an unwelcome responsibility.

In spite of the vague half-promises he was making, Jillian could see there was no future for them together. Ryder's responsibility to the past and to his cause held sway, preventing him from acting on whatever it was he felt for her, even now that he knew what Gerald had done to her. What they had shared during those halcyon days in Rochester, in these few dangerous stolen moments, was not strong or enduring enough to compete with his sense of right and wrong. And in her heart of hearts, would she have wanted a man who could so easily turn his back on his duty?

Jillian drew a long breath and looked past him into the darkness. Perhaps she had been deluding herself to think he might take her with him, offer her a future at his side. If that was so, she must accept his decision stoically and make a life for herself as best she could.

"You'll write me and let me know where you are, won't you?" he demanded, sensing her withdrawal. "I couldn't bear not knowing if you are well and safe."

His words surprised her, and in spite of understanding his motives, a challenge rose to her lips. "Does it matter so much where I go? Do you really care what happens to me?"

He saw her bitterness for what it was and knew he could not change what she was feeling without telling her things it would have been dangerous for her to know. Expressions of caring and concern sprang to his lips, but he could not give them voice. Gerald Walsh's actions were forcing him to silence when with all his heart he wanted to speak his words of love aloud. Even now when Jill needed reassurance so desperately, he had nothing to offer her, and he accepted her censure without defending himself.

Then, abruptly, she was sitting up beside him, seeking her clothes in the tumble of leaves and blankets, dressing quickly, with sharp, jerky motions. Realizing there was nothing he could do to ease her pain, he pulled his clothes on, too.

In a flurry of skirts she came to her feet, sweeping her cloak around her and gathering up the blankets.

He rose to stand beside her and caught her arm. "You must write me at the Queen's Hotel and let me know what's become of you," he whispered urgently.

She turned to look up into his eyes, trying to read something more than was revealed in the blazing cobalt blue.

"Must I?" she queried. "Must I really?"

The skepticism in her tone chilled him to the marrow.

"Damn it, Jillian, even though I can't offer you my protection, I care about you. I need to know you're all right," he reiterated, "now and in the future."

It was all he dared say; he could not make promises that might prove impossible to keep. He could not let her believe in a future he had no right to promise. It would have been cruel to give Jillian hope, then let circumstances snatch it away. And he knew he had given her very little in exchange for her precious words of love.

"Very well," she conceded with a shrug. "I'll write and let you know where I am. And I'm touched by your concern."

Her sarcasm bit deep, and he knew he had done many things this night to earn her rancor. But instead of trying once more to explain, he caught her against his chest, hoping that somehow he could convey the depth of his feelings through the tenderness of his touch, the fleeting intimacy of his embrace.

She remained impassive in his arms and, after a moment, pulled away.

This was not the way he had meant for them to part, with disappointment and disillusionment in her eyes, and regret in his heart. Again love words bubbled to his lips, but he ruthlessly silenced the vows. There was no way to explain the trials he must overcome before he could offer her the reassurance she was seeking, no way to change the tenor of his leave-taking without compromising everything.

"Tell me which bedroom is yours," he finally said. "I'll watch for you to light the lamp, just to be sure you're safe."

She stared at him a long moment, trying to reconcile what seemed like genuine concern with her feelings of abandonment.

"The long window is at the landing of the stairs," she conceded. "My window is the one beside it on the second floor."

Ryder nodded once. "I'll wait until you signal me."

Jill shook her head. "There's no reason for that. Gerald's study is dark. No doubt he's gone to bed."

"I'll watch anyway," he assured her, reaching out to touch her arm one last time before she left him. "I want to be certain you're settled for the night before I go to catch my train."

She left in a whirl of skirts, rushing up the yard, leaving him alone in the dark. He sighed softly as he watched her go. He understood what she was feeling, knew how much his lack of commitment was hurting her. But once he had completed the mission in New York, he would be back. In a few short weeks he would be able to give her all the things he had not been able to offer tonight. Until he returned, Jillian would have to be patient, and he needed to be patient, too.

He saw the back door to the house open and close, and a minute or two later a light went on in the window of Jillian's bedroom. The knowledge that she had reached her sanctuary offered little reassurance, but he had forfeited the right to ask for more. He had to trust in fate, had to trust in love, had to trust that Jillian would be waiting when he returned from New York City.

"Good night, sweet Jilly," he whispered into the dark. "One day soon I'll come for you, and then you'll know I love you, too."

Gerald Walsh lit what would be his final cigar of the evening and dimmed the light on his desk. He'd had a long session with his new clients tonight, and now that he had finished up his paperwork, he was decidedly weary. He seemed to be feeling his age now in ways he had never felt it before, in the fatigue that dogged him at the end of the day, in the lack of purpose that had plagued him for months on end. Perhaps it was losing his bid for reelection to Congress in 1862 that had robbed him of his vitality or the enduring grief over his son's death that had taken the zest from living.

Walsh flicked the ash from his cigar into the fireplace and moved across the office to the bank of windows that overlooked the yard. Jeff had died so needlessly in the carnage of Petersburg, he mused angrily, and all he had as recompense was an ungrateful, shrewish daughter-in-law. Walsh grimaced with the thought of the young woman who had been thrust upon him. It was bad enough that she had encouraged Jefferson to accept a position in the thick of the fighting instead of the one he had arranged for the boy at the War Department in Washington. But Jeff was hardly cold when she had descended like a plague, needing clothes, shelter, food. What was even worse, she had come without a grandson in her belly to repay him for his trouble. As he had come to know Jillian Chandler better, he found she was a callow girl, wanting free run of the city, unable to fathom the importance of his position here. He could hardly find words to express how he had come to detest her. Taking her in had been a grievous mistake, but one he could not bring himself to rectify. She had made an enemy of Elvira Pryor almost immediately, had done nothing to acknowledge his bounteous generosity. And her behavior at the dinner party several nights before had been completely beyond the pale.

Though they had never discussed politics, Gerald had assumed his daughter-in-law shared his views on the war. But in the company of some of the most influential people in this part of the state, she had glibly defended the Southern cause. Walsh could feel the blood rise in his face as he remembered. Jillian had spent her whole life in Pennsylvania, was the widow of a Union soldier, and yet the opinions she had voiced were little less than treason. It was shocking to discover that she wanted no revenge for Jefferson's death, that she had no desire to see the Southerners punished for their sins. She had been dead set against giving the rebs everything they'd bargained for when they fired on Fort Sumter. She was convinced that the way to an enduring peace was through tolerance not destruction, appeasement not total victory. He was nurturing a traitor in his home, and he could not countenance her views.

It had been all he could do to wait until the guests had gone before giving her a proper dressing-down. If she had been cowed in the face of his anger, or given even lip service to his views, he might have been able to maintain his self-control. Instead, the girl had argued with him, maintained her own opinions on the war in spite of his opposition. The blows he'd dealt her in anger were something she richly deserved, and he had taken perverse pleasure in venting his grief and frustration. After putting up with months of her insolence, it had felt good to see fear instead of contempt, respect instead of defiance, in Jillian Chandler's eyes. The emotions were interchangeable anyway, at least to the victor, and she had clearly been the vanquished in that confrontation. He smiled and remembered the power he had felt when he saw the bruises on her face the following morning, the wild satisfaction he had known when he saw that the incident had made her docile and solicitous. He rolled the cigar to the opposite corner of his mouth and smiled with the memory of the change in her.

Outside the window the wind was rising, stirring the trees behind the house. There would be a storm before morning, he surmised, maybe even snow, though it seemed a trifle early for winter to begin in earnest.

As he stood staring out into the night, he caught sight of a faint, furtive movement between two banks of bushes, and as he watched, a black-shrouded figure detached itself from the shadows at the end of the yard. He knew there shouldn't be anyone on the property at this time of night, and with mounting apprehension, Walsh watched the interloper approach. The figure was moving boldly, as if familiar with the house and grounds, assured that everyone inside had long since gone to bed. With features hidden by the deep cowl of the cloak, Walsh could not determine the intruder's identity, but as the person approached the rear entrance, Gerald slipped across the room and took a pistol from his desk.

He was waiting at the door to his study, poised and ready to defend his home, when the cloaked figure slipped inside. But as it did, the hood fell back, and Walsh recognized the intruder as his daughter-in-law. As Jillian paused to latch the door, he took in every scrap of her appearance. He saw that her lips were smudged and dark, that her clothes were in telling disarray, that bits of leaves were tangled in her free-flowing hair. Beneath her arm were two old quilts, and Walsh knew immediately where she'd been. Jillian was returning from a meeting with a man, from an illicit assignation.

The realization exploded between Walsh's eyes, and mindless fury swept him. He would kill her, he decided wildly, shoot her down where she stood. Murder was the age-old penalty for unfaithful wives. It was the only means to rectify the breach of her marriage vows, the only way to cure a harlot of her faithlessness.

He cocked the gun and prepared to follow Jillian up the stairs, knowing that swift retribution would right the terrible wrong Jillian Chandler had done his son. Yet as he stepped into the hall, Walsh hesitated, thinking that even such a justifiable course might be better cloaked in guile. Besides, it would be more enjoyable to catch Jillian with her lover, to hear them plead for each other's lives before he made them pay for their perfidy. With a whispered promise of redress on his lips, Walsh eased the hammer of the revolver back in place and returned to the dimness of his study.

As he put the gun away, he found himself wondering about the man his daughter-in-law had met. Who had had the temerity to seduce his son's wife? Who was brazen enough to brave a father's wrath? Was the fellow still about, still on the property somewhere? If the man was any kind of a gentleman, he would wait for some sign that his lady was safe before leaving the grounds himself.

Using the private entrance to his office, Gerald slipped out into the blowy night. He moved smoothly for a man of his proportions and years, silently working his way down the yard in the shadow of the hedgerow. It was abysmally dark in the garden, the moon's light shrouded by thickly billowing clouds. But as he crept along, his eyes grew accustomed to the dimness.

He had barely reached the arbor when he heard someone moving toward him up the slope. He had been right. The man Jillian had met was still abroad, and he planned to slip past the darkened house instead of retreating along the river. Gerald slid beneath the arbor's arch of tangled vines, but the faint sound of movement must have reached the stranger. The man froze not a dozen paces from where Walsh stood, tensed, listening, waiting.

Was the man armed? Walsh found himself wondering suddenly. Would he stand and fight if his presence was discovered? Gerald cursed himself for having put his gun away. Waiting to find the lovers together before extracting retribution was one thing, but facing his daughter-in-law's lover alone and unarmed was more than Walsh had bargained for when he'd crept into the yard. After several endless seconds, the stranger moved on, unaware that he had been observed.

Walsh heaved a sigh of relief. In spite of the momentary danger, he had found out what he wanted to know. Jillian's lover was a stranger, tall, black-haired, wild-eyed, and clearly dangerous. He had a hard, angular face, the kind some women found appealing. But Walsh saw in the man's taut expression only deceit and treachery.

Gerald remained in the bushes for several minutes more, then backtracked, following the stranger's path down the slope toward the river. It was not difficult to discern where the trail would lead. The place had a history of assignations.

Walsh came to the gazebo and paused at the foot of the steps, loath to enter the deserted structure. Yet there was evidence of recent habitation. The leaves on the floor had been disturbed, and as he stood staring, the wind fluttered something toward him. Walsh bent and caught a hair ribbon in his hand. It was inky black and silky, confirmation of his daughter-in-law's presence at the gazebo only minutes before.

The ribbon was evidence enough to seal the accusation of adultery, and as her judge and jury, Walsh knew the sentence he would pass. But he would not see it carried out just yet, not until he learned her lover's name, not until the man could be included in her punishment.

As he stood staring at the evidence of Jillian's infidelity, Gerald remembered other lovers curled together in the dark. He could almost hear the hiss of their whispered endearments, could almost smell the randy musk of their rising passion. Had he really stood here on the steps of the summerhouse more than twenty years ago with the same emotions rising in his chest, the same hatred beating in his brain? Was it possible another woman had betrayed Walsh himself, just as Jillian Chandler was betraying his son? The thoughts roiled and burned inside him, echoing with remembered pain.

"Bitches," he whispered softly, caught in a half-world of present and past. "All women are bitches—lying, cheating whores."

His small eyes glowed like pagan torches as he crushed night-dark ribbon in his fist, confirming a discovery he had made years and years before.

"Oh, yes, women are all the same," he whispered into the night, "always lovely, always grasping, always faithless. For the scope of their infidelities, for the vows they have defiled, those of us who've been betrayed have the right to recompense. We have the right to judge the adulteresses for their sins and meter out their punishment."

Chapter Twelve

RYDER COULD HEAR a distant clock chime the hour, the strokes lazy and strangely resonant, pealing through the heavy silence. It was three in the morning, and still sleep eluded him. He had been lying awake for hours, his mind clamoring with activity, his belly clenched in anticipation. He knew he should rest, but his nerves were strung so taut that the darkness seemed a physical presence against his skin, the quiet a constant roar in his ears.

Knowing there would be no sleep this night, he rolled to the edge of the bed and, with a moan of resignation, came to his feet. It was cold in the hotel room, and he pulled on his pants and shirt as he padded to the fireplace. He rattled coal from the scuttle into the grate, and while he waited for the embers to ignite it, he moved to the window.

Below him lay one of New York's quieter streets, lined with private residences and small hotels. The gaslights stood like sentries, casting pale elliptical patterns on the pavement and turning the sleety rain into driving streaks of silver. Ryder was not even sure what street this was, since he had moved often in these last weeks. It had seemed wisest to stay no more than a day or two at any establishment, and the men of Robert Martin's command had hopscotched across the city while they waited for something to happen.

Well, something would happen tomorrow, Ryder reflected, but it would not happen quite the way they'd originally planned. The mission they had discussed a month or more ago in Toronto could not quite be termed a failure, though what had finally evolved from it would hardly be the success they had hoped either.

The first obstacle had arisen with the arrival of "Beast" Butler and his troops. If the news stories were to be believed, Butler and his men had come to keep the peace on Election Day in one of the North's most volatile cities. But as time passed, hints that they had also been ordered to protect New York from Southern sympathizers began to appear in the papers. How the Yankees had got wind of the Confederate mission, Ryder could only guess. But the Union general's presence at the Hoffman House Hotel had sent blind panic racing through the Copperhead ranks, forcing postponement of the planned uprising and their mission as well.

Ryder had remembered Thomas Hines's harsh indictment of the Copperheads when the following day's headlines heralded the discovery of a Confederate plot in Chicago.

"Well, that tears it!" Martin exploded, when they met at the cabin he had secured in Central Park. "There will be no support for our cause in Chicago, and perhaps none in Boston or Cincinnati either."

Headley glanced up from reading the accounts in the morning papers. "It says that they've arrested General Marmeduke, Colonel Grenfel, and several other Confederate leaders, but there's no mention of Captain Hines. Do you think he got away?"

"Hines is a slippery fellow," Jamie put in with a touch of awe. "If anyone can escape the Yankees, I'd put my money on him."

"But how will those arrests affect what we've come to do?" Ryder wondered quietly.

"I suppose it will make the Copperheads as skittish as a maiden mare in heat," Martin answered pessimistically.

"It's damned irritating!" put in Robert Cobb Kennedy, another of the new recruits. "I came here to set New York ablaze, and I'm just not ready to give up and pack away my matches."

None of them had been ready to do that, but Martin counseled patience. "We don't have any choice but to wait," he told them. "With this news from Chicago, Butler and his troops are going to be more vigilant and the Copperheads more wary."

They had waited, but not patiently, their frustration growing day by endless day. They had waited through Lincoln's reelection, through the day Butler and his troops left the city, through Sherman's burning of Atlanta and the news of his plans to march to the sea. Under the weight of the blaring headlines in the *Times*, under the crush of the Confederates' impatience, the Copperhead support had finally collapsed altogether.

"They say now that the end of the war is inevitable," Martin had reported at a meeting in Headley's rooms at the Astor Hotel. "They say there's nothing to be gained by supporting Confederate efforts to burn the city."

"We've been trussed up like a Christmas turkey for weeks, waiting for McMasters and his cronies to make their move," James Chenault, one of the group that had come from Toronto, muttered in disgust. "Now at least we're free to decide our fate, to decide what we alone will do."

"I say we hightail it back to Toronto," John Price, another one of the raiders, put in. "We haven't heard a thing from the groups in other cities. I think it's just plain crazy to continue to risk our necks to implement a plan that has been doomed to failure from the start!"

It was a harsher indictment than any of the other Confederates were prepared to voice, and there were murmurs of discontent at the venom in Price's words.

"But we told Thompson he would hear from us regardless of what was done elsewhere," Headley argued. "He seemed to approve of our determination, and I don't think it's wise to fold before the last card's been played."

"I'd like to see the North pay for what they've done in the Shenandoah, what Sherman and his marauders seem determined to do in Georgia," Rob Kennedy put in.

"I agree with Kennedy," Ryder voted. "Without the help of the Copperheads, we may not be able to achieve the disunity that will bring the North to peace, but that doesn't mean the Yankees should go unscathed when there's no question that the worst is ahead for the South."

Jamie nodded in confirmation. "Let's do what we came to do. Let's make the Yankees feel the sting of Southern defiance."

Martin quickly assessed the feeling of the others around the room. They were in agreement with Jamie's sentiments.

"We'll have to revise our plans," their leader answered, speaking slowly. "There aren't enough of us here to take over the Federal buildings and set the town alight."

"The government buildings are always guarded, anyway," Headley observed. "We need to focus our attack on places where we're granted freer access."

"Like hotels," Chenault agreed. "These damned Yankee hotels are like palaces, with their dangling crystal chandeliers and oceans of plush carpeting. There's no one in the South living nearly as well as these stinking Yankee merchants on their ill-gotten gains."

It took a moment for the thought to sink in. They had all seen their share of hotels this trip and had been first awed and then offended by their opulence.

"The idea has some merit," Martin agreed, rubbing his scraggly beard.

"It does at that," Bradford replied. "But do we still have access to the explosives we'll need to set the town ablaze?"

Martin conceded with a nod. "Our contacts here in the city have told me where the Greek fire is being hidden."

"But will the mixture do the job it is supposed to do?" Ryder asked. "Do we even know how to detonate the compound?"

Greek fire, a mixture of phosphorous and bisulfide of carbon, had been used primarily in hand grenades thus far in the war, and none of the men in the group had any experience handling it.

"A little experimentation should teach us all we need to know," Martin assured them, speaking with what was perhaps greater conviction than he felt.

From the meeting at the Astor a second, less magnificent plan had been born, a plan a cadre of Confederate raiders would easily be able to implement.

Ryder took a turn around his chilly hotel room, considering what they meant to do. It was not all he had once wished they would accomplish, and the knowledge was edged with disappointment. But tomorrow, for good or ill, the Confederates would move, and he wished with all his heart that he had something stronger than water to drink as he waited for the dawn. In these past weeks, Ryder had had his fill of waiting. He'd had his fill of failure, and when the new plan came together, he had been ready to agree to almost anything that would give him another chance to forge into the fray.

The men of Martin's command had met earlier in the evening at the cottage in the park to await the arrival of Lieutenant Headley. He had been selected to pick up the shipment of Greek fire from a store near Washington Square. Smoldering tension had crackled around the shabby cabin as they waited, and the men passed the time with a game of cards. They gambled with matchsticks, betting with the bits of wood as readily as they were prepared to bet their lives.

"He's here!" someone finally called from the doorway, and the Confederates spilled out of the cabin to watch Headley's approach.

"I could hardly carry this damned thing," Headley panted, gladly handing over a huge valise that smelled suspiciously of sulfur. "And what's worse, I couldn't find a cab at Washington Square and had to take a streetcar. It was not an inconspicuous way to travel, and the smell from the valise drew lots of comments."

"It stinks, that's sure," Kennedy agreed, wrinkling his nose, hitching up his thick mustache. "It's worse than rotten eggs."

Martin opened the case gingerly, and the pungent smell grew stronger still. "One of the bottles has spilled," he reported to Headley. "If this concoction's as volatile as they say, it's a wonder the whole case didn't go up, taking you and the streetcar with it."

In spite of the noxious odor, the Confederates gathered close while Martin unearthed one of the bottles and held it to the light. The liquid inside was clear, the bottle sealed with plaster.

"Did the man who gave you these offer any instructions?"

The lieutenant shook his head. "He didn't say so much as a word to me."

Martin led the men outside, across the pelt of fallen leaves. "If this works the way we've been told, we simply have to crack the bottle and the contents will catch fire."

With a glance at his companions, he threw the vial toward a rock at the edge of the clearing, a dozen yards away. There was a satisfying smash of breaking glass, and for a moment nothing happened. The Confederates crept forward step by step, eyeing the broken bottle suspiciously. A flickering trail of smoke drifted upward from the bed of fallen leaves, and there was a sinister hiss of spiraling vapor before the ground erupted into flames.

A whoop of excitement burst from the Confederates, and they grabbed each other, yelling like victorious schoolboys. The explosive compound worked! After heartily congratulating themselves for their cleverness, they used several more bottles of Greek fire for experimentation. It didn't take long to discover that the phosphorus needed to soak in before it would burst into flame. But as the yellow fingers of fire crept over the ground toward where they stood, the men grew silent, as if suddenly realizing the awesome power of the weapon they held in their hands. Hurriedly stamping the fire to ashes, they retreated to the cabin to lay plans for the following day.

"We will meet here at six o'clock," Martin instructed as he carefully tucked the valise of bottles beneath the table by the wall. "Bring a satchel of some sort with you, and we'll distribute the explosives then.

"In preparation, I want each man to take rooms at several hotels, good rooms, on the second floor or the third, where the fires we set won't be readily discovered. We'll begin our work at eight, while most of the guests are at dinner. Our goal is to destroy property, not burn the Yankees in their beds."

Martin's instructions had been well thought out and clear, and as Ryder stared up and down the street, he couldn't help wondering if there was a chance for their plans to succeed. So much had gone wrong on this mission already, he was afraid to contemplate even a limited victory. Would they accomplish what they meant to, or would their efforts come to naught?

As Ryder stood considering all that could happen, a soft insistent scratching came at the door to his room. It seemed unlikely that anyone would be abroad at this hour of the night, and Bingham slipped the pistol from his carpetbag before going to greet his visitor.

Jamie stood outside in the hall, his fair hair tousled with sleeplessness and his gray eyes wide with uncertainty.

"I didn't mean to disturb you," he began in an apologetic voice, "but I haven't had much luck sleeping, and I wondered if you'd join me for a drink."

Jamie flashed the bottle of whiskey he had hidden inside his jacket, and Ryder greeted both the offering and his friend with a welcoming grin. As the smaller man entered the hotel room, he took note of the twisted bedclothes that gave mute testimony of Ryder's own restlessness.

"I couldn't sleep either," Bingham admitted sheepishly. "And you can't know how much I've been wishing for a drink to calm my nerves."

Ryder put the gun away and took two glasses from the washstand.

"Dutch courage?" Jamie asked, pouring three fingers of amber liquid into Ryder's glass.

"I told you before, I don't give a damn whose courage it is, as long as it gets me through."

They took a long deep swallow of the whiskey in a toast to courage, and another in toast to each other. Then, refilling their glasses, they settled back in the room's two mismatched armchairs to pass the night together. For a time they drank in silence, letting the warmth of the whiskey spread outward from their bellies, listening to the rain hissing against the glass, knowing that the minutes ticking past were bringing them closer to the dangers of the morrow.

Finally Ryder spoke, putting both their thoughts into words. "None of this has turned out quite the way we planned, has it?"

Bradford shook his head and cast a glance at his tall companion. "God! Do you remember how we felt when Thompson proposed this plan? We were filled with implausible dreams: that we would have the Union at our mercy with a few threats from the Copperheads and a couple of well-placed fires, that we need only give the Yankees a scare to make them sue for peace." He drew a long breath and exhaled slowly. "It makes you wonder, doesn't it, how we could have been so gullible."

Ryder heard the bitterness in Jamie's tone and felt the rise of an answering bile.

"I suppose we wanted to believe what Thompson told us," he offered with a shrug. "He gave us a renewed belief in an independent South, the sense that our actions could make that a reality."

Ryder ran a hand through his hair, and when he continued, his voice had taken on a lower, husky timbre. "He offered me a chance for the things I wanted to share with Jillian: a life, a home, a future. Perhaps that is why we embraced those dreams with such blind hope, why we cling to them so stubbornly still. Maybe it even explains why we are doing what we promised when it would be so much easier and wiser to simply give it up and leave."

"Damn!" Jamie lamented softly, fishing a cigar from the inside pocket of his jacket. "We harbored such foolish, foolish dreams."

"You do think it's over, then, the chance to accomplish all we fought for?"

Jamie shook his head despairingly. "I think our chance to make a difference is over. But the war won't be over for months yet, not for months. It won't be over until the Yankees have crushed the South to ashes, smothered the last embers of rebellion. What we plan to do here in New York is nothing more than a meaningless act of reparation, a defiant gesture that can serve no enduring purpose. It's so damned futile for men to risk their lives when there's nothing to be gained."

Ryder eyed his friend, seeing his dejection. "If that's the way you feel, Jamie," Ryder suggested gently, "perhaps you should leave New York tonight."

There was a moment of silence before Jamie answered, raising slitted eyes to Ryder's face. "Shall I go and let them brand me a coward?" he demanded in a hoarse whisper. "Shall I let them say that I'm afraid to die?"

In a flash of insight, Ryder knew that the overwhelming pessimism Jamie had voiced from the beginning of this endeavor was based in the fear of his own mortality.

"We're all afraid to die, Jamie," Ryder answered him. "But the fear's always worse before the battle than once the fight's begun."

Jamie stared at his friend incredulously. "You're not afraid, are you, Ryder?"

"Of course I'm afraid," Ryder admitted on a gust of laughter. "Any man in his right mind is afraid of going up against the enemy, of being killed or wounded. Or of turning tail when things go wrong."

Silence hung between them as Jamie rolled the unlit cigar between his fingers.

"I did that in my first battle," Jamie finally gulped in a voice thick with shame and self-loathing. "Instead of following my unit into battle, I laid down my arms at the sight of the Feds and let myself be captured."

Ryder turned to stare, stunned by Jamie's admission. He had no idea that Jamie had been in battle, no inkling that he had surrendered without a fight. But then, nothing they had done invited confidences, and there was much he didn't know about the other man.

"But you've risked far more than men in battle," Bingham burst out, "crossing and recrossing the border, traveling between the Union and Confederate lines! How can you think of yourself as a coward when you've been doing something so dangerous?"

Jamie put the cigar in his mouth and struck a match to flame.

In the flare of the wavering light, Ryder could see how violently Bradford's hands were trembling.

"I became Holcombe's messenger after I was exchanged. It gave me the chance to do the things I'm good at: being charming and guileless, or cunning and evasive. It's a useful talent, I admit, but it's no substitute for the courage it takes to face the thick of battle or to be a saboteur."

"Then for God's sake, Jamie, why did you volunteer to come with us to New York?"

Jamie shrugged, shrinking deep into his chair. "I came because I needed to prove something to myself, to be part of something so important. I came because I'd discovered that though my fear of dying is horrible, it's no worse than living with my cowardice."

Jamie's eyes met Ryder's across the space that separated them, and his voice was filled with urgency. "What I need to know, Ryder, is how I get past that fear."

Bingham shook his head, wishing he knew how to answer his friend, trying to convey some kind of reassurance. "You never do get past it. And in the end, it doesn't really matter. You do what you must because others are depending on you. If you don't do your part tomorrow, some of us will be caught burning the hotels, and for our crimes we'll be tried and hanged."

Disbelief shone in Jamie's eyes. "That seems unbelievably simple."

Ryder took a swallow from his glass and weighed his own apprehension. "War is a primitive activity," he finally replied. "In the end the decisions are easy because the options are so few."

There seemed nothing more to be said between them, and they sat drinking the whiskey in silence. The fire crackled in the grate, filling the room with glowing warmth. The rain pelted the window. The occasional clink of the bottle against the rim of a glass was the only sound that disturbed the quiet as they helped themselves to more of the liquor. There were no answers in the room that night, only boundless uncertainty. There was no respite from the fear, only the fleeting courage companionship gave them. There was only the deed before them to contemplate, not the past, not the future, not the possibility of heaven or hell. There was only the waiting and the promise of action to come. It wasn't enough for either of them, but it was all they had.

Toward dawn Ryder must have slept, for when he awoke, stiff and groggy in the leather chair, Jamieson Bradford was gone.

* * *

Sheets. Blankets. Pillows. Towels. Rug. Curtains. Chair. Drawers. Newspapers.

Ryder balanced the pile in the middle of the double bed and opened a vial of Greek fire. The pungent smell of rotten eggs assailed him, and he wrinkled his nose with distaste as he poured first one vial and then a second over the collection he had made of things in the hotel room that would burn. As the chemical compound soaked into the tangle of furniture and bedding, he gathered up his black valise and headed toward the door. He paused with his hand on the knob, wondering why the bed wasn't yet alight. He had used the Greek fire as Martin had instructed him, as he himself had practiced only the night before. But somehow standing in the deserted park, it hadn't seemed to take this long for the compound to ignite.

Ryder stalked back across the room, wondering if he would need to turn to something as basic as turpentine and matches to get the room to burn. But just as he reached the side of the bed, there was a woosh, and flames flared up through the center of the pile.

He leaped backwards and watched as the pillows and drapery caught, going smoldery and brown around the edges, curling slowly at the base of the flames. He stared for a moment in fascination as the fire crawled across the headboard, then leaped onto the wall, clawing its way toward the ceiling.

He could feel the heat on his face, hear the intimate crackle of flames, taste the smoke in the back of his throat as his eyes began to tear. He knew he had no time to stand here admiring his handiwork. Either he would be trapped by the fire itself, or he would be discovered watching it.

With self-preservation in mind, Ryder left and locked the hotel room door behind him. Once he was out in the hallway, he had to fight the urge to run. Instead, he took the stairs three flights down and calmly crossed the lobby. The reception area was crowded with men enjoying an after-dinner cigar, with couples queueing up outside the restaurant, with people requesting rooms. Ryder could not resist a backward glance as he approached the exit onto Broadway. How long before this hotel became a conflagration? How long before these staid people began to scream in panic?

He brushed through the door onto the street and gave the doorman a parting nod. Would the man be able to describe him to the police? Ryder wondered. Would the desk clerk remember him among the many others who had checked in to the hotel that day?

He walked more than a block before stepping aside and glancing anxiously over his shoulder to be sure he wasn't being followed. Across the street, he noticed a clock in a jewelry store window. It was eight twenty-three, and in the first hotel on his list a room had already been set alight.

Taking his satchel more firmly in hand, Ryder turned north and west, moving toward the second target on his list. When he reached it, he made his way up to the room he had secured earlier in the day. This room was not as large or as lavishly furnished as the first had been, but he went about the same preparations. He piled everything he could find on the bed and doused it with Greek fire. He waited only for the first streamers of smoke to appear, then locked the room behind him and left the hotel.

When he reached the street, fire bells were beginning to clang, a sound he hoped would be heard loud and often during the night to come. When he reached the corner at Broadway, he looked down toward the first hotel he'd visited, but there were no people in the street, no sign that an alarm had been given. Though he felt the prod of curiosity, he knew it would be dangerous and foolhardy to return to watch for evidence of his efforts. Instead, Bingham turned uptown, moving quickly past other people on the walk.

The street was crowded tonight, filled with many who had chosen to take advantage of the break in the weather. It had rained until nearly noon, but now the sky was clear and bright. There was a festive feeling in the air, perhaps the aftermath of the Thanksgiving holiday celebrated throughout the North the day before, or perhaps a reflection of New York's own commemoration of Evacuation Day, when the last of the British troops had left the city at the end of the Revolutionary War. Whatever the cause, people had come out in droves, to shop, to stroll, to see or be seen. They might well have been on their way to theaters to see the Booth brothers in *Julius Caesar* at the Winter Garden, or to hear Donizetti's new opera, *Don Sebastiano* at the Academy of Music. They perused menus posted outside restaurants up the block, and gathered in noisy groups on corners of the busy thoroughfare.

As he neared City Hall Park, he saw firemen in the street, reeling our yards of hose in front of Barnum's famed museum. Barnum's had not been on the list of sites to be burned, but as Ryder came closer, he could see that the place was already aflame, and his heart began to pound. Some enterprising soul among them had used his allotment of Greek fire to turn the place into an inferno. Terrified people were streaming out the doors of the museum, and flames were spitting skyward from the upper floors of the brick and iron structure. Smoke rose in gray-black billows, drawing a mob of onlookers from up and down the thoroughfare. Ryder stood across the street watching the melee, as caught up in the excitement as anyone else in the crowd.

Barnum's animals were being brought out the central door, an elephant on a chain, a boxing kangaroo and its trainer, a Bengal tiger in its cage. On the second story balcony a woman emerged from the burning building and stood silhouetted by the blaze. There was something both fascinating and horrific in watching her, in seeing the terror in her face, in hearing the crowd shout encouragement and suggestions to aid in her escape. But as soon as the firemen became aware of her predicament, a ladder was set in place, and one of the men scampered up to rescue her. Cheers greeted the successful completion of the mission, but the faces of the fire fighters were set and grim as they went on about their business.

The traffic on Broadway was in a snarl as carriages rolled to a stop, blocked by the tangle of fire apparatus and the crowd that swelled from the confines of the sidewalk out into the street. From the people in those stalled vehicles word began to spread that there were fires breaking out in other parts of the city as well. The cry of "Arson!" swept through the crowd like a wave, heads turning in nervous haste as the accusation was passed from mouth to mouth. With the news came speculation about the cause of so many fires, and the suspicion of a Confederate conspiracy was passed along as truth.

The mood of the gathering changed in the space of a dozen heartbeats. Faces that had been marked with curiosity and excitement were now shaded with suspicion and twisted with incipient panic. The mass of spectators began to seethe as people sought some means to escape the threat of a Confederate uprising. Slightly more than a year before, the city had been rocked by brutal riots, and where another place might have dismissed the charges of a conspiracy as unlikely, the people of New York were not so blissfully untouched.

The crowd's frantic movements were further hampering the efforts of the firemen, and when policemen carrying billy clubs appeared at the edges of the fray, Ryder decided he had seen enough. Sprinting between two carriages, he made his way down an alley that brought him out a block from the fire and the crowd. Bingham could still smell the smoke from the Barnum Museum fire and hear the roar of voices echoing between the buildings, but he was able to catch his breath before moving on to his next hotel.

As he headed north again, the fire alarms were clanging constantly in shrill, hysterical peals that seemed to echo the fear and trepidation that had begun to grip New York. Though theirs was a sound that might well herald Confederate success, Ryder found it somehow less exhilarating and less gratifying than he had thought he might.

In the lobby of the third hotel, the porters seemed particularly vigilant, as if word of what was happening elsewhere in the city had reached them and put them on their guard. They eyed him suspiciously as he entered, but when Bingham slipped up a narrow back stairway to the second floor, no one followed him.

But just as he was fitting his key in the lock to his room, there was the sound of footfalls at his back.

"Are you the man who wanted extra towels?" a soft voice asked.

With reflexes honed sharp by apprehension, Bingham swung around before he had time to realize the question was innocuous. Raising one arm to fend off an attack, he slammed his inquisitor into the corridor wall with brutal jarring force. He realized his mistake seconds later when he found himself staring down into the startled face of one of the hotel's maids. The towels she had been holding tumbled from her arms as she stared up at him, and Ryder recognized instantly that the violence of his unthinking response had drawn unwanted attention to his presence.

Immediately he stepped away, steadying the maid with one hand as he offered an apology.

"I sure am sorry, ma'am. Are you all right? Coming up from behind like that did give me an awful start."

He had never been more aware in his life of his rich Carolina drawl, and he wondered if the woman had the presence of mind to take note of it.

She did seem to regain her composure with remarkable speed, glaring up at him in irritation as she adjusted the bodice of her uniform.

"I'm fine, I suppose. Though I'm hardly used to such rough treatment," she scolded. "And on top of everything else, I suppose you're not the gentleman who's been waiting for his towels."

Not trusting his voice, Ryder shook his head, then bent to help her retrieve the linens from the floor. Once the maid had gathered the towels in her arms, she gave him a hard look and retreated down the corridor. As he watched her go, Bingham roundly cursed his own stupidity. The tensions of the night were beginning to tell on him, and Bingham found he was anxious to finish his assignments and return to the anonymity of his own hotel.

As he let himself into the room he'd rented, he wondered if the maid would report his actions and send someone up to question him. She would be able to identify him, at the very least, and he realized it would be both risky and unwise to set a fire after what had happened. For once in his life, Ryder decided to concede that discretion was indeed the better part of valor, and once he had checked to be sure that the hall was empty, he made his way out into the night.

Moving quickly along the side streets, he headed back toward Broadway. But as he walked, he noticed police and firemen routing people from their homes. The reason for the evacuations was abundantly clear, for as he approached the congested thoroughfare, the air grew dense with drifting smoke. He brushed past frightened women with crying children in their arms, saw men clutching their pitiful few belongings tight against their chests. Panic was as thick as the air, and it bothered him no small bit to see the effect the fires were having on the populace.

Ryder had not bargained on the feeling of remorse he found rising in his chest or on the guilt that dogged his steps as he traversed the smoky city. Though he called up the multitude of reasons the Confederates had given themselves to justify setting the town ablaze, now he found the arguments thin and unconvincing, expedient and dishonorable. There were few times in his life when he had so unequivocally seen the consequences of his actions or found them so appalling. Still his duty lay before him. There was one last hotel on his list, and if he was to complete the assignment he'd been given, he would need to fire that place as well.

But when he found himself in the room at last, Ryder hesitated, plagued by conscience. Was this really what he wanted to do? Were the reasons for burning the hotel as valid as they had seemed earlier in the evening in the company of his confederates? Before, he had held the conviction that he was doing what was right in light of the Yankee atrocities, that all they meant to do was avenge the terrible wrongs that had been done to the people of the South. He had seen this mission as a chance to even the score for Mitchell's death, but when he thought of the fine, gentle man who had been his younger brother, Ryder began to wonder if

Mitch wouldn't be dishonored by the form that vengeance had taken. When Ryder made the decision that brought him here, the Yankees had been a faceless mass, an army of vicious strangers. But on his way to this hotel, he had seen his enemies as frightened individuals. That jarring new perception was making it more difficult to do what he had pledged.

As he piled the chairs and drapery on the bed and opened the vials of liquid fire, he tried to block out the terrified women and children he had seen on the street, tried to erase from his mind the concern he had seen in the faces of their husbands and fathers. This was what he had agreed to do, what he had been ordered to do, he told himself. But the task had become vile and distasteful, shameful and barbarous. Bingham had to force himself to pour the chemicals over the pile of bedding, and even before the compound began to ignite, he hurried from the room and slammed the door behind him.

The mood on the streets was ugly, and though the police were patrolling the neighborhoods around Broadway, there were mobs of angry citizens marauding the streets. He dumped the empty satchel in an alley and tried to draw as little attention as possible as he sought the safety of his rooms, skulking along in the shadows like the criminal he had become.

It was well past midnight when Bingham reached his goal, and as he prepared to go inside, he could still hear fire bells clanging everywhere. Jamie had been in the back of his mind the whole evening long, and before he returned to his room, he rapped on Jamie's door, a few down the corridor from his own. At first he thought his friend had not yet returned, but after several interminable seconds, Bradford opened the numbered wooden panel.

He was pale as alabaster as he peered through the crack at Ryder, and there seemed to be a sickly green cast to the skin around his mouth. Jamie finally pulled open the door to admit his friend, and once Bingham was inside the room, he realized the reason for Jamie's appearance. The place smelled like a distillery, and there was an empty whiskey bottle on the table by the bed.

"Are you all right?" Ryder demanded with rising concern.

"I'm fine," Jamie slurred. "Did 'zactly what I was supose' t' do."

There was no triumph in the words, nor did Ryder expect to hear any. Jamie was not an insensitive man, and the deeds they'd done this night must have bothered him every bit as much as they had bothered Ryder.

"Why don't you go to bed, then?" Ryder urged gently. "We can talk about this in the morning."

"Bed?" Jamie muttered as if he'd never heard the word.

"You know, lie down, sleep."

Before Jamie could respond, his knees began to bow, and Ryder wrapped an arm around his waist and hustled him toward the bed. Once the smaller man was lying down, Bingham began to remove his boots and shirt in an attempt to make his friend more comfortable.

"Gonna be sick," Jamie warned, and Ryder went scrambling for the chamber pot, then held the other man's head as he relieved himself of his dinner.

Pale and sweating, Jamie finally flopped back on the mattress. "'S not glorious, like I thought it'd be," he muttered limpidly. "'S not glorious at all."

Ryder smoothed a shock of matted curls back from the blond man's brow. "I know it wasn't glorious. It wasn't even civilized."

"'Spected it to be glorious, actin' for the cause."

"Things are rarely what we expect," Bingham murmured consolingly, as much for his own benefit as for Jamie's. But Bradford's eyes were closed, and Ryder was not sure he'd heard.

It seemed wrong to leave his friend in such a state, and after disposing of his coat and overcoat, Ryder eased himself into a chair at the foot of the bed. Between his concern for Jamie and the fire bells that continued to peal, Ryder realized that there would be little sleep this night. But then, he hadn't really expected he would sleep well, anyway.

Chapter Thirteen

THE NEW YORK papers shrieked the news. The headline in *The New York Times* cried: "The Rebel Plot—Attempt Made to Burn the City—All the Principal Hotels Simultaneously Set on Fire— Prompt Arrest of Rebel Emissaries." The *Herald* added its voice to the chorus: "Attempt to Burn the City—Discovery of a Vast Rebel Conspiracy—Arrest of Four of the Principals—The Perpetrators to be Tried at Court Martial and Hanged Immediately."

Jillian spread the papers out on the floor of her bedroom and tried to quell her rising panic. Her concern was focused and clear: Had Ryder been involved in these atrocities? The possibility made her heart constrict until she felt cold and dead and breathless. Had he been on his way to New York when he had come to her? Ryder had seemed different then, somehow: calmer, gentler, more settled, as if he had made peace with himself at last. Did the onset of this mission explain the subtle change she had sensed in him? Was this the means he had found to revenge his brother's death? And, dear God, had he come to her to say good-bye?

There was a jangling uncertainty in the pit of her stomach as her eyes scanned the carpet of newspapers. It had been impossible to read the accounts of the aborted Confederate plot in Chicago several weeks before without wondering if Ryder was involved. But somehow she had known he was not, and as the names of those who were apprehended had been made public, the truth of her feelings had been verified. But whatever sixth sense had made her certain that Ryder had not gone to Chicago now seemed to confirm that he was tied up with the rebels who had fired New York. Contemplating what that meant left her giddy. The papers reported that men had already been arrested and that the police were on the trail of several others. They also said that the punishment for such a crime was execution, and she was terrified that Ryder would be arrested, tried, and hanged.

She pressed one hand to her mouth to stifle a sob while tears beaded and simmered at the corners of her eyes. She could be wrong, she tried to tell herself. Ryder might still be in Toronto or even on his way to Wilmington. But even as Jillian fought to convince herself, she knew it was unlikely.

No, Ryder had been in New York with these men, and he had known he was going there when he had seen her last. She was sure of that now, and that certainty was changing, congealing into paralyzing dread. Where was he now? Had he escaped from the city? Or would he be trapped, run to ground by Union detectives?

As Jillian stared at the field of headlines, pondering Ryder's fate, there was a knock at the door to her bedroom.

"Just a minute!" she called out as she scrambled around, attempting to tuck the papers out of sight. But before she could, the door opened and her father-in-law stepped inside. She swirled guiltily to face him, holding some of the crumpled papers behind her back, struck speechless by the fact that Gerald Walsh had invaded her bedroom. In the past when he had wanted to see her, he had summoned her to his study, and those were summonses Jillian had come to dread. What it meant to have him burst in here now Jill could only guess.

She took a step back, coming up hard against the side of the bed, and watched as he took in the disarray of newspapers spread across the floor.

"Taking a new interest in the war, my dear?" Walsh asked her quietly. "Or is your interest only in the plot to burn New York?"

"I— We— It does show incredible gall on the Confederates' part, don't you think? That they would try to set the largest city in the North ablaze?" In the split second she had to ready her defenses, outrage seemed the safest course. It would not force her to voice any outright lies, and righteous indignation was something easily riled. "That the rebels set fire to hotels while the patrons were in their beds is shocking, despicable. I can't imagine there's any way to sanction—"

Gerald Walsh came a step nearer, and the rest of the sentence stuck in her throat.

"I was under the impression that you would approve of such behavior," he drawled. "You as much as advocated acts like these the evening we had guests to dinner."

"No, I never—" Jillian began, but Walsh continued in spite of her objection.

"At the time I wondered at your sentiments, at your blatant sympathy for the South when you are a Yankee born and raised and the widow of a Union soldier. But now I understand the reason. After finding a stranger on the property a month or more ago, I did some checking, and your affinity for the Confederate cause was easily explained. You have a rebel lover, don't you, girl? He's an escaped prisoner, a blockade-runner, Captain Ryder Bingham."

For an instant, Jillian wasn't sure she remembered how to breathe, but as she finally sucked a deep draft of air into her lungs, her first thought was for her lover. "You haven't hurt Ryder, have you? You haven't turned him over to the Yankees?"

Walsh gave a sinister laugh at the confirmation in her words. "Not yet I haven't, but I will. And I mean to turn you over, too. Imagine having a rebel's whore in my own household. Imagine having her despoil her marriage vows before my very eyes. You've been meeting him down at the gazebo, haven't you? It's a good place for unfaithful wives, a wonderful place for lovers' trysts."

Even as she tried to form the words of a denial, she knew her protests would be fruitless. Everything he said was true. She had met Ryder at the gazebo, but she was a widow now, no longer bound by marriage vows she'd given to a dead man. But even as she railed against Walsh's accusations of unfaithfulness, it was the threat of Ryder's exposure that was the more clear and present danger. There was no way she could refute her association with the Confederate, even if she wanted to do so.

As she grappled for words to nullify her father-in-law's accusations, he continued. "It doesn't matter what you say, girl. I saw you coming in the last time you met him, with your hair tumbling down your back like a harlot's, with your face aglow in the aftermath of his lovemaking. There's no use denying it. It was only by the wildest chance that I came upon the man himself and found out who he was. Now I intend to make you pay for your indiscretions and your treachery."

A sudden paralysis seemed to afflict Jillian. Her limbs stiffened; her lips stilled, though she sought some magical combination of words that would refute the conclusions Walsh had drawn.

"He was with the bastards who fired New York, wasn't he?" her father-in-law went on. "Your interest in the papers confirms that. And now he's coming to get you, isn't he, on his way back to Toronto?"

"No!" Jillian managed to croak.

"No? You'll give me leave to doubt it. But then, you're usually a more accomplished liar than you seem to be today."

"I don't know anything about Ryder being in New York," Jill answered, recovering her powers of speech at last. "And I have no reason to think he'll come for me."

Walsh shook his head in disbelief. "They got out of the city, you know."

"Did they?" Jillian demanded askance, not knowing if she should be relieved or frightened by his assurance.

"Some suspicious characters took rooms in Albany last night. And it's my understanding they boarded the westbound train this morning."

"How do you know that?" she demanded.

"Oh, I have my sources."

Did he? Congressman Walsh had connections in every branch of the government. Could he possibly know what he was saying? Were Ryder and his comrades on the train headed for the border? And if they had been identified, as her father-in-law's information seemed to confirm, how had they escaped capture?

There was no reason for her to deny herself all the information he could give. "If the authorities know who and where the saboteurs are, why haven't they been arrested?"

"I didn't say the authorities had been informed. It was my own men who wired me this morning. I've been having your lover watched these last weeks, ever since I found out who he was."

Jill digested that bit of news in silence. "But if your men followed Ryder to New York," she finally asked, "why weren't they able to prevent the fires?"

Walsh paused, eyeing her as if he was loath to reveal the truth. "Your rebel lover is a discreet and clever man," he finally admitted. "My men lost sight of him a day or two before the arsonists set to work, but they caught up with Bingham again when he and several of his fellows boarded the train for Albany on Saturday night. Unlike the detectives in New York, my men knew whom they were looking for, and they have been trailing the captain ever since. I've told my men to intercept the Confederates before they make their way into Canada, but I intend to capture your lover myself, when he comes here to collect you."

"He isn't coming here!" Jillian insisted, knowing full well that she spoke the truth.

"Isn't he? Well, he'll be arrested with the others, then, though that will be a disappointment. But in the meantime, I intend to make certain you can't warn him of my trap."

Jillian retreated half a step. "What do you mean?"

Instead of answering her, Walsh went to the door of the bedroom and called for Mrs. Pryor. The woman must have been waiting at the foot of the stairs, for she arrived promptly, carrying a length of rope.

Without a word, Gerald took it from the housekeeper and dragged Jillian toward the bed. It was patently obvious that he meant to tie her to the bedposts, and Jill began to struggle doggedly against his far superior strength. Walsh gripped her arm with a force that threatened to crush her bones, but she ignored the jolt of pain that rippled toward her shoulder and continued fighting him. Still, he managed to wrestle her onto the bed, fitting her right wrist against the bedpost as he uncoiled the rope to bind her. Driven by desperation, Jill caught the skein of twisted hemp with her free hand and tugged with all her strength.

Walsh cursed as she jerked the end away from him, leaving splinters of rope embedded in his palm. As he tried to recover it, Jillian broke his grip and rolled off the far side of the mattress in a tangle of skirts and petticoats. She took the rope with her as she

moved and in a single flaying motion dumped the whole of it into
the fireplace. Dry and brittle, the rope caught immediately, flaring up in a flash of blue and orange flames. As she regained her
balance, Jillian assessed her situation. Her father-in-law was
standing fast on the far side of the bed while Elvira Pryor was
inching around the foot. Jillian was cornered, as helpless as a fox
amid a pack of braying hounds. As she waited, her muscles
trembling in anticipation, she prayed that when her adversaries
made their move, she could turn it to her advantage.

At last Walsh began to follow Mrs. Pryor toward the foot of
the bed, and when he rounded the post at the far corner, Jillian
dived beneath the sideboard. Her only hope of escape was to
make it to the door, but she had not counted on the housekeeper's
speed and strength. The woman caught her around the hips just as
she was scrambling beneath the bed and hauled her roughly to her
feet.

They all stood panting for a moment, and as Mrs. Pryor
twisted Jillian's wrists behind her back, her desperate struggles
subsided.

Abruptly Walsh wheeled toward the door. "Can you hold her
while I go and get more rope?"

"That's not necessary, Gerald," the housekeeper shouted, halt-
ing him. "There's a nearly full bottle of laudanum in the nightstand. If we make her drink the medicine, she'll be asleep when
her lover comes."

Jillian felt a dart of surprise at the woman's casual use of her
father-in-law's given name, but she had no time to consider what
it meant, for Walsh was already opening the drawer, removing
the brown glass bottle.

A slow smile curled his lips as he read the label, and Jillian
tried again to twist away when she realized that he meant to do as
the housekeeper had suggested.

With slow, deliberate movements, Walsh removed the cork
from the neck of the bottle and poured an inch of the thick, dark
liquid into a glass. Jillian's eyes widened when she saw the dose.
Laudanum was administered by the drop. He had poured out
enough to kill her!

"Put some water in with it," the housekeeper coached and
tightened her hold on Jillian's wrists. Gerald Walsh dutifully
complied and moved toward where the women stood.

"But that's too much!" Jillian cried as he approached her. "Are
you trying to put me to sleep or do me in?"

Walsh hesitated, but the housekeeper urged him on. "She's

only saying that, Gerald. Give the girl the laudanum and let's get on with the rest of this."

Jillian struggled furiously as Walsh pressed the glass to her lips. She could smell the bitter sting of the alcohol and opium mixture, taste the potency of the dose. But with the housekeeper holding her immobile and Gerald's fingers tangled in her hair, there was nothing Jill could do. She coughed and gagged as he made her drink, and she finally managed to free one hand. But before she could knock the glass away, Walsh had forced the larger portion of the liquid down her throat.

There was a look of satisfaction on the congressman's face as he stepped away. "When you awake, my girl, we'll have caught your rebel lover. Then we'll see how well you two can defend yourselves against the charge of adultery and the charge of treason I plan to make."

It seemed foolish to try to refute his words, and Jill hung her head as a shudder of despair moved through her.

"Stay with her until the drug has taken effect, Elvira," he told the housekeeper as he turned to go. "Then come downstairs. We have several things to prepare in order to welcome Bingham properly."

When Walsh was gone, Mrs. Pryor thrust Jillian onto the bed. "Now you lie there, girl, and I'll sit with you until you sleep."

Jillian crawled to the center of the counterpane, rubbing her bruised wrists and glaring at the housekeeper.

"Why did you let him give me so much laudanum?" she challenged the older woman. "Surely you're aware of the usual dosages. You let him administer enough to kill me."

Mrs. Pryor smiled and pressed Jillian's shoulders back into the bank of pillows. "I know the dangers of laudanum as well as you do, but then, you won't be the first woman to take more drops than you should, nor will you be the first to die by that mistake."

"You intended him to murder me?" Jillian gasped, as terrified by the admission as by the prospect of the deed's success.

"You have no place in this household, and we'll be the better off without you."

"But what will he say when he finds me dead? Whatever else Congressman Walsh is planning, I don't think he meant to murder me."

Elvira Pryor shrugged. "What difference does it make if you die peacefully in your sleep or at the end of hangman's rope. You should be grateful that what we've done will make your passing an easy one."

There was a twisted logic to the woman's words. If she and Ryder were turned over to the authorities, the only difference would be the trial before the execution.

"Besides," the woman continued in a confidential tone, "yours won't be the first killing in this house. He's done murder twice before, and I was glad to help him both times."

What the housekeeper meant by that, Jillian could not guess. Who else could Gerald Walsh have killed, and why had the housekeeper acted as his accomplice?

Putting the pointless questions out of her mind, Jill tried to concentrate on a way to warn Ryder of the danger before she succumbed to the effects of the drug. Though she was not convinced Bingham would stop on his way to Toronto, Walsh's certainty had begun to erode her own. What if Ryder came? What could she do to warn him away? And how long would she have before the laudanum rendered her helpless?

Remembering her father's response to the drug, Jill surmised that she might have twenty minutes from the time the drug had been administered, half an hour at the most. But would the larger dose she'd been given make the laudanum act more quickly? And with Mrs. Pryor standing guard, what could she do?

"Are you beginning to feel sleepy yet?" the housekeeper inquired as she bent above the bed. "That's the way it begins, you know. You'll feel tired, dizzy, peaceful. I'm told that an overdose of laudanum is really a rather pleasant way to die."

The woman's words were soft, almost crooning, as if they were meant to be a lullaby. Jillian let herself respond to the coaxing tone, loosening her muscles, letting herself sink back into the mattress. If she could counterfeit her response to the drug, there was a chance the housekeeper would leave before Jill was overcome in fact. It was a risky plan, as Jillian well knew. She might misjudge her own reactions or the housekeeper's gullibility. Still, it seemed the only course open to her, the only way she might have a chance to warn Ryder of the danger.

Jill let her eyes grow cloudy and unfocused, allowed her lids to sag and her lashes to flutter.

"You're feeling the effects of the laudanum, aren't you?" the housekeeper asked with a fiendish kind of glee.

"No," Jillian replied drowsily. "No, I don't feel anything at all."

She allowed her breathing to deepen, let her lashes fall. Through slitted eyes she watched the woman hovering above her. If only she would leave, Jillian thought desperately, forcing her body to relax in spite of the tension coursing through her. If only the housekeeper would go, before the playacting became reality.

Jill sighed, stirred, closed her eyes.

She could sense the woman standing over her, watching, waiting, gloating. Jill's eyelids twitched, and she cursed her lack of self-control. She tried again to school her face to blankness, made her body limp as a discarded doll. Was she succeeding in duping her captor? Would the woman ever leave?

After what seemed an aeon, she heard Mrs. Pryor turn. There was the crunch of newspapers under the housekeeper's sensible shoes, the creak of the opening door. Jill held her breath and heard the panel close behind the housekeeper. There was the scrape of the key in the lock and then the sound of Mrs. Pryor's tread on the stairs.

The moment for action was upon her. But as she tried to stir, Jillian realized the lethargy she had been feeling was not completely feigned. Her arms seemed weighted at the wrist and elbow; her head was beginning to ache. The bones in her legs had turned to jelly, and the drowsiness drifting over her was treacherously soft and welcoming. The drug was beginning to do in fact everything Jill had pretended.

Groaning, she rolled to the edge of the bed and forced herself to stand. She had so little time to act. In a matter of minutes she would be unconscious. In an hour, she'd be dead. But before she gave up her life, Jill meant to find a way to warn Ryder of the danger. Whatever signal she gave would have to be visible from outside the house; it would have to be a sign he could readily see and understand. But already her thoughts were going wispy, thin, and her ability to implement any plan she might concoct was swiftly being compromised. She had no idea what to do.

Jill staggered to the armoire and swung open the mahogany doors. What she was hoping to find inside she hardly knew, but she prayed for inspiration. As she stood gaping at the rack of hanging gowns and the carefully folded clothing on the shelves beside them, the need for a signal beat in her brain with the insistence of a litany. Then from among the folds of black peeped a small bright corner of something red. Jillian caught her breath. Red was for love, for truth, for danger.

With difficulty she focused her eyes on the bit of cloth. It was the heavy silk brocade of her mother's honeymoon shawl. Jill caught the edge between her fingers and pulled, the effort nearly overwhelming her. She watched stupefied as the shawl came toward her bit by bit, the pattern dancing, the fringe writhing as dark as blood against her wrist. The clothes that had been piled above it came, too, tumbling to the floor at her feet, floating downward, like the drifts of blackness that seemed ready to envelop her.

She stared at the bright red cloth drooping against the front of her gown, wondering where she could put the shawl so Ryder would see it and understand its meaning. Instinctively Jill moved toward the window, dragging the silken cloth behind her. Bracing her feet, she tugged at the sash, feeling the strain across her shoulders and down her arms. But even against her most dogged assault, the window refused to budge.

She leaned heavily against the frame, the warmth of her face frosting the smooth, cold glass. Tears of frustration and fear beaded against the pane and coursed helplessly down her cheeks. She had tried so hard to warn Ryder of the danger, had tried in the last moments of her life to provide a signal that could save him from recapture. Her knees began to melt beneath her and she sank helplessly to the floor, but as she grasped the casement in an attempt to remain erect, the window lock jabbed into her palm, and she realized that in her haste, she had failed to turn the window latch.

Urgency gave her strength, and she forced herself to snap the lock and pull at the lower sash. It slid upward slowly, inch by inch, and with a trembling sigh she spilled the shawl through the width of the opening.

The porch at the back of the house seemed miles below as she leaned out to secure the shawl, and the patterns of the paving stones undulated dizzily. With an effort she forced her eyes away, but her whole world had begun to spin, drifting hazily before her heavy-lidded eyes. In a last desperate act, she closed the window on the corner of the shawl as the potency of the drug overwhelmed her.

Through spinning, wheeling exhaustion. she stumbled toward the bed. In the last moments of her life she had given Ryder a chance to escape, and she knew a swell of satisfaction. But numbness was assailing her. She felt pale, transparent, as if she were dissolving in air. When the mattress came hard against her hips, she let her momentum carry her onto the bed. She lay there panting as the room swooped dizzily around her, as her thoughts grew even mistier and more confused. At the periphery of her vision the darkness began to spread, closing around her inexorably as she was drawn deeper and deeper into its terrible beckoning void.

"Damn it, Ryder, this is crazy! We've probably got every detective in New York trailing us and a few Pinkerton agents besides. If we had a brainin our heads, we'd hightail it across the border with Martin and the rest of them."

Bingham stepped down from the horsecar that had brought them from the Suspension Bridge depot to Niagara Falls. "There's not a thing in this world that says you have to come with me, Jamie. You can take the stage right back to the station and catch the next train to Toronto."

"I just don't understand why it's so all-fired important that you see your ladylove today," the smaller man continued, making a mighty effort to stay at Bingham's heels. "You can come back this way next week when things have cooled down some."

"I told you I'm worried about Jillian. The last time I was here, her father-in-law had beaten her. I thought I'd have a chance to check on her long before this, but my duty interfered."

In the end, his duty hadn't proved to be all that much more important than making sure Jillian was safe, Bingham admitted silently. The fires in New York had caused panic among the populace, but they hadn't made any appreciable difference in the chances for the survival of the South. The mission had been a failure, another in a long chain that had plagued the Confederates in Canada. It was a failure that might well have put Jillian at an even greater risk than she had been when Ryder had left her more than a month before.

"I suppose I'll tag along with you, anyway," Jamie drawled, breaking into Ryder's thoughts, "just to see if this woman's worth the trouble."

Ryder knew exactly why his friend was determined to stay, and he appreciated the other man's concern. He supposed it was foolhardy and reckless to make a two- or three-hour layover on this side of the border when there were probably either secret service agents or New York City detectives hot on their heels. He and Jamie had seen the men watching the Thirtieth Street train station on Saturday night, and it was only by sneaking into the sleeping car two hours before the train was scheduled to leave that they had been able to avoid discovery and arrest. They had no way of knowing how quickly the Northern bloodhounds had picked up their scent, but it was prudent to assume there were men in pursuit, and to act accordingly. But in spite of the danger of remaining on Northern soil, Jillian had been on his mind so much today he knew he had to see her.

All he wanted was a glimpse of her, he told himself. He wouldn't try to meet or talk to her. He just needed to know she was all right. How he was going to make certain of that without drawing attention to himself, Bingham was not sure. Perhaps he would be lucky enough to catch a glimpse of Jill returning from afternoon calls. Or once the lights were lit, he might be able to peer in a window and convince himself that she was fine. It was necessary to see her, that was all, and it made Ryder uneasy to feel that conviction so strongly.

It was a cold day, clear and militantly sunny, the best that could be expected at this time of year in these frigid northern climes. It must have snowed during the night, for patches of white lay in the shadows, and the grass at the edge of the walk was frosted stiff and silvery. Ryder shivered as he turned into the wind and headed east along the riverbank. From somewhere close behind him, he could hear Jamie's teeth begin to chatter.

It seemed wisest to approach the Walsh property from the rear, as he always had before, but with the lush summer foliage gone, the garden seemed naked, barren. Standing in the shadow of the gazebo, he could see the land sweep upward from the river, broken only by a bank of bushes and the curving tunnel of an arbor midway up the yard. The house itself was large even by southern standards, and seeing the structure in daylight gave Ryder a chance to study it. The original building on the site was the long narrow elevation at the center, with an elegant Greek revival addition to the right and a servants' wing on the back at the left. A tall, narrow door led directly inside from the yard, and he knew the multipaned window above it was on the landing of the stairs. The window to Jillian's room was directly to the right on the second floor.

Was she there now? Ryder found himself wondering. Was she working on her embroidery or reading a favorite book? As he stared up at the dark, blank panes of her window, he became aware that something was fluttering in the wind, caught beneath the sash. It looked like a piece of cloth, flaming red against the rough pale gray of the native stone. It flapped and danced in the breeze, but from this distance, he could not quite make out what it was. Why that piece of cloth suddenly took on such importance, Ryder could not say. It was something unexpected, and the unexpected made him wary.

"I'm going closer," he muttered, glancing at Jamie. "And limber up that Colt, will you? I don't like the feel of this."

Without waiting for Jamie's response, Ryder checked the load in his own revolver and moved quickly up the slope. In the brisk winter wind, leaves scuttled along before him like tiny fleeing animals, and the web of empty branches creaked and clattered overhead. When he reached the shelter of the arbor, Ryder paused to survey the house, and a moment later Jamie came dashing up beside him. Partially hidden in the tangled mass of vines, Ryder stared even more intently at Jillian's window.

The fiery cloth that hung snagged beneath the sash had been wrung by the wind until it resembled nothing so much as a twist of silken rope. But as he watched, a gust from the opposite direction sent the banner flapping free. As it unfurled, Ryder could see a square of red brocade with a long silky fringe streaming from the edges. He recognized it instantly; it was Jillian's mother's shawl. One night in Rochester Jilly had taken it from her trunk and wrapped it around her shoulders, snuggling into the shimmering cloth as if it were a warm embrace. Jillian would never treat the shawl so carelessly, and all at once the color of the fabric took on a new significance. It was red: red for love, for blood, for danger.

"Something's wrong," he whispered through narrowed lips. "Jillian's in trouble."

The smaller man nodded, realizing instantly how he knew. "Or perhaps she thinks that you are."

Though the warning Jillian had intended to convey was clear, neither man moved from where he stood.

"You think Walsh has laid a trap?" Bradford asked.

"I'd put money on it. But how did he know I was coming to Niagara Falls?"

"And if he knew we were coming, why weren't we arrested when we got off the train? Do you think Martin and the others are in jeopardy?"

Ryder considered the question for a moment, then nodded. "There's a good chance of it, I suppose. Do you want to go and warn them?"

Jamie quickly assayed his loyalties. "If there's going to be trouble on this side of the border, they're probably knee deep in it already."

Ryder frowned in agreement, pleased that Jamie intended to stay. If Walsh was indeed expecting him, it would help to have a friend at his back.

"How did you get word to Jillian before when you came to visit?" Jamie wanted to know.

"That only happened once, and I simply had a note delivered."

"That wasn't very ingenious."

"No, but it was effective, and it didn't seem much riskier than the other things I was considering."

"It might have aroused Walsh's suspicions."

Ryder was silent for a moment. Had his actions put Jillian in jeopardy? And if they had, what could he do to help her now?

"Suppose I write another note," he proposed.

"To let Walsh know you're here?"

"My guess is that he's expecting me, and I don't see any harm in giving him confirmation. What if I set up a tryst at the gazebo for after dark?"

"So we'll have time to prepare a welcome of our own."

Seeing that Jamie was in league with his plans, Bingham took a crumpled railroad schedule and a pencil from the pocket of his overcoat. While Ryder scrawled a message on the back of the timetable, the smaller man pulled a peaked cap from his pocket and dropped his coat and cravat to the ground. By the alteration of his clothes and some subtle shift in the way he carried himself, Jamie was transformed from a nattily dressed man in his twenties to a scruffy boy in his teens. Giving Ryder an audacious grin, he took the note and moved toward the front of the house, bent on delivering the message and learning what he could.

Though to Ryder it seemed forever, Jamie returned with surprising speed.

"There's something going on, all right. I could feel it the minute the housekeeper opened the door. Her eyes got all black and sparkly when I said I had a note for Mrs. Walsh."

"Did you see any sign of Jillian?"

Jamie shook his head as he struggled into his overcoat. "I tried to get into the house. I told her I was to give the note to her mistress myself, but she said Mrs. Walsh was lying down and could not be disturbed."

"Then there's nothing to do but wait."

They did wait, through suppertime, into the deepening twilight. But the appointed hour came and went without any sign of the congressman.

"Walsh wants this on his own terms," Jamie finally whispered, shivering in the wind.

"Well, since he's invited me to his lair, I can hardly disappoint him."

"Then give me time to circle the house, before you go a-calling."

With his concern for Jillian escalating, it was difficult for Bingham to wait even a few minutes more. All this time, there had been no sign of her, nor had any light appeared in the bedroom window. Where was she? Ryder agonized. Why hadn't she come to see if her signal was still in place?

Tension was singing in his veins as Bingham crept to the shelter of the arbor. He knew they didn't have much of a plan, compared to what Walsh must have had time to devise. But as far as they could tell, there was no one in the house but the congressman and his housekeeper. Jamie's judicious arrival was the only hope they had of outwitting Walsh, and when Ryder stepped from the slight protection of the arbor into the open yard, he knew exactly what he was risking.

There was still no sign of life as he approached the door, and a frisson of fear swept down his spine. Was Walsh waiting just inside? Was Ryder going to die for his temerity?

Unlocked, unbolted, the panel swung silently on its hinges, and he stepped into the elegant hall. He took note of the doors to his left and right, the lights left burning in the entry. The house was silent as a tomb, as if totally uninhabited, and he stifled the urge to shout Jillian's name, though he was wild for reassurance. He crept slowly toward the front of the house, past a coatrack decked with hats, past a pair of straight-backed chairs. His feet were silent as he stole down the strip of flowered carpet, but with every step he took, Bingham felt more vulnerable and conspicuous.

Just as he came even with the pocket doors at the front of the hall, a stocky woman emerged from the darkness, leveling a shotgun at his chest. In the same instant, Ryder heard a faint sound from behind him and whirled to find an armed man standing beneath the slope of the stairs. Ryder was caught defenseless, just as Walsh had intended.

"Captain Bingham, I presume?" the man intoned. "We've been anticipating your arrival since late this afternoon. Now, if you'll drop your weapon, sir, perhaps I'll feel more hospitable."

As he complied with the request, Ryder let his gaze skim over Gerald Walsh. He was tall, gray-haired, malevolent. Nor was there a question of his intent. His revolver was pointed at Bingham's heart, and there was murder in his eyes.

"Congressman Walsh, we meet at last. What have you done with Jillian?"

Walsh's mouth lifted in the semblance of a smile. "I have your lovely but traitorous mistress safely tucked away, since I wanted a chance for us to get properly acquainted. Your friends slipped past the guards I had posted at the bridge, so we have the arson in New York to discuss."

Bingham was glad to hear that Martin and the others had made it safely into Canada, though concern for Jillian was foremost in his mind.

"I trust you had a pleasant trip," the man continued. "And I'm very anxious to hear about your experiences. If you will follow me, Captain Bingham, perhaps we can have a brandy while we talk."

Walsh's manner was exaggeratedly polite, but Ryder had no illusions about what the congressman would do once their chat was over.

After retrieving Ryder's gun from the floor, Walsh turned and led the way to his study. As he followed, Bingham could feel the twin bores of the housekeeper's shotgun trained on the center of his back, and he began to wonder just how long Jamie intended to wait before coming to his rescue.

At just that moment, the front door banged back on its hinges as Jamie burst into the hall. "Stop where you are!" he shouted, training his gun on all of them.

At the sound of the opening door, Walsh wheeled back toward the front of the house, raising his revolver as he turned. But before he could squeeze off a shot, Jamie fired, his aim sure and true. Simultaneously, Ryder spun toward the housekeeper, knocking aside the twin barrels of the shotgun so that when she pulled the triggers, buckshot sprayed the furniture, ceiling, and walls. Shards of splintered wood, plaster, and broken glass exploded around them, as Bingham's momentum drove her to the floor. He hovered over the woman, waiting, but without the protection of her weapon, she quickly conceded the fight.

Bingham rose lightly and cast a glance at his companion. "You took your time about getting here," he complained as he confiscated firearms.

"I can't say a minute more or less would have made all that much difference."

Both Walsh and the housekeeper were struggling to rise, and when she had regained her feet, the woman hustled toward the older man.

"Gerald, are you all right?" she asked with great concern.

"My arm hurts like hell," Walsh told her gruffly. But in spite of the blood soaking the fabric of his sleeve, it was evident the wound was a relatively minor one.

Ryder felt no remorse for the congressman's pain. For in spite of the sound of the shooting, there was still no sign of Jillian.

"Where is she, Walsh?" Ryder demanded. "What have you done with Jilly? Why hasn't she called out to us?"

"You'll find her locked up in her room," Walsh conceded, not willing to risk further injury by denying Bingham information.

While Jamie nudged the two into the study and bound them with tasseled curtain cords, Ryder exhorted him to hurry. Once Walsh and Mrs. Pryor were tied, gagged, and locked in a closet, the two Confederates set off in search of Ryder's mistress.

"We haven't got much time," Jamie pointed out as they rushed up the stairs. "Let's find your ladylove and be on our way to Canada."

The lock on the door to Jillian's bedroom gave under Ryder's determined assault, and he burst into the room half expecting to find Jillian waiting for him. But as he stood frozen in the darkness, there was no noise, no sign of movement.

"Jillian!" he breathed. "Jillian? Are you here?"

Jamie followed him inside, then fumbled to find and light a lamp. As the wick flickered and caught, they could see the woman they were seeking was sprawled across the bed.

"Jilly!" Ryder cried, moving to gather her in his arms, and though he frantically called her name, there was no sign that she had heard. Her skin was parchment pale against the rich black of her gown, her features blank, void, still, as lifeless as a statue's. He touched her eyelids, fragile and delicate as a child's, brushed her parted lips and saw that they were faintly blue. She was so limp, so cold, so totally unresponsive. He could not even tell if she was breathing.

Ryder went dizzy with the panic burning upward from his belly, felt frozen with the dread leaping along his nerves.

"Oh, God," he whispered helplessly. "What has that bastard done to her?"

Jamie searched for a pulse along the white expanse of Jillian's throat. "They've given her laudanum," he answered Bingham, indicating the bottle on the nightstand. "I'd say the dose was pretty strong, but she's still alive and fighting it."

Ryder stared, stunned, empty, terrified, holding Jillian close.

"She's alive, Ryder," Jamie reiterated. "She's alive, but we've got to get her out of here."

The words might as well have been in a foreign tongue for all the sense Bingham could make of them. Still he trusted Jamie's judgment instinctively and gathered Jillian in his arms. As he rose, her head rolled against his shoulder, and she sighed softly in her sleep. That faint sign of life reassured him, enabling him to focus for an instant on the room in which she lay. There was the bottle of medication on the bedside table, a broken glass on the floor amid a tangle of bedclothes and newspapers. It gave evidence of the drama that had been played out some hours before, and it was clear Jillian hadn't given in to Walsh without a fight.

Brittle anger suffused him as he carried Jillian down the stairs. He would make Gerald Walsh pay for what he'd done, Ryder vowed. Not now, not tonight when Jillian's life hung in the balance. But one day he would come back to Niagara Falls, and when he did, Walsh would feel his wrath.

"We can't take her to a doctor here," Jamie mused, thinking aloud, as they made their way into the yard. "We'll have to get her into Canada before we dare seek medical attention."

With difficulty Ryder forced himself to concentrate on what the smaller man was saying. "But will she be all right?"

It was a question Jamie could not answer. "All I know is that if Walsh sets the border guards on us, she'll be considered as guilty of treason as we are."

Ryder nodded. Bradford was right about the danger of remaining in the North one minute more than necessary.

"But how will we get her across the border?" Bingham wanted to know, trusting to Jamie's inventiveness.

"I do have an idea," Jamie assured him as he led Ryder toward the stable.

Once they had overpowered and bound the coachman, Jamie hitched up the team while Bingham loaded Jill inside the sleek closed carriage. Climbing in himself, Ryder was again struck by how still and white she was. There was no color in her face, no animation. There was no hint of a living person behind her stark, smooth features. The blankness terrified him anew. People died from overdoses of laudanum, and Jillian's shallow breathing and blue-tinged lips did not bode well for her recovery. The thought of losing Jilly left a void where his heart should have been. It was a void so deep and vast that it seemed to suck all the warmth, all the energy, all the determination, from his body. He had long since realized that Jilly was the only woman he would ever love, the only woman with whom he could share his life completely. What would he do if Jilly died?

And how would he live with himself? He had known that Walsh had beaten Jillian, that she was endangering herself by remaining in Niagara Falls. Why had he listened to her assurances when she said she was preparing to leave Walsh's home? Why hadn't he insisted on taking her to Canada? He should have realized that Jilly's safety was still in jeopardy. He should have realized that her well-being was more important than going on the mission to New York, more important than either duty or revenge. Instead, he had gone ahead with his plans, and now Jillian might die for that mistake.

He was distracted from his grim thoughts a few minutes later when the carriage rolled to a stop in a dark, narrow alley.

"Follow me," Jamie whispered as he helped Ryder get Jillian out of the carriage. He led them to the door at the back of a warehouse and quickly picked the lock. Inside it was dark and stale and resinous, piled high with the hulking shape of boxes. When Jamie finally found and lit a lantern, Ryder could see that the oblong shapes were coffins. A hearse stood at the far side of the warehouse near a door that, judging from the sounds beyond, housed the funeral home's horses.

A shudder ran the length of his spine, and he clutched Jillian tighter, as if protecting her from their macabre surroundings.

"Put her down," Bradford ordered in a burst of efficiency. "We've got lots of work to do before we'll be able to cross the border."

"But where should I put her?" Ryder asked and was dumbfounded as Jamie raised the lid of one of the caskets.

"This will do for the moment," he answered and then, seeing Bingham's reaction, went on to reassure his friend. "God, Ryder, put her down. This isn't going to be her final resting place."

Anger shot through Ryder at the grim humor in the other man's tone. "You're proposing we take Jill across the bridge in a coffin, aren't you? Pretend she's dead to rescue her?"

"I thought we'd take her across in a hearse," he confirmed. "But if you've got a better idea, I'd be very glad to hear it."

Ryder stared, appalled. Putting Jillian in one of these contraptions, for any reason, was grizzly, barbarous, terrifying. But Ryder had to admit he didn't have a better plan. They could hardly take an unconscious woman across the border on the train or even in a carriage. This was the safest course for all of them. Cursing softly, he settled Jillian on one of the worktables.

"How did you know about this place?" Ryder demanded.

"I thought I was being followed one night while I was waiting for the train to Toronto, so I stopped in to pay my respects to a gentleman laid out in the front parlor of the funeral home attached to this establishment. When I left by the back door, I discovered that by cutting through the workshop, I could make my way into the alley."

As he finished his explanation, Jamie scooped up a drill from one of the worktables and handed it to Ryder. "You're good with your hands," he observed. "Put holes in the lid of that fancy coffin there. The guards are less likely to question us if we're taking some rich Yankee to Canada for burial."

Ryder did as Jamie had instructed, boring holes at six-inch intervals along the lid of the rosewood box, cleaning them out with his fingers so the air could flow more freely.

While Bingham worked, Jamie was busy rummaging through a desk in the far corner of the warehouse, then scribbling on papers that looked important and official. When his job was done, Ryder moved to where Jamie was finishing up his handiwork.

"What are those?" he asked, peering at the forms.

"I'm just putting together the papers I suspect we'll need to cross the border: a death certificate, an order of transport, a pass from the provost marshal."

"Are you forging them?" Ryder asked incredulously.

"Of course I'm forging them," Jamie answered with a wry smile. "It's a useful talent, forgery. Where do you think the papers I gave you came from?"

That revelation did nothing to calm Ryder's nerves, but there wasn't time to discuss it. They had to get into Canada before Walsh and his housekeeper slipped their bonds and raised a warning. Working together, they laid Jillian out in the casket and packed their carpetbags around her. More shivers slid down Bingham's spine as they closed the lid. It was as if the worst had already happened and he was bidding Jilly good-bye. He could hardly think, could hardly breathe for the swell of dark regret. He felt parched and brittle inside. Though the hearse and the coffin were a sham, the sense of loss was devastating.

"You're sure she'll have plenty of air to breathe?" Jamie asked, as they lifted the casket into the hearse that stood near the doorway of the workshop.

"That box would do credit to a swarm of termites," Ryder answered grimly, closing the wide glass door at the back of the van.

After hitching a team of jet-black horses to the vehicle and donning the black cloaks and hats they found hanging on pegs, the two Confederates opened the doors to the warehouse and drove out into the night.

The streets were deserted as they made their way toward the bridge at Niagara City, and the horses' hooves clattered hollowly on the paving stones. From where they sat on the high box seat, Ryder could see the black plumes on the harness bobbing as they jogged along and feel the trim of fringe at the edges of the seat brush against his calves. He looked back often to check on the coffin housed in its ornate glass enclosure, praying that Jillian was still alive.

His muscles tightened as they approached the carriage level of the Suspension Bridge and pulled up before the Customs House. The building was new and made of the same native stone that studded the escarpment behind it. Setting the brake on the hearse, Jamie jumped down.

"You coming or staying here?"

Jamie's voice had taken on the nasal intonation of Yankee speech, and Ryder knew that if he was questioned, his drawl might give them away. Still, he could not remain with the hearse, waiting for Jamie to return. With a last worried glance at the coffin, he jumped down and followed the smaller man inside.

There were two customs men yawning at their desks, and the younger one rose wearily as Jamie and Ryder entered.

"You're out late tonight," he commented, as he took the death certificate and provost marshal's pass from Jamie.

"We've got a corpse to take across for burial early tomorrow morning."

"Seems an unlikely time to be taking it."

"I'd say it was damned appropriate, crossing in the dead of night."

The customs agent laughed at Jamie's unseemly jocularity. "Have you a transport order for me to sign?"

"I think I've got it here somewhere," Jamie answered, patting at his pockets.

While he searched, Ryder could feel the sweat bead up across his brow. Why the hell hadn't Jamie kept everything together? Did he have a transport order prepared, and how could he have misplaced it when their lives depended on the document?

"Have you got it?" he asked Ryder, wicked humor glinting in his eyes.

Ryder's heart slammed against the wall of his chest as he

shook his head, afraid to say anything that might make the customs men suspicious.

"Ah," Jamie finally said, pulling the paper from inside his coat. "I knew I had it somewhere."

The customs man glanced at the form, then scrawled his signature on the bottom line. "Young woman," he observed.

"And she was pretty, too, I'm told. She took more laudanum than was wise, but high-strung women seem to need it to calm their nerves."

Ryder thought he might need a dose himself before this interview was over.

But finally the customs agent handed the papers back. "You may as well be on your way, though you've got a damned grim job to do."

"Oh, you get used to driving a hearse," Jamie quipped, slipping the forged papers inside his cloak. "At least your passengers never complain about the ride."

The customs men were still laughing as the Confederates left, but Ryder was unnerved by Jamie's flippancy.

"This is hardly the time for humor," he whispered severely as he climbed back onto the seat. His knees were quaking from the encounter with the customs men, and his clothes were soaked with sweat.

"Those men had no more desire to come out here and examine a corpse than we have to show them one," Jamie muttered under his breath. "Sometimes playing the buffoon is the easiest way to allay suspicion."

Bradford didn't tell Ryder that he meant to convey a deliberate carelessness in his manner, to distract the customs men from studying the papers too closely. He wasn't sure how convincing his forgeries were, and there was no sense tempting fate by giving the officers time to study them. From childhood he had known the importance of distracting his marks' attention from the real purpose of his scams, and although his actions had unsettled Ryder, they had helped him achieve his goals.

As they rumbled onto the wooden deck of the bridge, he could sense Bingham's desire for greater speed. It had been a trying night for his friend, and things might be far worse before the new day dawned. Still, Bradford held the horses to an easy lope, knowing that every inch they traversed without drawing attention to themselves brought them closer to safety and freedom.

Since Canadian customs might well be a repeat of Jamie's

performance, Ryder elected to remain with the hearse. But they were passed with remarkable speed and hunted up a doctor's office only a few streets beyond the bridge.

What the doctor's patients thought when they saw a death cart pulled up in front of the house at daybreak, neither man knew nor cared. The woman they had smuggled into Canada wasn't going to have need of such a vehicle for years to come, and that was all that mattered to either of them.

Chapter Fourteen

JILLIAN SEEMED TO exist on the far side of a curtain. It was a curtain that was sometimes dark and opaque and sometimes a filmy veil between her and the rest of the world. It distorted what she saw and heard: disjointed scenes that flickered over the surface of her mind, nonsensical words that drifted past her, conversations that had no beginning and no end. Sometimes by an act of will she managed to push the curtain aside and the images would clear. But she could not sustain the effort it took to keep the darkness at bay, and the world would swirl and recede as if through a gathering mist.

Once when she struggled toward the surface of consciousness, Ryder was beside her, his face pale and drawn with worry, his eyes hollow and dark with fatigue.

"Ryder?" she murmured, and was rewarded with a gentle touch and a weary smile.

"Yes, Jilly, I'm here," he answered. "Are you feeling better?"

Though she tried to form an answer, the curtain dropped between them before she could find words to reply.

When she came to herself a second time, there was a stranger at her bedside. He was fair and small and gentle, with a kindly face and warm gray eyes.

"Where's Ryder?" she asked in a voice dry and husky with disuse.

The man smiled and pressed a glass of water to her lips, letting her drink deep before he responded.

"I put him to bed more than an hour ago. He's been camped at your bedside ever since we brought you back. But once you started to come around, I managed to convince Ryder you'd be all right without him."

"Have I been sick?" she asked with an effort, the creeping exhaustion assailing her.

"In a manner of speaking, you have. But you'll be fine in a day or so."

The blond man's words faded away, but they had reassured her.

When she rose from the depths again, she felt sunlight warm and orange on the screen of her eyelids, recognized the scratch of flannel against her skin, and smelled the sharp scent of carnations. For the first time, Jillian became aware of her surroundings: of the iron bed on which she lay, of the blood-red flowers in a vase on the nightstand, of the slanting rays of a golden sunset streaming through a bank of windows. She let her gaze drift around the room, noting the neat but sparse furnishings, the man's jacket and shirt hung on pegs by the door, the tiny wooden animals lined up along the windowsill. There was the essence of Ryder here, his smell, his clothes, his carvings. Only the man himself was missing. He was not standing by the windows, nor was he sitting in the straight-backed chair beside the bed. Ryder's things were here, but he was gone, and she had no idea what had become of him.

She stirred ineffectively on the feather bed, her limbs hollow and heavy with lethargy. She felt stale, achy, weak. She was tired and confused, and there was no one to explain what had happened. Jill had nearly slipped back into her somnolent world when she heard the door open. Struggling to shake off her drowsiness, she turned her head and stared up into the careworn face of a woman well into middle age.

"Awake again, are you?" the woman asked, her voice thick with a Scottish burr. "That's a sign I'm glad to see. Are you up to taking some nourishment? I've some broth brewing in the kitchen."

As the woman came into the room, Jillian eyed her with a mixture of curiosity and suspicion.

"I'm Mrs. Moire, if you were wondering. Mr. Bingham brought you here yesterday."

"Where's 'here'?" Jillian murmured in confusion as the woman sat down beside the bed.

"You're in Toronto, lass. Toronto, Canada West. You've been asleep for three days all together."

"Toronto?" Jillian repeated in disbelief. "And Ryder brought me here?"

"Aye," the woman answered. "It'd hardly have been fitting for him to leave you with that scalawag father-in-law of yours after what he nearly did to you."

Jillian's head was clearing. She remembered that Gerald had meant to lay a trap for Ryder, that he and the housekeeper had forced her to drink laudanum. Yet in spite of the effects of the drug, she had managed to hang a signal out her window to warn Bingham away.

"Ryder's safe, then?" she murmured.

"He's safe, all right. It's you that gave us a terrible start, me and Mr. Bingham and Mr. Bradford. But you're out of danger now, and if you can manage, a bit of broth might help you."

Jillian assayed her condition again and realized she was hungry. "Yes, I'd like that very much."

The older woman rose, answering with a nod. "A bite of food is what you need, lassie. You'll feel more like yourself once there's something in your stomach."

When the woman returned, she found that Jillian had crawled to the edge of the bed and was trying to sit up.

"Don't be doing too much just yet," she warned as she settled Jill back on the pillows and put a tray on her lap, "or Mr. Bingham will have my hide for letting you."

"Where is Ryder?" Jillian managed to ask between spoonfuls of soup and bites of bread and butter.

"He's asleep at last, poor man. He's been with you ever since Monday night."

"And this is . . . ?"

"Wednesday, all day. Mr. Bradford only got him upstairs and bedded down a couple hours ago."

Jillian took in everything the woman said, finding it hard to believe that she had been unconscious, drugged and unaware, for three whole days. She would have liked to ask a myriad of questions about Ryder, about the man called Mr. Bradford, and about her own presence here. But she was getting sleepy again, and Mrs. Moire took note of it.

"You get a good long rest tonight, my girl, and you'll be right as rain tomorrow."

Jillian did feel more like herself when she awoke the following day, and as she lay watching the early morning sun filter through the curtains, her mind was busy with all the questions she had been too tired and dull-witted to ask the night before. Had Ryder indeed come to Walsh's house? Had her signal warned him of the danger? What had happened when he arrived? How had they managed to get to Canada? They were questions she had no one to ask until Mrs. Moire put in an appearance with a breakfast tray.

As she ate porridge thick with cinnamon sugar and drowning in cream, Jill received some of the answers she'd been seeking. But with a determined practicality, the woman put aside the rest, more intent on getting her to eat and helping her with her bath. The warm, sweet-scented water did far more than get her clean, and when her hair was washed, brushed dry, and tied back with a ribbon, when she had been hustled into a clean nightdress and bundled back into bed, Jillian felt like herself again.

Ryder came by a few minutes later, looking freshly bathed and shaved and uncertain of his welcome. She thought he must have been watching her from the doorway for some time before she noticed, but he made no move to approach until she raised one hand to beckon him. Without a word, he came to sit beside her on the bed, put his arms around her, and drew her close against his chest. He held her gently, silently, cherishingly, resting one cheek against her hair.

As her arms crept around his back, she gave herself over to his embrace. He was solid and strong beside her, enveloping her in his warmth. His clean masculine scent was in her nostrils, his body hard against her softer one. He held her so tight and so long, she wondered if he ever meant to let her go. But at length he settled her back in bed and, with painfully gentle motions, smoothed her hair across the pillows.

"Are you comfortable? Is there anything I can get for you?" Concern etched his face and shone in his deep blue eyes.

Jillian smiled to reassure him. "The bed's as soft as sponge cake, and I'm not in need of anything now that you are with me."

"The doctor told me once the laudanum worked its way out of your system, you'd wake up. But after you'd been unconscious so long, it was hard to believe what he said."

"I'm fine," she confirmed and smiled at Ryder.

He cradled her hand in both of his, and for the first time since they'd come together, he didn't seem to know what to say to her.

Jillian broke the silence, giving voice to the questions she had been wanting to ask. "What happened, Ryder? How did I get here? I don't remember anything after hanging my mother's shawl out the window in the hope of warning you away."

He took a deep breath and began to talk, speaking slowly, reluctantly, because the words were hard for him. He told her the shawl had been the signal she had intended it to be, explained how he and Jamie had overpowered her father-in-law and his housekeeper, how they had spirited her across the border. He did not say that he'd never in his life been more frightened than when they burst into her bedroom and found her sprawled lifeless on the bed. He did not tell her he had been utterly terrified during the endless hours when she had lain insensible. The experience had marked him far more deeply than he cared to admit. It had brought home his need to protect her and keep her safe, made him want to take her into his arms and hold on to her forever. Yet he allowed none of those emotions to shade his voice as he spoke, explaining what had happened in Niagara Falls, reviewing the incidents that had brought them to Toronto, answering her questions. He did not want Jillian to realize how close she had come to death or how distraught he had been at the possibility of losing her.

He watched her as he spoke, seeing the life and light in her gold and green eyes, the animation in her face. She was so beautiful lying there, her tawny hair curled against the pillows, her skin pink and creamy against the well-washed flannel of Mrs. Moire's nightdress. Though to him she seemed somehow more fragile than before, it was clear Jillian was going to be fine. It was evident in the return of her vitality, in the renewal of her good humor, in the clamor of her curiosity.

And Ryder was unspeakably glad.

"Is Jamie the man who was with me the second time I awoke? Is he the man with the blond hair and kind eyes?"

Ryder smiled at her description of his friend, knowing Bradford would be flattered. "We owe him your life, and mine, a dozen times over. Without him, I'm not sure we'd have made it into Canada."

"Well, I'm not sure I fancy doing any more traveling in a hearse." Jillian laughed, tickled by the means they had used to spirit her away. "Trains and carriages offer much more comfortable accommodations, don't you think?"

Ryder remembered much too clearly how he had felt when they closed her in the coffin three nights before to be able to treat the incident so lightly. He merely nodded in agreement, and silence fell again.

When he finally spoke, he had difficulty meeting her eyes.

"I'm so sorry for what happened, Jilly. I should have brought you to Canada long before this. When I found out your father-in-law had beaten you, I should have known you'd be in danger."

She saw the strain around his mouth, the guilt in the droop of his broad shoulders. It was his curse to take the blame for things he could not control, to accept responsibility for everything that happened for good or ill.

Her fingers curled more tightly around his palm. "You had no way of knowing what would happen, but I would have come if you had asked me."

"I should have asked you; I wanted to. God knows, I've wanted you with me since that last night in Rochester."

"Then why didn't you ask?"

Ryder paused, reconsidered what he had been about to say, then bravely met her gaze. "Do you know where I've been?"

Jillian nodded.

"I couldn't tell you about my New York trip, because it was a secret mission. All of us who had volunteered knew how dangerous it was going to be. When I found out what Walsh had done, I wanted to bring you here. But, Jilly, how could I do that when I knew I had to abandon you to a world of strangers, when I knew I was leaving on a mission from which I might never return?"

It was a moment before she spoke.

"I understand, Ryder," she began slowly, "why you couldn't ask me to come to Toronto. I understand why you didn't offer. But what I fail to comprehend, and what offends me most, is why you set fires in New York, why you made war on women and children."

Ryder caught his breath. He had known she would not approve of the mission to New York, but in this context her censure was unexpected, devastating. He fumbled for a reply and found it impossible to mouth the platitudes that had seemed so valid a month before. The mission had not achieved its goals, and that weakened his defense. There was no justification in failure, only in victory, no vindication in what might have been nor any in what was.

"Jillian, you must try to realize that when we went to New York, we were only trying to bring the hardships of war into Northern homes, to repay the Yankees for burning the Shenandoah Valley and Atlanta." The words sounded hollow in his ears, defensive, unconvincing. He tried again. "The women and children of the South are suffering every bit as much as the soldiers in the field. There isn't any reason why the Yankees should remain unscathed."

Jillian lay back against the pillows and closed her eyes. Ryder felt a jab of concern, but before he could express it, she looked up at him again. As she did so, he could see the conflict in her face, the shimmer of tears that dimmed the golden gleam in her eyes.

"Do you know why Gerald Walsh struck me?" she asked suddenly, continuing before he had a chance to reply. "It was because I had defended the South for not engaging in such atrocities. I told him and a roomful of his cronies that the North was wrong to take out its bitterness on the South, that burning Confederate homes and farms would only deepen the separatism and hatred, postpone the advent of peace."

Ryder saw the disillusionment in what she said, the contradictions clearly laid out before them. The war was as universal as it was personal, a conflict of nations as well as individuals. It was the clash of larger issues and personal beliefs. It demanded compromises of policy on a national scale and the sacrifice of integrity that could destroy men's souls. This war had put the sword to honor, loyalties, compassion, and somehow it was hard to mourn the passing of such virtues when it was a struggle to stay alive.

Bingham simply did not know what to say to Jillian. He could not further defend his actions, nor could he chide her for her condemnation. They would never surmount this philosophical impasse, and there were more pressing matters to resolve.

Jillian seemed to understand that, too, and when she spoke again, she had somehow overcome the barrier between them. "And what will happen to me now?"

It was a new consideration for Ryder. He had not been able to think past the point where Jillian was awake, aware, and herself again.

He hesitated for a moment as he searched his mind and heart for an answer. "I don't know," he finally said.

Jillian blinked and caught her breath. Waking up here with Ryder in attendance had given her certain expectations. Perhaps they were expectations she had no right to entertain, but his answer confused her and made her fearful for the future.

"You brought me here, then, without any intention of marrying me?"

Ryder stared at her. "I brought you here because your father-in-law tried to kill you."

Her voice broke on the next words, though she knew she had to hear his answer. "And you don't . . . love me?"

There was a moment of startled hesitation before Bingham replied.

"Yes, of course I love you!" he declared, making the concession almost angrily.

Ryder had never expected to say those words for the very first time in his life as rebuttal in an argument. He should have whispered them into Jilly's mouth as they clung together in the deepest throes of passion, breathed them against her skin in the joyous aftermath. It was wrong to say them now when they could bring no comfort, no resolution.

"But if you love me," Jillian continued earnestly, trying to quell the joy that had surged through her at even his reluctant admission, "why don't you want to marry me?"

It was a bald question, but one she had to ask. She waited for his answer, torn by hope and dread.

Ryder stood and made a circuit of the room, as if a physical distance was necessary for what he had to say.

"Damn it, Jilly, how can I propose when I haven't anything to offer you?"

Jillian took a shaky breath and answered carefully. "You do have something, Ryder. You have yourself to give."

"Myself!" Bingham gave a grunt of derisive laughter. "And what a poor offering that is! My honor's compromised, I have no home, no way of supporting you. I have half a dozen obligations to discharge before I could even consider asking you to be my wife."

Jillian was stunned and strangely disillusioned. It had not occurred to her that Ryder might have thought about marrying her and then discounted it for the sake of his responsibilities. And somehow those obligations seemed the poorest kind of excuse when Jillian was willing to brave so much. She would do anything to share Ryder's life, to keep his home, to bear his children. She was willing to accept whatever the future held if she could face it at his side. Why couldn't he believe that they would find a way around the obstacles? Why was it impossible for him to realize that his love for her was all that mattered?

But then the larger question arose: If he wasn't going to marry her, what on earth was going to become of her?

"Well, I won't be your kept woman, Ryder," she warned, pride forcing her to make the declaration. They might have been lovers once, coming together because of feelings too strong to deny, but if he was not willing to risk the future, she would offer him no half-measures. If he wasn't willing to make her his wife, she would make her own way in the world, somehow learn to stand alone. She had been prepared to do that when Gerald Walsh mistreated her, and she would have to prepare herself to do it now, only it would be so much more difficult to establish herself here, away from everything familiar and comfortable.

It was a second before he responded, and his voice was soft and low. "Nor would I shame you by asking you to be my mistress."

Ryder seemed to understand her need for independence more clearly than Jillian understood it herself. Or perhaps he was merely relieved to be absolved of the responsibility. He could hardly continue to seek retribution for his brother's death, follow his duty wherever it took him with her as a liability. He could not continue to risk his life for the South if she maintained a hold on him.

There was a discreet cough, and they both started, looking up to find Jamie in the doorway.

"Getting everything settled between you?" he inquired.

"I suppose it's settled, after a fashion," Ryder commented dryly. "And now it's time you met our mentor, Jillian. This is Jamieson Bradford, my fiendishly clever, overwhelmingly ingenious, outlandishly talented friend."

The smaller man approached the bed and, with a flourish, took Jill's hand. "May I say, Mrs. Walsh, you're even lovelier awake than you are when you are sleeping."

Jillian returned his smile. "I'm pleased that you are finally seeing me at my best, Mr. Bradford."

"You were a sleeping beauty, to be sure. Just like the princess in the fairy tale."

Jillian was fully prepared to like the man who had helped rescue her from Niagara Falls, and she basked in the warmth of his personality as if in rays of welcome sun. "It seems I owe you my thanks, Mr. Bradford, for helping to bring me here."

"You're very welcome, Jillian. May I call you Jillian, since I've come to think of you that way? And if you grant me that liberty, I hope you'll call me Jamie."

Jill nodded in assent, and Jamie settled in the chair beside the bed as if planning an extended stay. But before they could include Ryder in their conversation, he was edging toward the door.

"I have some things to do," he murmured. "And since you have Jamie for company, this seems like a good time to take care of them. I'll stop by later, Jillian, to see how you're getting on."

Before either Jill or Jamie could protest, Ryder made a hasty exit. Jillian sighed softly as she watched him go, and when she turned, there was a knowing light in Bradford's eyes.

"I take it things are far from resolved between you," he observed, taking a cigar from the inside pocket of his frock coat.

Jillian shook her head. "Now that I'm here, I don't think Ryder knows what to do with me." The man beside her was a stranger, but he seemed determined to be her friend.

"He didn't ask to marry you, then? Damn, I was afraid his pride would get in the way."

Jillian stared at Jamie, startled by his perceptiveness.

"Well, Ryder loves you, that's sure. I don't think he realized himself how much until these last days. He's been nearly wild with worry."

Jillian digested that news in silence. "He may love me, Jamie," she admitted after a moment, "but he's not going to ask me to be his wife."

"Let me guess," Bradford observed, lighting his cigar. "He doesn't have anything to offer you, no place he can take you that's home." When Jillian remained silent, Jamie frowned. "Well, that doesn't surprise me. He's as stubborn as a mule, as stiff-necked and proper as a maiden aunt."

Jillian was forced to smile at the characterization of the man she loved. It was succinct and painfully accurate.

"And you aren't willing to be his mistress, even if he asked you."

"Were you listening at the door?"

Bradford shook his head and laughed, a warm, comforting sound. "No, I just know how Ryder thinks. He's all trussed up with pride and honor and obligations. And he loves you enough to want what's best for you."

"But he doesn't think that's him."

"Not now, not when there is so much gnawing at him."

"Then what am I to do here in Toronto?"

Jamie paused and eyed her. "What do you want to do?"

She could never remember another time in her life when anyone had asked that question. It was rife with fears and possibilities.

"I'm not quite sure," Jillian answered earnestly. "I haven't had much time to consider it. I'll need to find a way to support myself, I suppose, though heaven only knows how."

"Well, you've had some schooling, haven't you?"

"As much as many men."

"Then we'll find something for you. Don't worry. I've got a

prospect or two that might work out once you're feeling better."

"And in the meantime how will I live? I didn't have much money to call my own before I left Niagara Falls, and now I have none at all."

Bradford regarded her through the haze of smoke from his cigar. "Would you permit me to float you a loan? You'll need a few new clothes, I guess, since we neglected to pack a bag for you. And after the first of the month, you'll need to pay for accommodations here."

It was an indelicate question, but Jillian asked it anyway: "Do you have the funds to do that, to extend me a loan?"

Jamie laughed again. "You're direct; I like that in a woman. Yes, I have all the money I need. Before the war I was a gambler, and I've never met men more willing to part with coin than these Confederates. If you give them two pennies, they'll lose one betting on a long shot and the other backing a sure thing."

When Jillian seemed unconvinced, Jamie continued. "Whether he admits it or not, Ryder wants you here. He'd be eaten alive with regret if he let you get away. He'll come 'round soon enough, Jillian. I'm just saving him from himself by offering to help you."

Jillian was as warmed by his understanding and generosity as she was by his blatant charm. "You're a good friend to him, Jamie. I'm very glad you're here."

"I'm no better friend to him than I'm prepared to be to you," Bradford acknowledged and patted her hand as he rose to leave. "Now you go ahead and get some rest, and don't let all this bother you. We'll get it sorted out, you'll see, and in the end that ornery fellow will do exactly what we want him to."

They were comforting words, and Jillian longed to believe them. She had no choice but to put her trust in fate and in Jamieson Bradford's friendship. She was in Toronto to stay, and she would have to make the best of it.

Jillian tied a black silk ribbon beneath the wide lace collar of her gown, then made a final attempt to sweep the baby-fine tendrils of hair at the nape of her neck into her heavy chignon. Tonight Ryder and Jamie were escorting her to a reception in Jacob Thompson's rooms at the Queen's Hotel, and she was determined to look her best. The gathering was being held to celebrate Jamie's twenty-eighth birthday, and she was looking forward to meeting some of the men Jamie and Ryder had talked about. They had run across a few of the Confederates already: John

Headley and Rob Kennedy while she was shopping with Jamie on King Street, Phillip Sheppard and William Cleary the previous Sunday afternoon when Ryder had taken her for a buggy ride. Since she had come to the city, her life had fallen into a pleasant but dull routine, and she was looking forward to both the festivities and the introductions.

Jillian pirouetted before the mirror, inordinately pleased by the new gown she had purchased with her first earnings from the mercantile exchange. She was also pleased with the job Jamie had managed to find for her and proud that she had acquitted herself so well in her new position as a clerk. It had been difficult at first to be a woman in a man's world, but her ability with figures and her diligence had helped her gain the attention of her superiors and the respect of the other clerks. For the first time in her life she was on her own, independent of any man's care and filled with burgeoning self-confidence.

She only wished that her relationship with Ryder were going as smoothly. After their argument the day she awakened in Toronto, he had withdrawn from her, moving his belongings to a garret room upstairs, trying to hold himself aloof. Yet as much as he had tried to maintain his distance, what they had shared made that impossible. She had found in Ryder an attentive confidant, willing to listen to the frustrations and joys of her new position, willing to offer advice and reassurance when she needed them.

As news from the South continued to worsen, she had tried to help Ryder through this difficult time, to buffer his disappointments, to allay his fears. Petersburg was still under siege, Sherman was closing in on Savannah, and the armies in the West were just barely holding their own against far superior numbers. Hope for Confederate independence grew dimmer with every passing day, and there was nothing for the men in Canada to do but read the newspaper accounts of the battles and despair at the dissolution of their cause. She only hoped that at the party this evening the difficulties of the war might be set aside. Surely they all needed a chance to enjoy themselves, a chance to set thoughts of the conflict aside.

Just as she was putting a touch of cologne behind her ears, there was a knock on the door to her bedroom. When she opened it, she found Ryder and Jamie standing outside, bathed, barbered, and dressed in their very best clothes. As her gaze moved over them, she knew a swell of deep affection. Jamie was dapper in a deep gray coat and pants, with a gray brocade vest and a silky string tie. The fabric complemented his fairness and clung to the breadth of his shoulders, making him seem more imposing than his diminutive size would indicate. Ryder stood tall and solid beside him, dressed conservatively in black. But somehow the deep color of his clothes, in contrast to the snowy shirtfront, pointed up the rugged cut of his features, the indigo blue of his eyes. He was the only man she had ever met whose smile could steal her heart, and the warmth in his expression tonight made her go breathless and tingly.

"Come in a moment, will you?" she invited. "I have a birthday gift I'd like to give you before we leave for the party."

Taking a small tissue-wrapped parcel from the top of the chest, she placed it in Jamie's hands.

"For me?" he breathed and attacked the wrappings with characteristic haste. He slipped the ribbon and tore at the paper, then exclaimed over the three monogrammed handkerchiefs tucked inside.

"Why, these are far more elegant than I deserve." Jamie beamed, fingering the fine linen squares with their hand-rolled hems and embroidered initials. "And I'll warrant you sewed them yourself. I'll have to save them for something special, perhaps drying a lady's sentimental tears or tucking in my breast pocket."

Jamie's evident delight at the simple gift pleased her, and Jill bent unselfconsciously to drop a kiss on his cheek. "Happy birthday, Jamie, and my wish for many more."

They took a carriage to the Queen's Hotel and made their way to Thompson's rooms. Though there had been no attempt to decorate for the occasion, someone had moved a piano into the room, and a group of men had gathered around it singing. As the chorus of a bawdy ballad filled the air, Jamie secured a glass of punch for Jillian and something stronger for Ryder and himself. While she sipped at her drink, Jillian took note that she was one of the few women present and that most of the others were the kind few ladies came to know. But Jillian no longer held the prejudices of her sex where such women were concerned. She had learned firsthand how difficult it was for a lone woman to make her way in the world, and she harbored no illusions about what she might have become without her education and Jamie's connections to bolster her.

As they stood a little way apart, Jamie pointed out the people she had come to know by reputation. Captain Thomas Hines was there, recently married but without the woman he had taken as his bride. Robert Martin and John Headley, who had been with Ryder and Jamie in New York, were blending their voices with the others around the piano. John Beall, of the Lake Erie raid, was conversing with Jacob Thompson and Phillip Sheppard. William Cleary was bustling around to see that the food and drinks were in good supply, and from the far side of the room Rob Kennedy raised his glass in greeting.

But as they stood by the windows looking out across the snowy bay, few of the men came to talk to them. It was several minutes before Jillian realized the Confederates were uncomfortable to have a Yankee at their gathering. But as the evening progressed and the liquor flowed, some of the men began to approach. Among the first was Rob Kennedy, anxious to renew his acquaintance with the lovely woman he had met on the street. The Louisiana native was the epitome of gentlemanly charm, complimenting Jillian on her gown and beauty, commenting on the increasingly frivolous nature of the birthday celebration.

From a few steps away, Ryder watched the interchange with a jaundiced eye. He conceded that Kennedy was a handsome enough man, strongly built and stocky, with thick brown hair and a full mustache. He also noted that Rob had a pleasantly infectious laugh, though his high spirits seemed enhanced by the amount of liquor he'd consumed. Still, Jillian seemed fascinated by the stories of Louisiana life Kennedy was telling, and she smiled with genuine amusement at the good-natured banter between Rob and another Confederate whose name was John Ashbrook.

While they were exchanging pleasantries, the man at the piano broke into a waltz, and when several couples began to dance, Kennedy offered his arm to Jillian.

"I must confess, since I took that Yankee bullet at Shiloh, I'm not the dancer I once was. But if you're willing to overlook my infirmity, Mrs. Walsh, I'd be most honored to partner you."

Jillian cast an inquisitive glance at Ryder, and he nodded in response. Though he could not withhold his assent, it galled him to see Jill cross the floor on another man's arm. But then, he had forfeited his right to interfere with Jilly's dancing partners the morning he had refused to marry her. Ryder watched them move stiffly through the first turns, but as the handsome couple were caught up in the swell of music, their dancing seemed to improve.

Ryder went to the bar to replenish his drink in the hope that it would divert him from watching Kennedy and Jillian. It was only a dance, after all, he told himself impatiently as he sloshed whiskey into his glass. Considering the ambiguous nature of their relationship, he could hardly begrudge Jilly the company of other men. Still, he could not take his eyes off them. But was it necessary for Jillian to look up at Rob through her lashes like a practiced coquette or smile quite so beguilingly at everything Kennedy said? Wasn't the Louisianian holding her closer than was proper? And what was it he was saying that Jill found so damned amusing?

"It seems our lovely Yankee is having a pleasant time, now that a few of the others have deemed it expedient to talk to her," Jamie observed quietly, coming up beside his friend. "Kennedy seems quite smitten, don't you think?"

Ryder's mouth tightened at the comment, but his reply was carefully neutral. "We've all needed a chance to relax a bit. I'm glad to see Jillian enjoying herself."

"Well, she's made a conquest of Kennedy, that's sure," Jamie continued, lighting his cigar, "and now it looks like Jacob Thompson himself is going to dance with her."

Bingham found Thompson a more acceptable partner for the stunning honey-haired woman on the far side of the room, but he was not so pleased when one by one the others asked her for a dance. When it appeared that Kennedy was about to claim her a second time, Ryder slammed his drink down on the table.

"I think I'll dance with her myself," he announced, then made his way across the room.

Jamie hid his grin behind the rim of his glass as he watched Bingham execute a gracious bow, then summarily claim Jillian's hand and drag her onto the dance floor.

"I thought I'd take a turn with you myself," Ryder muttered as he took her in his arms, "since you've deemed it necessary to dance with every other man in the place!"

Jillian stared in astonishment at her disapproving partner. She had never known Ryder to behave in such an ungentlemanly manner, and the grip he maintained on her hand was firm and blatantly possessive.

Why, he was jealous of the attention the other men had been showing her, Jill realized with a jolt of surprise. At the implication of that discovery, she was torn between the desire to nettle Bingham all the more and a wish to smooth his ruffled feathers.

"Ryder, I've been looking forward to dancing with you ever since the music started," she admitted, smiling coyly up at him. "These other men have been doing nothing more than keeping a lady company."

He looked down at her to measure her response. But her simple honesty and her evident enjoyment undermined his peevishness. Holding her close beside him brought complex feelings to the fore, and Ryder was not sure if he was more irritated at Jillian for being friendly to his compatriots or at himself for feeling compromised.

My God, she's beautiful, he found himself thinking, his rational side totally at odds with his emotions. He had never seen anyone quite so ravishing as Jillian, with her caramel-colored hair shining tawny and bright in the lamplight and her face aglow with pure enjoyment. Her pale exotic features seemed at once both vital and serene, and her gold and green eyes were as dark and mysterious as polished agate. As possessiveness overwhelmed him, he tightened his arm around her, drawing her far closer than decorum allowed.

In spite of his best resolves, his gaze strayed to the curve of her mouth. It was full, pink, and hopelessly inviting, mere inches from his own. The need to kiss her spread through his mind like a fog, obscuring propriety and self-consciousness, shrouding his loyalties and responsibilities until he could hardly remember what they were. He wanted to crush her to his chest and cover those soft, dusky lips with his own, claim Jillian as his woman here, in front of everyone. Desire roused inside him, seeping warm and honey sweet through his veins, stirring strong and demanding through his loins. He longed to lower his head and taste her mouth. But if he permitted himself that single concession, he knew he would sweep her up in his arms, take her somewhere far away, and spend the night making love to her.

Finally reality reasserted itself, diminishing his need, forcing control over his confused and irresolute emotions. It would be foolish to give in to an impulse that could only lead to misunderstandings, succumb to feelings that could only end in disaster. He loved Jillian and wanted her for his own, but he could not give her the security or future she deserved. He had nothing at all to offer her, and the thought brought stinging disillusionment.

For a time he could not even look at Jillian, not until his needs began to subside, not until he banished from his mind the fantasies of a life with her. But he had never been more aware of a woman than in those fleeting moments when he danced with Jilly in his arms.

When the music was over, he escorted her across the room to where Jamie was awaiting them. But before they reached the window alcove, Rob Kennedy was asking Jillian for another dance.

During this waltz a messenger arrived, shivering and snow-covered, as if he had ridden a long distance to reach Toronto. William Cleary immediately alerted Jacob Thompson to the man's appearance, and the three retired to the adjacent chamber to discuss what appeared to be urgent business. Nor did the messenger's arrival go unnoticed by the others who had gathered for the evening's festivities. The dance music abruptly halted, and the crowd milled around the main room of the suite. Was the messenger bringing word of a new mission to be undertaken for the cause? Had he come through the snowy night with news that the war had ended? His arrival cast a pall on the evening, and though the Confederates lit cigars, replenished their drinks, and conversed on a variety of subjects, the tension in the room escalated palpably.

Finally William Cleary emerged from the adjacent room. At first he went to where Phillip Sheppard stood and, after a few minutes' consultation, turned to the guests at large.

"We have intercepted a message bound for Washington, but it is in a code we cannot break. If any of you have had experience with the Signal Corps or with cracking ciphers, we desperately need your help."

The Confederates looked from face to face around the room, but no one volunteered.

"Lives may well be at stake if we can't get this message decoded," Cleary pleaded.

Jillian drew a long, slow breath. One of the games she and her father had played during her growing-up years was to leave notes in codes they'd devised to stump or trick each other. They had been notes that passed on the most basic kind of familial information. "The piano recital will be on Wednesday, April 12, at four o'clock," Jillian might have written to her father in a cipher she'd devised. "I will be late for dinner Tuesday night. Why don't you make something simple?" he might have written before leaving the message on the breakfast table for her to find and unravel.

Now the Confederates had a code they could not crack. Could Jillian's early training help her unscramble the Yankee cipher? Would her loyalty to the North be compromised if she offered her assistance? Jill looked around the room at the men she'd danced with this evening. She glanced at Ryder, whom she loved, and at Jamie, whose friendship meant so much to her. William Cleary said that lives might be forfeit if the code could not be broken, and they might well be the lives of the very men about her. How could she deny them her help when some of them might die without it?

"I—I have some experience with ciphers," she offered in a very small voice, fully aware of what she was committing herself to do.

One by one the men turned to look at her. Both Ryder and Jamie stared with the same question in their eyes.

"I don't know if I can crack the code," she offered softly, "but I would be willing to try."

Cleary hesitated only a moment before crossing the room to where she stood. "You realize, Mrs. Walsh, what you might be doing by helping us."

"If there are truly lives at stake, Mr. Cleary," she repeated more determinedly, "how can I refuse?"

With a nod, Thompson's secretary led Jillian toward the doors to the adjacent room, and as she followed him, she snagged Ryder's hand.

"Come with me, please" was all she was able to whisper, but he readily understood her need for reassurance and fell in step with her.

"Can she be trusted?" someone murmured as Cleary led Jillian through the doors to the adjacent room.

"How can a woman break a Yankee code when neither Thompson nor Cleary could do it?"

Thompson seemed as surprised by Jillian's offer as the others had been, but he gave her the paper and pencil she requested and allowed her a seat at his desk. She turned up the lamp and studied the single sheet of rumpled paper that was set before her on the blotter. The message was printed in a small neat hand and took up less than half a page.

After studying the writing for a moment, she turned to where Thompson sat beside her. "Have you a Vigenère tableau," she asked him, "a basic cipher square?"

Thompson looked startled by the request and did not reply.

"Surely you've been sending your messages to Richmond enciphered in some manner or another," she pressed him. "I can make up a square of my own, but if you have one here at the hotel, it will save time to let me use it."

Thompson agreed reluctantly. "William, get her the cipher square."

A moment later Cleary handed over the deciphering instrument she had requested. On a pasteboard card, the letters of the alphabet were printed across the top and in a vertical column at the left side of the page. Arrayed between these two legs of the square were letters in descending order so they formed twenty-six-character lines.

"Now," Jillian continued as the men looked on, "I wonder if you have any idea what key words the Yankees might be using."

The Confederates eyed the woman warily before Thompson answered her. "For a time at least, they were using 'death before dishonor.'"

After writing the words at the top of the paper, Jillian began to match the letters of the message along the left side of the page to those across the top. She needed to decode no more than a word or two to determine that the key Thompson had suggested was not the one to unlock this puzzle.

When she realized that, Jillian drew a long breath, wondering how to proceed. Trying to decode a message of this complexity without knowing the key was very nearly impossible.

"May I please see the envelope the message was in?" she asked softly. "Perhaps there is some clue to the code written on the envelope."

At Thompson's nod, Cleary gave her what she needed.

Jillian took the bright red envelope in her hands and stared at the address: Edwin Stanton, Secretary of War, War Department, Washington City.

Nothing about the address seemed more than what it should be, and she turned the envelope over, seeking some clue to the key. There was nothing else written on the outside, and when she peered into the envelope, she saw nothing inside, either. She turned the packet over and over in her hands, noting the size, the weight, the color of the paper.

Nibbling at her lower lip, she laid the envelope aside and wrote "RED LETTER" at the top of a clean sheet of paper. Laboriously, she found the "R" at the left margin of the cipher square, followed the line to the right until she came to the "L," which was the first letter of the message. Following the line of letters upward to the alphabet at the top, she wrote "U," hoping she had guessed the key, hoping "U" was the first letter of the message. She continued the process until she had spelled out "USUAL ARREST ADVISE."

"I think we have stumbled on the key, gentlemen," she offered with cautious optimism.

There was a moment of silence following her pronouncement before Phillip Sheppard challenged her. "How can you be sure of that, Mrs. Walsh? It's not as if you have vast experience with ciphers, and the words don't make any sense."

"Let her finish," Ryder put in quietly from behind her. "This is a damn sight more than the rest of you could do."

"Yes," Thompson agreed, watching the young woman with new respect. "Let's see what she comes up with before we draw any conclusions."

During the next half-hour, Jillian continued decoding the ciphered message. As she did, names began to appear, Jamie's name, Ryder's name, the names of other Confederates in Toronto. The men stood over her while she worked, staring in amazement, mistrust, skepticism. But when the words were all decoded, the message remained a jumble. It was frustrating to have come this far, to be sure the message was about the group here in Toronto, without being able to make sense of the words.

"You see. I told you," Sheppard crowed. "She hasn't been able to make any more of this than the rest of us."

Jillian stared up at the man, and something in his penetrating gaze made her shiver.

"I believe a second cipher was used," Jillian went on after she had studied the words a moment more. "Unless I miss my guess, the sender used a route cipher to further obscure his meaning."

"What does that mean?" William Cleary asked, clearly impressed by what this young woman had been able to do.

"It means that there is a pattern to the way the words have been enciphered, a way to find the correct order and make sense of what's been decoded already. For example, there are nine letters in the key phrase, 'red letter.' If I write the message in nine columns left to right across the page, perhaps the way to read the message will come clear to us."

"This is preposterous," Sheppard huffed. "She's making this up as she goes along. After all, she's a Yankee. Why should she offer to help us?"

The gentle pressure of Ryder's hand against her shoulder gave Jillian the courage to answer Thompson's aide.

"Mr. Cleary said unless this message was decoded, lives might be lost. I've offered my help because I hate to see those lives wasted uselessly. I think that is something, Mr. Sheppard, on which Yankees and Confederates agree."

"Go on, my dear," Thompson encouraged her. "There's nothing to be forfeit but some time, and you've already made far more progress than we'd have been able to make without you."

Jillian divided the page into nine columns and began to write one word in each column. Her concentration was deep and fierce as she worked, carefully copying the words, praying that she was right about the second solution to the puzzle. When she was done, it was clear how the message was to be read, from the lower right-hand corner up the columns toward the left. She carefully rewrote the words into a clear and concise missive for all of them to read:

THE CONFEDERATES INVOLVED IN NEW YORK CITY RAID STILL IN TORONTO ARE: ROBERT MARTIN, JOHN HEADLEY, JAMES CHENAULT, RYDER BINGHAM, JOHN ASHBROOK, ROBERT KENNEDY, JAMIESON BRADFORD. TOM HINES AND JOHN BEALL HERE, TOO. PLEASE ADVISE OF YOUR PLANS TO ARREST THESE PERPETRATORS. CONTACT AS USUAL.

"There must be a spy in our midst," William Cleary exclaimed, "to have this kind of information!"

"That's ridiculous!" Thompson's other aide burst out. "We've been very careful about whom we allowed into the inner circle of our planning."

Jacob Thompson rubbed his eyes, distressed not only by the message but by the implication that his group had been infiltrated by a spy. It explained a great deal of what had happened: how the Yankees had known about the plot to capture the *Michigan*, why "Beast" Butler and his men had been dispatched to New York, how Tom Hines and his men in Chicago had been betrayed. Slowly he nodded and and took the paper from Jillian's hands.

"We thank you for your efforts, Mrs. Walsh. You've done a great service to the Confederacy."

Jillian inclined her head by way of acknowledgment and once again became aware of Ryder's hand, warm and reassuring on her shoulder.

"I only did what I thought was right," she answered carefully. "I helped only because Mr. Cleary said men would die if I didn't. Now you have the proof you need, Mr. Thompson. There is a Northern spy in your midst. If you and your men are to survive until peace is declared, it is up to you to find him."

Chapter Fifteen

"IT WILL BE fun," Jillian said enthusiastically, "really it will."

Jamie cast a skeptical glance at the other two Confederates who were loping along in the woman's wake. "I can't imagine how anything that takes us from a warm fireside on such a day could be considered fun."

"I can't understand why you Northerners are so dead set on enjoying the cold weather," Ryder echoed Jamie's sentiments. "If God had intended us to frolic in subzero temperatures, he'd have covered us with fur!"

"Maybe she does think it will be fun," Rob Kennedy put in. "But then, there's no accounting for Yankee tastes."

Jillian glanced back at the trio who had agreed to accompany her on this Sunday afternoon outing and continued her encouragement. "The ponds have been frozen solid for weeks, and once you get the hang of it, you'll enjoy skating as much as I do."

"Balanced on those little narrow blades?" Jamie shook his head. "I beg your pardon, Jillian, but give me leave to doubt it."

Ryder smiled down at the lone woman in the group. Her eyes were shining and merry, and it was evident she was enjoying the good-natured bickering. The chilly weather seemed to enhance Jillian's natural beauty, pinkening her nose and cheeks, warming her smile. It made her seem vibrantly alive, deliciously frolicsome, nearly irresistible. Seeing her like this made Ryder want to have her to himself, to take her somewhere warm and snug for an activity that required vastly fewer clothes than they were wearing now.

"Well, I'm willing to give skating a try," Rob put in, "though sliding over a field of ice seems like something no Southern boy was meant to do."

The heavily traveled paths crunched beneath their feet as they crossed the snowy expanse of Queen's Park to the spot where Taddle Creek widened just enough to be called a pond. The vendors had obviously known where the skaters would gather, and there were a number of men bundled up against the cold, selling pastries, waffles, and hot chocolate. There was the warm, tantalizing scent of roasting chestnuts in the air, borne by the silvery clouds of steam that rolled upward from the roaster.

"Why don't we just eat some chestnuts and watch the brave ones skate?" Jamie proposed, as he tucked his collar close around his ears.

"Just think how much better those chestnuts will taste," Jillian countered amiably, "after you've done something to work up an appetite."

Since she had brought it up at breakfast, Jillian had been adamant about how she, Ryder, and Jamie were going to spend the afternoon: She was going skating, and they were going with her. Rob Kennedy had been dragooned as part of the expedition when he had stopped by for a visit, and now that she had managed to get the protesting Confederates to the pond, she wasn't about to let them stand idly by and watch her. She led her trio of escorts to the man who was renting skates, paid him for her own, and found a log at the edge of the creek where they could sit to strap them on. Jillian finished first and stepped out onto the ice, making a quick circuit of the pond with all the frisky exuberance of a horse turned out to pasture.

A smile crinkled the corners of Ryder's lips as he watched her skim across the ice. Her movements were swift and sure, and there was a graceful flowing rhythm to her unencumbered glides. She flashed along the length of the creek bed with surprising speed, her skirt and the tails of her scarf flaring out behind her, like a tribute to youth and freedom. Jill made skating seem smooth, easy, natural, and Bingham was suddenly eager to join her on the pond.

He got his feet steadied under him before he tried to stand, then came upright with an effort, feeling shaky and uncertain. But once he was balanced on the blades of his skates, moving seemed only logical. He extended his right foot gingerly and pushed with his left, moving forward in a wavery glide. It took less courage to press his slight advantage, and by the next push, the next glide, he was feeling a bit more confident.

When Jillian came sweeping up beside him to offer instruction and encouragement, he dared to spare a glance for something besides his skates. But just as he gave her a this-isn't-so-difficult grin, his feet went flying out from under him. Ryder sat down with a plop, and Jillian was forced to clamp a mittened hand over her mouth to keep from laughing down at him.

"I was doing all right there for a minute," he declared defensively, though there was humor in his eyes. "Don't just stand there, Jilly. Help me up. You're the one who got me into this!"

Jillian flitted over beside him and offered him her hand, but getting up from the ice was trickier than Ryder expected. His skates seemed determined to skid off in opposite directions every time he put weight on them, and even with Jillian's help, he couldn't manage to get both feet under him. Finally he set his skates determinedly and tightened his grip on Jillian's fingers. She hauled and he tugged, but in the end all their efforts did was bring her down on top of him.

"Now see what you've done!" she scolded in mock severity as she rolled away.

"I declare," he snapped back at her, "you Yankees have the most peculiar notions about how to spend your time."

But before he had finished carping, Jillian was up again, and after several abortive attempts, Ryder managed to duplicate her movements.

"Here now," she offered. "Just hang on to me, and I'll pull you across the pond."

"I've been trying to hang on to you for weeks, pretty lady," Bingham quipped, with an overbright grin, "but you've been bound to keep your distance."

Jillian ignored his comment and with a flash of skates, began to tow him after her. They made what seemed to Ryder remarkably fast progress across the creek, and he found himself clinging to Jill's outstretched hand as if it were a lifeline. As she pulled, he stood teetering but erect, afraid to move his feet for fear of falling over them.

"Go ahead and push," she coached, "one foot and then the other."

Cautiously, Ryder tried to emulate her movements, and as they skated together his confidence grew. Sailing across the ice, he was beginning to enjoy the rhythmic repetitive motions, the simple natural harmony of coordinating his glides with Jillian's. Though he was still shaky and unsure, Bingham felt a heady sense of pride at even this slight accomplishment. He liked the cold wind that brought tears to his eyes, the economy of motion that gave a sense of flying free, the realization that he had begun to master an activity that was both challenging and exhilarating. Now that he'd had a taste of it, he was beginning to understand why skimming over the ice held such appeal for Jillian.

She was smiling up encouragingly when they encountered a

rough patch of ice, and anticipating the effect it would have, Jillian threw her arms around Ryder's waist in an attempt to steady him. Though he managed to keep his balance, his arms came around her, too, and only when she tried to loosen her hold did Jill realize what she'd risked by helping him. A slow smile stole over his face, a twinkle of laughter shone in his eyes, and then Ryder was lowering his mouth, his goal to capture hers.

Scoured by the frigid wind, his lips were stiff and cold, but the kiss he pressed upon her mouth was deliciously sweet and summery. It was as soft as the touch of a butterfly's wing, as perfect as a cloudless sky, as warm as the hazy sun, as fresh as new-mown clover. As they kissed, joyous welcome came in a burst of wild delight, sending a sweep of raw emotion welling up between them. In the relative privacy of the far side of the pond, Ryder bound Jillian closer than before, and she leaned into his embrace, homing to the shelter of his tenderness. That they loved each other still in defiance of all that had conspired to keep them apart was wondrous, giddy, life-affirming. It gave a hope for whatever the future might hold. But they simultaneously realized that this was neither the time nor place to try to resolve their differences.

Jillian lurched back abruptly, pulling free from Ryder's arms, leaving him stunned and wavering, breathless and faintly disoriented. Their eyes met, touched, held, filled with nascent promises.

Then Ryder broke the spell, his mouth curving in a grin that was both confident and happily lecherous. "I see where the fun of skating comes in," he told her with a wink. "I think I'm beginning to understand at last."

Jill chose to ignore his comment. With a flip of her skirt and a clatter of blades, she whirled gracefully away, casting a capricious glance over her shoulder, taunting him to follow her. It was too intriguing a challenge to refuse, and he stroked along behind, concentrating on keeping his feet untangled while he did his best to catch her. But before he had reached either Jillian or the opposite bank, his ankles began to bend while his knees went as limp and wobbly as lengths of rubber tubing. To make things worse, he took a second spill, and Jillian was not there to rescue him. When he finally clambered to his feet, he sought the safety of the log, only to be greeted by Jamie and Rob, who were laughing with great hilarity.

As Ryder reached them, Jamie mopped a tear from the corner of one eye. "Well, thank you, Ryder, for demonstrating how this skating's supposed to be done. Your efforts were certainly entertaining and a credit to our cause."

"God, Ryder! You looked so funny," Rob broke in. "You kept flapping your arms like some great bird. Though I noticed you sometimes found it expedient to cling to whatever means of support was nearest you."

A darker flush rose in Ryder's cheeks at the mention of the kiss he had given Jillian, and he sent a withering glance in Rob's direction. What passed between Jilly and him was not Kennedy's concern.

"Suppose you fellows give skating a try," Ryder countered with the confidence of someone who had attempted a difficult feat and was aware of all the pitfalls. "I don't think you'll find it nearly as easy as Jillian makes it look."

Jamie nodded, tightened his skate buckles, and made a valiant attempt to stand. His feet immediately slid out from under him, depositing him at the edge of the ice.

"No, no, Jamie," Ryder chuckled, beginning to see the humor in the situation. "You're supposed to glide on those little blades, not skim along on your behind."

The smaller man glowered at Bingham and tried again to stand. For a moment it looked as if he might succeed, but he overbalanced at the critical moment and went sprawling flat on the ice.

"Those blades are tricky, aren't they?" he inquired, sitting up slowly and carefully.

"Oh, in time you'll get the hang of it," Ryder promised from the stature of his relative expertise. "A little practice is all it takes. You shouldn't be discouraged."

"Well, it's a good thing you don't have far to fall, my friend," Kennedy added, chortling at Jamie's misfortune. "If you were a few inches taller, you might be in real danger of hurting yourself."

"I don't see you taking a turn on the ice," Jamie countered, trying the maneuver with somewhat more success.

"Well, you can bet, Bradford, that when I do, I'll be better at this than you are."

When Jamie had finally made it to his feet, Ryder skated over to offer suggestions.

Rob finally moved off the log and balanced on the blades of his skates. There was an expression of incipient triumph on his face as he propelled himself in Ryder's direction. But the thing Kennedy had managed to overlook was that he had no idea how to stop himself. Backpedaling and yelling, he flailed his arms, but to no discernible avail. He went careening into Ryder, sending them both sprawling across the ice in a tangle of arms and legs. Bingham laughed and Rob cursed as they struggled to get up. And when Kennedy had finally regained his feet, he stroked cautiously in Jill's direction.

Ryder remained with Jamie and tried to share what little he had learned, but whatever Bradford's accomplishments, skating was not one of them. He did try his luck several more times before the afternoon was over, but either his feet, the skates, or the ice itself was totally uncooperative. Muttering about this being the most dangerous thing he'd undertaken since the war began, Jamie finally crawled back to the log in ignoble defeat to wait for the others to tire.

Rob Kennedy continued to struggle until late in the day, gliding for a few yards, then sitting down abruptly, struggling to his feet and gliding a few yards more. His determination was to be admired, and Jillian said as much when she skated over to help him.

"It gets easier the more you do it," she encouraged. "Try to relax and enjoy yourself."

Rob grinned in response to her words. "If I try to relax and enjoy myself, these damned skates sneak off in the wrong direction."

Jillian smiled and reached out to catch his hand. "Come skate with me awhile. I'll show you how easy it really is."

Rob hung on while Jillian towed him beside her, and as she did, his movements became looser and more graceful.

"Perhaps this isn't so difficult after all," he finally conceded. "But it's sure not something we'd be able to do in Louisiana in the wintertime."

"And what do you do at home in the wintertime?"

"We stay close by the fire mostly. We mend tack or broken tools, see to the animals. The women sew. There's not a whole lot to be done on a farm in the winter."

"Do you miss it, Rob," she asked him, "as much as I miss Pennsylvania?"

Kennedy nodded sadly. "It's beautiful where I'm from, particularly in the spring when the lilacs and azaleas are out. And if you go into the woods, there are blooming redbuds and dogwood sprinkled all through the trees. I'd give anything to be back there in time to see the woods in flower and help my pa with planting."

"Will you go back once the war is ended?"

"To tell you the truth, Jillian," he admitted reluctantly, "I've been thinking of going back even before we've signed a proper peace."

"But won't that be dangerous, traveling through Yankee territory before the war is over?"

Kennedy shrugged and eyed her consideringly. "I've been thinking that traveling with a woman might even the odds a little."

Jillian remained silent, knowing what he was about to ask.

Rob continued, his voice edged with entreaty and wistfulness. "They say you traveled with Bingham earlier in the war. They say you saved him from Union detectives by saying he was your husband."

Still Jillian said nothing, wondering what Kennedy knew about Ryder's escape.

"If I decided to go back to Louisiana, Jillian, would you consider coming with me? It would only be for a little while. You could come right back here afterward."

Jill looked into Kennedy's earnest face. She could see the loneliness and desperation in his eyes.

"Oh, Rob, I can't—" she began. But why couldn't she go with Rob to Louisiana? Was it that she couldn't leave Toronto? Leave her job? Leave Ryder? Bingham said he loved her, left her warm and weak with the fervor of his kisses, yet he was not willing to marry her, to offer her his name or a future as his wife.

Rob was not asking her to do anything she had not done for Ryder already. He only wanted her help in eluding the Yankees, just as Bingham had.

"Think about it, Jillian; that's all I ask. It's something I've been considering ever since we returned from New York."

Jill nodded. She could not agree to accompany him, but she refused to extinguish his hope.

On the far side of the pond, Ryder sat frowning and watching them. "What are they talking about so seriously?" he murmured under his breath.

Jamie shifted on the log beside his friend and offered the bag of roasted chestnuts. "They may well be discussing something as innocuous as the weather, and even that would bother you. Admit it, Ryder, you're jealous of any man who so much as looks in Jillian's direction."

Bingham accepted one of the chestnuts and snorted in disgust. What Jamie said was true. He didn't want anyone he didn't trust within fifty yards of Jillian.

"Damn it, Ryder. This is silly," Jamie continued. "You love Jillian, and she loves you. Take what happiness you can, while you have the opportunity."

"There's more to it than that," Bingham began. "I have things I must accomplish before I—"

Jamie raised a dismissing hand. "Oh, God, Ryder! Spare me the details. Have you ever thought that you might be well past the point where duty becomes obsession? I can't imagine that your brother would want you to throw away your future to rectify something that's over and done. Forgive yourself for Mitchell's death, admit that you made a mistake while running the blockade and lost your ship as a consequence. And once you've done all that, put the rest of it out of your mind. There's nothing to be gained by forfeiting your life when such a glorious future is beckoning."

Was what Jamie said true? Bingham wondered. With the war drawing to a close, was it finally time to put away the things he had tried and failed to rectify? He wanted a life with Jillian, a home, a family, security. She meant the world to him. Was it really only his sense of duty that was keeping them apart?

He pushed the thought aside and popped the chestnut in his mouth. He would think about what Jamie had said when he had more time to consider it. But now it was getting late. The sun was going down. The tips of his fingers were tingling with cold, and his feet might as well have been chunks of ice. He set aside his skates and glanced out across the pond. Rob Kennedy was limping toward them, one skate dangling from his fingers. It was time to go back to the boarding house, time to return to their daily lives.

Only Jillian, alone on the silvery glaze, seemed unwilling to give up the afternoon's adventure. The circles she inscribed on the ice were gilded by the sinking sun, while the snowy bank behind her shone amber, mauve, and powder blue, hemmed by the darkening sky. Against the glowing snow, she spun and twirled with the fey mysterious movements of a stranger.

Ryder's eyes followed her as she swooped gracefully across the pond, capable, unencumbered, and glorious, filled with life and vitality. It seemed suddenly as if she was indulging a part of herself that circumstances never allowed her to be. She seemed young, frivolous, beautiful; pagan, wild, and free. As he watched her solitary figure flare past him toward the farthest reaches of the pond, he felt an unfamiliar sting at the back of his eyes and a poignant tightening around his heart.

* * *

When Jillian left the mercantile exchange late Friday afternoon, Jamieson Bradford was leaning against a lamppost waiting for her.

"Jamie, what a pleasant surprise!" she burst out when she saw him. "Have you come to walk me home?"

He nodded and fell in step beside her. "I wanted a chance to talk to you," he told her, "to have a few words with you alone."

Jamie's uncharacteristic seriousness filled Jillian with misgivings. "Is something the matter, Jamie? Is Ryder all right?"

Bradford wasted no time in coming to the point. "John Beall is putting together a party to rescue some Confederate officers who are being transported from Johnson's Island to Fort Lafayette. He plans to waylay their train south of Buffalo and spirit the men into Canada."

"And Ryder is going with them," Jillian murmured, following the trend of Jamie's thoughts.

There was no question in Bradford's mind that Jillian could be trusted with the particulars of this new Confederate operation. She had long since proved her loyalty to Ryder and had decoded the message meant for Secretary of War Stanton the night of the party in Thompson's rooms.

"I wouldn't ordinarily interfere with something Thompson and his men are planning," he went on, "but I have a bad feeling about this. I tried to dissuade Beall and the rest from committing themselves to this mission, but to no avail. I don't want Ryder involved, and I thought you might be able to change his mind."

"What makes you think that Ryder will listen to me," she challenged, "if you've already tried to talk him out of it?"

A grin split Bradford's face. "Oh, I think you have powers of persuasion far beyond those I'm able to bring to bear."

When she looked skeptical, Jamie continued more seriously. "Ryder loves you, Jillian. Perhaps he'll listen to what you say. It's worth a try, at least. This whole thing stinks of disaster."

She said nothing for a moment but tightened her grip on the edges of her cloak as if newly aware of the chill.

"When are they going to leave?"

"Some of the men will cross the border tomorrow; the rest are planning to go on Sunday."

Jillian drew a long breath and let out a sigh. "I'm not sure Ryder will listen to me, Jamie. You know how strong his sense of duty has become since his brother's death. And when it comes to anything involving Fort Lafayette, he simply isn't rational."

"I'm not saying he should put his duty aside, Jillian, but there's no reason for him to be a part of every mission the Confederates plan. And I especially don't want him involved in this one."

Jill inclined her head in agreement. She did not want Ryder risking his life needlessly either. At the mere thought of what he was planning to do, Jill could feel the fear crystallize inside her chest. What if the mission failed? What if Ryder was captured? The newspapers were filled with threats about what would happen if the New York City arsonists were arrested. It seemed to be tempting fate for Ryder to cross the border again when he had already risked so much for the South. Was the prospect of rescuing a few Confederate officers worth all he was preparing to gamble for their freedom?

There wasn't any question about approaching him; she was only glad that Jamie had seen fit to warn her about what Bingham planned to do. As they walked through the heavy winter twilight, Jillian tried to decide what arguments she could use to persuade Ryder to remain in Toronto. It was disheartening to realize that Jamie must have fruitlessly employed the most logical ones already.

If she was honest with herself, Jill had to admit she had only one advantage in dealing with Ryder, and she was loath to use her feminine wiles against him. Using them seemed devious, unfair. It would demean what they felt for each other, somehow change the quality and substance of their love. Besides, in the past neither her feelings for Ryder nor his for her had been sufficiently compelling to keep him from doing what he felt he must. She could only hope that if she tried hard enough, argued strongly enough, enticed him sweetly enough, Ryder might give up the mission and stay with her.

While she was busy with her own thoughts, Bradford plodded along beside her, taking her silence as assent. If anyone could change Ryder's mind about going to Buffalo, Jillian could. She was an extremely clever and resourceful woman, and there was no doubt that Ryder loved her. Though Jamie hated asking Jillian to intercede, the end would justify the means if she was able to make Bingham reconsider taking part in the raid.

Shivers spilled down Jamie's spine every time he thought about the attempt to rescue the Confederate officers, and he could not shake the feeling that the mission was going to end badly for everyone involved. There was no rational reason for his concern. Beall was a good and careful officer, and this mission had as much chance for success as any the Confederates in Toronto had undertaken. But that knowledge did not quell Jamie's uneasiness. In revealing the plan to Jillian, he was doing nothing more than trying to avert disaster.

When they reached the boarding house, Jillian bade Jamie good-bye and went directly to her room. While she removed her outerwear and washed her face and hands, she continued to puzzle over what she would say to Ryder. Since she could not speak her mind in the company of others for fear of compromising the mission's security, she would have to see Ryder in his room before supper was announced.

After tidying her hair and adding a pretty lace collar to her plain black gown, Jill mounted the steps to the third floor of the boarding house and knocked on the door to Ryder's room. While she waited in the drafty hall, she prayed that once they were alone, she would find the words she needed to dissuade him.

There was surprise in Bingham's eyes as he opened the rough wooden panel, but he did not hesitate to offer his hospitality. As she stepped across the threshold, Jillian suddenly realized how much Ryder had given up by letting her have the room on the floor below. This tiny, freezing chamber tucked up under the eaves had no fireplace of its own, and the ceiling was so low he could barely stand erect. The furnishings that had been clubbed together for his use were rude and Spartan at best: a narrow iron bedstead, a washstand stained and rickety with age, and a small upended crate that held a single oil lamp.

Her eyes swept around the small enclosure, coming to rest on the neatly packed valise in the center of the mattress. Her gaze rose from the bag to the contours of Ryder's face, and she knew, as she stood staring up at him, just how difficult a task she had agreed to undertake.

"Jamie told you about the mission, didn't he?" Ryder asked softly and read the confirmation in her face. "It's useless to try to talk me out of going. This is something I'm bound to do."

"Is it, Ryder?" she began. "Why is it necessary for you to risk your life when there are others who could venture into Union territory without jeopardizing everything?"

His voice took on a more resonant timbre. "Are you asking me to countenance cowardice, Jilly?"

Jillian shook her head. "No one will call you a coward if you decide to remain in Toronto."

"Perhaps it's a man's opinion of himself that determines what he's called."

"But, Ryder, this operation seems ill-advised at best. It won't change the course of the war; it won't alter the South's destiny. Why must you gamble so much when even complete success will accomplish something so insignificant?"

Anger puckered the corners of Bingham's mouth and narrowed his eyes. "What I'm going to do isn't insignificant if it frees even one man from his imprisonment."

"Of course, the freedom of the officers is important," she conceded. "But this late in the war, it will gain them nothing but a few months' liberty."

"Isn't it my sworn duty to aid my brothers-at-arms, regardless of the prospects?"

"Oh, Ryder, please, what you're planning frightens me. I'm only asking you to reconsider. Jamie is convinced the mission will end badly, and I—"

Ryder's derisive laughter cut her short. "Jamie's worse than an old woman when it comes to assessing risks. What we're doing isn't all that dangerous."

"Isn't it, Ryder? Aside from Jamie's concerns, aren't you taking your life in your hands every time you cross the border?"

He looked down at her impassively, calm and resolute in the face of her rising agitation.

"Don't you realize that nothing you can do will change the past?" she went on. "No matter how many times you volunteer, no matter how many times you put your life in jeopardy, you can't bring Mitchell back."

"I know that."

"Do you? Then why do you continue to take such chances? Why must you continue to try to change something that's clearly irrevocable?"

Bingham drew a long breath. "You know there's more to it than that. My God, Jilly, there's a war on. Battles are being fought; the future of my country is being decided in a hundred skirmishes every day. What I'm doing may not have the impact it would have had once, but helping those officers escape is part of what I've sworn to do. Would you have me walk away because it's expedient, because I might be asked to forfeit my life in the name of the cause?"

Jillian knew that what he said was true. Countless others had sacrificed their futures in the hope of securing an independent South. But those others were not her concern—Ryder was. And she meant to do her best to save him from himself.

"Since I've been in Toronto," she told him, "I've done everything I could to understand your views, to accommodate your allegiances, to show you how much I love you. I've made friends of your friends; I've decoded a ciphered message in the hope that by aiding your cause I might prevent the useless loss of lives—"

"And I appreciate what you've done, Jilly. I know how hard you've tried to make a place for yourself here. But my participation in this mission simply isn't negotiable."

Her voice broke with frustration as she brought her last argument to bear. "Please, Ryder, I haven't asked much of you since we first met, not when we were together in Rochester, not since I've been here. But I want you to remain in Toronto, if only to save me from worrying."

Bingham looked down into her face and understood that it was love and concern that had brought her to his room, understood that it was love and concern that were driving her to demand concessions now. Why wasn't his love and concern for her enough to allow him simple acquiescence? What prevented him from giving Jilly what she wanted by staying in Toronto? He did not doubt that he should do as she asked. But even knowing she had saved his life, had risked her own to send him north to freedom, he could not give her his promise.

"Then don't be afraid for me, Jilly," he offered simply. "I give you my word that I'll come back to you."

The audacity of his reply offended her, and she stood staring up at him, hating his blind tenacity, hating his empty assurances.

"Damn it, Ryder!" she cried. "Stop and think about what could happen if things go wrong!"

A smile touched the corners of his lips. "If we stopped to consider every chance we take in life, we'd give up every hope we have for living."

His eyes were as dark and vast as a midnight sky, implacable, distant, cool. As she stood glaring up at him, futile arguments clogged her throat; disappointment stung like acid in her veins.

Angry and frightened, disillusioned and frustrated, she turned on him, challenging the invisible barrier between them, braving his intimidating physical presence. With impotent rage singing in her head, she lashed out at him, intent not on hurting him but on expressing how much he was hurting her. Whether to quell her resistance or offer recompense, Ryder gathered her in his arms, trapping her hands between them.

For the span of a long drawn breath, they stood staring into each other's eyes. She could see pain and regret in his, and she realized suddenly that she was not really fighting Ryder's need for revenge, not fighting his sense of duty, not fighting to make him acknowledge and act on his love for her. She was not fighting Ryder at all. She was fighting the inevitabilities of war. In war men died, sacrifices were demanded, the normal flow of life was violently disrupted. And in war the most basic differences between men and women were exacerbated.

To men war offered a chance to prove themselves, to measure themselves against some masculine ideal. For them it was valor and glory, patriotism and devotion to a cause. It was an attempt to resolve irreconcilable differences. But women saw war in more personal terms. Women understood instinctively the exact price and value of every life expended on the field of battle, saw beyond the fierce high-mettled charges, beyond the hopes for victory. They recognized the brutality, the destruction, the pain. Women could imagine the vast dark future when the true forfeit of war would come due, knowing it would be paid in loneliness, bitterness, and isolation.

In the most intimate way possible Jillian was addressing age-old conflicts, struggling with questions of life and death, probing the very essence of male and female. She saw the larger issues for what they were and, with a shiver of resignation, acknowledged that they were conflicts she could never hope to reconcile.

The enormity of the defeat sapped Jillian's strength, and she sagged against the breadth of Ryder's body. Now that she had recognized her inability to change their fate, she needed to address another question: How would she send him off to seek his destiny? She could spend the next hours at odds with the man she loved, or she could use those hours to express her feelings. She could extend the conflict between them, or she could make peace in the most tangible way she knew. She saw the question clearly and made her choice without reserve. In spite of their differences in mind and heart, she wanted this last chance to be with Ryder.

As she leaned into his embrace, she became aware of the sharp tang of shaving soap that lingered on his skin, the warm familiar musk that was so much a part of Ryder. She saw that the collar of his shirt lay turned back against the yolk, that tufts of night-dark hair were curling from the opening. With a noose of bittersweet tears tightening around her throat, Jillian lifted one hand to the base of the closure, gently touching the whorls of silken hair, the warm honey-gold flesh that lay beneath it.

Ryder dropped his arms to his sides and retreated a step, misunderstanding the sudden intimacy.

"Jilly, don't," he whispered. "Don't."

In spite of his warning, she closed the distance between them, pressing the stark black bodice of her gown to the pure white cotton of his shirtfront as her fingers skimmed up along the placket, tracing the edge of the widening opening.

Jill had not come here to seduce Ryder; she had staunchly refused to consider bartering her body for his acquiescence. But if he was going to risk his life, she wanted one last chance to show him how much he meant to her, one last chance to find happiness in his arms, one last chance to savor the magic of their unique and wondrous rapture.

She saw dark emotions cloud his eyes as her hand reached the base of his throat; as her thumb brushed the shallow half-moon hollow; as her fingers fanned into the long, thick hair waving at the nape of his neck. She bent nearer than before, and her tongue scoured the heated skin exposed by the opening of his shirt. She felt him swallow, heard his breathing accelerate.

"Jillian, please," he murmured in a voice gone suddenly deep and husky. "You know I can't change my mind now that I've committed myself to go with them."

"I know," she murmured, "and I've accepted that. But won't you grant me a few more minutes of your company, a few more minutes when we can be alone together?"

Even hearing her assurance, Ryder was not certain he believed her. But as he tried to weigh the sincerity of her words, her tongue became a dart of heat moving along the midline of his body, up from his breastbone, searing his skin. He clenched his teeth as she nibbled along the angle of his jaw, drove his close-cut nails into his palms as she feathered kisses to the corner of his mouth. He had to be sure her actions were not a ploy to gain his acquiescence before he could take what she was offering. But a wave of sensation was zigzagging along his nerves, kindling a fire in his loins. The web of her allure was tightening around him, and he went breathless and light-headed with the force of denying both himself and her.

"Oh, Jilly, love," Ryder groaned, half mad with the sight and scent and feel of her. "You cannot win your way like this."

"I'm not trying to persuade you to change your mind," she told him in a wounded tone. "I only want to be with you. Can you deny us that, Ryder? Can you deny that you want to make love as much as I do?"

His answer was clear in the taut planes of his face, in the splash of hectic color at the crest of his cheekbones, in his arrested waiting posture. His eyes were tightly closed, the lacy lashes meshed, while his mouth was slightly open, tempting, taunting, vulnerable. She could see the curve of his upper lip, the gentle dip at the center of the lower one. He looked like a man who could be damned by the mere brush of a kiss, a man who would welcome that damnation.

She came on tiptoe to offer what they both wanted, and she saw his mouth widen, soften, bow in unwilling anticipation. With instinctive sensuality, Jillian hesitated just short of her goal, sensing that the need was never so fierce as in that instant of impending pleasure. Her lips hovered a hair's breadth from his, and she could feel his warm breath wash across her skin, sense how his heartbeat was fluttering. At last, she covered his mouth with hers, kissing him deeply, letting the inner surfaces of her lips caress him with gentle but devastating persistence.

A ragged moan rose in his throat, and she felt it vibrate against her. In it was both joy and resignation, both regret and sweet surrender. Whether he believed that it was love and nothing more that was driving her to seduce him, she did not know, but as one hand clamped hard at her waist and the other furrowed upward into her hair, it didn't seem to matter.

With joy swelling in her breast, she warmed and budded with a passion to answer his. She curled closer in his embrace, running her hands up his back to settle between his shoulderblades, contouring the swell of her hips to the juncture of his legs. As she acceded to the yearning in her blood, she opened herself to him, wanting to share all she had to give, wanting to prove the depths of her feelings in the most selfless way she knew. She needed to savor once more the love that had brought such joy to both their lives, find expression for emotions that were so difficult to put into words.

Clothes were no impediment to their escalating need, and they scattered them on the floor, dispensing with layer after layer of fabric and lace and inhibitions. Finally they were kissing naked, unencumbered, bare. As they brushed mouth to mouth and thigh to thigh, Ryder's manhood sought a haven at the joining of her legs. His hands stroked the contours of her body from shoulders to flanks.

Giving lie to all restraint, they surrendered to the magic that had always been between them, reveling in delight, losing themselves in the splendor. Their tongues touched, slick, soft, and faintly nubbly. Their breath merged, sweet-scented and warm. Each drank in the wild intoxicating essence of the other. Neither the cold nor the meanness of the chamber mattered, for they were transported beyond their physical surroundings. They were alone, together, in love. Nothing else existed for either of them.

At last Jillian drew away and leaned back secure in Ryder's arms. The pale yellow glow of the oil lamp limned the contours of his features, haloing his dark hair and lashes with crimson and amber. The highlights and shadows cast across his face turned him into a stranger, but the tenderness and longing that flowed between them was comforting, infinitely familiar.

Their eyes held as she stared up into his face: his heavy-lidded and dark as polished lapis, hers shining with a golden glow.

"I love you, Jilly," he whispered, lost to the promises her body was making to his.

"And I love you, Ryder. I love you with all my heart."

Vivid awareness spread along Ryder's skin from the places where their bodies touched, like ripples across a pond, like warmth radiating from a blazing fire. It was a curling, spreading ache that sent tendrils of sultry anticipation to the farthest reaches of his body. He raised one hand to graze her cheek, to trace the extravagant curves of her pale pink lips.

He had never been more aware of his need for Jill, for the sweetness of her body, for the sustenance he found in her arms, for the momentary forgetfulness only Jillian could provide. But before he could succumb to the pleasure and claim Jillian as his own, he had to be totally sure she had accepted the truth.

"This won't matter, Jilly," he warned, his voice breathless, slurred, and soft. "Even this won't change my mind about going with Beall and the others."

With tears rising in her eyes, she reached up to caress his cheek, stroke the strong sculptured column of his throat.

"I may have come to try to change your mind," she reassured him, "but that's not the reason I've decided to stay. With all my heart, I wish this could deter you from this course. But if you must follow the dictates of your conscience, I want this chance to prove how much I love you."

As she gave herself in the act of love, the supplication of her body became so much more than what she had intended. It became salvation, joy, elation; commitment, serenity, contentment.

Being with Ryder tonight was all that mattered; she could not let herself think about the rest.

Convinced at last, he bent his head to claim her mouth, his lips moving gentle and sweet against her. But the kiss presaged a burst of inner fire that flared like an arcing charge between them. It was incandescent, unchanneled, as wild and basic as summer lightning. It blazed like sparks in the darkness, a conflagration in the night. It rose beyond the confines of normal restraint, enhancing and redefining the scope of their feelings for each other.

In spite of the urge for consummation, they held back, pushing themselves toward the plane where pain and pleasure merged, reveling in the want rising desperate and hungry in their blood. But passion restrained was not passion denied, and at length they moved to the narrow bed, succumbing to their destiny.

The springs of the cot screeched in complaint as they pushed aside the valise and tumbled onto the lumpy mattress. The completion of the act was swiftly beckoning, and the sound of the protesting metal might as well have been a love song.

Ryder trailed his hand across her belly to the apex of her thighs, and the heat and need within her rose up against his palm. He stroked her, pleased her, whispered her name, until she was dewy and moist, aching to receive him. As his fingers probed deep into her welcoming warmth, her hands moved over him, too, teasing him with the exquisite languor of her touch, offering him the potent enticement of her infinite tenderness.

When at length he drew his hand away, she felt his rampant maleness brush the threshold of her body and opened herself to welcome him. He came slowly, sinking into the sweet, hot well of her femininity, pressing deep and deeper still, until they were wholly, wondrously joined. The unity was stunning in its perfection. It was profound, limitless, vast, unrivaled by any other kind of love. It was the giving of every essence of self, the denial of any reality but this.

They sank down and down into the transient world of unencumbered bliss, discovering and discounting the wisdom of reserve. They put the problems of the world from their minds as their lips touched, as their skin brushed, as their hearts thudded and beat as one. They moved with boundless swelling abandon: unified; together; joyously, mystically joined.

But as they moved together each touch compelled another; each stroke demanded a stroke to answer the last. Every shuddering breath brought them nearer the ultimate ecstasy, the moment of ending and beginning. They fought the sweeping sensation. They held back and yet surged on until the crest rolled over them in a devastating, melting completion that was infinitely right and satisfying. Consciousness shattered, emotions swelled, passion ran white-hot and shimmering through their veins. They clung helplessly loin to loin and heart to heart while bliss and love and hope became the only reality.

They lay tangled together, shuddering with the faint sweet tremors still bursting through their blood. They reveled with the sense of wholeness and satiation. They snuggled, stroked, dreamed in a half-world of latent slumber. But at last the flares of passion ebbed away, receding, drifting, leaving them huddled and spent with the waiting world before them.

Jillian stirred slowly and looked into Ryder's face. She smiled and kissed his lips. "I love you, Ryder."

"And I love you."

"Then please, my darling, stay with me." The words were on her lips before she could stop them, born of her love and concern for him. It did not matter that her passion had not been meant as an inducement, that she had given her word not to make their loving more than what it was. The plea reflected her stark terror at what the future might hold, and every instinct urged her to try once more to protect Ryder from himself.

Resignation kindled in his eyes. "I told you making love wouldn't change my mind. I have a duty to discharge, responsibilities to others and to myself. Can't I make you understand the difference between duty and dishonor?"

Jillian sat up beside him on the bed, her hair tumbling around them in flowing silken ropes, her skin shining ivory and gold in the feeble light of the oil lamp. "I do understand, Ryder," she told him wearily. "I understand far more than you know. It's just that I'm so afraid, so afraid that I'll lose you, that we'll lose what we've finally found together."

He pulled her down beside him and buried his face in her hair.

"I know, Jilly," he acknowledged quietly. "I'm afraid of losing what we've found together, too."

He held her close all through the night, whispering endearments, showing how much he loved her. But no matter how he sought to please her, no matter how sweetly he pledged his love, they both knew it would not change his decision or what would happen on the morrow.

Chapter Sixteen

THE BOARDING HOUSE parlor was quiet, and after a busy day at the mercantile exchange, there was about the place a contented air that Jillian found renewing. It had become the custom for the women to gather there after supper, to read, to sew, to gossip by the warmth of the fire. Mrs. Moire often sat as she did tonight, working on household accounts, while Mrs. Claremont, one of the other boarders, prattled on about everything under the sun. Huddled in the pools of mellow lamplight, Mrs. Claremont's niece and Jillian nodded or shook their heads in keeping with her subject and continued their sewing. This evening Jillian was busily knitting socks to give to Ryder and Jamie for Christmas, only three days away.

Nearly a week before, Ryder had come to her room in the dead of night to advise her of his safe return from Buffalo. His knock had awakened her from a sound sleep, but somehow that hadn't mattered.

"I wouldn't normally disturb you at such an hour—" he had begun when she opened the door.

"No, it's all right," she whispered and motioned him inside. "I'm glad you came to let me know you're back."

While Ryder collapsed into one of the armchairs, Jillian lit a lamp and added coal to the fire in the grate. She had been wild with worry since the news came through that two of the men who had gone to Buffalo had been captured in the Suspension Bridge station, and she was unspeakably glad to see Ryder now.

"I'm not sure how much you know about the outcome of the mission to Buffalo," he began, "but Jamie was right about its chances for success. We waited and waited for the train with the officers to come through, and even managed to stop one on its way into Buffalo. But the men we were seeking were not on board, and after that we had no choice but to abandon our plans."

Jillian finished stirring the fire to life and, since Ryder seemed to feel like talking, settled herself in the armchair opposite his.

"We heard that much from Martin, Headley, and the others. And that Beall and George Anderson were captured."

Ryder wearily shook his head. "Anderson wasn't feeling well when we reached the Suspension Bridge station, so while the rest of us scattered, Beall stayed with him at the depot. I still don't know how they were spotted, but about half an hour after we left them, someone came into the saloon where Holt and I were having a drink and announced that two Confederate spies had been arrested. We went right over to the station to see what had happened, but with the number of guards buzzing around Beall and Anderson and the alarm their presence had aroused, there wasn't anything we could do."

"What happened then? How did you get across the border?"

"Holt and I decided to separate, and I took a room at one of the hotels."

"There in Niagara City, where they were bound to be looking for you?" Jillian was incredulous.

Ryder's head lolled against the back of the chair. "There wasn't much choice at that time of night. I figured I'd draw less attention holed up in a hotel room than wandering the streets, though I can't say I got much sleep.

"The next day I made inquiries to see if there wasn't some way to break Beall and Anderson out of jail, but they were trussed up tighter than a Christmas turkey. I also learned Beall was to be tried for piracy in New York, and that Anderson was being sent with him."

Jillian didn't say that it was the kind of fate she had feared would befall Ryder. She didn't need to say it. She didn't need vindication, and Bingham wouldn't welcome the reminder that her concern for him had been well founded.

"Once I was sure there was nothing I could do, I figured I had better head north myself. I knew the border guards would be particularly vigilant at Suspension Bridge, so I took the train to Detroit and crossed into Canada by ferry."

Ryder didn't tell her how conscientious the border guards at Detroit had been, how close he had come to being exposed. He did not need to tell her about the dangers he had faced; Jillian seemed to know.

"So the mission came to naught," she observed quietly.

Ryder nodded. "The mission came to naught, and we lost two more of our best men."

Jillian could read the disillusionment in Ryder's face, the defeat, the exhaustion. Without a word she moved to the arm of his chair, driven by a need to offer comfort.

"Oh, Ryder, I'm sorry," she breathed. "I wish the mission had ended differently."

"Jamie was right," he conceded, his voice slurred and soft. "You were right. I should never have gotten involved with this."

She raised one hand to stroke his hair. "You did what you had to do, Ryder. You did what you thought was best."

He nodded wearily and drew her into his arms. She went willingly, eager for the closeness, eager to soothe his disappointment. They kissed, the embrace tender and consoling, but it was tinged, as always, with the wondrous excitement they found together. She felt the magic growing between them, felt the need to act, to offer all the solace she could give.

It had been difficult to ask the question after the night they had spent together, after the pledge Ryder had made not to make her his mistress. But she had voiced the words, knowing full well what an affirmative answer would mean.

"You look exhausted, Ryder. Would you—would you like to come to bed?"

Ryder hesitated, studying her face, the need for succor evident in the dark blue depths of his eyes. He recognized what she was asking, what she was offering, what she felt compelled to do, and he slowly shook his head.

"I can't stay with you, Jilly," he whispered, his voice husky with a mixture of promise and regret. "Not now. Not yet."

His decision made so selflessly lit a soft insistent glow inside her chest. It made her understand just how important she was to him, how much their future mattered. When he left her to seek the solitude of his own room, he left her with a gentle promise, a fledgling hope for a final resolution between them. The implied commitment in his words had grown to a nebulous hovering joy that warmed and sustained her through the following days. And those days had proved difficult ones for all of them.

News from the South was universally bad; the end of the war was inevitable. The future the Confederates had fought so hard to make a reality was crumbling before their eyes. But since the night Ryder had come to her, Jillian knew that once the South surrendered, once the war was resolved, she and Ryder would find a way to make a future together.

As Jillian turned her attention to the sock she was knitting, she remembered Ryder's unspoken promises and took comfort in all he had not said. As she worked over the small linked stitches, a smile came to her lips, hovering at the corners, widening the lavish bow. With hope for the future growing in her heart, she found that the sacrifices she and Ryder had made seemed less desperate, more reasonable.

Her thoughts were interrupted by a knock at the front door, and Mrs. Moire went to answer it. When she returned to the cozy parlor, Rob Kennedy was trailing after her. He had become a frequent visitor in these past weeks, and Jill smiled to welcome him.

He greeted the other ladies, then turned to address Jillian directly. "I was wondering if I could speak to you alone. There is a matter of some importance I need to discuss."

"You can use the dining room if you like," Mrs. Moire offered. "There's still a fire lit in there."

Jillian was glad for the suggestion since it would have been an unthinkable breach of propriety to take a gentleman to her bedchamber. She set her knitting aside and led Rob into the adjoining room, closing the doors behind them.

He stood for a moment watching her, turning his hat in his hands.

"What is it, Rob?" Jill inquired, sensing his uneasiness. "Is something wrong?"

"I've come to a decision," he told her softly, his trepidation showing in his eyes. "I've decided it's time to go home."

His revelation was not a surprise; he had spoken longingly of Louisiana the day they had gone skating and on several occasions since. Jillian also knew it would take courage for Rob to run the blockade into Wilmington or to travel overland through the Union.

"Is that wise, Rob?" she asked softly. "The war can't go on much longer, and it would certainly be safer to wait until peace is declared before heading home."

"I know that," he admitted. "But I'm anxious to see my people, anxious to put the war behind me."

They were sentiments she could readily understand. While she had found some measure of contentment in Toronto, she hated having her life ruled by events she could not control, hated being barred from the land she loved, hated living in exile. Rob must have had those reservations, too, and he must have felt them even more strongly than she.

"Since running the blockade into Wilmington is growing more difficult every day, I am planning to take the train as far as Detroit and make connections south from there."

An unexpected shiver moved through Jillian at the thought of what he meant to do. Surely he was aware of the dangers the Confederates faced if they were caught on Northern soil, of the forfeit he would pay if he should be recaptured.

"I came to ask you, Jillian," he continued, "if you would be willing to accompany me."

For an instant Jillian stared at the sturdy young man before her, seeing the hope and desperation in his face. She liked Rob; his welfare mattered to her. But she did not want to leave Toronto, and searched for words to tell him so.

He raised a hand to forestall a reply. "When I asked you this before, you refused me, but I was hoping you might have changed your mind. I'm convinced I would be safer traveling with you as my wife than I would be alone, and I think any detectives who might follow me would be confused by a woman's presence."

What he said was largely true, but Jillian clung to the many reasons she had for refusing him.

"I have money to pay for our passage," he went on, "and I would buy a ticket for your return. I don't expect any more than your company, and I'd be pleased if you'd consider helping me."

Jillian studied the brown-haired man before her, thinking how lost and unhappy he seemed. Yet in spite of it, he had been the soul of consideration. He had offered her his company, his humor, his friendship when the other Confederates had not.

"You would be gone hardly more than a week, three or four days going and the same coming back," he argued.

"But, Rob, I have a job here, and I can't afford to jeopardize it."

"You could make up some story about having to go to a funeral or to visit a sick relative. Surely they would let you leave for that."

Jillian reconsidered his request. Would it be so difficult to say yes to what he was proposing? Hadn't his consideration and friendship been worth the risk he was asking her to take? And how would she live with herself if he went alone and was taken by Union detectives?

Jillian knew Ryder wouldn't approve of Rob's plan, but there was no reason to ask Bingham's permission to do what she thought was right.

Rob watched her face as if sensing her conflict. "I know you traveled with Bingham earlier in the war," he put in, "and Ryder says he would never have reached Canada without your help."

Jillian nodded absently, remembering very clearly all she'd done to send Bingham on his way. Now another man was asking for her help, and it was becoming increasingly difficult to refuse him. If she agreed to do as Rob asked, she wouldn't be taking any risks she hadn't taken already.

"If I were going to accompany you, Rob, when would you want to leave?"

Hope eclipsed the doubt in Kennedy's face, but he was careful not to push her. "I thought a few days after Christmas might be a good time, perhaps the twenty-seventh or twenty-eighth."

Jill nodded again, and considered the dates. She might well be able to accommodate him and return to Toronto just after the first of the year.

"We'll need passports to cross the border, won't we?" she asked. "There have been several articles about them in the *Globe and Mail.*"

"Jacob Thompson has promised me everything I need."

"And is he willing to get me papers, too, even though I am a Yankee?"

Her tone was skeptical, but Rob hastened to reassure her.

"Jacob knows how desperately I want to go home. He'll do everything in his power to help me."

Jillian plucked restlessly at the gathers in her skirt. The gamble seemed worth the risk, and Jill suddenly wanted to help this young Confederate in any way she could. Ryder had done what he thought was right in going on the mission to Buffalo. Surely in this case, she was every bit as bound as he to act on her convictions.

She expelled her breath on a sigh. "I'll go with you, Rob," she told him, "but you mustn't tell anyone except Jacob Thompson what we're going to do."

"Would Ryder try to dissuade you?" Kennedy asked, showing genuine concern.

"Neither he nor Jamie would let me go. That's why we can't give them any inkling of what we're planning. But I can't imagine I'll be facing any real danger. I've been born and bred a Yankee, and there's no reason why I can't travel anywhere I choose."

Rob clasped her hand in both of his and squeezed it gratefully. His eyes were warm and bright, and he looked as if a tremendous weight had been lifted from his shoulders.

"I can't tell you what this means to me," he bubbled. "I thank you, Jillian, with all my heart."

The joy in his face and his simple words of appreciation did a great deal to seal Jill's determination.

"It seems the very least I can do," she assured him quietly.

"I'll be back to talk to you in a few days' time, once everything is settled with Thompson."

Jillian nodded and escorted Rob to the door. But as she watched him disappear into the snowy night, she wondered if the decision she had made in haste was one she would repent in leisure. There seemed to be no way to judge the wisdom of accompanying Rob to Louisiana, and she returned to the parlor and her knitting, brimming with new uncertainties.

Ryder returned to the small cold room under the eaves and shrugged out of his snow-covered coat. He had been with Jacob Thompson most of the day discussing senseless, futile plans to prolong the Confederacy's life. That Thompson still believed such a thing was possible undermined Ryder's faith in the commissioner and gave proof of his own disillusionment. With Sherman's capture of Savannah and Hood in full retreat, there seemed to be little hope of avoiding the inevitable. The war was ending; their cause was lost. Soon they would all be going home. But what would they find when they arrived? Would their houses be burned, their plantations in ruins? Would the darkies have run off to celebrate their freedom? Would there be anything left in the South on which to build a future?

Thoughts of home made Ryder remember the letter he'd tucked into the pocket of his overcoat. Mrs. Moire had handed it to him when he came in, but he had been too preoccupied to give it more than a passing glance. He retrieved it, then lit the lamp beside the bed and fingered the battered envelope. A myriad of emotions snarled in his middle as he recognized the writing. The address was in his brother's hand. Would Wade's news be as bad as he anticipated? Was Ryder ready to learn the truth of what was happening in the South, to face the fate that had befallen his own family?

As he stared at the envelope, he had to acknowledge that in spite of his concern for the land he loved, in spite of his worry about the remaining members of his family, his greatest fear was for himself. For months he had blamed himself for Mitchell's death, for the loss of his ship and crew, and Ryder was not sure he was prepared to accept Wade's comments on his failures. Bingham stared at the missive for a very long time before tearing open the envelope.

October 20, 1864

Dear Ryder,

We received your letter from Windsor only the day before yesterday on a blockader in from Nassau. It is growing increasingly difficult for the runners to elude the blockade fleet, and the number making the trip has dropped off dramatically in these last months.

I am pleased that you managed to escape from Fort Lafayette and make it safely into Canada, but it grieves me to learn of Mitchell's death. He was the kindest, gentlest soul I ever knew, and we will all miss him terribly in the years to come. But as deep as my loss is, I know yours is even deeper. The bond between the two of you was something very special, and over the years it has troubled me no small bit to be excluded from that camaraderie. I sense you feel a deep responsibility for Mitchell's death, and I understand your pain, your frustration in having been helpless to alleviate his suffering, but there was nothing you could have done to avoid the inevitable. When God sees fit to call one of his children home, there is no way to prevent an answer to the summons. My thoughts and Vivien's are with you in the hope that they will help you through this difficult time.

Ryder closed his eyes against the swell of sudden tears. Wade didn't blame him for Mitchell's death. Wade understood how painful it had been to stand helplessly by and watch his younger brother waste away. He even recognized the special bond that Ryder and Mitch had shared and was able to accept it without the jealousy that had plagued them during their childhood. Relief moved through Ryder like a slowly breaking wave, and the tears that misted his vision were as much from joy as from grief. He felt closer to his older brother now, when they were separated by half a continent, than when they had shared a home. He had not realized how the fear of Wade's censure had weighed on him, had not acknowledged how much he had dreaded receiving word from Wilmington. An exhilarating freedom came with Wade's comforting words, a healing power that radiated from the closely written page. It was a forgiveness he had never been able to grant himself, a reprieve he had never dared to contemplate.

Bingham drew a shaky breath and wiped his eyes. Perhaps, now that Wade had absolved him of the terrible responsibility for Mitchell's death, Ryder could find a way to accept that absolution. It was a pardon of which he was sorely in need, a pardon that could lead to a final acceptance of his actions. It gave him the sense that there was indeed a future ahead of him, a chance to make peace with the world at large and finally with himself. As he sat clutching the single rumpled page, the silence that swelled around him was soft and soothing, gentle and comforting, an unexpected balm.

Finally he began to read again.

News of your exploits on Lake Erie has been in all the papers, and I regret that the mission did not reach its full potential. I was unaware that there were Confederates in Canada, and the work you seem pledged to do is vitally important to the cause.

We are maintaining our life here to the best of our ability, and the stump of my leg is finally healing properly. I have begun to wear a wooden peg that increases my mobility, though riding and walking any distance are still difficult for me. As a result of my infirmity, we have had to cut back on the crops we are growing, turning from cotton to foodstuffs for ourselves and for the army. They take such a large percentage of what we grow that Vivien says she is not certain we will make it through the winter without tightening our belts another notch. Some of our people have run off since you last were home, but perhaps that is just as well since food is proving to be so scarce.

One matter I meant to discuss with you the next time you visited is an inheritance from Mother's English relatives that you and Mitch were to have shared. Just what it entails I cannot quite make out, but there is an estate somewhere in Sussex on a fair amount of land. Since Father willed Riverview to me, and the shipping concern has been all but decimated by the war, Mother was determined that you and Mitchell would have something to call your own. If you write to her solicitors in London, they can tell you more about the legacy and what you must do to claim it.

In the meantime know that our thoughts are with you. Come back safe, Ryder. We will need your strength and energy here at home once the war is done.

Vivien, your nephew Charles, and baby Rebecca send their love.

Your brother,
Wade Bingham

Ryder read the letter a second time from start to finish, then sat digesting the news. Things might well grow worse for Wade and his family now, with Sherman and his men marauding along the coast. Surely it would only be a matter of time before even Wilmington fell. He hoped that there would be no further hardships for his brother's family, but it seemed likely things would worsen before the war was over. The thought of their vulnerability and the new and fragile peace between Wade and him deepened Ryder's concern.

The legacy in England was a total surprise. He had known his mother came from landed gentry and that his father had met her on one of his trips abroad. There had been talk about her relatives in England when he was growing up, but his mother seemed content with her life in North Carolina and had never gone back to visit. Ryder had even passed up his chance to make the grand tour after he graduated from college in favor of shipping out on one of the family-owned vessels, and somehow it had never been convenient for him to meet any of his mother's family when he'd been in London. Now after all these years, his mother's holdings across the sea had finally come to him.

It took another long moment for Ryder to realize the implications of the bequest. It meant he still had something tangible in his life, assets, property, the chance to rebuild his future once the war was over. At last he had something to offer Jillian if she would agree to be his bride. A sweep of gratitude to his mother moved through Ryder at the realization of what she had done for him. Alysse had always known what he needed or wanted before he knew himself, and even in death she had provided for him. The knowledge warmed and comforted him. Her legacy gave him the means to make Jillian his own, gave him the chance to start his life again. Confidence surged through him, and he was suddenly eager to share his news.

Pausing only long enough to brush his hair and straighten his tie, Ryder made his way to the room Jilly kept on the floor below. He rapped impatiently, wanting to share the contents of Wade's letter, wanting to offer Jillian the secure future that had seemed all but impossible.

Surely she was inside, he thought as he knocked again. It was well past time for her to have returned from work at the mercantile exchange, and she was undoubtedly preparing for supper.

"Jillian," he called out softly, "it's Ryder. May I talk to you for a moment or two?"

There was no sound from inside the room, and on impulse he

turned the knob. The door was unlocked, the room dark and empty. Jillian must have gone downstairs, Bingham reasoned, though he found it odd that she would give up her few moments of treasured solitude at the end of a busy day.

Just as he was turning to go, the shaft of light from the hallway fell across an envelope, stark and white against the bright pattern of the bed quilt. With a lurch of uncertainty in his chest, he stopped and picked it up. His name was written on the outside in Jillian's clear copperplate hand. As he held the missive between his fingers, the hairs on the back of his neck began to stir, and chills flickered down his spine. He lit the lamp and opened the note with mounting trepidation as he read her simple sentences.

> Dear Ryder,
>   I have left Toronto to accompany Rob Kennedy to his home in Louisiana. He feels he will be safer traveling as a married man, and I am inclined to agree with him. The trip as a whole should take a little more than a week. I should be back just after New Year's. Don't worry while I'm gone, and please don't try to follow us. You, more than anyone, should understand that in this war there are things we simply have to do.
>
>   Jillian

Ryder sank to the side of the bed as cold fear sluiced beneath his skin and robbed him of his breath. Did Jillian know what she was risking in accompanying Kennedy south? Didn't she realize that if Rob was captured, she would be imprisoned, too? The thought of what could happen brought out gooseflesh along his arms, and he swore that if he ever got his hands on Kennedy, he'd tan the bastard's hide.

Jill hadn't given any indication of how they were traveling, and he looked around the room as if there might be some clue in the simple furnishings. But the room was scrupulously neat, singularly bare, totally uninformative. It seemed suddenly hollow and empty without Jill's presence to give it life.

Ryder felt hollow and empty himself.

He was still staring into space, vacillating between anger and despair, when Jamie appeared in the doorway.

"Ryder, where's Jillian? Is something wrong?"

Ryder handed the note to Bradford without saying a word.

"Shit!" Jamie exploded eloquently when he had read it

through. "God damn Kennedy for taking her. God damn him for even asking her to go. It's bad enough that he's risking his own neck crossing into the States at a time like this, but to ask Jillian to risk hers, too, is totally insufferable."

Sharing the news with his friend seemed to shake Ryder from his daze. "And what am I to do about it?" he demanded in frustration. "I can't wait here as she requests, not knowing where she is, not knowing if she and Kennedy are going to be able to elude the border guards and detectives."

Jamie knew what Ryder was considering and did his best to change Bingham's mind. "You can only hope and pray that they get through. You don't have any choice about staying here. If you try to cross the border yourself, you'll be as good as dead, and your going after Jillian might put her in even greater jeopardy."

Bingham recognized the wisdom in Jamie's words. It would be lunacy to follow Jill, but it was going to be sheer hell waiting here for her to return. He saw the irony of his situation and accepted it with markedly poor grace. Jillian had done what she felt she must, and for once it was Ryder who would wait while she paid her debt of honor.

The clatter of the train on the rails was muffled by the deep snow that lay in drifts on either side of the track. Beyond the window, a thick swath of white subdued the rural landscape, turning stone fences into humpbacked dunes, houses and barns into eerie shapes that rode the crests of an alabaster sea. The dark sky was speckled with fine feathery flakes that swirled in the wind, soaring and spiraling until they were batted against the glass to melt in shimmering streaks of silver.

Jillian looked out on the wintry panorama and willed her clenched muscles to relax. They had passed into the United States without incident and were wending their way south and west toward the city of Detroit. Once the customs agent at the border had checked and stamped their papers, Rob had begun to doze. He was nodding beside her now, his breathing measured and sonorous. Somewhere toward the rear of the car, Lieutenant John Ashbrook had also taken a seat. He would travel with them as far as Kentucky before setting off on his own.

Still nettled by her fears, Jillian turned back to stare at the snow. Had she done the right thing in accompanying Rob and Ashbrook into the United States? Would her presence make it safer for the two Confederates to travel through the North? Would she and Rob reach his home in Louisiana without drawing the attention of Union detectives?

She expelled her breath in a ragged sigh, thinking of all she had left behind in Toronto. By now Ryder must have found her note, and she could not help wondering how he had greeted the news of her departure. Had he been angry, concerned for her safety? Would he be as worried about her as she had been about him when he went on the mission to Buffalo? Her fair brows drew together in a frown. She had not intended to make him feel the same kind of fear for her that she had felt while he was gone.

To escape her thoughts, Jillian focused on the dual images visible both on and through the window. Winter raged beyond the pane, but the passenger coach reflected in the glass was amber hued and cozy. Glowing brass lamps swung in baffles, their chimneys trailing smudges of smoke toward the ceiling. The passengers' baggage loomed in the overhead rack, while men and women sat lumped beneath, shifting and turning in their seats as they tried to get more comfortable. Beside her she could see that Rob was sleeping peacefully, while on the far side of the aisle a woman with a child in her arms was humming a familiar lullaby.

Jill watched the tender scene with a soft, sweet ache around her heart. How much she wanted children, a home, and a man to love. It worried her that Ryder had never talked about having children, when she so desperately wanted to join her life to his, to cradle his seed within her loins, to carry his children under her heart. She wanted to be everything to this man, as he was to her. When peace came to the country at last, would she and Ryder indeed find a way to be together?

She blinked the thought away as two men crossed her field of vision. As they swayed down the aisle past where she and Rob were seated, the men seemed to hesitate, looking back intently. A flicker of alarm moved through her, but by the time she had swung around, the two rough-looking fellows had taken seats toward the front of the car. She tried to tell herself that their interest might well have been in her imagination, that she was making more of their behavior than what it was. When she glanced over her shoulder to see if Ashbrook had noticed them, she saw that John's seat was empty.

Finally Detroit came into sight, looking like a dozen other northern cities under a blanket of graying snow. Chimneys puffed coal smoke into the cold, dark sky until the stars turned pale and murky and the lamplight that filtered from more than a hundred windows seemed filmy and wan.

As they pulled into the station, Kennedy awakened. "You ready to find a place to lay your head?" he asked as he lowered their baggage from the rack. "I must confess, I'm a little tuckered myself."

"I'm tired, too," Jill agreed, "but shouldn't we find Lieutenant Ashbrook before we take rooms at a hotel?"

"Don't worry about him, Jillian. We're going to meet in the morning. It's just as well we're splitting up. It'll be safer for all of us that way."

Kennedy led Jillian up the aisle, across the slippery platform and through the crowded waiting room. The two men from the train had disembarked at Detroit, too, and though they were standing some distance away, they seemed to be eyeing Rob and her. Were the men Union detectives? Had they been on the train since Toronto? Fear closed Jillian's throat, making breathing all but impossible. Should she tell Rob about the men? How would they get away if they were being followed?

When next she risked a glance across the depot, she found that one of the fellows had disappeared. With that, her apprehension eased a little. Perhaps they were nothing more than what they seemed, men returning home after a Christmas journey. Still, Jill meant to tell Kennedy what she'd seen once they were safely away from the station.

Rob took her arm and steered her out onto the snowy street, but before they had walked a block, the man who had remained in the station caught up to them.

"Do you have a pass, sir? Proof of your identity?"

Rob stiffened in response to the request but took the papers Thompson had given him from the pocket of his overcoat. "They're in perfect order, as you'll see," Kennedy assured the fellow.

Without further comment the man took the passports and examined them in the glow of a street lamp.

While he studied the forms, fear lay like a cold, heavy hand on Jillian's chest. The man hadn't offered any explanation for his demands, and there wasn't any reason for this stranger to be examining their papers. Still the fellow continued perusing them.

"It says here your name is Cobb," he began, turning to Rob, "but I believe there are others in New York who know you better as Mr. Stanton."

Stanton was one of the aliases Kennedy had used during the incendiary raid more than a month before, but before Jill could think how to respond to the name, Rob was pushing her aside and reaching for his revolver. As he whirled to aim, the second man came dashing up beside him. The two strangers struggled with Kennedy for several moments before they wrestled the gun away, and as they subdued and manacled him, Jillian took to her heels.

She raced toward the depot, thinking that if she could find Lieutenant Ashbrook, they might be able to free Kennedy from his captors. But just before she reached the station doors, one of the men caught up with her. He grabbed her roughly from behind and pulled her around to face him. As she turned, she drove an elbow into his ribs and heard a satisfying grunt of pain. Using her feet and her fists, she fought to get away. But Jill was no match for the detective's burly strength, and he finally managed to force her to her knees.

"Real wildcat, ain't ya?" he demanded as he clamped icy-cold manacles around her wrists. "Your fighting didn't do no good though, did it? We got the both of you anyway."

Jillian glared at the man as he hauled her to her feet, and was unduly pleased to discover that she had managed to bloody his nose.

"You'll be sorry you've treated me this way, you great barbarous ruffian!" she threatened. "I'm a United States citizen, and I demand to be released immediately!"

"I don't know yet what kind of citizen you are, missy," the fellow snarled as he hustled her up the street toward where Kennedy and the other man were waiting. "But you're traveling with a Confederate spy, and that don't bode well for you at all."

Chapter Seventeen

"THE ACCUSED WILL rise to hear the charges brought against her." The judge advocate's voice boomed through the small room in New York City where the military commission had gathered to consider the case of Jillian Chandler Walsh, being tried for treason in a military court as was prescribed by the Articles of War. It was a bare, bleak room, suitable to such dire proceedings, located in the building on Bleecker Street that had been turned over to the Military Department of the East.

Slowly the fair-haired woman came to her feet and stood straight and tall beside her court-appointed counsel, Captain Frederick Winchester.

Major John Bolles, who had been judge advocate for the courts-martial of John Yates Beall and Robert Cobb Kennedy, cleared his throat before he began to read. "The prisoner is first accused of having violated the Articles of War by giving aid to the enemies of the United States, specifically to agents of the insurgent states of the Confederacy.

"In this that Jillian Chandler Walsh did, between August 12 and August 19, 1864, aid and abet the escape from Fort Lafayette of the Union prisoner Ryder Bingham, blockade-runner and captain of the captured ship *The Wraith*.

"In this that Jillian Chandler Walsh did, on December 6, 1864, decode a message intended for Secretary of War Edwin Stanton to aid those agents of the insurgent Confederate States in Canada.

"In this that Jillian Chandler Walsh did, on December 28, 1864, accompany Confederate agent Robert Cobb Kennedy into the sovereign territory of the United States of America with the purpose of abetting his return to his home in the insurgent Confederate States.

"The second charge is that the prisoner violated the Articles of War by procuring information for the agents of the insurgent Confederate States, acting as a spy.

"In this that Jillian Chandler Walsh did, on numerous occasions between August and November 1864 while residing in Niagara Falls, meet with Captain Ryder Bingham for the purpose of passing information to the agents of the insurgent Confederate States in Canada.

"How does the accused plead to these charges?"

Jillian cast a glance at her counselor before giving her reply. "Not guilty," she answered clearly.

"You may be seated, Mrs. Walsh," the president of the court-martial instructed. "Major Bolles, please call your first witness."

"We call Lieutenant Wood, commanding officer of Fort Lafayette Prison."

A slight, dark-haired man made his way from an adjoining room and took the chair beside the long table at which the six members of the military commission were seated.

"Do you affirm that the evidence you shall give in the case now in hearing shall be the truth, the whole truth, and nothing but the truth, so help you God?" the judge advocate swore the witness.

"I do," Wood replied.

"State your name, rank, and current appointment."

"Lieutenant Charles O. Wood, commander of Fort Lafayette Prison."

"Would you please state for this commission any knowledge you have of Captain Ryder Bingham," Bolles began.

"Captain Bingham was a blockade-runner brought to Fort Lafayette October 14, 1863. He was held in confinement until August 11, 1864, when he escaped from the prison."

"How did Captain Bingham escape?"

"He removed sufficient masonry from a second-tier casemate, at the barbette level, and made his way to the roof of the fort. He then lowered himself on blankets and swam ashore."

"Was any attempt made to recapture him?"

"Yes, sir. Sentries on Long Island fired on him, but in spite of the wound he received, he managed to elude them. After that, we had detectives check all the means of transportation from the city of New York."

"And was Captain Bingham recaptured?"

"No, sir."

"In your opinion, Lieutenant Wood, could Bingham have managed to escape without assistance?"

"No, sir. I believe he had help from the earliest phase of his escape."

"And could you describe Captain Bingham for the commission?"

"He is a tall man, six feet three or four. He has black hair, a full beard, and blue eyes. He is a tough-looking fellow, built big and rangy. Not someone I'd like to confront."

"Thank you, Lieutenant Wood."

Though Major Bolles offered Jillian's counsel the opportunity to question the witness, Captain Winchester declined.

"The next witness we would like to call is Archibald Snow."

The man took the witness chair and was sworn in by the judge advocate.

"What is your occupation, Mr. Snow?"

"I am a conductor for the New York Central Railroad."

"What was your position during the month of August 1864?"

"I was on the run between Albany and Niagara Falls."

"And in your capacity on that train, did you ever see the accused?"

"Yes, sir, I did. She was traveling to Niagara Falls with her husband, 'bout the middle of that month."

"On August 12 to be specific?"

"I couldn't say the date for sure."

"And was there any particular excitement on the train on the night in question, or do you have any particular reason for remembering the defendant?"

"Yes, there was some excitement," the man recalled. "We received word that there was an escaped Confederate on the train."

"How did you come to know this?"

"It was telegraphed to us from the Albany station."

"Go on."

"When word come through about the escaped prisoner, we searched the train, but we couldn't find anyone who seemed to be the man we were looking for."

"What did the accused tell you when you questioned her about the news you had from Albany?"

"She said she didn't know any escaped prisoner but that her husband was ill and needed care."

"What was wrong with her husband?"

Snow fidgeted for a moment before answering. "She said it was a relapse of malaria, and he did look mighty sick. I suggested she take rooms with Mrs. Marshall in Rochester instead of taking her husband through to the end of the line."

"Did she take your suggestion about getting rooms from Mrs. Marshall?"

"Yes, she did." Snow nodded vigorously. "We wired ahead and had a wagon meet them."

"And what did her husband look like, to the best of your recollections?"

"He was a tall fellow with black hair."

"Do you remember anything else about the man?"

"No, sir, not anything I can recall. Except that he was sick, like I said."

Major Bolles took his seat at the table beside the one Jillian and her counselor occupied, as Captain Winchester rose.

"Do you know how the authorities found out there was an escaped Confederate on the train?" Winchester asked.

"Not at the time, I didn't. But afterwards I heard they found a note in the backhouse at the ferry."

Several men on the panel snickered, but Winchester continued.

"Have you any idea how the note got there?"

"No, sir, no one knows as far as I can tell."

"It's not possible that Mrs. Walsh wrote the note when she passed through Albany?" Winchester pressed him.

"But why would she do that, then claim the Southerner as her husband?"

Why indeed? In retrospect, the actions made as little sense to Jillian. Leaving the note in the privy in Albany had been a desperate bid for rescue. But so much had happened between Albany and Rochester that she had been forced to revise her feelings for her captor. By the time she had been asked to claim Ryder as her husband, he had proved himself strong, courageous, and worthy of her concern by saving a child from drowning. But she knew she couldn't explain that to the military commission, knew that by their definition he was still a criminal.

"In your opinion, might Mrs. Walsh have been forced to help Captain Bingham in his escape?"

"It's possible, I suppose. But it sure didn't look like that when I came upon them."

Winchester nodded in resignation and dismissed Snow.

The next witness, Mrs. Marshall, cast a sympathetic glance at Jillian as she took her place at the front of the room. She settled her heavy skirts around her and gave her name and occupation.

"Mrs. Marshall, have you ever seen the accused before?"

The woman nodded. "On the twelfth of August last year I rented a room to Mrs. Walsh and a man she claimed to be her husband."

"How can you be so sure of the date?"

"She signed the register at my boarding house before I gave them a room."

"And is this the page from the register that bears Mrs. Walsh's signature?"

"It is."

Bolles handed the register page to the court-martial reporter for identification as evidence.

"How long did Mrs. Walsh and her husband stay with you, and what were the circumstances of their visit?"

"Mr. Walsh—the man she claimed was Mr. Walsh—was sick when they arrived. She told me he had a recurrence of malaria, and I helped her get him up to their room."

"Did you have any reason to doubt her word?"

"No, sir, not then. But she seemed awfully worried about him."

"Isn't it normal for a wife to be concerned for her husband's health?"

"Well, it seems to me, now that I think of it, that if his was a recurring illness, she should have known more of what to do for him."

Bolles leaned closer to Mrs. Marshall. "And she didn't?"

The woman shook her head. "No, sir, not really. I believe I suggested the use of quinine to her myself."

"How long did Mrs. Walsh and her husband stay with you?"

"Until he was better, nearly a week. And I was glad to have them. They were good guests and kept to themselves. I thought at the time that they must not have been married very long." The woman cast Jillian another sorrowful glance. "They seemed so very much in love."

Jillian bit her lip at the woman's words. She and Ryder had been in love then, though neither of them had been aware of it. It was telling that this woman, a virtual stranger, had noticed how they felt long before either of them had known. Might things have been different if they had realized it sooner? Would she and Ryder have had more to share than the days in Rochester and the weeks in Toronto if they had realized the scope of their feelings from the start?

"Could you describe Mr. Walsh?" the judge advocate continued.

"He was a very handsome man, sort of rakish-looking, with black hair and deep blue eyes. And he was tall. Mrs. Walsh is a good deal taller than most women, and he fairly towered over her."

Smugly Major Bolles took his seat, and Winchester asked no questions of his own. There didn't seem to be any point, since it was clear that Jillian had been with Ryder and had aided in his escape. That particular charge was well founded, and there was no way to refute it.

Jillian saw that she was in grave danger of being found guilty of aiding Ryder, but when she had made up her mind to help him, she had been fully aware of the consequences.

It was the other charges she had more of a chance to disprove, though the competence of the judge advocate frightened her, and her confidence in the abilities of her court-appointed counsel was dwindling with every minute that passed. Still, she had no money to hire lawyers and could not expect help from the Confederates in Canada when none had been forthcoming for either John Beall or Rob Kennedy. Already Beall had been hanged at Fort Columbus for piracy on Lake Erie, and Kennedy would probably draw a like sentence for his part in burning New York. Could she expect the same condemnation? Would she die for what she'd done?

Winchester seemed to think that no military commission would pass a death sentence on a woman. Neither Mrs. Greenhow nor the notorious Belle Boyd had been sentenced to death for her intrigues. Still, Jillian was worried. In these last months, there seemed to have been a change of attitude in the North, a new grimness and determination to win the war, a new ruthlessness in the methods employed by both military and civilian leaders to achieve that end. Jillian had lain awake in her cell many nights, grieving for John Beall and Rob Kennedy, worrying about the outcome of her own court-martial. Above all else, she prayed that the onset of her trial would not bring Ryder to the city in a vain attempt to help her.

She had spent hours thinking about Ryder, taking refuge in the memories of the brief time they'd had together, remembering without regret all the things she had done to keep him safe. She wondered what he had thought when he found the note telling him that she had accompanied Rob south, wondered if he understood her reasons for having agreed to go with Kennedy. Half a dozen times she had considered writing to him, exhorting him to remain in Canada, but she had suspected that her letter would be intercepted. She had to trust that Jamie would dissuade Ryder from doing anything rash. Two men had already been tried for the missions he had engaged in, and there was no question that he would fare far worse than she should he be tried for his activities.

But as the judge advocate called his next witness, Jillian felt a curl of apprehension in her middle.

"I would like to ask Gerald Walsh to take the witness chair."

Sending a withering glance at Jillian, her father-in-law made his way toward the chair from the adjoining room. His hatred for her was palpable, and she had no doubt that he would do everything in his power to convince the military commission of her guilt. As he took the stand, Gerald seemed somehow older, thinner, less vital than he had the last time she had seen him. But in spite of the change in him, it was clear that his distaste for her was as sharp and bitter as ever.

"Please state your name and occupation," the judge advocate instructed once the oath had been administered.

"My name is Gerald Walsh, and I am a lawyer practicing in Niagara Falls, New York."

"Let the record show, by way of establishing the witness's credentials, that Mr. Walsh also served as a county judge for twelve years prior to his election to the United States House of Representatives in 1852.

"Now, Congressman Walsh," Bolles went on, "what is your relationship to the accused in this case?"

"Jillian Walsh is my daughter-in-law," Gerald answered, "the widow of my only son, who was killed last year at Petersburg. She lived with me from late August 1864 until she left with her rebel lover toward the end of November."

"And what is the name of the man with whom your daughter-in-law was involved?"

"The man's name is Ryder Bingham."

"Have you seen him?"

"Yes, I have, prowling around the garden of my home."

"Would you describe him for the commission?"

"He is black-haired, tall, and well built. He's rather hard-looking, dangerous."

"You're sure his name is Ryder Bingham? The same Ryder Bingham who escaped from Fort Lafayette in August?"

"I found the man on my property uninvited and made a point of having him investigated."

"What did you discover about the man in question?"

"I hired detectives to find out who he was. When they could find no one in the city who fit the man's description, they brought me some wanted circulars put out by the Army. I was able to identify Bingham from the picture on one of them. In the drawing he was bearded, but I didn't have any trouble picking him out. That's how we discovered he had escaped from the prison at Fort Lafayette. The provost marshal later informed me that Bingham was suspected of being involved with Commissioner Jacob Thompson and his Confederates in Canada."

"Did you discover anything else?"

Gerald nodded. "My men watched for Bingham to cross the border after that, and they followed him to New York. That is how we discovered his connection with Robert Cobb Kennedy and the men who burned the hotels last November here in New York."

Bolles smiled and paced back and forth in front of the witness. "How did you learn of Captain Bingham's involvement with your daughter-in-law?"

"I saw her returning to the house one night with her clothes in disarray, and a few minutes later I found Bingham in the yard. It didn't take a genius to surmise what they had been up to. And after she ran away, my housekeeper and I found a note from him in her belongings."

"Is this the note of which you speak, Congressman Walsh?" the judge advocate asked, holding up a crumpled piece of paper.

Jillian gasped in recognition.

"Would you read the message for the commission, sir?"

Gerald took the paper from Bolles and read: "'Dearest Jilly, I must see you tonight. Meet me at the usual time and place. R.B.'"

"Is the note from Ryder Bingham?"

"I can't be sure, of course, but the initials would seem to indicate that it is."

Bolles handed the paper to the recorder. "I would like this marked as Exhibit Two."

Once that was done, the judge advocate moved toward Walsh. "Why was your daughter-in-law meeting Ryder Bingham?"

"They were lovers," he accused.

"Did you see them together?"

"No, I never did, but she admitted that he was her lover when I confronted her."

"What exactly did she say?"

"I don't remember exactly. I was terribly upset by her infidelity. It was more that she didn't deny the accusation, rather than admitting it."

Bolles drew a long breath and scratched his ear. "Now, Congressman Walsh, from the wording in the note would you say that your daughter-in-law's meetings with Bingham were fairly frequent?"

"Well, I took 'at the usual time and place' to mean they were."

"And when you discovered your daughter-in-law's trysts, did you think she was involved in anything more than a love affair?"

"Knowing that she was involved with a man so soon after my son's death was terribly unsettling for me, but until I found out who the man was, I had no other suspicions. When I learned that Ryder Bingham was involved with the Confederates in Toronto, I began to wonder about her loyalties, and she expressed pro-Southern views one evening at a dinner party. Then, too, my housekeeper and I found the proof of her activities."

"Proof?" Bolles's impressive wedge-shaped eyebrows lifted in a classically dramatic expression. "Proof of what?"

"Proof that she was spying for the Confederates."

"He's lying!" Jillian whispered to Winchester, but her counsel only continued watching the proceedings without giving any sign that he had heard. "I said he's lying," she tried again, finally succeeding in getting the captain to turn to her.

"And what would you have me do about that now?" he whispered back. "My turn to question him will come during cross-examination. And why should a congressman perjure himself in such a case as this?"

Jillian stared at the man beside her. She had not had much faith in Winchester from the moment he had been assigned to defend her, but she had at least believed that he had her best interests at heart. Now, when it was too late for her to object, the only man who might be able to help with her defense was unwilling to believe that Gerald Walsh might lie to the commission for reasons of his own.

"And what proof of spying did you find, Congressman Walsh?"

"We found notes about troop movements rolled inside balls of yarn in her sewing bag. And in the mourning picture she had been doing, there were a number of encoded designs that seem to relate to strategic information."

"That's not true!" Jillian spoke aloud, since Winchester seemed unwilling to refute the testimony Gerald Walsh was giving.

The president of the court-martial glanced up and fixed her with a glowering stare. "Captain Winchester will have a chance to question this witness, Mrs. Walsh. I suggest you keep your comments to yourself in the future or face action by this court.

"Proceed, Major Bolles."

The judge advocate sent a sliver of a smile in Jillian's direction, then returned to questioning Gerald Walsh.

"Are these the papers you found secreted in the balls of yarn, Mr. Walsh?" he asked, producing two narrow strips of paper with writing on one side.

"They are."

"And would you be good enough to read them for the court?"

"The first one says: 'Thomas reinforcing defenses around Nashville, Pulaski, and Columbia.' The second reads: 'Schofield's men arriving with orders to dig in around Duck River.'"

"Where would your daughter-in-law have obtained this kind of information?" Bolles prodded Gerald.

Walsh had the effrontery to look abashed. "Even though I am no longer active in the government, I am still privy to certain information. Jillian must have been intercepting the communiqués I received by wire. It is an oversight for which I am heartily sorry. If I had been aware of her perfidy, I would certainly have been more careful with the information afforded me."

"Is this the embroidery of which you spoke earlier?" Bolles asked, taking up the mourning picture Jillian had worked on for months. "Is it the one with the information sewn into the pattern?"

"Yes, it is."

"Will you elucidate for this court the things that led you to believe that the design conveys military information?"

Gerald took the embroidery from Bolles's hands. "If you invert the picture, you can see that the pattern of the branches in the willow roughly approximates a map of the Shenandoah Valley. The leaves sewn in darker green mark the locations of Martinsburg, Winchester, Strasburg—"

"That's preposterous!" Jillian exclaimed, no longer able to hold her peace. "That mourning picture is nothing more than a memorial for my father!"

"Mrs. Walsh!" the president of the court-martial admonished her sharply. "If you continue to break into the court's proceedings, I will order you gagged!"

"But he hates me!" Jillian burst out. "He is lying about my involvement in spying. I learned nothing more about the war in his house than what I was able to glean from the newspapers!"

The president of the court-martial motioned one of Jillian's guards forward as if ordering him to gag her as he'd threatened. But Captain Winchester was on his feet.

"Please, sir. I can assure you that my client's outbursts are the result of extreme emotional distress. If I may ask for a brief recess, perhaps Mrs. Walsh will have a chance to regain her composure before we proceed."

"Very well, Captain Winchester." The president nodded. "Let's take an hour for dinner and reconvene at one o'clock."

When they resumed the questioning, Jillian was feeling a bit more confident. She'd had a chance to talk to Winchester in private and had explained about the enmity between Gerald Walsh and her. She was not convinced that he could use the information to provide her with a more competent defense against the charge of spying, but he had at least listened and made note of what she said.

"Have you any more questions for Congressman Walsh, Major Bolles?" the president asked when they had gathered.

"Nothing else in the line of direct questioning, sir," the judge advocate put in. "Though I would have the notes found in the balls of yarn and the embroidery marked as Exhibits Three and Four."

Winchester nodded his acceptance, and the reporter made note of the evidence.

"Congressman Walsh," Winchester began, approaching the chair where Gerald sat. "What was your relationship with your daughter-in-law while she was living under your roof?"

"We got on, after a fashion."

"Didn't you blame her for your son's death?"

"No," Gerald lied.

"Didn't you disapprove of her behavior in wanting to involve herself in the women's relief organization in Niagara Falls?"

"I didn't think it seemly for her to engage in such activities so shortly after my son's death, but eventually I allowed her to join the women's efforts."

"Didn't you disagree with her opinions on the war?"

"I daresay that no two people in the North share exactly the same opinions, beyond the wish to see the Union triumph."

"Didn't you strike her on one occasion for voicing opinions different from your own?"

Gerald swelled with feigned indignation. "No gentleman ever strikes a lady, no matter what she does to provoke him!"

It was not a direct answer, but Winchester broke off that line of questioning.

"You said that the notes on military maneuvers secreted in the balls of yarn were put there by your daughter-in-law."

"Yes."

"But are you conversant enough with your daughter-in-law's hand to be sure that she is the one who wrote them?"

"I think I am. Yes."

"Then if the court will indulge me for a moment, I would like Mrs. Walsh to write the two sentences found in the balls of yarn."

Jillian took up the pen that had been placed on the table and dipped it in the inkwell. Carefully she wrote the two sentences on a sheet of paper, blotted them, and handed the paper to Winchester.

He in turn handed the sheet and the two messages to Gerald Walsh. "Do these look as if they were written by the same person, Congressman Walsh?"

Gerald considered the specimens of handwriting. "They look different, to be sure. But it would be in Jillian's best interest to make her hand as dissimilar as possible."

"I would like to enter Mrs. Walsh's copy of the notes into evidence and have it marked as Exhibit Five," Winchester intoned.

"But who else would write the notes my housekeeper and I found in Jillian's rooms?" Gerald burst out, reddening slightly. "And why would someone forge her handwriting?"

Winchester gave Gerald a long, hard look. "Yes, Congressman Walsh. Why indeed?"

Jillian was wild for Captain Winchester to continue, but he resumed his seat with nothing more to say. She whispered to him volubly, exhorting him to press Gerald Walsh for answers, but her counsel shook his head.

"You are excused, Congressman Walsh," the president said after a moment's hesitation. "Major Bolles, do you have another witness to call?"

"I do, sir. I call Phillip Sheppard."

Jillian caught her breath as the judge advocate spoke the name. The Confederates in Toronto had known there was a spy among them, and since the charges against her included decoding the note in Jacob Thompson's rooms, she should have expected that same spy to give evidence against her; but it had not occurred to her that the spy might be someone so highly placed in the Confederate organization. Still, it made perfect sense. Sheppard would have known about the attempt to capture the *Michigan*. He would have been privy to the missions to Chicago and New York. With a shiver she recalled how he had questioned her expertise the night she had decoded the message, remembered the challenges to her ability and the inexplicable menace she had felt. Now Sheppard was going to seal the case against her, and there was no hope of discrediting him or the testimony he was about to give.

Phillip Sheppard came to sit in the chair before the court and swore to tell the truth. And there was no reason for the man to lie when veracity would condemn her.

"Mr. Sheppard, please state your name and occupation."

Sheppard cast a long frigid glance in Jillian's direction before he answered. "My name is Phillip Sheppard, and I am a special agent for Secretary Stanton."

"Please tell the court how you came to be in Canada."

"In the summer of 1864—in July, I think it was—the secretary asked me to go to Richmond on a special assignment. I was to approach the Confederate secretary of state, Judah Benjamin, and ask for an assignment out of the country."

"What made Secretary Stanton think you might be granted such a position?"

Sheppard cleared his throat. "I was a minor official with the Georgia state government before the war, and I had known Secretary Benjamin in that regard."

"Did Secretary Benjamin offer you the position you were seeking?"

"He gave me a note to Jacob Thompson, assigning me as his aide in Toronto, Canada West."

"And when did that occur?"

"In late August last year."

"While you were in Thompson's employ, did you have an opportunity to meet the accused?"

"Yes, I did. She came to Canada in late November and lived as Captain Ryder Bingham's woman in a boarding house on St. Ann Street in Toronto."

"Was she Bingham's mistress?"

"I have no intimate knowledge of her relationship with Bingham, but I have reason to believe she was."

Bolles nodded thoughtfully. "Now, Mr. Sheppard, I would like you to recall the evening of December 6, 1864. Do you remember seeing Mrs. Walsh that night?"

"I do indeed. There was a party in Thompson's rooms, and she attended with Captain Bingham and Mr. Bradford. During the evening's festivities, a messenger arrived. Someone had intercepted a coded note addressed to Secretary Stanton in Washington."

"Could Thompson or his aides decode the message?"

"They could not. Nor was I willing to help them, since I had written the message myself."

Jillian gave an audible gasp at the revelation. That explained the confrontation with Sheppard as she had tried to decode the note. It also explained so much more that had gone wrong for the Confederates in Canada.

"How did Mrs. Walsh come to offer her services?"

"Thompson's other aide, William Cleary, asked the guests at large if any of them was able to decipher codes, and Mrs. Walsh volunteered."

"Did she break the code successfully?"

"Indeed she did. Whatever else she is, Mrs. Walsh is a very clever woman."

"What happened then?"

"Well, Thompson was alerted that there was a spy in their

midst, and it wasn't long before things got too hot on the other side of the border. Late last month I was forced to flee Toronto for the Union."

"Would you say that Mrs. Walsh's decoding the message aided the Confederates in any way?"

"There is no doubt about that, sir. Her help was invaluable to them."

"Very well, Mr. Sheppard," Bolles concluded with a nod. "Captain Winchester, have you any questions for the witness?"

Winchester rose slowly as if he was not sure just what to ask. "Did Mrs. Walsh offer aid to the Confederates in any other capacity?"

"Besides accompanying young Kennedy south, you mean?" Sheppard paused. "No, not that I know of personally, though it was reputed that she had helped Captain Bingham escape."

"Do you know that as a fact, sir?"

"Not as a fact. It is hearsay; that is all."

Winchester nodded and sat down.

"There is one more witness we would like to call," the judge advocate continued. "But as it is growing late, I believe we could adjourn until tomorrow."

"That seems a capital idea, Major. Have you any objection, Captain Winchester?"

"None at all."

"Very well. The court-martial of Jillian Chandler Walsh will reconvene at nine o'clock tomorrow morning."

They gathered again the next day in the same room, but somehow it seemed even more stark and grim, closer and more confining. The men come there to decide her fate seemed more impersonal and intimidating, the judge advocate more menacing, her counselor less competent. Jillian faced the day's events with rising anxiety.

During the night she had spent alone in her cell, she'd had time to review the first day of the trial, and she had begun to despair at what the findings of the court-martial would be. She had indeed helped Ryder to escape, decoded the message for the Confederates in Canada, accompanied Rob Kennedy in the hope that her presence would enable him to reach his home in Louisiana. It was only the charge of spying that she had a chance to refute, but with the testimony Gerald Walsh had given and the trumped-up evidence he had provided, even that charge appeared to be valid. With every witness who gave testimony her situation became more untenable. A weariness of the spirit assailed Jillian.

It was as if the court-martial was nothing so much as a formality and her guilt a foregone conclusion.

Once the preliminaries were over, Major Bolles called his last witness to prove his case, one of the men who had arrested Jillian and Rob Kennedy in Detroit.

"State your name and position for the record," Bolles began.

"My name is Christian McDougall. I am a detective with the city of New York."

"Were you one of the two men who arrested the accused and Robert Cobb Kennedy in Detroit?"

"Yes, sir. James Bennett and myself arrested them."

"Would you explain how the arrest came about?"

"We heard from one of New York Police Chief Kennedy's men in Toronto that two of the fellows involved in the incendiary raid on New York were about to cross the border, and the chief sent us to Detroit on the chance that they might cross the border there. On December 28, 1864, we received a wire that the men were on the eleven o'clock train, and we went to the rail junction about three miles outside Detroit. We boarded the train and spotted Robert Cobb Kennedy and Mrs. Walsh in one of the cars. There was supposed to be another man, John Ashbrook, with them, but he must have given us the slip."

"What happened when you reached the Detroit station?"

"Bennett went on ahead and waited outside, and once Robert Cobb Kennedy and the woman left the train, I trailed them onto the street. Bennett and I stopped them outside the station, in case they offered any resistance. Kennedy did try to fight, but the two of us subdued him. When the woman saw there wasn't anything she could do to help Kennedy, she took to her heels."

"Mrs. Walsh, you mean? She was with Kennedy, then?" Bolles clarified.

"Oh, yes. When we came upon them, they were talking about where they'd spend the night."

"Mrs. Walsh couldn't have been an innocent bystander?"

"No, sir. She was with the Confederate, all right, both on the train and in the station."

"Do you have any idea why Mrs. Walsh was with him?"

"Well, she never did say right out, but I believe it was to offer him protection. I suppose he figured he would be safer traveling with a woman—"

"I object," Winchester spoke out. "Mr. McDougall has no way of knowing why Mrs. Walsh might have been with Kennedy. Perhaps she encountered him on the train; perhaps she had some business in Detroit that had nothing to do with Kennedy. Any answer Mr. McDougall might give would be idle speculation."

Bolles nodded, satisfied that he had made his point. "I withdraw the question," he conceded.

But when it was Winchester's turn to cross-examine the witness, he had nothing more to say.

The only person to be called on Jillian's behalf, as a witness to her character, was the man who had taken her father's place as headmaster at the private school in Harrisburg. He seemed to be embarrassed at having to appear at such a proceeding and took the stand reluctantly.

"How long have you known the accused, Mr. Rouse?" Winchester inquired.

"I've known her most of her life. Ever since I came to Fairfield Academy in 1848."

"And what kind of a woman is she, in your opinion?"

"She's always been quiet and modest in her actions, deliberate and obedient. She took very good care of her father in his last years and seemed reluctant to leave Harrisburg when he died."

"In your own mind, can you reconcile the actions Jillian Chandler Walsh has been accused of in this trial with the behavior of the woman you have known for nearly twenty years?"

"Why, heavens, no! Jillian has always been the soul of propriety, a little reticent, if anything. I cannot reconcile the bold things she has been accused of with the girl I knew before."

"Did you ever hear her espouse support of the South?"

"No, never!"

"Did she in any way show herself to be the kind of a woman who would involve herself in political intrigues?"

"I should say not! As a matter of fact, I never heard her voice an opinion of her own on any topic, except when she admitted to sharing her father's views."

"And what were her father's views on the war?"

"Benjamin thought the South was wrong to secede from the Union. He had abolitionist leanings, too, though he was never very vocal in supporting the more radical factions of the movement."

"And Mrs. Walsh never gave you any indication that she was in sympathy with the Confederate cause?"

"Never, sir."

"And to your knowledge, she never had any connections with Confederates?"

"Never. No."

"Thank you, Mr. Rouse. Your witness, Major Bolles."

Bolles stood at the table and addressed the witness. "The accused seems to have been very much under the control of her father when she lived in Harrisburg, is that correct?"

"Yes."

"And she gave at least lip service to everything he said?"

"I think it was more than that. She honestly believed in her father's views."

"Is it possible that once she passed from his protection, she rebelled against all her father stood for?"

"I'd say it was possible for some women to act that way, but I doubt if Jillian would." Rouse seemed adamant in his defense of his old friend's daughter, and Bolles was clearly not willing to debate the point when his case was more than sound.

Still, he pressed Rouse. "What do you think would make a woman revise her views on the war?"

"I don't know that I could say, sir."

"Might Jillian Walsh's mind have been changed by an intimate relationship with a Confederate? Might her mind have been changed by her abiding love for Ryder Bingham?"

"I don't know the man of whom you speak. But Jillian is not an impetuous girl. I doubt that she could be swayed, though it is debatable if another woman could. Women are such impressionable creatures."

"Then you are saying that a woman could easily change her mind?"

"I'm saying that some women might be swayed to the opinions of the men in their lives."

"And are we to believe that Jillian Walsh , a woman who had never voiced opinions of her own, would hold fast to her father's views on the war when she was confronted with a man who held views contrary to her own? You have stated that women are 'impressionable creatures.' Couldn't a strong, passionately opinionated man like Ryder Bingham change her views?"

"I object," Winchester finally spoke up. "Major Bolles is asking the witness to speculate about things he cannot know."

"Very well, then," Bolles conceded. "You need not answer the question, Mr. Rouse. If Captain Winchester has no redirect, I suggest we move on to his next witness."

Winchester had no other witnesses. It was against the law for Jillian to take the stand in her own behalf, and though she would have liked to refute the charge of spying, there was nothing she could do.

Now Jill sat with a feeling of impotence as Winchester rose to make his final statement. No matter how eloquent he was, Jillian knew that Bolles had been both skillful and clever in building his case. In being barred from testifying to her own actions, she had been denied the chance to air an opposing view. Her fate lay now in Winchester's ability to undermine the judge advocate's case and convince the court of her innocence. She faced the prospect with little hope that he would be able to do either one effectively.

"Jillian Chandler Walsh is a rare woman," Captain Winchester began. "She held her father's home together from the time she was ten. She was a good and dutiful daughter, and she was an obedient and faithful wife. The untimely death of the two men who had been the larger part of her existence left her with no resources of her own. It left her vulnerable to the actions of ruthless men: an escaped prisoner who victimized her, men who told her that unless she helped them in their cause lives would be uselessly expended, another who convinced her that the only way he would ever see his home would be by her cooperation.

"Her actions might not have been all that we would have wished them to be in the face of the disunion in this nation of ours, but any actions Jillian Walsh might have taken were motivated by misplaced faith in others, by the desire to do what they told her was right. If she is guilty of anything, she is guilty of caring too much, trying too hard. Jillian Chandler Walsh is a woman who was caught up in situations beyond her control, and in judging her you must take those situations as much into consideration as her reactions to them. And in the light of those situations, you must acquit her of the charges against her."

Captain Winchester had not told her what he would say in the summation of her case, and she found his words—though they might serve to lessen the consequences of her actions—insulting, condescending. Jill had acted of her own free will, and when she made those decisions, she had been prepared to accept whatever came as a result of them.

As Winchester spoke, Jillian felt a flush rise in her cheeks, felt anger flare like sparks in her blood. She had not been a spy, but she had done the other things of which she stood accused, and she did not want Winchester or these men to see her as a victim, as someone easily swayed by others. She wanted them to view her acts as something she had done because she believed in them. She was not sorry she had acted as she had, and if she was damned for doing so, she would make restitution for her crimes.

There was no time for her to express her displeasure to Winchester before Major Bolles took his place before the military commission. He drew a long breath before he began to speak.

"Captain Winchester would have you believe that Jillian Chandler Walsh was a pawn in the larger game of politics, a careless innocent who was swept up in concerns beyond her understanding. I do not believe that is so.

"Mr. Sheppard testified that Mrs. Walsh was clever enough to decode a carefully enciphered message. Congressman Walsh testified that his daughter-in-law was cunning enough to take the intelligence coming into his home and turn it to the Confederates' advantage. Mr. Snow and Mrs. Marshall told you that this woman before you was skillful enough to save an escaped prisoner, a wounded man, from his pursuers.

"Jillian Walsh was never duped, never cajoled, never misinformed about where her activities might lead. She is a strong, courageous woman, and while we might laud her for those attributes, the fact remains that she acted against her government, violated the Articles of War. She did so knowingly and repeatedly, driven by beliefs and passions we cannot know. She did help Ryder Bingham escape. She did pass information to the Confederates in Canada and deciphered a message whose contents jeopardized the Union cause. She accompanied Robert Cobb Kennedy with the hope that her presence would enable him to escape retribution for his crimes.

"We have heard witnesses who gave evidence of her actions, and while we might feel compassion for her motives, respect for her daring, the fact remains that these witnesses have given clear proof of her guilt, and you must judge her accordingly."

With the conclusion of the judge advocate's statement, the court-martial prepared to decide Jillian's fate. And somehow as she was returned to her cell, she felt a certain sense of triumph that Major Bolles had seen her acts for what they were.

Jillian could guess how the military tribunal would rule. In a way, she had known it from the moment she heard the charges against her. She was guilty of three of the four things of which she had been accused, and she could not expect the members of the commission to do more than accept the evidence against her. While she sat alone in her cell, doing battle with the fear that she would disgrace herself when the verdict was announced, the judge advocate came to see her.

"Mrs. Walsh," he began, standing in the hall outside her cell. "There is a distinct possibility that the court's findings will go against you."

"I suppose I've accepted that possibility," she replied, trying to discern the reason for the judge advocate's visit.

"And I hope, if they do, you will not hold my efforts at the trial against me."

Jillian stared at the middle-aged man on the far side of the bars. Was he asking for her forgiveness in the role he had played in convicting her? It seemed unlikely. But it also seemed unnecessarily harsh to refuse him absolution.

"You were only doing the job assigned to you, Major Bolles," she offered generously.

"I thank you for understanding my position, ma'am," he acknowledged. "And if the court's decision should go against you, as I believe it will, I think there may be some concessions in the sentence if you agree to cooperate with the court."

So that was his game, Jillian thought as she studied him. Bolles wanted something from her, something she had not given her captors during all the weeks since her arrest. She could guess what Bolles was going to ask, and she decided to hear him out, if only for the diversion it would provide.

"And what form would that cooperation take?" she inquired.

Bolles's dark eyes gleamed at the question. "It would take the form of certain information, certain favors you might do for the Union once your sentence was commuted to—probation, let's say."

"What information would you need?" She could play this speculative game as well as he, and she was curious about what he was empowered to offer her.

"We would want you to tell us certain things about the Confederates in Toronto: what they're planning, when those plans are going to be implemented."

"I should think that Mr. Sheppard had given you more than enough of that kind of information."

Bolles inclined his head in acknowledgment. "Yes, that's been true in the past, but Sheppard's usefulness is over. He has declared himself for the Union, and his ties with Thompson and his cronies have been severed."

Jillian shrugged. "A pity, that."

"We need ongoing information, information from inside Thompson's organization, information you could provide if we allowed you to return to Toronto."

Jill gave no outward sign of the agitation she was feeling. "You mentioned favors, Major Bolles," she said, baiting him. "What favors would you want in return for my safety? And how would we fool the Confederates in Toronto into thinking I had somehow escaped the Union's wrath?"

"You are a very beautiful woman, Mrs. Walsh, and it would be understandable for a jury made up of men to take that into account in their deliberations. Perhaps they will find you guilty of only one or two of the charges. Not of spying, surely, the one charge I know you would most like to refute. Instead of recommending the death sentence or years of imprisonment for your actions, they might send you into exile until the war is over."

"They would send me back to Toronto? Is that what you're saying? Aren't there enough spies reporting the Confederates' activities already?"

"It's true that both Chief of Police Kennedy and Colonel Lafayette Baker have men in Toronto who report on the Confederates' schemes, but as I said before, we need someone who has gained the trust of Thompson's band."

When Jillian made no reply, Bolles continued, trying to convince her. "Belle Boyd was exiled from the North and is happily residing in England now. She's writing her memoirs, or so I'm told. But, yes, Mrs. Walsh, we would want you to return to Toronto to provide the special kind of information you alone could give us and . . ."

Jillian drew a long breath. "And?"

Bolles's eyes narrowed. "We would want you to lure certain Confederate raiders over the border."

"So they can be captured and tried for their crimes?"

"As Mr. Sheppard said, ma'am, you're a very clever woman. You were born and raised in the North, and surely you can see the advantages in cooperating with us now."

Jillian swallowed hard, trying to maintain a hold on her temper so she could hear what more he had to say. But what he was asking, what he believed she was about to agree to do, was too underhanded and despicable for her to keep her peace.

"Why, you sneaky son of a bitch!" she raged suddenly, allowing her temper free rein. "You're asking me to betray my only true friends as well as the man I love. What you're suggesting is loathsome, disgusting. For the sake of victory, you and your ilk have sacrificed every one of your principles, and for the sake of expediency, you expect others to do the same."

"Shall I tell the court you are not willing to accept their offer of leniency?" Bolles seemed unruffled by her outburst, and his calm fed Jillian's fury.

"You have dishonored me and yourselves in asking me to do this deed. You are engaging in the most vulgar form of blackmail, offering to trade my freedom in exchange for Southern lives!"

There were no words vile enough to hurl at him; she did not know invectives stunning enough to express her indignation at what he had proposed.

In frustration she spat at him, behaving like a common woman for the first time in her life. "That is what I think of the offer you have made me! Tell them that is my answer to what they would have me do!"

Bolles mopped the moisture from his face before he answered her. "Then you've made your own decision, Mrs. Walsh. And it's a pity that you're determined to be so uncooperative. I warn you, you'll be sorry you have turned aside this offer. I suggest you prepare yourself to hear the commission's findings. I doubt you'll be pleased by what they decide."

When he had left with the slam of doors and the angry stamp of footsteps, Jillian made her way to the cot against the wall and sat down heavily. She had no second thoughts about her answer to what Bolles had proposed, nor had she any illusions about what the effect of refusing him would be. She expected the worst, and as she sat staring blankly ahead, she tried to prepare herself for the court's decision. Somehow she would have to find the courage to accept retribution for her crimes, to hear the verdict and sentence stoically.

How well she had succeeded in that when her two burly guards came to get her an hour later, she was not sure. But for good or ill, she would accept her fate.

When she was returned to the courtroom, she saw that the commander of the East, General Dix, had arrived to hear the verdict in her trial and that newspaper reporters had been allowed to stand along the back wall for the same purpose. Her arrest and trial had drawn considerable notice in the press, and now the reporters gathered like raptors to await the outcome of her case. To her mind they were an insensitive, despicable lot. Caught up in the sensationalism of her story, they had no understanding or concern for the motives behind her actions. As she took her seat beside Winchester, she wished that the newsmen had been barred from this phase of the proceedings as they had from the bulk of the trial. But their presence only made her realize the ruthlessness of the Yankees in trying to sway her to their terms. They would not stop with the offer Bolles had brought to her. They would go on questioning her, badgering her until she was too broken or weary to refuse them. The trial had been a sham from the start; she knew that now. It had been a means to force her complicity, just as the verdict and sentence they passed would be.

As she sat waiting for the commission to come to attention, she did her best to ignore the reporters. But as her eyes swept across the room, she saw Gerald Walsh and Elvira Pryor standing together by the wall. They looked like a pair; she did not know why she hadn't noticed it before. There was the same avid malice in their eyes, the same cunning determination in their faces. Had Elvira Pryor been a party to Gerald's other schemes? She had been part of Gerald's plan to capture Ryder; she had been the one who had urged Walsh to give Jillian the overdose of laudanum that had nearly taken her life. Had Mrs. Pryor indeed helped Gerald cover up a murder, or even two? How horrible and far-reaching were the deeds they had done together?

Jill shivered and turned away. Gerald and his housekeeper would glory in what was about to happen, and she could not bear to see the satisfaction in their faces.

"Mrs. Walsh, would you please stand to hear the court's findings?" the president of the commission requested.

Jillian rose slowly to her feet, her face pale, her hands clasped tightly before her. Beside her, Captain Winchester stood impassively, as if he, too, knew the decision the commission would render and meant to accept it quietly, though he had far less to lose than she.

The judge advocate read the charges one by one. "On the charge of aiding the Union prisoner, Ryder Bingham, to escape, how find you?"

"Guilty," answered the president of the court-martial.

"On the charge of offering information to the Confederates in decoding a captured message, how find you?"

"Guilty."

"On the charge of abetting Robert Cobb Kennedy's return to the South, how find you?"

"Guilty."

"On the charge of acting as a spy for the Confederates in Canada, how find you?"

"Guilty."

Jillian bit her lips and tried to remain calm, though with each successive guilty verdict, a heavier weight seemed to press down upon her. She felt demoralized, crushed, overwhelmingly weary.

"Before the sentence is passed, has the accused any statement to make in her own behalf?"

In spite of the terrible lethargy that seemed to envelop her, Jillian raised her head and let her gaze pass over the men of the court. She looked long and hard at the judge advocate.

Finally she spoke, her voice low but very clear. "I am no spy. I denounce that charge against me. And whatever else I did that has here been construed as a violation of the Articles of War, those actions were done for love."

There was a moment's silence in the small, dismal room, and she could almost hear the squeak of the newsmen's pencils as they moved across the foolscap pages, taking careful note of her words.

Finally the judge advocate spoke again. "What sentence do you pass on the accused before you, Jillian Chandler Walsh, who has been judged guilty of all charges brought against her?"

The president of the court-martial drew a long breath. "For her crimes against the government of the United States of America, we sentence Jillian Chandler Walsh to death by hanging."

It was exactly what Jillian had expected.

**BEAUTIFUL
CONFEDERATE SPY
CONVICTED OF TREASON
DEATH SENTENCE
INVOKED BY MILITARY
PANEL**
Woman Maintains Her
Innocence in Spite of
Verdict

New York City—Jillian Chandler Walsh, beautiful Pennsylvanian turned Confederate spy, was today convicted by a military tribunal on four counts of treason. Accompanied by her court-appointed counselor, Captain Frederick Winchester, Mrs. Walsh betrayed no emotion as the president of the commission read the verdict in the trial. When asked if she cared to make a statement in her own behalf, Mrs. Walsh declared herself innocent of spying and claimed that whatever she had done, she had "done for love."

Mrs. Walsh did pale visibly when the death sentence was pronounced, though she seemed composed when she was led from the courtroom some minutes later. The death sentence is rarely invoked on women in such crimes against the state. When asked about the severity of the punishment, the president of the proceedings replied that the reason was Mrs. Walsh's involvement with the perpetrators of the hotel fires set in New York City during November 1864.

When asked for his opinion of the verdict in the case involving his daughter-in-law, practicing lawyer and former United States Congressman Gerald Walsh said: "Jillian Walsh is a fiendishly manipulative woman, and I believe she deserves to be hanged. She took advantage of my son in forcing him to marry her and of me in abusing the hospitality I offered her after my son's death. She used her position in my home to gain information to pass on to the Confederates now taking refuge in Toronto. It is only right that she pay for her crimes." Walsh gave evidence against Mrs. Walsh during her trial.

This same military panel also sentenced John Yates Beall, whose execution recently took place at Fort Columbus, and is still considering the fate of Robert Cobb Kennedy, accused of spying and arson. Appeals for executive clemency were made to the President on Beall's behalf, and it is expected that a similar plea will be made in Mrs. Walsh's case.

While awaiting her execution Mrs. Walsh will be imprisoned at Fort Hamilton in New York Harbor.

With a curse, Ryder crumpled the paper in his fists, then flung the sheets away. The worst had happened. The thing he had dreaded from the moment Jillian was arrested in Detroit had come to pass. Jill had been sentenced to die, as much for his intrigues as for her own. She was guilty of nothing more than having loved him, guilty of nothing more than having used her courage and intelligence to help those in fear for their lives, guilty of nothing more than having wanted to see a friend safely home to Louisiana. For those things, Jillian was going to be hanged as a traitor, and there was nothing Ryder could do to prevent it.

Oaths rumbled in his throat as he threw himself into the arm-chair, thinking what hell these past two months had been. He had been wild with worry when he learned that Jill had crossed the border with Rob Kennedy and furious when he realized that on pain of death he could not follow her. The situation had grown worse when word came through that she and Rob had been ar-rested. Bingham had been prepared to throw caution to the winds and go to her right then, but Jamie and Jacob Thompson had restrained him. They had convinced him that her scant involve-ment in their activities and her gender would protect her from the consequences of whatever charges were eventually lodged against her. The two men he trusted most had made him see that he would be taking a far greater risk in crossing the border than Jillian would by standing trial.

Reluctantly, Ryder had done as they counseled him; he had waited and read the accounts of her imprisonment and trial in the New York and Toronto papers. Because Jillian was beautiful and a Northerner by birth, the press had taken a particular interest in her case, homing to the drama like vultures to a corpse. The documentation of her trial had been minute and painful for him to read, but at first it had appeared that Jamie and Thompson were right: that her background and her sex would protect Jillian from retribution. But when Walsh had testified, providing trumped-up evidence of her involvement in spying, when Phillip Sheppard had added his damning account of Jillian's breaking the Yankee code, the tenor of the trial had abruptly altered. Ryder had gone to Thompson then to plead that the commissioner disavow Jil-lian's involvement with the Confederates in Canada. But on orders from Richmond, Thompson had been unable to help either John Beall or Rob Kennedy, and he claimed he could not aid Jillian either.

So Ryder had waited, impotent and impatient, praying that some miracle would save Jillian from the hangman's rope. But the verdict was in now. There had been no miracle; Jillian was sentenced to die.

Bingham closed his eyes and thought, as he had so many times in these last days, of what she must be going through. He knew what prison was, knew about the loneliness and despair, and Jillian had no friends or family in the North to help her through the ordeal. There was no one to act as her advocate, no one to make sure she had decent food or accommodations, no one to listen to her fears or offer comfort. He had been able to see to those things for his brother when he and Mitch were at Fort Lafayette. He had made certain Mitchell was warm and dry, had seen that his brother had enough to eat even if he himself went without. He had spent hours talking to his brother about better days when they had been growing up or about the excitement of successfully running the blockade. As Mitchell's condition worsened, Ryder had listened to his fears of death and had done his best to assuage them.

It hurt Ryder to know that Jillian had no one to see to her welfare or confide in, no one to help her prepare for her impending execution. She would be facing death alone, a violent, shameful death of miscarried justice. Did she have the strength to sit in her cell, knowing how she would die, knowing she had not maliciously undertaken the crimes of which she had been convicted?

The bedroom grew dark as thoughts churned in his head. What could he do to help her? How could he save Jillian from the gallows? Was there a way to cross the border without being caught, a way to break Jilly out of the stockade at Fort Hamilton? And if he succeeded in freeing her, whcrc could they go to be safe from the long arm of Yankee extradition? The answers to his questions were elusive, the risks overwhelming, but he could not bear to sit idly by and read of her execution.

Looking back, Ryder could see the stunning difference Jillian had made in his life. At a time when there was nothing inside him but hatred and vengeance, she had shown him tenderness and compassion. She had reminded him that gentility and selflessness still existed in the world when his own experiences had robbed him of that belief. She had shown him how to give and love again, even when he was sure there was no room in his heart for the gentler emotions.

In his mind's eye, he could see Jilly as he had on that day months ago, sitting quiet and demure in a railroad car, her beauteous features screened from his view, her kindness and generosity unhoped for and unexpected. He had not known that this stranger would change his life from that day on. He had not known that she would bring warmth and sweetness to his stark existence. She had feared him, then cheered him for saving a child's life, and taken responsibility for him when by rights he should have been her enemy. She had drawn compassion and concern from the well of her own emptiness and filled him with all the love and caring he could hold.

How clearly he could recall the halcyon days they had spent in Rochester, the bittersweet nights when they'd made love. He had never expected that a chance meeting would change the way he viewed the world, alter the scope of his existence. But it had; it had changed it irrevocably. Jillian had made life worth living again, given him hope like a gift, wrapped in tenderness and tied up with a bow of wondrous dreams. She had given him back his life in more ways than she knew, and he loved her with a deep, abiding love he would carry with him into eternity. The gratitude he felt to her was deeper than he could ever express, and now that she was facing a danger more terrifying than any he had ever known, he had to find a way to save her. If he failed to do so, the miracle Jillian had wrought with her steadfastness and her loyalty, her sweetness and her love, would be destroyed. He could not bear to see that happen.

Bingham was sunk so deep in thought that he was hardly aware of the knock on the bedroom door.

When no one came to answer it, Jamie stuck his head inside. "Ryder? Are you here? Why are you sitting in the dark?"

Receiving only a vague murmur of acknowledgment, the smaller man entered and lit the bedside lamp.

The flare of light made Bingham blink, and it was a few seconds before his eyes adjusted to the brightness. When they did, he noted the same undiluted grief on Jamie's face that he was feeling himself.

"You know they've sentenced Jillian to hang." It was a statement, not a question.

Jamie nodded in reply. "I'm sorry, Ryder. I know how much she means to you."

"It is my fault she's come to this," Bingham began, giving voice to his inevitable recriminations. "If I hadn't brought her to Toronto, she would never have met Kennedy. If I had told her I wanted to marry her, she might never have—"

"It's not your fault," Jamie broke in. "You could hardly have left her with her father-in-law after what he'd done, and she might have gone with Kennedy anyway. She did what she thought was right, just as all of us have done."

Ryder stirred in his chair, suddenly aware of the ravaged expression on Jamie's face. "You know you shouldn't blame yourself for what's happened, either."

The smaller man sank into the other chair. "It's not just Jillian, Ryder. I received a letter from Richmond not an hour ago." The words were flat and toneless, though as he continued, the control he had maintained over his voice began to disintegrate. "Laura's dead. She died from a fever that has been sweeping through the Richmond hospitals."

Ryder flinched with the impact of the news.

"Her mother wrote me," the smaller man continued, "under duress, I suppose. The woman never thought I was good enough for her daughter."

Ryder reached across to touch his friend's arm and offered his condolences.

Jamie continued as if he had not heard. "I swear, Ryder, Laura was the only good thing that ever came into my life. I didn't deserve her, God knows, but she loved me anyway." He looked up as if for reassurance. "But why would she love me? I had nothing to offer her. I was a liar, a cheat, a gambler, always one step ahead of the law. I wasn't the kind of man a sheltered Southern lady was supposed to marry."

Empathy twisted in Ryder's chest, and he swallowed hard. "There's nothing to be gained by deriding yourself, Jamie."

A frown pinched Bradford's fair brows together and drew the corners of his mouth. There was the darkness of tears on his lashes. "Laura gave me hope, you know? She made me believe that once the war was over, I could start again. She made me believe I could make myself into the kind of man who would deserve a woman like her."

On levels Jamie could not fathom, Ryder knew.

Bradford fumbled for a cigar in the pocket of his coat, then held it absently between his fingers as if he did not know what to do with it. Bingham struck a match and leaned closer, cupping his hands around the flame. Jamie's eyes narrowed as he accepted the light; then he receded into the comforting embrace of the armchair opposite Ryder's.

"I met her at one of the big charity balls they had in Richmond at the beginning of the war," Bradford offered, seeing a crowded, candlelit hall draped with patriotic bunting instead of the rented room in which they sat. "It was not the kind of event a man like me was usually invited to attend, but I was a soldier, and in those days a uniform took you anywhere. I met Laura during the Virginia reel. She came swishing up beside me in a butter-yellow gown, and she smiled at me in a way no other woman has ever smiled. I arranged an introduction to her that very night and began courting her in earnest. Her family didn't approve of me, but that didn't seem to matter. Laura said love was what counted, not background, not riches, not a place in society. She said she'd follow me anywhere, do anything I wanted her to do. She made me believe in the future, and now that she's gone . . ."

In his own mind, Ryder finished the sentence for his friend: *Now that she is gone, there isn't any hope, any warmth, any meaning in life.*

"Jamie, I'm sorry." Saying the words was like dropping a stone into a deep, dark well. It took a long time for them to hit bottom, and when they did, the impact was negligible. But words were all Ryder had to offer.

The two men sat for a very long time in the quiet room, watching the shadows creep across the wall, smelling the meal being served downstairs, for which neither of them had any appetite, feeling the chill in the air as the untended fire died to embers. Jamie's cigar burned between his fingers, trailing thin whorls of smoke into the silence. Ryder's body sagged with the weight of the disasters that had befallen each of them. The clock on the landing struck eight, eight-thirty, nine, and still they sat unmoving.

Finally Ryder roused himself. It was useless to be immobilized by grief, to succumb to the lethargy of blighted hope.

"I'm going to New York," he said, not sure he had even made the decision until he gave it voice. "I'm going to find a way to rescue Jillian or die in the attempt."

Saying the words aloud gave the act conviction, gave it momentum, gave it life. Ryder nodded once and sat up straighter. He was going to do something to help Jillian, and no one on either side of the border was going to keep him from it. And if he did not succeed, the consequences did not frighten him. He had nothing left to lose.

With the announcement, Jamie's head came up. Anger and pain were mingled in his eyes, but his jaw was set stubbornly. "Then sure as hell I'm going with you."

Ryder did not argue. He knew why Jamie wanted to come, knew that his need to volunteer went beyond courage, beyond friendship. It was rooted in Jamie's basic optimism, in the belief that life and love would triumph over evil, adversity, and even death. In the moment of his greatest tragedy, when he had lost the most important person in his life, Bradford was willing to do what he could to see that Ryder had his chance for happiness. Jamie's offer was a tribute to the man he was, to the strength of his philosophy, to the depth of his character. His words brought a tightness to Ryder's throat, but he said nothing in reply.

Instead, his mind was stirring, the blankness and grief being replaced with possibilities. What they meant to do would depend on preparation, planning, timing. It would take days, perhaps weeks, to devise some scheme that would work to their advantage. But they would find a way; there was no choice about that now.

Across the width of the room, blue eyes met gray, conveying determination, single-mindedness, devotion to duty. With the contact Ryder felt a stir of honest hope. And in that instant he believed that, with Jamie at his side, he would succeed in rescuing Jillian.

Chapter Eighteen

"AN EXCELLENT MEAL, Elvira," Gerald Walsh commented, leaning back in his chair with an air of satisfaction.

The housekeeper bent above him, pouring more coffee from the silver pot. "I'm glad you enjoyed it, Gerald."

He glanced up. "Why don't you sit down and join me for a moment? I received a bit of interesting news from New York this afternoon."

The woman's eyebrows rose at his suggestion, and she hastened to take a cup from the china cabinet for herself. Surely whatever word he'd received pertained to the fate of his daughter-in-law. They had both been waiting impatiently since the trial several weeks before to learn if the death sentence the military commission had handed down would actually be enforced. Now Gerald might have some indication that it would, and Mrs. Pryor was fully prepared to gloat over the particulars.

The woman poured herself a cup of coffee and settled beside the congressman at the long mahogany table. "Tell me, Gerald, what have you learned about Jillian's fate?"

"I received word today that young Kennedy's hanging has been scheduled for the twenty-fifth of this month at Fort Lafayette, and Jillian has been moved to a cabin at Fort Hamilton so that she can be there to watch him swing."

"Does that mean her execution will follow his?"

Walsh dipped sugar into his cup. "It brings it that much closer, to be sure. I believe the authorities are still trying to persuade Jillian to turn traitor to her friends in Toronto. They think that seeing Kennedy die may tip the scales in their direction."

"Do you think their plan will work?"

Gerald sighed, shrugged, and set his spoon aside. "You know how stubborn Jillian can be. Witnessing Kennedy's execution will either turn her to their way of thinking, or it will seal her doom."

The housekeeper did not try to hide the gleam in her coal-black eyes. "She's such a callow girl, Gerald. Surely she will agree to what they want once she sees how the government deals with those who refuse to aid their cause."

Walsh sipped from his cup before continuing. "Well, Kennedy will die in either case. The authorities aren't all that interested in what he has to offer them. It's only Jillian who can lure Ryder Bingham and his cronies onto Northern soil."

Mrs. Pryor nodded with satisfaction. It would be the perfect irony if Jillian Chandler Walsh was forced to betray her rebel lover.

"There won't be any chance for executive clemency, will there?"

"Not with my connections in the government. I can make very sure of that."

"But if the war ends before she can expose the traitors in Toronto, won't those men be pardoned?"

Gerald shook his head and reached across to pat her hand. "I have it on good authority that there will be no amnesty for the men who acted as spies and saboteurs. The Confederates in Canada will still be fugitives, no matter the outcome of the war. They are special cases every one and will be subject to prosecution regardless of a truce."

"And will Jillian share their fate?"

"If she doesn't cooperate with the government, she will be long dead when peace is proclaimed."

Mrs. Pryor smiled, thinking that in a way she was grateful to Jillian Walsh and her intrigues for the renewed closeness between Gerald and her. Not since shortly after Serena Walsh's death had Gerald been so attentive, so careful of her feelings. They had been lovers then, she and Gerald, driven by their complicity in concealing the truth of his wife's demise.

She could remember the incident as if it were only yesterday. It had been her warning that sent Gerald to the summerhouse that evening more than twenty years before, and Elvira had watched from behind the screen of lilac bushes as he confronted Serena and her lover. They had been totally compromised when he arrived, clutching, panting, whispering endearments as they gave themselves in passion. Gerald had come upon them with gun in hand, bursting into the gazebo with all the fury due a wronged husband. He had torn Serena's lover from her arms, driven by a passion of his own, a passion, Elvira had seen, that clearly edged on madness. Serena had gone to the man's defense, and in the scuffle, she had been thrown back against one of the structure's wooden uprights. Gerald had turned on her hapless lover then and had shot him at point-blank range. The man was dead before he hit the floor, a fitting retribution. As Elvira watched, Gerald had dragged the body to the riverbank and, after firing into the man's face to obscure his identity, dumped him into the water. When Gerald returned to the gazebo, he found his wife dead, too, her skull crushed by the force of the blow he'd dealt her.

It was then that Elvira had made her presence known, and instead of grieving for her mistress, she had helped Gerald dress Serena in her nightclothes and arrange her at the foot of the stairs. They made it look as if she had missed a step and fallen during the night, and in front of Serena's friends and family, Gerald had grieved like a man possessed. Torrential rains had come to obscure all evidence of the murder, and four days later when Serena's lover had been washed up at the foot of the Falls, there had been no one to mourn his passing. From that day to this, Elvira and Gerald had shared a special bond, forged by the conspiracy of that night so long ago.

Now Jillian Walsh had renewed their need for each other. Elvira's help in arranging the evidence against his daughter-in-law had again put Gerald in her debt. It was something she had been wont to do, for she hated Jillian from the moment she arrived, hated her ladylike airs, hated her attempts to usurp Elvira's own place in the household. That Gerald hated Jillian for what she had done to his son had reasserted his need for his housekeeper's help, and Mrs. Pryor was glad. They were bound anew by more hatred, more treachery, more secrets, and it appeared that all they had done to rid themselves of Jillian Walsh was moving toward fruition.

"There's no way for Jillian to escape retribution, is there?" the housekeeper asked, hoping for further reassurance.

"Come into the study, if you like. I'll let you read the letter for yourself," Gerald invited, rising to his feet.

Elvira followed him, making a mental note that because the other servants had left for the night, she would have to clear away the cups and saucers when she was finished with Gerald.

As they moved down the hall toward his office, Walsh laid a hand against her arm and she felt the old familiar tingle of excitement at even his lightest touch. He was a ruthless man, a powerful man, and she loved him for the very attributes that caused others to revile and condemn him.

He opened the door and moved to light a lamp, and when the golden glow illuminated the room, they could see there was someone sitting in the high-backed chair behind Gerald's desk. Elvira's eyes widened and Walsh's narrowed with sudden recognition. Seated behind the desk, big as life and twice as bold, was a man they'd never thought to see again. It was Ryder Bingham.

They stood staring for a long moment, frozen with surprise. Then Bingham gestured to the man beside him and spoke in a voice that was both casual and polite.

"Congressman Walsh and Mrs. Pryor, I don't believe I had the opportunity to introduce my companion properly the last time we were here. This is Jamieson Bradford, lately of Toronto."

Shaking off his shock, Gerald Walsh stormed toward the desk. "What the hell are you doing here, Bingham? Why have you come to see me?"

Ryder's brows rose as if he were confused by the congressman's wrath. "I think you know as well as I do that we have some unfinished business to resolve."

"The hell we have! The hell we have!" Gerald shouted.

"I've come to make you pay, Congressman, to make you pay for what you've done to Jillian, for what you tried to do to me."

"Then you'll hang for your audacity, Captain Bingham!" Gerald threatened. "Now that you're on this side of the border, the detectives are bound to pick up your scent, and when they catch you, you'll hang, like Beall, like Kennedy, like your faithless Jillian."

A frisson of anger spiked along Ryder's nerves, but he shrugged with every semblance of nonchalance. "Perhaps I will, Congressman Walsh, but not before I've had my way with you."

"You mean to kill me, then?"

The younger man shrugged again. "I'd like to kill you, yes. But I won't do it in the treacherous, cold-blooded manner you seem to favor. Nor will I let others do the deed. I mean to give you a fighting chance, which is more than you were prepared to give me when I came here in November."

Gerald seethed with malevolence as he glared across the desk, but Ryder maintained his calm.

"Jamie, will you make certain the congressman isn't armed before I address myself to him?"

Bradford crossed from where he had been standing behind the desk and swept his hands along Walsh's sides.

"He has no weapons," Jamie reported, then took a place beside the housekeeper.

Ryder stood, laid aside his gun, along with the derringer from his boot and a wicked-looking knife. Moving with calculated lazy grace, he rounded the corner of the desk to stand before his adversary.

As he faced his worst enemy and what he knew would be one of the most difficult battles in his life, Ryder was well aware of his advantages. He was younger, stronger, and leaner than the older man, but he had no illusions about Walsh's guile or cunning.

"I mean to beat the hell out of you, Walsh," he promised softly. "In truth, I'd like to kill you with my bare hands, but I'm giving you a chance to defend yourself. It's more of a chance than you gave Jillian."

Walsh made no reply, but suddenly launched himself at Ryder. Doubling his fist and leading with his right, the congressman caught Ryder on the cheekbone with a vicious punch, and the two men crashed onto the desk in a flurry of arms and legs. Pens, papers, and Bingham's weapons went skittering onto the floor as the two men rolled, and an inkwell overturned, spewing ink across the desk's worn leather top. Walsh forced Ryder's head back into the growing puddle, and he came up a moment later with a smudge of black beside his ear. Bingham had not been expecting the older man's aggressiveness, and a rush of feral glee moved along his nerves. As he broke Gerald's grip on his left arm, he threw a punch that drove Walsh back.

Gerald staggered under the force of the blow but righted himself with surprising speed. Just as Ryder was regaining his feet, Walsh lowered his bullish head and butted him in the stomach. Bingham doubled over with the pain in his ribs but recoiled from the blow's momentum to send Walsh tumbling backwards. With fists and elbows flying, they thudded to the floor, flailing in the space between the two heavy chairs that faced the desk. There was the thump of landing blows, a livid spate of curses, gasps of sudden pain. Walsh seemed to be gaining an early advantage over his younger opponent, and as he rolled on top of Ryder, he used a deep-drawn breath to trumpet, "You'll have a long way to go before you kill me, boy, a very long way indeed."

Bingham saved his wind for fighting, and taking advantage of Walsh's bravado and his own whipcord strength, Ryder flipped Gerald over his head, slamming the older man onto his back in the center of the rug. Ryder was on him in an instant, dropping his full weight on Walsh's body, driving the air from the other man's lungs. He landed several bruising blows before Gerald recovered, but Ryder did not see the older man lash out until the punch knocked him sideways into the rung of one of the chairs. It crashed sideways with the force of their movements, one of the blocky legs driving hard against Ryder's spine. Walsh made the most of his momentary advantage and struggled to his feet. He kicked savagely at Ryder's ribs, driving the breath from his body with a groaning whoosh. But when Gerald raised his foot to kick again, Bingham caught and twisted it, toppling Walsh to the floor.

Ryder was on top of him again in a matter of seconds, pounding his fists into the congressman's ribs in a flurry of flying punches. Gerald snatched at Bingham's throat, and they rolled over and over, bunching the run beneath them, sending a potted palm smashing to the floor. There was the thud of falling furniture, the tinkle of shattering bric-a-brac. The smell of oil from the reservoirs of the overturned lamps hung over the room like a haze.

With a grunt of effort, Ryder came to his knees and staggered upright. Walsh followed his example. They stood facing each other for an endless moment, bloodied, panting, wavering with the force of the battle they had joined.

Walsh was tougher than he looked, Ryder acknowledged, and he fought like a cornered tiger. There must have been a history of brawling in Gerald's past that Ryder had not anticipated. He stared at the older man with new respect, measuring his abilities, his ruthlessness, the vigor of his movements. Still, Bingham was pleased that the man had chosen to defend himself. It made the blood lust run cleaner in his veins, made the fight between them a fairer one. Each stood waiting for the other to make some aggressive move, each eyeing his opponent, measuring his feints, the reserves of strength still left inside him.

"Get him, Ryder!" Jamie crowed. But in the instant when all his concentration was on the men circling in the center of the room, Mrs. Pryor reached around for a tall brass vase standing on the table to her left. She brought it up in an arching swing that caught Jamie just above the ear, and with a clang of ringing metal, Bradford dropped to the floor like a stone.

Ryder saw the housekeeper's move from the corner of his eye, and as he turned to shout a warning, Walsh came at him a second time. Bingham went down with the force of the older man's assault, collapsing a graceful gate-legged table beneath him as he fell. This attack was more measured and shrewd than the earlier ones had been, and Ryder guessed that Walsh was conserving his strength for what was yet to come. Ryder was tiring, too, but he knew the longer they fought, the greater his advantage would be. He had more stamina than a man nearly twice his age, though he was aware that without Jamie to monitor the housekeeper's movements, the opening of a second front was more than possible. He rolled, taking Walsh with him, so he could see what the woman was doing, and there was wisdom in the move. She was still clinging to the huge brass vase, looking for a chance to heave it, but before Bingham could respond to the newest threat, Walsh was hitting him again. The older man's punch glanced off Ryder's chin but with enough force to make spangles of light dance behind his eyes. As he shook his head to clear it, he saw that Walsh was staggering to his feet, readying himself for a new attack. Bingham moved swiftly to undercut Gerald's efforts, and they rolled left and right and left again, thrashing in the direction of the hearth. The glance he shot above his head showed the fireplace utensils to be the congressman's goal, and Ryder caught the older man's wrist just short of the lethal iron poker.

They reversed directions again, and as they lurched toward the center of the rug, Ryder finally managed to gain the superior position. Straddling the congressman's chest, he closed his hands around the older man's throat, tightening them in a surge of righteous rage. Walsh cursed and bucked and gagged as Ryder closed his grip relentlessly. But just as the congressman's face began to redden and his struggles began to wane, Bingham caught a glitter of light at the corner of his eye and was abruptly reminded of the housekeeper.

He forfeited the death grip and jerked aside as Elvira Pryor dashed the heavy brass vase in his direction. But her aim was less than true, and instead of hitting Bingham, it toppled the lighted oil lamp in his direction. The base grazed Ryder's shoulder, but caught Gerald square in the chest, shattering the fragile etched glass globe and spattering burning oil everywhere. It fell around them in a hellish rain, pelting the rug, sending licking tongues of fire across the floor. Other lamps had been upset in their struggles, and the sparks leaped from one splotch of splattered oil to another, flowing in molten rivers, flaring up around them like torches in the night.

Beside Ryder, Gerald Walsh was sitting up, staring down at his clothes. His oil-soaked shirt had already begun to burn, and small darts of flickering yellow light were moving across his chest. As Gerald beat at them ineffectively, a scream of pain and horror rent the air, filling the room with his agony and echoing off the walls. The cry sent a jolt of mindless panic ripping along Ryder's nerves, and driven by the sound, he scrambled in the opposite direction.

But even as Bingham fought to escape the flames, Elvira Pryor flew past him toward the very thick of them. When he looked back to where Gerald Walsh lay, the housekeeper was kneeling at his side. Clutching her employer to her breast, she was desperately shrieking his name, weeping as if her falling tears could somehow drown the blaze. They huddled in the very core of the erupting holocaust, and Ryder could see the fire that was consuming Walsh was eating at her, too. It was gnawing at the flaring skirts that swirled across the floor, curling back the skeins of trailing hair that had straggled to her shoulders. Through the conflagration, Ryder could see an unholy light reflected in her eyes, and he suddenly realized that she would rather die here, with Gerald Walsh in her arms, than flee and live without him.

The carpet had turned into a sea of seething orange and red, and spires of flame were scaling the paneled walls when Bingham found Jamie, still sprawled insensible. Hauling his friend across his shoulders, Ryder staggered to his feet. Their only hope of escape from the heat and thickening smoke was the door at the end of the study that led out into the yard. Ryder lurched in that direction through a hail of burning brands as the lambrequins and shutters at the widows melted to the floor. But the acrid smell of burning flesh that bit at Ryder's nostrils and scoured the back of his throat drove him on relentlessly.

The fire whooshed around them, the crinkle of spreading flames transformed into a steady, growling roar, and at the far end of the room the wall came down with a screech of giving timbers. Sparks fluttered upward like a million fireflies dancing in the air, while intense heat buffeted and assaulted him like a bursting, breaking wave. It scorched his face and hands, seared his lungs, and stole his breath. He felt stunned, dizzy, weak, and even Jamie's slight weight seemed a burden he could not abide.

* * *

Still he knew he had to make it to the door or both he and Jamie would die here with Walsh and his housekeeper.

A tufted chair went up in a flare of light, threatening to block his path, and he felt a singe of pain run up his wrist as he thrust the barrier aside. He did not pause to beat out the flames until he had staggered into the yard and could feel the cold night air on his skin as he dragged Jamie outside with him.

Sinister smoke trailed after them, drifting like specters across the lawn, hovering in a cloud of murky gray over the pale and frozen earth. When they were a safe distance from the house, Ryder lowered Jamie to the ground and sprawled, coughing and gasping, beside him. He felt the sting of frigid air in his raw, parched lungs as he tried to catch his breath, felt an insistent throbbing pain from the burn along his forearm. Still, they had managed to escape the blaze, and he whispered fervent, raspy thanks to whatever forces had protected them.

As Jamie began to moan and stir beside him, Ryder mopped the tears from his eyes and turned to look back toward the house. The fire had gained purchase everywhere, evident in the glowing panes of glass on the lower floor and the shuddering flickers of light against the curtains on the one above. Then with a blast that shook them where they lay, the windows exploded outward, spattering crystal shards of glass through the night. They came to rest on the frozen ground and lay glittering like rubies and topaz, reflecting the brilliant hues of the flames.

Spears of fire loomed through the broken-window frames on the upper floor, charring the wide white cornice that hemmed the high stone walls. The blaze had reached the front of the house, where it was shooting out the door, and the pillars along the portico stood like martyrs being sacrificed with flames around their feet. Fire shot up the columns, surging toward the pediment, and in a burst of luminous orange, the roof shuddered and gave way. A brilliant, glowing aura was cast up into the cold, dark sky, limning the clouds above with saffron, orange, and red.

As the two men sat huddled in the shadows of the bushes at the edge of the drive, there was the sound of voices, the silhouettes of people streaming in from the street. Drawn by the sound and midday brightness of the yard, they stood mesmerized, frozen in awe by the savage spectacle of ancient power and destruction.

In the confusion, Ryder and Jamie melted into the trees, seeking the solace and anonymity of the dark. They were scorched, singed, and covered with soot, but somehow they had managed to escape the seething hell Gerald Walsh's mansion had become.

Inside, the man and his accomplice had been chastened and destroyed, and in an hour there would be nothing left of the magnificent home but an empty, smoldering shell. There would be nothing to give testimony to the mansion's elegance and grace, nothing to give testimony to the cruelty and evil that had been nurtured within its walls. Standing on the riverbank, staring back at the house engulfed in flames, Ryder knew a sudden peace as if his need for retribution and revenge had finally been satisfied.

Chapter Nineteen

IT WAS A perfect day for an execution, or so Jillian Walsh's guards contended as they escorted her across Fort Hamilton's broad parade ground. There was no doubt that it was a fine March day. The sky was clear, the sun was bright, though the wind that swept across the field stung her cheeks with cold. Still her guards were wrong. There could be no good day for what was about to transpire, no good day for a man to die.

As they escorted her through the fort's main gate, Jillian paused to look across the Verrazano Narrows toward their destination, the infamous Fort Lafayette. Completed just after the War of 1812 on a broad rock reef six hundred yards from shore, it was a hulking red stone fortification, guarding the entry to New York Harbor. It had been the site of Ryder's long imprisonment, the place where Mitchell Bingham had died. Today it would add another ignoble chapter to its history: It was where her friend Rob Kennedy would be hanged as a Confederate spy.

Jill drew a long, slow breath as they made their way down the slope toward the expanse of gray-blue water. Already a crowd was gathered on the dock awaiting passage, and an army captain was checking passes, much to the chagrin of people who had paid fifty dollars a head for the privilege of watching the Confederate swing. She was shocked at their prurient interest in this afternoon's proceedings, appalled that anyone should be so eager to watch a man go to his death, but she would gladly have forfeited her place at the hanging to anyone who wanted it.

She clearly understood the reason for her mandated attendance at Rob's execution. The Department of the East deemed it expedient for her to witness the consequences to those judged guilty of treason. It was a threat the Yankees were using in the hope of convincing her to inform on the Confederates remaining in Toronto. If she did as she was told, they intimated, she would go free. But the price of her freedom would be the arrest and eventual conviction of Ryder and his comrades.

In these last weeks it had become clear that her own sentence was a ruse, a means of keeping her in close confinement while her inquisitors tried to wear her down. Officers came daily to badger and threaten her in the hope of enlisting her aid. Thus far she had managed to resist them, but the grim accommodations, the uncertainty, the boredom and loneliness, were beginning to take their toll. Perhaps they sensed her resolve was weakening; perhaps they suspected that seeing Rob die would overwhelm her last reserves. And if she was honest with herself, she wasn't sure that they were wrong.

As she waited with the rest for the steam barge that would take them to the prison, the knot of cold, hard panic lodged deep inside her chest seemed to grow, making breathing difficult, making rational thought impossible. She longed for the nightmare of her imprisonment to end. Yet she could not betray the people she loved, could not bear the thought of finally succumbing to the Yankees' threats.

Jillian shivered in the wind blowing in across the channel and dreaded what the next hour would bring. Where would she find the fortitude to witness Rob's execution? And afterward, would she have the strength to continue to deny her inquisitors the complicity they were seeking?

The steam barge to Fort Lafayette approached the dock, and a single man disembarked before the captain allowed the crowd to board. Jill would have refused to go if she thought it would do any good. But she knew her two guards had their orders, and they would brook no resistance from her. As she and the guards stood by the rail near the stern of the vessel, she felt the other passengers' eyes upon her, saw them whispering among themselves when they noticed the manacles on her wrists, the two burly soldiers beside her.

Mercifully, the trip was a short one, and when they reached Fort Lafayette, Jillian was escorted through the sally port and into the commandant's office. The room was crowded with soldiers and civilians, and among them Jill recognized several of the newspapermen who had been present at her trial. In the confusion, she tried to recede against the wall, hoping no one would recognize or notice her. But eventually an officer approached.

"Are you Mrs. Walsh?" he asked, without offering her the courtesy of his name. "Captain Kennedy asked to see you when you arrived."

From the way he spoke, Jillian knew she had no choice but to accede to Rob's request, nor would she deny him her company if he wanted it. In a way, she did indeed want to see her friend before he died. She wanted a chance to say good-bye, a chance to offer him what encouragement she could. But she also dreaded the reunion. She did not know what to say to a man who was to be hanged within the hour, did not know how she could bear to see him, knowing it was for the very last time. The lump of ice in her chest seemed to be growing larger, colder, more intrusive.

As they traversed the prison yard, Jillian wondered how she would find Rob. Would he be much changed by all that had befallen him? Would he be terrified of facing his own mortality? Was there anything she could do or say that might offer him comfort in the last minutes of his life? She did not know why Rob wanted to see her. He might expect something of her, but she couldn't imagine what it could be.

The door to Rob's cell was unbolted, and Jillian was led inside. As she entered the casemate, its chill and dampness enfolded her, seeping through the fabric of the thick, dark cloak she wore. The room was like a close, dark cellar, like a cave far beneath the earth, like a premature entombment. There were a number of men at the mouth of the cell, and stealing herself to face the condemned, Jill threaded her way through the gathering to where Rob was seated at a table.

He rose when he saw her and came forward to take her hands. His were every bit as cold as hers.

"Jillian!" Rob greeted her with a smile. "I am so very glad you're here."

They had not been allowed so much as a moment together from the time they had reached New York, and even in these grim circumstances it was good to see him again.

In the moment of silence that followed the greeting, helpless tears rose in Jillian's eyes. She could not think what to say to Rob, nor he to her.

Finally he spoke, and she blessed him for his fortitude.

"I've been eager to see you," he told her. "I've wanted so

much to apologize, to tell you how very sorry I am for having gotten you into this. You were brave and good to agree to accompany me when I asked, and I wanted you to know that if I'd had any idea how things would turn out, I would never have put you in such danger."

Jill studied the man before her, seeing the sincere regret in his soft brown eyes.

"None of us could have foreseen what happened, Rob," she murmured around a sob. "You must not blame yourself."

He nodded once. "You forgive me, then?"

"Of course I do, but there's really nothing to forgive. I agreed to go with you because I wanted to help. It is to my eternal regret that my protection could not see you safely home."

They stood for a moment with their hands linked between them, and she willed a measure of her own infinitesimal courage to be communicated through the press of flesh to him.

"And for yourself," he finally asked. "Is there some resolution to your difficulties?"

"I doubt that I will pay the price that you are paying," she told him in a whisper, "though they seem determined to keep me confined until I agree to help them with their schemes."

"Do not help them, Jillian. Do nothing they ask," he urged. "I have given them a confession, but I did not implicate any of our friends. And now I believe I am prepared to die for the Confederacy and the cause."

She wanted to say more, wanted to say something that would remind him of happier days. She wanted to ease his fears, to laud his courage, but there were no words to express what she was feeling.

There was a rustle of footsteps in the direction of the door, and someone touched her shoulder. "Say your good-byes, Mrs. Walsh. There isn't any more time."

Rob stiffened and drew his hands away. "I have something for you, Jillian," he offered, turning to the table. "It is only a lock of hair and a photograph they let me have taken several days ago, but perhaps they will help you remember me as a soldier of the gallant South."

He put an envelope into her manacled hands and placed his arms around her. He was trembling and smelled of liquor, but she leaned close in his embrace.

"I won't forget you, Rob. I promise," she whispered against his shoulder.

"Nor I you, my lovely Jillian."

She touched his bearded cheek, smoothed the lapels of his wrinkled gray jacket, before clasping his hands once more. But the guards were pulling her away, and she left the casemate woodenly, her vision blurred by tears.

Outside, the crowd was waiting, the ranks of the garrison flanking two sides of the parade ground, the prisoners in lines behind them. The military and civilian observers were on the second level of the fort, and her guards led her to a vacant place against the rail at the end of the narrow parapet. The wooden gallows had been erected in the middle of the field, a stark, ungainly monument to cruelty and inhumanity.

Shuddering, she turned her eyes away. But the files of soldiers with their crisp uniforms and polished buttons, the ragged prisoners standing silent and bowed behind them, and the avid faces of the visitors offered her no respite from the knowledge of what was about to happen.

An execution must bring out the worst in all of us, she thought, *that vile, uncivilized monster alive in every woman and man. It makes us so much less than what we are, so much less than God must have intended us to be.*

Yet when a stir of excitement moved through the crowd, Jillian looked toward the door of Rob's cell to where his final procession was emerging. An army lieutenant led the way, with Rob, a cleric, and another man close behind him. Colonel Burke came next with a few others completing the fragile, somber line. Rob looked justifiably terrified, staring at the ground and trembling like a willow in a gale. He seemed so thin, so frail, so helplessly human as he traversed the few yards to the foot of the gallows. A noose was curled around his neck, the free end trailing down his back like a braid. The black hood that would mask his features as he died was already in place, rolled back against his forehead like a sultan's turban.

Jillian's heart thudded against her ribs as if it were trying to escape the confines of her body. Her temples throbbed; her mouth went dry. She felt cold and dead inside. She, too, began to tremble.

While one of the officers read the sentence, Jillian turned the white-rose ring on her finger, trying to draw on the strength and comfort of Ryder's love to help her through this ordeal. But Ryder seemed inaccessible, so very far away, and she knew she would have to face what was to come with nothing but her own stubbornness and courage to sustain her.

The chaplain's voice echoed from the walls of the yard as he began to recite a prayer, but the words seemed blurred and far away as Jillian stared at the man on the scaffold. She felt totally attuned to Rob's rising fear, his impotent anger, and his flaring regret. Her thoughts seemed to touch his terrified, turbulent ones.

She closed her eyes and tried to pray. But the question, "Why, God, why?" played over and over in her brain. Rob was not wicked, was not evil. He had done nothing more than what the war had forced so many men to do. He had fought for a cause he thought was just, and his deeds were no worse than what others had done in the name of patriotism and victory. Why was he being forced to pay so high a price for his convictions?

There were no answers to the questions; there was no comfort in the words the chaplain was saying. She clung to the icy iron railing, trying to conjure up her happiest memories of the man who was about to die. She thought back to her first days in Toronto, remembering Rob's gallantry, his courtesy, his kindness to her. She recalled the afternoon they had all gone skating at Taddle Creek, the good-natured teasing, the fun they'd had. She remembered his seriousnesss, his loneliness, and his burning desire to go home. As she did, tears seeped from beneath her lowered lashes, searing against her cheeks. She would mourn Rob Kennedy all of her days, as a friend, a compatriot, a man who loved the South.

Finally, the parson's prayer drew to a close and silence fell over the prison. No one spoke, and she could hear the wind moaning along the ramparts of the stark old fortress, hear the flag snapping sharp and loud overhead. The iciness inside her was fed by the silence.

Then, suddenly, singing was borne across the courtyard. It took her a moment to realize it was Rob's voice that was raised in song. He was singing one of the bawdy ballads she had heard him sing that night of the party in Thompson's rooms. The song that had once made her blush now fed her memory of the evening they had spent together. They had talked, danced, joked. They had been happy and carefree, but then the war had intruded as it always did, bringing pain and death and sorrow. Rob's voice was sweet and clear and true, soaring in the wind. But in midbar the singing stopped, and there was a sudden, deafening quiet.

The cold that had lain inside her seemed suddenly to spread, sending tendrils of ice along her limbs, whorls of frigid fear sweeping to her head. Her thoughts spun like snow in an arctic wind, like a hoary gale blowing in from the north, and she readily gave up her hold on consciousness for a darkness that was far warmer and more comforting.

When she came to herself, she was lying on a cot in the commander's office surrounded by a circle of curious officers. One of them was on his knees beside her, solicitously patting her wrist. As soon as he saw she had opened her eyes, he took up a glass and began pouring brandy into her mouth. It seared, stung, and dribbled down her chin. Jillian gagged and pushed his hand away, glaring up at the man ineffectively.

"Are you feeling better, Mrs. Walsh?" he asked.

Was she feeling better? Would she ever feel truly well again?

Wearily, Jillian forced herself into a sitting position, fighting down the sickness inside her.

"I'm feeling a bit better, yes," she answered him, but her pallor belied the brave words.

Though she felt that they owed her an apology for what they had forced her to endure, no one spoke, and she tried to summon her anger to banish the weakness and futility assailing her.

"Are you up to returning to Fort Hamilton?" one of her two guards asked.

"Let her sit quietly for a few minutes more," someone advised as the group around her began to thin.

She sat alone on the cot, shattered, exhausted, spent, trying in vain to recoup her strength. She hated the men who had made her come here today, hated them with a single-minded animosity that was foreign to her nature. But even using the hatred as a goad, she could not seem to banish the weakness and lethargy. Yet as she waited to be transported back to her prison at Fort Hamilton, she was aware of a subtle change in her.

The Yankees had made her attend Rob's execution because they thought it would break her, force her to bend to their will. Instead, it seemed to have hardened the kernel of defiance inside her, hardened it in a way even she had not anticipated. Seeing the reality of a hanging had firmed her resolve; she would never be the cause of another man's execution. Nothing she did would lead a brave man to such a degrading end. As the conviction took root inside her, she knew it would condemn her to an indefinite imprisonment, perhaps even death. But Rob Kennedy had given her the determination to refuse to help her captors with their vile plans.

It was the war, its futility, its senselessness that had brought them all to this, and she mourned for all the men who had died in the meaningless struggle for Southern independence. There was no valid excuse for this useless loss of life, no excuse that could be given to the women who would pass the rest of their lives alone, no excuse that could be offered to children who would never know their fathers. The war was a sin against humanity that could never be absolved. What good were bravery, patriotism, and devotion to duty when they led to such as this? It would have been better if the Confederacy had been allowed to go its way, better for the Union to have been divided forever than for all these lives to have been expended needlessly.

For Jillian's part, the loss of life would end with her. She would not bow to the Yankees' demands, would not sacrifice even one man to gain her freedom. Though her politics might have led her to sanction the Union cause, her humanity would not allow anyone else to pay the price for her actions, her beliefs. She would steadfastly refuse to help the Federal government, and perhaps one day the war would end.

Her guards allowed her to remain in the commander's office for the best part of an hour, and when they finally made their way back to Fort Hamilton, it was evident that a storm was blowing in across the harbor. The bright spring sun was gone. The sky was lowering, and there was snow in the air. It hadn't turned out to be so fine a day for an execution, after all.

When her guards returned to the cottage at Fort Hamilton, Jill made her way inside, feeling ancient, brittle as parchment, and nearly as translucent. It took some minutes for her to muster the ambition to strip off her cloak, some minutes more to find the strength to light the lamp. As the brightness blossomed, she looked around the tiny cabin, seeing her sewing where she had left it on the corner of the narrow pine table, the half-finished book propped open on the chair. She felt as if her life had changed since she had left the tiny cabin. In many ways it had.

The decision to continue to thwart the Yankees should have given her resolution, strength. Instead, her mind was blank, stunned, void. She could not face the ramifications of that decision now. Tomorrow she would be fierce and strong, she told herself, but tonight there was only disillusionment.

Standing in the middle of the room, she began to weep, hot

tears seeping down her face, pearling at the curve of her jaw before they spattered onto her bodice. Her sobbing filled the cabin, and she made no attempt to muffle the expression of her grief. Her chest heaved, her shoulders shuddered convulsively as she cried, mourning the fate that had befallen all of them. She wept for all the people she had lost: her father, Jeff, Ryder, and Rob. She wept for the end of her security, the betrayal of her idealism and her dreams. She did not know how to cope with the emptiness. It was vast, unchartered, devastating, absorbing her courage, challenging her fortitude.

How long she wept she hardly knew, but in time Jill made her way to the bed. With an effort, she peeled back the blanket and bent to remove her shoes before settling gingerly on the narrow, lumpy mattress. As she lay there, she tried not to think about the afternoon's occurrences, tried not to think how lonely and abandoned she felt.

Like a cat settling down for a nap, she rubbed her cheek against the fabric of the pillowcase before pulling the blanket up around her shoulders. Wearily she sought the balm of sleep, stirring, snuggling deeper, sliding one hand beneath the pillow as she sought a more comfortable position. But as she did so, her fingers encountered several unfamiliar objects.

Puzzled, Jill sat up and lifted the pillow off the bed. There beneath it on the rough cotton sheets were two gifts, delivered with who knew how much difficulty. She stared at them for a very long time, afraid to believe that they were really there, desperate to believe in their significance. Slowly, she reached out to touch the smooth silver bottle, the long twisted chain. It was indeed her mother's silver vinaigrette necklace, the one she'd pawned in Rochester. With hope thawing the ice around her heart, she slipped the chain around her neck and touched the lovely silver vial where it lay gleaming against the bodice of her gown. The necklace was once again where it belonged, linking her to the past in a tangible way, and that link filled Jillian with hope.

At last, she picked up the other gift. It was a delicate wooden carving. She turned it this way and that to examine the craftsmanship and subject more carefully. It was of a tiny, perfect bird, its feathers minutely detailed and artistically arranged, its head raised and its beak open as if in song. And in the pose the carver had chosen, the bird was poised and ready for flight.

Chapter Twenty

"You HAVE VISITORS, Mrs. Walsh." It was midmorning of the day following Rob Kennedy's execution when the captain of the guard came to see Jillian in her cabin.

"Visitors?" she asked, trying to control the tremor in her voice. Since the night before, she had been filled with a strange mixture of hope and dread, and this bit of news elicited a whole new spectrum of responses. Diligently she strove for nonchalance. "But the two gentlemen who come every day to question me aren't due until this afternoon."

The captain smiled and stroked his beard. "Well, I believe these visitors will be somewhat more welcome than the ones you usually see. It's your aunt Jane and the parson from your church in Pennsylvania, Reverend Mathews, who have come to visit you."

Jillian's heart lurched and began beating double time. She didn't have an aunt Jane, and the pastor of her church was Reverend Purcell, not Reverend Mathews.

"Aunt Jane and Reverend Mathews are here?" she asked incredulously around the bubble of emotion swelling in her chest. "They came all the way to New York to see me?"

"Yes, ma'am, they did. They're in Colonel Burke's office just now. Shall I bring them over?"

Jillian's eyes filled with delight. "Oh, yes, Captain. Just give me a moment to tidy up."

The man smiled as his prisoner's hands flew up to smooth her hair and straighten the collar of her gown. It was the first time since this young woman had been under his care that he had seen anything but sorrow and resignation in her face. Happiness changed her completely, turning a pale and somber girl into a beautiful, vibrant woman with color in her cheeks and a sparkle in her eyes. He was instantly glad he had come himself to break news that could so cheer and transform her. It was especially gratifying to see her despondency of the previous day changed to eagerness and excitement. But then, Confederate or not, the man who had been hanged had been her friend, and he could guess how it must have felt to witness the execution when she knew she would likely share his fate.

"You know I must have one of my men here while you're visiting, Mrs. Walsh," he warned her.

Jillian nodded and smiled at him. "That doesn't really matter, Captain. I've grown so tired of my own company. Please hurry and bring my guests to me. I'm so eager to see them both."

The captain locked the door behind him, leaving Jillian to collect her thoughts. She had spent a sleepless night, torn between delight at the gifts she'd received and the knowledge that Ryder was in New York, risking recapture or worse. There was no question that the gifts were Bingham's doing. Only he had known about the vinaigrette in the pawnshop in Rochester; only he could have made the tiny wooden carving. In spite of the irresolute way they had parted, in spite of the terrible danger of being on Northern soil, Bingham had come to her. She had lain awake all night staring into the dark, with the silver vinaigrette around her neck and the tiny carving clutched in her hand like a talisman.

Before her visitors arrived, she did make some attempt to see to her appearance, but her hands were shaking so badly that her best efforts to straighten her hair and smooth her skirts were all but ineffective. Soon there was the sound of the key scraping in the lock, and the thick wooden door swung open.

A diminutive woman entered first, and when Jillian saw the round, fair face beneath the brim of the feathered bonnet and the twinkling gray eyes that met her own, a giggle fluttered to her throat, and it was all she could do to keep from laughing. Jamie was dressed to the nines in a fashionable deep purple gown with frills of blond lace tumbling down the front and rows of inch-deep ruching in scallops along the hem. Tendrils of his fair hair peeped from beneath the brim of the splendid scoop-front hat, and he carried a shawl, a beaded reticule, and a parasol as if he had been born to them. For an instant Jillian could do little more than stare, but finally her eyes rose to the tall, dark man who stood behind him. Ryder was dressed in a fine black suit, a hat, and a clerical collar. He carried a prayer book and looked somber and proper with newly grown muttonchop side whiskers and a luxuriant mustache liberally streaked with silver. His hair had been whitewashed, too, making him look staid and distinguished, though the rakish light in his deep blue eyes was not at all seemly for a man of the cloth.

One of the young privates who acted as her guard followed the two visitors inside and closed the door behind them.

"Jillian, child," Jamie trilled, in a voice that was at once both feminine and strangely familiar, "aren't you glad to see us?"

The smaller man's words roused her from her stunned surprise, and in an instant, she was across the room in Jamie's arms.

"Oh, Aunt Jane," Jillian gasped, hugging the man who looked oddly at home in his disguise. "I never in this world expected you to visit me."

"My poor, dear Jillian, what are family for but to help in times of trouble? I was so distressed when I heard what had befallen you, I hardly knew what to do. But when Reverend Mathews said he'd accompany me to New York, what choice did I have but to catch the very next train?"

Jamie paused to catch his breath before continuing, hoping he was giving Jillian a chance to catch hers, too.

"Goodness, girl, let me look at you. You're as pale as whey and as skinny as a stick! Aren't they feeding you in this wretched place?"

Jillian was beginning to recover herself and beamed at him. "Oh, Aunt Jane, I'm so very glad you came. And Reverend Mathews," she murmured, turning to Ryder, "how very kind of you to accompany her."

She submitted to a gentle kiss on the cheek before Ryder deemed it necessary to answer her. "Well, my dear, I could hardly let yor auntie come all this way alone, when I was nearly as distraught to learn of your troubles as she was."

Ryder was trying valiantly to subdue his Carolina drawl, though with only limited success, and Jill realized it would not be wise to let him say too much.

In an attempt to turn the focus from Ryder's unseemly accent, Jillian addressed her guard. "Private Sayers, could we please have another chair or two for my visitors?"

She hoped the request would buy them a few minutes of solitude so Ryder and Jamie could advise her of their plans, but the guard was too accommodating.

"There are some chairs right here on the porch, Mrs. Walsh. I'll bring them in."

While the private fetched a chair, Ryder took in the woman before him, trying to ascertain how the months of imprisonment had affected her. She was thinner, that was sure, and as pale as alabaster, as if she never saw the sun. But more distressing was the air about her of someone who had given up all expectations of release. Fury pounded in his head when he saw that the Yankees had robbed her of her spirit, her vitality, her hope. He longed to take her in his arms, longed to comfort her and share his strength with her. But he resolutely stayed in character, seating Jillian's aunt solicitously, procuring a second chair for himself.

While Ryder was watching Jillian, Jamie took in the sparsely furnished cabin. It was small and dismal, with a table, a chair, a bed, a chamber pot, and a basin. Seeing that the shutters had been nailed in place to secure the cabin for use as a prison, he realized the door was the only exit. For all the options he and Ryder had considered, the choices had abruptly dwindled down to the most forthright and dangerous one.

Once they were settled, the young private closed the door again, and there was the scraping of keys as the locks were snapped in place.

"Well, Jillian," Jamie began brightly, "tell me what on earth has happened to you to bring you to such as this."

Jill took a long breath before she spoke, trying to discern what Ryder and Jamie had planned. Were they really going to help her escape? Had they come to size up her situation, or were they going to act today?

"I don't know what you read of my trial in the newspapers," she replied distractedly, trying to follow Jamie's lead, "but the military commission that tried me found me guilty of all charges and has sentenced me to hang."

"Hang! Oh, my dear child, tell me it isn't so! They've sentenced you to hang! Oh, dear!" Jamie gave a fair accounting of himself as an older woman with the vapors, raising one lace-gloved hand to his cheek, breathing in painful little gasps. "Oh, please, I need my smelling salts. I believe they're in my reticule."

Jillian grabbed for the small beaded purse dangling from Jamie's wrist. While she fumbled with the bag, Ryder bent over his companion, fanning Jamie with his hat. The young private had been drawn into the drama, too, and was hovering over Jamie ineffectively. In the split second when the soldier bent to loosen the top buttons of the woman's bodice, Jamie doubled his fist and punched him. Ryder administered the coup de grace by bringing his heavy prayer book down on the fellow's head. As the private's knees gave under him, Bingham caught the man under the arms and eased him to the floor.

"Undress," Jamie ordered Jillian in an undertone. "You're going to put on that Yankee uniform and escort us out of here."

Doing as she was told, Jill began to tug at the top fasteners of her gown, and in the most chivalrous gesture she'd ever seen, Ryder spun Jamie around so that she could disrobe in relative privacy. While she hastily stripped off her clothes, Jamie pulled two pistols and a length of rope from beneath his froth of petticoats.

"Thank God there's some chivalry left, even in these Yankees," he mumbled under his breath, lowering his wide skirts to the floor.

In the meantime Ryder was busily relieving the private of his clothes, and once they had him stripped to his drawers, the two men hastened to bind and gag him.

"Damned stays," Jamie gasped as he stood up. "I don't know why women wear them."

Jillian was too busy scrambling into the soldier's uniform to answer him and, when she was fully dressed at last, turned to face her rescuers. Because she was tall, the private's uniform fit her tolerably well, but even with his hat crushed down on her head to hide her hair and the shirt bunched around the waist, there was no question she was a woman.

"You couldn't have been flat-chested, could you?" Jamie grumbled, as his eyes ran over her.

Ryder had reasons of his own for being pleased with Jillian's attributes and quickly offered a solution. "The man on the porch is wearing an overcoat. Perhaps if she puts that on, she'll be better able to pass as one of the guards."

Bradford nodded and moved toward the door. "Sergeant Hargrave," he called out through the wooden panel, mimicking Private Sayer's voice almost perfectly. "Mrs. Walsh's visitors are ready to leave."

There was the thud of boots on the narrow porch, the rasp of the key in the lock, and when the hapless sergeant opened the door, Ryder greeted him with pistol drawn.

"Make no sound and step inside," he instructed quietly, and when the man did as he was told, Jamie hit him over the head with the butt of his gun. Removing the soldier's overcoat, they passed it to Jillian.

While the two men tied and gagged the second soldier, Ryder gave instructions. "We were supposed to return to Colonel Burke's office when the visit was over, but you're going to escort us directly to the gate."

"But what if someone tries to stop us?" she mumbled, buttoning herself into the bulky coat and taking up one of the muskets.

"Then run like the devil's at your heels, since that's exactly where he'll be," Jamie answered her.

Jillian was tingling with excitement and shaking with dread as they prepared to leave the cabin. But Ryder took a moment to clasp her hand and bring it to his lips.

"I owe you this, Jilly. You've earned it more times than you know."

Reluctantly, she took back her icy fingers and opened the door. Ryder threaded Jamie's arm through his elbow, though it was Jill who was most in need of his support.

They left the vicinity of the cabin quickly, but without appreciable haste, moving straight across the parade ground in the opposite direction from the colonel's office. As they strode along, Jillian tried to adopt a military bearing, squaring her shoulders and striding along as if she were a man. As they traversed the expanse of hardened, snow-dusted earth, their feet beat a desperate tattoo that matched the pounding of her heart. All around them the military post moved with its usual efficiency: platoons marched, gunners practiced their drills, sutlers sold goods from their heavily laden carts. The soldiers guarding the outbuildings seemed to take no notice of the people crossing the field, though in her jury-rigged disguise, Jillian felt conspicuous and vulnerable. Every step they took brought them nearer their goal, the gate that led to the water, the landing, and the dock.

There was the crush of the gravel drive beneath their shoes as they reached the road, the breath of an ocean breeze wafting through the columned opening. She could see the bulk of Fort Lafayette and Staten Island across the water far beyond it. The portal was mere yards away; safety was just beyond their grasp when a voice cut through the air.

"Wait! Wait, Reverend Mathews, Mrs. Chandler, where are you going?" It was the captain of the guard crossing the parade ground after them.

Beside her, Jamie stiffened and muttered, "Damn!"

They made no move to slow their pace even when the captain cried out again. There was the sound of hurried footfalls, and with Ryder's tug against her arm, Jillian tossed aside the heavy musket and broke into a run. The three sprinted through the gate and down the slope that led to the dock. As they ran, Jamie hauled his encumbering skirts up around his thighs, giving anyone who cared to look a clear view of his lacy pantalets.

Behind them the captain's voice was rising in alarm: "Damn it, they're escaping! Quickly, you men! After them!"

There was the sound of running feet behind them, spurring the three fugitives to a faster pace. They heard the captain's order to fire and felt clods of dirt pelt their legs as shot slammed into the earth at their feet.

None of the three of them faltered as they raced toward a small steam tug bobbing beside the dock. Its lines were already freed; its engine was on and idling. They threw themselves toward the deck as the engines flared, and they landed with a thump on the foredeck as the bow swung wide, heading toward the open channel.

"Go!" Jamie shouted at the captain. "Get this bucket out of here!"

The steam tug whined and picked up speed, but the Fort Lafayette barge was also at the dock, and the captain and his men were piling on board. As the three fugitives turned back to look, they could see the barge was coming about, swinging away from the landing to follow them.

There was the sound of firing from the trailing boat, the flare of flames and the blossom of thick, dark smoke borne up and away by the wind. Bullets sliced into the rough water around the tug and thudded into its wooden hull. The waves were making accurate shooting impossible, but still the pursuers kept volleying.

The deck of the steam tug bucked beneath their feet as the boat crashed through the breakers, sending spume leaping high, flaring sternward from the bow. The wind tugged the hat from Jillian's head and tore at her long fair hair, and although she knew that they might be recaptured, she was enjoying the semblance of freedom. The Yankee barge remained in hot pursuit, battling the waves in the turbulent channel, smacking into the wake of the smaller vessel. But at last the tug began to pull away, slicing out into the open water just ahead of a sleek ocean steamer.

"I guess the gold we paid for speed was money well spent," Jamie finally conceded, and produced a cigar from inside his reticule. Standing in his feathered hat and gown, he looked so ridiculous lighting his smoke that Jillian began to giggle.

But when the giggle became a sob, Ryder put an arm around her shoulders and pulled her close against his side. Cupping her chin with his free hand, he turned her face to his and bent to kiss her gently.

Jill turned suddenly desperate in his arms, burrowing against his chest, twining her arms around his waist, pressing closer, seeking reassurance.

"Oh, Ryder, you came," she gulped, "even though I didn't want you to."

"Yes."

"You came!"

"There wasn't any way I could do otherwise."

"I was so frightened," she whispered brokenly against his chest. "I was so worried—"

"Hush."

"So worried—"

"Hush."

"—that you would try to rescue me." She was crying so hard her words were all but unintelligible.

"You mean you didn't want to be rescued?" he teased her softly. "This a hell of a time to tell me so."

She raised her head and smiled up at him through the tears.

He smiled, too, touching her cheek as if she were not the only one in need of reassurance. "It's all right, Jilly," he whispered, guiding her head to the hollow of his shoulder. "It's all right now. Everything turned out the way we planned."

"But, Ryder, the risks you and Jamie took—" she murmured against his shirtfront.

"Mean nothing now that everything is settled."

"But if you'd been caught—"

"We weren't."

"But if you stand trial—"

"We won't."

Her arms tightened around him again. "Oh, Ryder, I love you so."

He had no time to respond to the woman huddled in his arms because the pitch of the engine changed, and Jillian turned to see what was happening. Far behind them the barge was riding the swells, its quarry having outdistanced it. But the tug was slowing, too, pulling up beside the ocean steamer as a ladder unfurled slowly down the side. As the tug captain held the launch steady, they clambered aboard the larger boat.

Jamie immediately disappeared down a companionway, and Ryder took Jillian's arm and led her toward the bow of the ship which was now headed out to sea.

In silence they watched the land fall away, watched until Long Island was nothing more than a smudge on the western horizon, watched until the wide, bare ocean lay before them. Finally, Jillian turned to the tall, dark man beside her. She touched the gray streaks painted in his hair, the muttonchop whiskers and full mustache. Then she raised her eyes to his and stretched on tiptoe to kiss him.

The kiss was deep, long, searching, fired with fierce intensity. It was all a kiss should ever be and left them both aching and weak with the pain of long separation.

"Are you sorry?" he finally asked.

"Sorry?" she murmured incredulously. "Sorry about being rescued from hanging, about being saved from a life in prison?"

She sounded as if she had regained control of her emotions, and Ryder felt a surge of relief. "Are you sorry about being forced to leave the country of your birth, about giving up so much to help me?"

"I'll only be sorry if you tell me I can't be with you."

He smiled, stroked her cheek. With Jillian beside him, he felt complete, as if all he needed for peace and contentment was here in the circle of his arms. He stared down into her face, reveling in the exotic beauty that had held him enthralled from the first moment he had seen her, noting the strength and courage that had enabled her to endure hardships no one should ever have to face. This lovely, brave woman had changed his life the day he sat down beside her on the train. She had shown him tenderness when his heart was filled with hate, made him see the beauty in the world when he was blind to everything but his own misery. She had taught him how to love again when he was terrified by all he'd lost.

There was a shadow of uncertainty in her eyes, and he knew it mirrored the uncertainty in his own. It was time to resolve the questions that still lay between them, time to see if Jillian was indeed willing to share the future he had finally begun to plan.

Ryder drew a shaky breath. "There have been some changes in my life since you left me in Toronto."

Jillian's stomach dipped with apprehension, but she fixed her unwavering gaze on his, waiting for him to explain to her what course their lives would follow after this.

"I have an inheritance in England," he began. "It was my mother's legacy. I don't know quite what it entails, but I finally have something to offer you."

Jill caught her breath and tried to be calm.

"I'm not sure what kind of life I can make for us, Jilly, but I'll try to make you happy."

"Are you asking me to marry you, Ryder?"

He nodded slowly, a smile dawning in his blue eyes. "I want you with me always. I want to make a life with you. I want to give you a home and children and security. I want to wake every morning and find your sweet face on the pillow beside me. I want to kiss you and hold you and sleep each night with you by my side. I want—"

"But do you love me, Ryder?" Her question cut him short. He stared at her as if she was mad to ask him that after he had risked so much to rescue her.

"Of course I love you!" There was a catch in his voice that made the words all the more eloquent. "I love you more than anything, more than life, more than—"

Happiness fluttered in her chest, turning her giddy, warm, and breathless.

"Then that's enough," she murmured curling into his embrace. "Your love is all the security I'll ever want. Your love is all the promise I'll ever need. It's enough to build a life on, Ryder. Love is always enough."

Author's Note:

WHILE I WAS doing research on my last book, *Let No Man Divide*, I ran across an incident in September of 1864 when troop ships along the St. Louis waterfront were burned by Confederates from Canada. Confederates from Canada? I thought. What on earth were Confederates doing in Canada? When that book was finished, I began to research the topic and turned up the incidents that are the basis for *From This Day Onward*.

In my research, several books were of particular help. The first, *Canada and the United States in the Civil War Years* by Robin Winks, gave me an overview of the relations between England, Canada, the United States, and the Confederacy during the War Between The States. I also found invaluable *Confederate Agent* by James Horan, a book that outlines the Northwest Conspiracy and the associated plans through the exploits of Thomas Hines. I drew heavily on Nat Brandt's *The Man Who Tried to Burn New York* for information and for the characterization of Robert Cobb Kennedy. I hope Mr. Brandt will feel I remained true to the portrait of Kennedy he created in his nonfiction work. Kennedy's capture, without Jillian as his accomplice, is based in fact, as are the events surrounding Kennedy's execution. The information for these incidents is drawn primarily from Mr. Brandt's book. The quote from the *Richmond Whig* in chapter ten was taken from this source, also, since I had no direct access to the paper.

As I researched the section of the book that dealt with the incendiary plot to burn New York in 1864, I had a host of sources, including some of the ones mentioned above. I also drew on the memoirs of John Headley, *Confederate Operations in Canada and New York*, and contemporary newspapers from New York City, Toronto, and Niagara Falls. The arson plot, its frustrations, and eventual execution are well documented, and everyone involved, with the exception of Ryder, Jamie, Phillip Sheppard, and possibly Clement Clay, did indeed play the roles they are assigned here.

The Lake Erie raid is less cleanly documented. In many cases secondary accounts varied, often contradicting one another. Even the records of John Yates Beall's court-martial leave some intriguing holes in the story. With this event, I tried to incorporate the occurrences where two or more authors agreed. Where there was no positive documentation, I took the course that seemed most expedient for the development of my narrative. For example, the planning of the raid may or may not have taken place at Windsor, Canada West, and there is conflicting evidence about who was involved in this phase of the operation. I hope the reader will realize that in telling the story as I have I am not attempting to rewrite history, only to weave a cohesive plot from the somewhat sketchy facts handed down to us.

Writing the scene of Jillian's court-martial was something of a challenge, too. Since I have little familiarity with military law, discerning the finer points of this kind of a proceeding was difficult. I based most of my information on the references to Robert Kennedy's trial in Mr. Brandt's book, on the transcript of John Beall's trial, and on the *Army Court Martial Manual* of 1906. If there are any inaccuracies in the way Jillian's case is presented, it is not for lack of trying to make it accurate and authentic.

The social history also is as true to life as I could make it. I did a great deal of research into the mourning customs of the time, with the aid of Sheryl Lang at the Missouri Historical Society and Joyce Schiller at the St. Louis Art Museum. The clothes, food, and decor are of the period. The Walsh home is based on the Whitney Mansion, which still stands in Niagara Falls.

Writing accurate historical fiction is not something to be undertaken lightly, and as I put words into the historical characters' mouths, I felt the responsibility of what I was doing very keenly. What I hope I have done in this book is expand the reader's understanding of a complex and painful period of United States history through the telling of a compelling story. If I've succeeded, both the historical figures and the fictitious characters should be more real to the reader now, as should the complex motives that drive us all.

In the end, historical fiction should be an attempt to make the events of the past live for people in the present. Only the reader of this work can judge the extent to which I have achieved that goal. But it is my most fervent hope that John Yates Beall, Robert Cobb Kennedy, Jacob Thompson, Jillian Walsh, Ryder Bingham, and Jamieson Bradford have become as strong a link with the past for the reader as they have for me.

Elizabeth N. Kary
P.O. Box 30026
St. Louis, Missouri 63119
February 1988